PRETTY BOY

Pretty BOY

A Sam Jones Novel

LAUREN HENDERSON

THREE RIVERS PRESS
NEW YORK

Published by Three Rivers Press, New York, New York.
Member of the Crown Publishing Group, a division of Random House, Inc.
www.randomhouse.com

Three Rivers Press and the Tugboat design are registered trademarks of Random House, Inc.

Originally published in Great Britain by Hutchinson, London, in 2001.

Printed in the United States of America

Designed by Karen Minster

Library of Congress Cataloging-in-Publication Data

Henderson, Lauren, 1966–
Pretty boy : a Sam Jones novel / Lauren Henderson—1st ed.
1. Jones, Sam (Fictitious character : Henderson)—Fiction.
2. Women sculptors—Fiction. 3. England—Fiction. I. Title.
PR6058.E4929 P74 2002
823'.914–dc21   2002075448

ISBN 0-609-80866-4

10 9 8 7 6 5 4 3 2 1

First American Edition

PRETTY BOY

EVER SINCE I'D BEEN KIDNAPPED, I HAD INSISTED THAT Hugo wear the handcuffs. The restriction was beginning to chafe on him, though scarcely, I pointed out, as much as it had on me. My ribs had healed perfectly, my nose was the same as it had ever been—which was to say it still had that damned bump, even after having been broken—but those scars around my wrists were still there. They were faded white and, fortunately, not that noticeable unless you were looking for them. Hugo said they made me look like the most incompetent suicide in existence.

Hugo was in a bad mood generally. The handcuffs were just the excuse for him to launch into a general tirade.

"I'm not going to come no matter what you do," he said sourly.

"Don't tell me that's the fault of the bloody cottage too."

"Not everything's the fault of the bloody cottage. Quite a lot can be laid squarely at the door of the person currently straddling me, who insisted, for some Godforsaken reason which utterly escapes me, that we spend New Year in the English countryside in, yes, now that you mention it, a nasty damp little cottage with insufficient hot water for my elaborate bathing rituals."

Hugo pronounced the words "English countryside" with enough bitterness to be a total giveaway. Despite his accent and diction, he was born to lower-middle-class parents in Surbiton rather than the landed gentry, and every so often one of his attitudes would make this clear. A really posh person would have derived a large part of their income from mulching a complicated cocktail of pesticides into the English countryside, besides spending their weekends down there shooting anything that had managed to survive the chemical onslaught. They would never have dreamed of referring to it in such disparaging terms.

"Unlock me," he said pettishly. "I want to go and bathe in a few inches of tepid water."

"Oh, *Hugo,*" I said reproachfully, reaching for the key. "The boiler's not that bad."

I unlocked the handcuffs and removed them from the headboard. Hugo swung himself to a sitting position as I climbed off him and folded the handcuffs neatly on the bedside table. I contemplated the long pale lines of his back. His shoulders were slumped sulkily, but he was still beautiful. I wanted to run my thumbnail down his vertebrae, which were a little more exposed than they should have been—he had just finished filming a TV film which had required him to be elegantly wasted—right down to the shadowy cleft between his buttocks, but I knew it would just irritate him. Normally that would have been an extra reason for doing it, but I was full of the milk of human kindness right then, and I abstained womanfully.

"At least we've got a decent headboard," I offered in consolation. "Nice and sturdy. With a good crossbar for handcuffing purposes."

"The mattress sags," Hugo said dismissively, standing up and shrugging his shoulders forward to stretch them out after having his arms pulled back. "We'll be rolling into each other all night."

There was no pleasing him. Literally. Luckily, however, there had been an awful lot of pleasing me. I curled up on the bed, as satiated as I ever get, and, with tremendous aesthetic pleasure, watched him finish stretching out. Hugo was so white he glimmered against the wall, which was unfortunately painted the colour of smoked salmon; it matched his nipples, which were standing up, pointed as thumbtacks. His skin was smooth and almost hairless, like a marble statue, and he had the firm high buttocks of a David—Michelangelo, not Donatello—or the Rodin I had seen in the Sculpture Garden at the Met in New York, the Three Shades. Being still erect, however, he had the advantage on practically any statue I had ever seen. Absentmindedly he pulled on his cock, as if he were contemplating something else entirely and the manual exercise was merely helping him to clear his thoughts.

"Someone ought to sculpt you like that," I observed.

He turned to look at me.

"You're always objectifying me," he said. "Quite literally in this case."

"Wish I could. What a shame I'm not representational. I'd get a nice slab of marble and start carving."

"Your cockroaches are representational."

"Well, up to a point."

"My little cockroach queen," Hugo said more affectionately. Compliments had a way of restoring his good mood like nothing else. Hugo was an actor right down to his bone marrow.

He hadn't been hitting the gym for a while, in the interests of being elegantly wasted, and his pecs were flatter than usual, minimal breastplates, convex under my hands. Looking at him naked, even after having had prolonged sex with him, still made me want to run my hands all over him. Perhaps that was one of the many advantages of us being apart so often for long periods; absence made, if not the heart, then certainly various other portions of my anatomy grow fonder.

Hugo pulled on his dressing gown and headed for the bathroom. Various expensive smells gradually began seeping under the door and filling the corridor with a heady blend of bath foam, body lotion and cologne. Those were only the ingredients I knew about; there were probably more. Hugo was, in that respect, much more of a girl than me.

Certainly he was having a major pout at the moment. And if he kept it up, he would rapidly start to get on my nerves, no matter how much I tried to keep my temper. There had been many good reasons why we had come down to the countryside for the New Year's Eve weekend, chief among them that we were visiting my best friend, Tom, whom I had hardly seen since he moved out of London. Finally I was getting a chance to see his life down here and meet his new friends, and I was excited at the prospect. I was damned if Hugo was going to ruin it for me. Although we had been squabbling for the past few weeks—all right, months—I had assumed that, once we got away from our all-too-familiar surroundings, things would improve. Wasn't that what the women's magazines always said? Take a holiday together to renew the excitement in your relationship?

When I started believing the pap they fed you in women's magazines, I knew I was in trouble. So far it had been completely untrue. Hugo had been grumpy all the way down here, making only the most feeble stabs at navigating, and one look at our cottage had been enough to send him into a sulk so almighty and overpowering as to make the most spotty, discontented, sexually frustrated pubescent seem a ray of sunshine by contrast.

Shagging him senseless had seemed like a foolproof plan to ensure his overall contentment with life in general and our surroundings in particular. Obviously, it had also had fringe benefits for myself. Utter selflessness was not a concept with which I was familiar.

I stared up at the timbered ceiling and fervently hoped that Hugo and I weren't going to spend the weekend either bickering nastily or ostentatiously ignoring each other, like couples I had observed and despised in the past. God, relationships were really hard work. No wonder I'd never had one before. I was getting a headache just thinking about it.

And I liked the cottage, despite Hugo's snarky comments on its lack of amenities. It was cosy. Tom had booked it for us. Hugo, naturally, had wanted to stay in the most luxurious hotel the village could boast, but, luckily for our finances, there was no hotel of any description closer than a ten-minute drive. And clearly neither Hugo nor I would be doing any driving on New Year's Eve, or in fact on any other night which involved going out drinking with Tom. Proximity was crucial. We had turned down bed-and-breakfasts—lack of privacy, plus restrictive curfews—and had thus been left with the choice of a holiday cottage versus a room above the local pub. Naturally, I had opted for the latter, which was probably why Hugo had nixed it. He thought I would just spend the entire holiday in one long lock-in and have to be mopped off the carpet and poured into the car when leaving time came around.

A nasty thought struck me. I went to bang on the bathroom door.

"You'd better leave your water," I called. "God knows if the boiler can do two baths in an evening."

"Why don't you just get in with me, then?" Hugo called back, sounding unexpectedly approachable. "If you're going to be sitting in my fetid water anyway, you might as well have the advantage of my company to distract you."

"Fair enough."

I pushed open the door. The small and—luckily for Hugo's mood—nicely appointed bathroom was so thick with steam that I could hardly make out Hugo or the bath through the cloud of perfumed vapour.

"Keep talking so I know where you are," I said, crossing the room. "I can't see a thing."

The mirror above the sink was frosted over with steam; it looked silvered, like a tarnished antique tray. I dropped my dressing gown and stretched out one foot in what, by logical deduction, had to be the direction of the bath. A hand caught mine and pulled me towards a wet, smooth body. I slid down its length so he was spooning me.

"Typical," Hugo said with mock-annoyance. "Now I have to wash your back."

He soaped it thoroughly and proceeded to draw patterns in the lather with one long finger.

"Remind me again what we're doing in this provincial hell-hole?" he said amiably.

"Spending New Year with one of my oldest friends," I said reprovingly. "Having a long weekend in the country."

"Yes," Hugo sighed. "Odd—it sounds perfectly understandable when you put it like that."

"Think of all those New Years spent racing round London in a frantic round of one party after another, like playing pass the parcel," I said. "Always knowing that you're risking ending up at the dud one at midnight. And then you have to wait three hours at the fag end of the night for a violently expensive minicab and try not to throw up on the driver's beaded seat cover."

"Speak for yourself," Hugo said, shuddering.

It hadn't actually been that hard to convince Hugo to get out of London. He had spent the last few months filming there and was completely sick of it. And though he had wanted to book some last-minute trip abroad to some hot beach destination where the trained waiters anticipated your every cocktail need before you had even quite articulated the desire to yourself, this had been financially impossible. The film had been so low budget that the actors had practically been asked, as an economy measure, not to wash their faces after shooting in case any makeup might stay on for the next day. Hugo had spent the last few weeks on an increasingly virulent campaign (via his agent, who hadn't wanted him to do the film in the first place—extra humiliation) to get his travel expenses covered. To add insult to injury, he was firmly of the opinion that the film would turn out too bad to ever merit a cinematic release.

All of which meant that the funds for that kind of lavish holiday were unavailable. I couldn't help out; I hadn't sold any sculptures for longer than I cared to remember and was working on a new project for which I had had to put up some of the funds myself. My gallery had advanced me a small amount, as I had been lucky enough to get some money, too, from the local council who funded the arts centre where I was showing, but there was still a shortfall I had to cover. Even renting a holiday cottage had stretched my non-elastic credit card to its limit. And Tom had got us a special deal on it, as it was owned by a friend of a friend. We were lucky even to have this. I didn't point it out to Hugo, though, as it would have annoyed him too much. Usually, annoying him was one of my favourite hobbies, but that had been when the relationship was going better. Over the last few months we had hit some black ice and had been skidding around ever since. Though we had made an unspoken pact not to discuss it over the holidays, I was too aware of potential problems to want to pick a fight unnecessarily. I was nervous enough of what would happen when we got back to London, settled into normal life and everything came to a head once more.

"So what's the plan for the evening?" Hugo said, sketching ever more elaborate swirls on my back.

"Well, now we've achieved Step One—Getting Clean—we move on to Step Two—Getting Dressed and Having Some Champagne. Then we load up with more champagne and stroll across the village green to Tom's house for a lavish meal, before doing the rounds of various street parties in the village and

winding up at the church at midnight for a firework display and
bell-ringing."

"God, how bucolic," Hugo said.

I bit my tongue hard. If I snapped back, we would just have
yet another fight, and we were due at Tom's for dinner shortly.
With a huge effort, I tried to think of something positive about
the countryside that might put Hugo in a better mood.

"Tom thought we could go riding tomorrow," I said hopefully.

"Not a bad idea." Hugo perked up. "I could do with some
more practice."

Riding was a skill that all actors said they had, for obvious
reasons. Few actually bothered to learn till they had been cast
in the latest Jane Austen adaptation and had a month before
shooting started to learn to look as if they'd been doing it all
their lives.

Hugo's hands had slid around to the front of my body and
were now soaping my breasts in a distinctly suggestive manner.

"Am I just fantasising, or are you soaping my breasts in a distinctly suggestive manner?" I said.

"The latter."

"Hmn. And either the soap's slipped down my back and has
got wedged against me—and grown quite a few inches—or . . ."

"It's not the soap," Hugo said into the back of my neck.

I reached back.

"No, it certainly isn't," I said happily.

· · · · · · ·

It was nice and soapy, though. Positively slick. Which we
weren't. Any choreographer of porn videos would have rejected
our efforts out of hand. The tub was small and increasingly
uncomfortable; we progressed through a series of awkward,
though entertaining, positions to our final, exhausted, resting
place on the bathroom floor. Mercifully, it was carpeted.

I was glad, in retrospect, that I didn't know it was the only good sex we were to have that entire stay. It would have completely ruined my enjoyment of the New Year celebrations.

Night had thoroughly fallen by the time we finally locked up the cottage and headed out. It was cold outside, but we had come prepared for the country. Overcoats, scarves, hats and gloves. We were wrapped up as snugly as a pair of children allowed out to play only after a careful mother had bundled them into layers of warm clothing. I almost felt that I should have my gloves connected by a string running through the arms of my coat. Actually, come to think of it, that was a pretty good idea. I was always losing my gloves. The only incongruous touch was that, instead of an assortment of plastic toys, we were carrying ice-cold sweaty champagne bottles.

"This is the city equivalent of being out hunting all day and coming home with a brace of grouse apiece," Hugo commented, clinking his pair of bottles together meditatively.

We had already cracked a bottle while we got dressed and had a line of coke apiece. In short, we were sexually satisfied, bathed, clad in smart clean clothes, pleasantly fuelled up and ready to negotiate the hurdle of festivities with a load of people we had never met before. It felt almost like the high point of the evening.

Which was precisely what it turned out to be.

I was glad to have got Hugo out of the cottage. The more we stayed in there, the more faults he found with it. Certainly the narrow staircase had not been designed, as he pointed out, for anyone who did not have the compact dimensions of a medieval peasant stunted by an inadequate diet of onions and turnips, with the occasional potato on Sundays by way of a treat. It was lowering to reflect that, despite the strides humanity had made in nutrition since then, I was still short enough to negotiate the staircase with consummate ease and expected it to present no problems even when I returned in an advanced state of intoxication. Hugo, however, had already banged his head on the ceiling three times and was distinctly peeved. He had spent the last hour in a continuous commentary as he moved from one room to the other: the furniture was rickety, and cheap pine to boot, the heating unsatisfactory and moths had been feasting for years on the rug in the living room. There was no stereo and the TV was the size of a house brick, only with inferior reception.

Instead of taking issue with this list of complaints, I bit my tongue yet again—it was getting very sore—and mumbled a sort of agreement, which was more than enough to satisfy him. If I had tried to be soothing and concilatory, he wouldn't have believed it for a moment. Thank God for the champagne. Without it I would have exploded already. Still, I was bubbling underneath. If he didn't cheer up soon, I wouldn't be responsible for my actions.

The village, thank God, was very pretty without being twee. We turned up the street, heading towards the green. I was already struck by the apparent lack of inhabitants; we were not only alone on the street, but I could barely hear any noise at all. No cars, no footsteps, no music playing in the distance.

"It feels like a ghost town," I said.

"Maybe Tom's turned into a zombie and they're going to feast on us for New Year."

"They won't get much off you right now," I said. "Except your bum."

I squeezed it affectionately. It was a great comfort to me that, no matter how much weight Hugo lost, his bottom still remained relatively round and firm.

"Last place it goes," Hugo said. "God, I'm looking forward to eating. I'm doing nothing else all the time we're down here, I warn you. I have at least half a stone to put back on. Cheese and pâté and roast pork and Belgian chocolate . . . Christ, three months of living on grilled chicken breast and salad! Do you know, I used to pass McDonald's and get cravings for a Big Mac? Can you imagine how low I must have sunk, how desperate I was for calories?"

"I love Big Macs," I admitted, hanging my head. It wasn't the lack of nutritional value that was mortifying me so much as the environmental issues; as far as I was concerned the more additives in my food, the better. They were an excellent energy source.

"The shame! I can't believe I sleep with you. Ah well, as long as they contribute to your luscious hips."

Hugo smacked the nearest hip with one of his bottles. His mood had definitely improved.

"I'm starving now," I said. "All that talk about cheese and chocolate. I hope we get a good dinner."

"God, yes." Hugo cast a wry glance around him. "It's not like we can just pop out to a late-night chippy if we're still hungry. Jesus, look at that pub. Have you ever seen anything so frightening in your life?"

We were just passing it. A more austere frontage for a building whose function was to entertain the public I had never seen. The windows were tiny and darkened still further by being so heavily leaded that at a cursory glance they looked barred. Only the faintest chinks of light—so pale and cold it suggested that it was being emitted by bare bulbs—emerged through the slivers of glass. The door, flush to the outside wall, was firmly closed and looked as if it had every intention of staying that way. If it hadn't been for the faded sign hanging overhead, which proclaimed it to be the George Coaching Inn, I would have taken it for the village jail.

"I'm almost tempted to go in," I said, pausing. "Just to see what they're getting up to in there."

"Are you mad?" Hugo said incredulously.

"What if it's just really well insulated, and actually they're having a raving karaoke evening with flashing lights and theme cocktails?"

"Believe me, the high point of entertainment in a place like that is a local game of darts known as Pinning the Tourist to the Wall. Haven't you seen the films? Don't you know what happens to Londoners in remote rural pubs?"

I allowed myself to be drawn away.

"It didn't even sound like there was anyone in there," I said, looking back over my shoulder, as if expecting the George to burst into life once we were at a safe distance. "Where are all the people?"

"Let's not start saying that kind of thing so early in the evening," Hugo advised. "We should wait till about eleven-thirty, and we should be in the middle of—that."

He pointed to the village green, which we were just approaching. It was less flat than tradition dictated, almost hilly in places, and surrounded by a breast-high stone wall. Beyond it rose the church, back-lit by gentle orange footlights, a glittering Christmas tree on its castellated roof. Benches were scattered around it at intervals, and on one I could see a black shape, sitting in splendid isolation in the middle of the bench, its head slumped forward. Maybe it was a dead body. I did hope not. I had found enough of them over the past few years to last me for the rest of my life.

"We decide to take a short cut across the green," Hugo was saying, warming to his tale, "and one of us—you, you're the girl—says nervously, 'Darling, where are all the people?' Then we see a gravestone crack open"—he indicated the little cemetery to the side of the church—"and all the zombies start crawling out of their tombs, while the villagers suddenly flood out of their houses carrying burning crosses and howling like wild beasts—and then we turn to flee and see two huge pyres built by the side of the church—"

"Why not wicker effigies?"

"We would have noticed those. We're not blind."

"I think you've rather overdone it. Zombies *and* burning crosses?"

"You just wait till you're turning on the spit. 'Ah,' they're murmuring, looking out from behind their lace curtains. 'That'll be tonight's dinner. She looks like she'd roast up nicely.'"

"I survive," I pointed out. "The girl always survives. I just have to run around the churchyard screaming for a couple of hours."

"In a nightie."

"Obviously."

"As the flames crackle around my pyre," Hugo said, "the smell of my burning flesh ripe in your nostrils—"

"Don't," I said. "You're really making me hungry now."

We rounded the church. The black figure on the bench seemed to have shifted position slightly, sitting up a little straighter, or maybe that was just my wishful thinking.

"I hope we aren't going to dine on shepherd's pie and chips," Hugo said snottily. "You know how I feel about provincial cuisine."

I had the impression that he was deliberately trying to provoke me so I would finally snap back and start the argument that was waiting to happen. It was nothing to do with the countryside or visiting Tom; though maybe the fact that it was New Year's Eve might be bringing matters to a head for Hugo. It was a time of year when, if you weren't getting on well with your loved one, all the relationship's flaws loomed much larger under the magnifying glass of enforced festivities. The knowledge that in a few hours you would be expected to fall into each other's arms at midnight and cement the relationship for another year with a symbolic kiss was enough to make any couple tense and twitchy. Following my usual pattern, I just wanted to shove everything under the rug and not think about it. Hugo—being the girl in the relationship, if not the zombie film—wanted to Talk It Over, and needling me was the only method he had of getting me to open up.

I knew all that. I could even put myself in his place and see how frustrating it must be to have me as a girlfriend. Still, his timing was terrible. I wasn't going to have a major row minutes away from seeing my best friend after months of separation.

"I'm sure the food'll be good," I assured him. "Tom says Emma—his landlady—is a great cook."

Hugo sniffed.

"Tom's scarcely a gourmet, after all. Just as long as he gets his daily ration of starch, he's perfectly content."

God, he was being unbearable.

"You should hear the description of what she's been feeding him over the last few months," I said patiently. "He's practically been ringing me up to recount every detail of his dinners."

Tom had been living in co-op houses, where the main meal of the day tended to be something involving large quantities of lentils, for so long that it sounded like Emma's kitchen was pretty much Paradise Found. From his vivid descriptions, I had images of shelves of much-loved cookbooks, a table heaped with just-risen fresh bread and an Aga brimming with simmering saucepans of home-made jam. My stomach rumbled happily in anticipation.

"Don't landladies limit themselves to beans on toast and ham with salad dressing?" Hugo said.

"Emma's not really a landlady," I explained. Hugo had been so busy filming in the last few months that I hadn't had the opportunity to catch him up on all my friends' gossip. "She's an old friend of the headmistress at the school where Tom's teaching.

Her husband died a while ago, and apparently she's been knocking around in this big old house ever since. The headmistress was looking for somewhere for Tom to live and thought Emma might like to have someone to look after."

"A man to cook for," Hugo said rather cattily.

"I think she wants the company," I said. "Apparently there are a couple of other people staying there too. Americans. One of them's the daughter of an old friend of Emma's. Tom hates them. Says they're work-shy hippies leeching off her."

"Hasn't taken Tom long to develop right-wing tendencies, has it? I expect it's an occupational hazard of living in the country."

I had bitten my tongue so many times by now it felt as swollen as if I were having an allergic reaction. Still, I managed to stay silent, which unnerved Hugo into trying to be a little nicer.

"I'm looking forward to meeting Tom's new blonde," he commented. "Isn't that partly what we're down here for? To observe the latest love-object?"

"She's called Janine," I informed him. "I think Tom's hoping that New Year's Eve will do the business."

"Oh, they haven't—" Hugo said pruriently.

"No. She's a single mum—she's got a four-year-old boy; that's how they met. He was in Tom's class at school—and apparently she's pretty wary about getting involved."

"Been loved and left once already?"

"Something like that."

"Well, for goodness' sake, how much better could she do than a primary-school teacher?" Hugo said with impatience. "He's actually trained in looking after small children! How much more responsible could you get? What's the woman holding out for?"

"Well, it's a small village," I pointed out. "I expect you have to wait to be sure before you start up something. Otherwise the gossip would be a nightmare."

"Mmn."

"And besides, you know, sometimes Tom gets these big unre-
quited crushes," I said, shrugging. "Maybe this is just one more of
those."

To my surprise, I found myself remembering Julia—whom
Tom had been madly in love with years ago—one of his usual
skinny, pretty blondes, with whom he had been more than usually obsessed. Sometimes I thought Tom had a death wish when
it came to relationships. It had been a particularly nasty shock to
him to find out Julia was gay. Whoops. At least Janine, being a
single mum, could be presumed to be straight. Though nowadays
you never knew, I presumed that in a small country village a les-
bian with a small son would attract so much attention that even
Tom, who could be very dim of perception when faced with a
blonde of the type he fancied, would have her sexual orientation
forced on to his notice.

I remembered that for a while I had actually suspected Tom of
killing Lee, the woman Julia had been in love with. I couldn't
believe I had ever really thought Tom capable of that, but he did
have a temper, rarely though one saw it. I had once seen him
deck a guy in a pub who was coming on to yet another skinny
blonde on whom Tom had a crush. Admittedly, Tom had had a
few drinks, but it had taken three guys to hold him back while I
threw a pint of beer in his face to shock him into a state more
closely resembling sobriety. The guys had been pretty good
sports about being soaked in beer, considering.

I rarely thought about Lee nowadays. It was too painful. I still
missed her. And I shivered when I thought of who had really
murdered her. Not to mention how her killer had died at my
hands. It was ruled as self-defence at the inquest; I had never had
to go to trial. Still, it wasn't my most pleasant memory. I shoved
it back into the furthest cubbyhole of my brain and slammed the

door on it hard. As I just said, I was good at not thinking about things I really didn't want to think about.

We had reached the far side of the green by now. And there, sure enough, was the signpost Tom had told me to look out for, flush against the stone wall that ran along the side of the lane. The right pointer bore the legend: "Much Deeper 3m." The left simply read: "Toilet."

"I thought he was joking," I said, my jaw dropping open.

"Fabulous," Hugo said appreciatively. "We should photograph ourselves under this in the daytime. It should sum up our weekend in the country perfectly."

"You won't be alive in the daytime, remember?" I said shortly. "You'll be a charred heap of cinders."

"Heap them into a neat pile with my hat on top," Hugo suggested.

Ominously, everything that cheered Hugo up was a joke at the expense of Lesser Swinfold. And the more high-spirited he became, the more depressed I got. I was worried that he was going to refer to the village as Lesser Swinefold in public, as he had already done driving down here. Nowadays Hugo and I seemed like the man and woman in the little weather-house: when one of us was outside and happy, the other one was sulking indoors in a foul mood. Our *entente cordiale* in the bathroom had been a rare moment of mutual content. Generally we were much more likely to keep missing each other.

"Third house on the left from the sign," I said.

"Ah, the toilet."

I ignored him. The toilet was perfectly obvious, a squat cement outhouse marooned on the edge of the green, looking incongruous and uncomfortable. In London it would have smelt of stale urine, been carpeted with old syringes and condoms and been home to at least four unfortunates sleeping rough. Here, no doubt, it was merely a little damp. Probably the council budget was even extensive enough to run to toilet paper. Lesser Swinfold was, by the looks of it, a village not short of a bob or two. Every other house had a shiny Range Rover parked on its drive. The others had Volvo estates or BMWs.

"Here we go," I said. "Gate in the hedge. Stone stairs to left. All as described."

"It would be much too common to have street numbers, darling," Hugo purred. "Or, God forbid, plaques with the house names. How vulgar."

Ignoring him, I unlatched the gate and started up the steps without looking back. There was a short gravel path up to the house, which was, like all the others around the green, big, made of stone and well kept without being overly opulent. If there were any *nouveaux riches* in Lesser Swinfold, they had shaped up or shipped out pretty fast.

The front door was a little ajar. I pushed it, and it yielded.

"Hello?" I said, stepping into the hall. Polished floorboards and garlands of dried flowers, a kilim hanging on the wall. Pretty and welcoming. At least Hugo couldn't complain about this.

No-one answered. I could hear music coming from downstairs, though. Tentatively, I crossed the hall and was brought up short by the sight of a large living-room opening to my left, filled with sofas and armchairs in a wide circle around the fireplace. Bookshelves lined the walls. The floors were heavy with rugs and the sofas with cushions. It was the kind of room that immediately made me want to curl up in a big armchair, like a cat, and watch the flames flickering in the huge stone hearth.

Two men were slumped on the largest sofa, watching a film on TV. Though they must both have seen me standing there—if they hadn't heard me call out—neither of them so much as raised their heads to greet me.

"Hi," I said. "I'm looking for Tom."

"Downstairs," one of them grunted without taking his eyes off the screen.

Charming. Hugo, behind me, gave a shrug so expressive that it was almost audible and gestured towards the staircase.

Music rose around us, soothing soft jazz, as I picked my way carefully down the stone treads, each one worn concave in the centre by centuries of use. They led directly into the kitchen, a huge and cosy room, which at first sight seemed to be filled with people. No, not people: women. There were women everywhere. At the sink, by the fridge, at the Aga, in the larder, sitting around the table. It was like entering a Women's Institute harem. In the far corner of the room a group of small children was sitting on the floor, absorbed in play, surrounded by a sort of *cordon sanitaire* of bright plastic toys strewn all around them.

Finally, I picked out Tom, whose large, masculine presence balanced the oestrogen factor to some degree. Catching sight of us, he jumped up from the kitchen table, where he had been slicing something, and crashed towards me, knocking a couple of wooden chairs aside in his passage.

"Sammy!" he practically yodelled. "Hey, great to see you! Welcome to Lesser Swinfold!"

And he enfolded me in a great, woolly hug. No matter how many great, woolly hugs I had had from Tom over the years, I couldn't get enough. He was my sort-of-brother, and I loved him to death. I threw my arms around as much of him as I could reach—Tom had never been svelte—and hugged him back just as enthusiastically. Tom was my rock. I hadn't realised till now just how much I'd missed him. Suddenly, I found myself hoping, almost praying, that things with him and Janine would work out, that she was a nice person who loved him back. Tom, more than anyone else I knew, really deserved to be happy.

2

"HUGO! ALL RIGHT, MATE?" TOM SAID, THROWING HIS ARMS
around Hugo in turn.

Hugo wasn't a big hugger. Instead he patted Tom's shoulder
with one hand, as if reassuring a disturbed mental patient. Moving out of the way to let Tom past, I tripped over the legs of a
woman sitting at the table smoking, who made not the slightest
effort to shift over for me. I chalked a black mark up against her.

"Everyone," Tom announced happily to the assembled group,
"this is Sam, one of my best mates, and her boyfriend Hugo."

I couldn't help shuddering, and looking over I saw that Hugo
was having much the same reaction. We were averse to the
words "girlfriend" and "boyfriend." Particularly at the moment.

"Found it all right, then?" Tom said to us.

Hugo hated this kind of banal question.

"As you see," he said, making it quite clear by his tone of
voice that he did not consider this the happiest of eventualities.
I could have slapped him.

"I should introduce you to everyone," Tom said enthusiastically.

I braced myself, looking over at the children with a certain
dread. I couldn't imagine he meant this literally; he knew perfectly well how little interest Hugo or I had in people under the
age of sixteen (when they became legal).

"Yes, why don't you, Tom darling," drawled the smoking woman.

Everyone else in the kitchen seemed to be busy stirring pans on the stove or setting the table, but Smoking Woman was using her cigarette to indicate clearly how far removed she was from anything as mundane as preparation for dinner. I hadn't warmed to her, as will be obvious. I didn't like the proprietary, slightly patronising air with which she had addressed Tom, or the big ethnic bracelets, which clanked on her wrists like manacles whenever she made the slightest movement.

"Well, first and foremost, this is Emma," Tom said, crossing to the woman standing by the Aga. He sank his hands into her shoulders and rocked her back and forwards fondly. From having been embraced by Tom, I knew that his hands were greasy from the smoked salmon he had been slicing, but Emma seemed not to mind at all. She reached up and patted one of his hands, turning her head to smile up at him with great fondness.

"Emma's preparing a feast for us this evening, aren't you?" he said to her. "We're not going to be allowed to leave the table till we're stuffed like geese."

Emma was exactly what I had been expecting, a kind-looking woman who looked as at home in her cooking apron as if she put it on automatically every morning over her clothes. She was well into her fifties, her short unkempt hair thickly woven with grey, her body heavy with middle-aged spread, the kind of country woman who had long relinquished any vanity about her appearance that she might once have possessed. Still, when she smiled up at Tom, she was almost pretty, her eyes sparkling.

"I'm so glad you two could join us for New Year," she said, crossing the kitchen to shake hands with us hospitably. "Do take off your coats and hang them on the pegs, won't you? There's lots of space. Sam." She squeezed my hand. "Tom's told me so much about you. He says you're his best friend. It's lovely to meet you."

"He says you've been taking very good care of him," I said, smiling at her. The warmth and friendliness she projected were clearly genuine. I could see why Tom was so happy living here.

"Oh," Emma said, "it's been a positive pleasure. It's so nice having a—someone else to cook for."

I could tell that she had wanted to say "man," and caught herself at the last moment. To my right, by the table, I noticed Smoking Woman smirking unpleasantly.

"Emma's been feeding me up," Tom said unnecessarily.

I had already noticed that. The vegetarian diet in his London co-op house, combined with vigorous physical exercise (clearing the junkyard of a garden had been his house task) had caused him to lose the excess pounds he always complained about. Now he was almost chubby. Emma had doubtless been dishing up roast beef and Yorkshire pudding, with apple pie and cream to follow, three times a day for the last few months. Still, although a little more portly than was necessary, he looked blissfully happy. His skin colour was good and he moved with confidence. Tom was prone to sinking into depressions, during which he slumped around devoid of any energy, but maybe the countryside had picked him up. That, and having a job which paid a decent wage—at least compared to writing poetry, which he had done ever since I had known him. Even though he had been published, his income had always been pitiful. A steady job he liked doing, plus a budding love story—I hoped—would be enough to lift anyone's spirits.

I observed too that he was wearing a new sweater. Or rather, allowing for Tom's personal habits, a sweater that had been new some weeks ago. It was already beginning to acquire that patina of frays and stains which was Tom's signature look. I was willing to bet that Emma was responsible for the sweater as well.

Women always wanted to mother Tom. And at least this one was an appropriate age.

Smoking Woman was stretching out her hand to me and Hugo, rather like the Pope expecting us to kiss his ring. This was definitely not Janine. She was thirty years too old and two stones too heavy. But her hair colour would have been enough to settle the matter; its grey had been thoroughly covered by a mixture of expensively applied high- and low-lights in shades of bronze and auburn.

"I'm Sheila. Tom seems to have forgotten about me, so I'll do the honours myself," she said with a ghastly mixture of archness and hostility.

"Sheila's my sister," Emma hurried to explain. "Not that you can see the resemblance, I'm sure," she added self-deprecatingly, with a little laugh that Sheila echoed patronisingly.

I couldn't, or at least not yet. But I assured Emma that the resemblance was obvious simply because I knew it would wind Sheila up, and I was pleased to see that it did. Sheila, with her heavily streaked bob of hair, her lashes thick with mascara and her wrists laden with elephant off-cuts, clearly disliked being compared to her more frumpish sister. Emma, without a dab of make-up on her face and her figure settled comfortably into late middle-age, was probably anathema to Sheila, who was fighting the ageing process with every means known to womankind. It wasn't this I objected to; it was her attitude to her sister, which was immediately obvious. Sheila wasn't even helping out; she was just sitting on her dieted arse while Emma cooked a meal, which Sheila would probably smoke her way through. I smiled at her politely. Sheila glared at me and lit another cigarette.

"And this," Tom said, moving around to the other side of the wide old dining table, "is Janine."

He pronounced her name with a bashful tenderness, which I immediately recognised. And as I looked across the table at

Janine, who was sitting at it folding napkins, I recognised her too.
Not her, but the type: Tom's type. She was a perfect example. No
wonder I had hardly noticed her at first; she was small and delicately boned and looked very shy. Sitting next to her was a larger
woman with strawberry-blonde curls, bright red lipstick and a
manner so ebullient that Janine almost disappeared by contrast,
like the moon when the sun comes out. Janine's pale-blonde
hair was drawn back into a ponytail, and she wore hardly any
make-up, but she didn't need it. The more I looked at her, the
more I realised how pretty she was.

Tom was standing behind her chair, his hands leaning on the
top rail, almost looming, a big, goofy, beaming smile on his face.
Sometimes Tom felt like my older brother, when he lectured me
about my character flaws, but right now he was a much younger
one, presenting his latest girlfriend for approval and quite unable
to control his enthusiasm.

Janine looked a little embarrassed by how obvious Tom was
making the introduction. I could feel everyone else in the room
watching the little scene with considerable interest.

"Hi, I'm Sam," I said, smiling at her. It seemed ridiculously
formal to lean across the table and shake her hand, so I didn't.

"I'm Janine," she said. "Well, you know that already."

I was expecting her voice to be quiet, as shy as she looked, but
it was clear, unexpectedly confident and as pretty as her face. I
was impressed. There was character there. And now I looked
more closely I could see that there was a nice determined set to
her jawline.

"And this is Tamsin, my sister-in-law," she said, indicating
the woman with the strawberry-blonde hair.

"Welcome to Lesser Swinford!" Tamsin said, standing up and
sticking out her hand. She pumped mine with great enthusiasm,
despite the fact that we were both off-balance from leaning
across the table. Her ebullience was such that I suspected she

had been hitting the pre-dinner drinks in large quantities. Her eyes were bright and her lipstick a little smudged.

"And you're Hugo, right?" Tamsin leant still further across the table to grab Hugo's hand, wobbling a little. Janine removed a tray of appetising-looking cheese balls seconds before Tamsin's cardigan trailed across them.

"Happy New Year and all that," Tamsin went on. "Well, it's a bit early, but you know what I mean. You've come from London, haven't you? You lucky sods. Ooh, what I wouldn't give to be in London right now. See a bit of life for a change."

I had been resolutely avoiding catching Hugo's eye up till now, but I couldn't help glancing over at him. His expression was agonised. It was obvious that he was so at one with Tamsin that the struggle not to say "Me too!" was so acute that it had rendered him completely speechless. Lesser Swinford had won a victory, of sorts.

* * * * * *

After that I tried not to look at Hugo at all, in case his grimaces drove me so crazy that I picked up a meat cleaver and started hacking random pieces off him. We were only here for two days; it was ridiculous for him to drift around the place sighing for London as if he were a character in *The Three Sisters* pining for Moscow. I bet if Hugo were ever cast in a Chekhov play he would use this experience, though. He looked as if he had the sense of isolation down pat.

Champagne helped. It always did. If Irina, Masha and Olga had been able to hit the fizz every evening at the cocktail hour, there would have been fewer lamentations and considerably more affairs with officers, which would at least have proved a nice distraction from the whole Moscow question. After two glasses, which barely touched the sides of my throat going down, I was considerably more relaxed and able again to concentrate on Tom, rather than my deeply annoying boyfriend. The kitchen smelt wonderful, roasting meats and simmering berries mingling into a rich full scent so delicious that it almost felt as if I could taste it. Tom was slicing smoked-salmon strips and rolling them up with a cream cheese filling. Mellow jazz issued from the stereo, though its effect was slightly diluted by the variety of piercing beeps emitted by the children's toys. The kids had been briefly introduced by Tom—two were Tamsin's and one was Janine's—but mercifully they seemed as little interested in us as we were in them, and we had not been required to go through any ghastly, halting ritual involving their ages and their favourite subject at school.

"What's with the hats?" Tom asked me as I hung them on the pegs.

"Hugo got his first," I explained, "and I kept nicking it. So he got me one for Christmas."

I stroked my hat lovingly. It was Russian-style, with earflaps tied over the top, black fake fur soft as silk.

"Wasn't his too big for you, little pinhead?" Tom said, patting my crown as I came to sit down next to him. He had forgotten about the salmon grease, and so had I till it was too late. Hugo's wince of anguish was almost palpable. Ah well, bugger him. He didn't have to touch my hair if he didn't want to.

"She lost the hat she bought in New York," Hugo explained. It was such a surprise to hear him speak that everyone turned and stared at him. Little did they know that fashion was one of the few subjects that could coax Hugo out of a sulk.

"I loved that hat," I said wistfully.

"It was very Portobello Market," Hugo said. "She looked like a little street urchin."

"Hugo thought it was a bit trendy," I said.

"This one suits you much better," he agreed.

"Tom says you both live in London," Emma said from the Aga.

"Yes, I have a studio in Holloway and Hugo lives in Spital-fields," I said, glaring at him to indicate that he should make conversation.

"Oh, I hear that's really fashionable now," Emma said to him. "How long have you been there?"

"Nearly ten years."

"Really? You must be very disappointed at all the changes."

"Not at all," Hugo said with relish. "It was an absolute slum before. Now there are lots of lovely wine bars and restaurants, and my flat has gone up in value so many times I can't even tell you what it's worth."

Emma was slightly taken aback by this response. I think she had expected the usual complaint about yuppies moving in and ruining the area.

"You're an actor, aren't you?" Sheila said, leaning forward to get a closer look at him.

"*Omigod!*" Tamsin yelled, so loudly that Hugo, who was sitting next to her, flinched back as if she had just honked a horn in his ear. "*I know you! I saw you on the telly!*"

"Those two statements," Hugo said snottily, "often tend to be mutually exclusive."

Sheila sniffed with laughter at this to show how sophisticated she was. But Tamsin rode roughshod over it.

"*You were on* The Bill! *You were a poof!*"

Tamsin was definitely a little drunk. Janine, I noticed, looked embarrassed.

"Gosh, fancy you remembering that!" Hugo said, hugely flattered. "That must have been years ago. I was rather fatter then," he added modestly.

"*And I saw you just the other day! In one of those little thingies!*"

"Trailers, Tamsin," Janine said, catching my eye with an apologetic shrug. She needn't have worried. Hugo was such an exhibitionist that he relished practically any kind of attention.

He extracted his cigarette case and removed one of his pastel Sobranies. I noticed that he was now leaning back in his chair so that Tamsin could get an even better look at his face.

"You were beating someone up!" she recalled enthusiastically. *"And then you shagged this girl!"*

"My life on television is always full of incident," Hugo said cordially.

"Hugo's in a BBC series coming out next month," I explained. "They're running lots of trailers because they think it's going to do really well."

Hugo tried to look bashful and failed completely. Tamsin, having temporarily run out of steam, just sat and gawped at him. Hugo accepted this adulation complacently. I thanked God for Tamsin. She might just have saved the evening.

Everyone had their gazes fixed on Hugo by now. Even Emma, who was piping filling into what looked like hundreds of miniature quiches, had her head turned to take him in.

"I'll watch out for the series," Janine said. "What's it called?"

"Driven," I said.

"What're you doing now, mate?" Tom asked him. I supposed it was sweet of him to keep addressing Hugo as "mate," a token of goodwill, but it always seemed so inappropriate.

"Just finished shooting this appalling film," Hugo said. "Art for art's sake. Well, never again. I'm longing to sell out to Hollywood and play nasty English baddies for the next twenty years. Or Germans. I have the right profile."

It was true. Hugo's looks—tall and pale, with an imposing nose, cold, grey eyes and a slick of blond hair—were archetypal Aryan. He kept begging his agent to put him up for evil Nazis and was very disappointed when she told him they were currently out of fashion. He was hoping to play some international terrorists of indeterminate nationality instead. Hugo would do a lovely Bond villain.

"What was it about? The film?" Sheila asked, lighting another cigarette, her bracelets smashing into each other like fighting rhinos locking horns.

"God knows. Love and death in Acton. I have no idea, and I improvised most of it."

"Improvised?" Sheila said.

Hugo shuddered in recollection. "I loathe impro," he said confidentially. "I accepted this poorly paid, poxily run piece of amateur-league nonsense because they sent me a rather wonderful script, which the retarded teenage director then proceeded to throw away because he wanted 'reality' instead. *Really*." He grimaced. "I said, 'Darling, you can have all the reality you want, but could I please only have one chin?' It can come out a little soft from the side," he explained, with great solemnity, "and I didn't trust them to look out for it. It wasn't a good start. He thought I wasn't taking him seriously."

"And you weren't," Tom pointed out.

"Well, no. It was such a good script," Hugo sighed wistfully.

"What's it called?" Sheila asked.

"Oh, don't bother. Straight to video if it's lucky. An early part of my œuvre. One for the biography."

I was watching Tamsin and trying hard not to giggle. I could see that everyone apart from Tom was fixing Hugo with that baffled stare I had observed so often on people newly exposed to the full Hugo effect. They thought he was gay. I couldn't blame them; I had thought the same when I first met him. But Tamsin was by far the most blatant. She was positively goggling. Lesser Swinfold could never have seen anything like Hugo before. Which, as far as I was concerned, was Lesser Swinfold's great good luck.

"Anyway, enough about me," Hugo said complacently, having made his effect. "Tell me about yourselves."

This not unnaturally reduced the assembly to a silence finally broken by Sheila.

"Oh no," she purred. "You sound so much more interesting. Tell us more about your adventures in the film world."

Mercifully, however, at that moment a distraction afforded itself. Footsteps resounded on the stone stairs, and a girl clattered down them into the kitchen.

"Hi, everyone!" she said cheerfully, in a light American accent. "It's lovely outside! I just went for a walk round the village."

She was wearing an assortment of clothes which looked as if they had all been bought years ago from a charity shop at the scummier end of Kentish Town Road. Oversized jeans, layers of tattered sweaters and a beaten-up, ancient, man's linen jacket over the top, much frayed at the lapels and cuffs. Its shoulder-pads drooped well past her own shoulders, and its hem came to mid-thigh. I would have known who she was from her accent alone, but her style of dress confirmed it. This must be one-half of the hippy couple Tom had mentioned, the ones he didn't like. I wondered why. She seemed very friendly.

"You didn't go out in just that, did you, Laura?" Emma said maternally. "You'll have caught your death!"

"Oh no," Laura beamed. "I borrowed your warm coat. It was really toasty."

"Did Ethan go with you?" Sheila asked with an edge to her voice.

"Oh no," Laura said. "He was watching some action film on TV with Andy."

She smiled at Tamsin. I assumed that Ethan was Laura's boyfriend; we had already been informed that Andy was Tamsin's husband and Janine's brother. From the way they had both grunted at us from the sofa when we came into the house, I was in no particular hurry to meet either of them.

Laura pulled up a chair and sat down at the table.

"There was someone sitting out on the green, on a bench," I said, despite my better judgement. "They must have been cold."

"Oh, that was Alan," Laura said easily. "Looking at the church."

"Being existentialist," Sheila added indulgently.

"Alan's our local Angry Young Man," Tom explained.

As long as Alan wasn't their local Dead Young Man, I had no further interest in him.

"So!" Laura said. "You must be our guests from London!"

"How could you tell?" Hugo enquired.

She laughed. On closer examination of Laura I realised that she wasn't a girl at all. She must have been in her mid-thirties. The easy, tomboyish way she moved had fooled me; also the red flush to her cheeks, from being out in the cold evening air. She wore no make-up at all, and her skin was weatherbeaten. I doubted she ever moisturised. There was a sort of hippy innocence to her—no, not innocence, ingenuousness. Her hair was a tangle of unbrushed reddish curls and her eyes a washed-out blue. She was the kind of person who looked as if she would be relaxed in any surroundings, and her presence certainly lightened the atmosphere in the kitchen, as if she incarnated a breath of fresh air.

"Wow, there's enough food here to feed the village," Laura said, looking around the kitchen at the various platters of mini-quiches and Tom's rapidly accumulating smoked-salmon rolls. "What a feast!"

Tom, to my surprise, glared at her. And Emma's only response was a distracted smile.

"Oh God, I said I'd make an apple pie, didn't I!" Laura jumped up. "I'll do it now. I completely forgot."

Emma looked horrified.

"It's a bit much . . ." she demurred, trying to sound polite. "We've got loads of food already . . ."

"No, I said I would! I can't let you down!"

"The oven's very crowded as it is—" Emma started.

But Laura was already pulling over a big bowl of apples and rummaging around for a knife.

"Can I use this chopping board?" she said to Emma, indicating the one on which the massed ranks of tiny quiches were neatly arranged.

"Well, that's really for the—"

"I'll put them all on a big plate. Don't worry; it'll be fine!"

Laura dragged a huge serving platter off one of the shelves.

"That's for the meat," Emma said, sounding a little frazzled now.

"Oh well, I'll sort it out—don't worry; it'll be fine—"

Laura crashed around in cupboards for a while, making unnerving rattling noises. Finally, she brought the chopping board over to the table, having stacked the quiches messily on some dinner plates, and proceeded to start slicing apples.

"Aren't you going to peel them, dear?" Emma hinted politely.

"No, no, I never do," Laura said breezily. "It's a waste of time. Besides, all the vitamins are in the peel, right?"

"And all the pesticides," Sheila said dryly.

"No, they're organic!" Laura said. "I got them from the van! Bought them specially!"

Tom, beside me, muttered something I didn't completely catch. The only words I heard were "two months."

"So when are we eating?" Laura asked.

"Soon," Sheila said shortly, more to the ever-growing pile of roughly chopped apples than to Laura herself.

"Oh, no problem. The pie'll be in the oven while we eat, and then we can have it for dessert, right?"

I quite admired Laura's laissez-faire attitude to cooking. I wouldn't have been able to make an apple pie if I had had all day, twenty recipe books, the measured-out ingredients in front of me in little glass bowls and a celebrity chef on hand to trouble-shoot, so I was impressed by the way she was now emptying flour on to the board and kneading it up with water and butter without even measuring out quantities. It was so . . . authentic.

But I had the feeling I was in the minority. Tamsin and Janine were both staring at the dough with barely concealed expressions of distaste, like fastidious gourmets forced to enter a fish-and-chip shop and contemplating with horror the plastic container of mushy peas. The pastry, which Laura was now pressing into a ceramic dish, was oddly pale, with an unpleasantly sweaty sheen. Perhaps that wasn't what it was supposed to look like. Even Sheila, who didn't strike me as much of a baker, cast it one appalled glance and turned her head pointedly away, scattering ash from the end of her cigarette in a long arc as she went, which just happened to graze the edge of the apple pile.

Emma, realising that the apple pie was a *fait accompli*, said faintly, "I'll start rearranging things in the Aga so it fits in, shall I?" and bent yet again to the oven doors.

I revised my earlier opinion about Laura; that sunniness of disposition now seemed almost wilful, a blithe disregard for any opinions which contradicted her own. Emma could not have made it clearer that it was far too late for Laura to start baking a pie, and Laura had ridden roughshod over her hostess with a vague, happy smile. Having decided that cooking would be a nice, helpful thing to do, Laura was going to ignore any evidence to the contrary. I wondered if she was always this insensitive.

3

DINNER TURNED OUT TO BE EVEN MORE LAVISH THAN I HAD been expecting. Like a conjuror, Emma kept producing more and more dishes; when the oven had been emptied of roast meats and their accompaniments, she would emerge from the larder with brimming bowls of prawns and courgette couscous and a couple of Gruyère roulades with avocado and rocket filling. I tucked in like a starving jackal. The only problem was Emma's Augean-stables approach to catering. As soon as one dish had been finished, she would whisk away the serving plate, bundle it into the sink and whip out another from where it had been hiding in the fridge. This meant that it was impossible to pace yourself, as you had no idea of what, or how much, might be coming next. We just kept eating until we all passed out or exploded.

Tom and I spent the whole meal with our mouths crammed to bursting. Even Hugo was moving, more slowly than us, but just as steadily, through the massed onslaught of food under which the table was groaning. I was happy for him. He was usually on such a rigid diet that to see him able to give himself completely to the pleasures of gourmandising was a rare treat.

The quality of the food had perked him up tremendously, thank God. Being recognised had been a huge starting-point; the restaurant quality of the dinner added to the effect, and the final touch came when he had reached for the nearest champagne bottle only to find it empty.

"Is that the last one?" he said. "Damn. Maybe I should pop back to our cottage and get some more."

"Oh, don't worry," Emma said, setting down a serving platter thickly covered with overlapping slices of cold chicken breast in what was later explained to be a parsley velouté. "I've got cases and cases in the cellar. And there's a very nice Blanc de Blancs and some really good Californian Pinot Noir, if you'd rather have wine."

Hugo's expression was sublime. If a Hollywood director had just rung him personally to request that he accept a colossal fee to play a horribly perverted Roman emperor, with a fabulous series of togas, in a sweeping and lavishly expensive epic with plenty of location filming in Italy, he could scarcely have looked more content.

"Actually, we are running low. Maybe I should just pop down and get another case of the red—" Emma was saying anxiously.

Tom was already pushing back his chair, ready to help. But Sheila cleared her throat so loudly it could only have been meant as an interruption. She turned pointedly to Laura's boyfriend, who was sitting next to her.

"Ethan, why don't you help Emma out by getting another case up?" Sheila said. Though phrased as a suggestion, it came out much more like an order. Sheila was making a point. "You know where it is, don't you?" she added with what sounded to me like considerable sarcasm.

The subtext couldn't have been more obvious: Sheila was indicating that Ethan didn't pull his weight in the household and was something of a drink scrounger to boot. Well, they say you always dislike people who have the same faults as you. So far, all I had seen Sheila do this evening was sit in her chair and lift a wine glass to her mouth. But Ethan didn't seem at all resentful. He favoured Sheila, and Emma beyond her, with a wide, no-problem smile identical to Laura's, and said, "Sure," in an easy American drawl.

His heels clicked on the tiles as he crossed the kitchen and headed down the cellar stairs. He was wearing cowboy boots. I wondered if this was because he needed the extra height. He was definitely on the short side, smaller than Laura, even with the stacked heels. Or maybe it was just the image. Tom had called Laura and Ethan hippies, but I didn't think that description quite fitted them. They could have been brother and sister: they had the same skin, aged before its time by exposure to the weather, the same hazy blue eyes, the same relaxed, guileless air, which said that nothing was worth getting stressed or strained about. It was a kind of cowboy effect. Only cowboys, ideally, had a sense of purpose, which was the one thing that both Ethan and Laura signally lacked. Maybe Ethan was what cowboys turned into when they burned out and started bumming around Europe instead, being bad house guests.

"How are you kids doing?" Tom said, leaning over to the children's table. "Need anything else?"

The corner table under which the three children had previously been playing had been set up for their dinner. They had been fed roast potatoes, ham sandwiches and fizzy drinks, the last two produced by Tamsin and Janine from plastic bags they had thoughtfully brought with them. Tamsin's husband Andy was clearly one of those men who considered anything to do with children his wife's responsibility; having been summoned downstairs for dinner, he had hardly acknowledged the presence of the kids, beyond complaining about the noise they made yelling for more fizzy orange. Now, however, they had been silent for a good forty minutes. They were sitting in a sandwich-stuffed trance, their systems slowed down almost to coma by the act of digestion.

Janine shook her head vigorously at Tom, but it was too late.

"Ice cream!" the little girl demanded, springing immediately to life.

"Ice cream!" chorused the two boys. Their mouths were smeared and sticky with orange from the drinks, their faces flushed, their hair messed into clumps. Though dazed with food and the heat of the kitchen, the mere mention of ice cream had been enough to galvanise them.

"Tom, Tom," Janine said reprovingly. She was smiling at him, but still shaking her head. "Haven't you learnt anything yet? Never interrupt them when they're all nice and peaceful! And you don't ask 'em what they want, you tell them what they can have, when you're ready to give it to 'em."

She tutted in mock-disapproval.

"That should be the first thing they tell you when you're training to be a teacher," she added.

She was teasing Tom affectionately, but it seemed to me her manner was more that of one friend to another than lovers' banter. Still, there was enough intimacy in her voice to make Tom blush up to the roots of his hair and look simultaneously abashed and happy. It was obvious that Janine liked and felt comfortable with him. I felt encouraged about Tom's prospects—in the long term. But right now, if he didn't get some ice cream into those kids fast, he was in big trouble.

Emma prodded him urgently. I had noticed before that she had a worry crease between her brows, deep enough to insert the entire tip of one of Sheila's manicured nails into. Now the crease was intensifying as her brows drew together, till it was almost black. This was where one's third eye was supposed to be located. It couldn't be good karma to have a stress mark there instead.

"Tom, there isn't any IC!" she muttered. "Or at least"—she shot a glance at Janine and Tamsin, clearly torn between wanting to be a perfect hostess and the demands of her menu—"it's not for the small fry. It's home-made. They wouldn't like it," she added desperately. "I'm so sorry, I should have thought to get some in from the supermarket—"

"No, don't you worry," Janine said calmly. "It's nice enough of you to have them round for dinner as it is without going to extra trouble. Tamsin and I brought some of their videos—is it OK if I take them upstairs and settle them in front of the TV?"

Emma looked hugely relieved.

"Oh yes, that would be fine," she said. "But won't they—you know—"

But Janine was already on her feet. She cast a quick glance at Tamsin, but her sister-in-law had been hitting the wine at dinner with great brio and for the last half-hour or so had relapsed into a happy state of almost semi-consciousness, nodding her head with owlish seriousness at stray comments made by her immediate neighbours, but clearly with a minimal idea of what they had actually said. Next to her was her husband, Andy, a large man with a head like a potato, bearing no resemblance to his sister Janine apart from the family colouring. He was already going bald, though he couldn't have been more than thirty, and the top of his head was pink and shiny with heat. I had the perfect opportunity to observe it at that moment, because he hadn't even raised it to participate in the discussion about his children. He was too busy forking cold chicken into his mouth, as oblivious to the noise his own kids were making as if they weren't even in the same house as him.

No wonder Tamsin had overindulged a little. Looking at what she had to go home with that evening, I considered she had practically been a model of restraint.

"Come on, you lot," Janine was saying to the kids. "We're going upstairs to watch the box and play with your toys. I've got lots of Christmas chocolates in my bag for you. And I've brought a Disney video we can put on."

The children followed her like lambs. Chocolate and Disney films: that was probably what the Pied Piper had promised the children of Hamelin. Tamsin and Andy's daughter, who looked a little older than the boys, seemed to be the ringleader: she bounced off her chair yelling, "Christmas chocolates!" gleefully, eyes sparkling, curly hair tossing, like a miniature version of her mother. The boys charged along, following her lead. Janine, standing at the bottom of the stairs, shepherded them past her one by one, like a teacher checking off her pupils. The last one was her son, who, we had already learnt, had the unfortunate name of Pitt. He took a few steps up the stairs and then paused mid-stride, looking suddenly worried. Curling one leg behind the other, he scratched his head, tilting it a little to one side. It was a curiously adult pose. Take him out of the bright dungarees and stripy T-shirt and put him in a floppy lace shirt and bloomers and he would look just like one of those Victorian photographs of children, the ones with the twee titles like "A Little Angel Contemplates" or "A Thoughtful Moment on the Stairs." His blue eyes and cornsilk-blond hair added the final touch—even though the latter was matted around the edges with ketchup.

"Mum," he said doubtfully, "isn't there any ice cream, then?"

"We've got lots of lovely chocolates," Janine reassured him. "Now up you go, quick, quick! Go on, or Courtney and Marc'll get the best places on the sofa!"

"I'll come and give you a hand," Tom volunteered. I had been expecting this; I was only surprised it had taken him so long.

Turning back to the table, I caught Emma's eye. She looked almost in physical pain. The third-eye crease was so dark it was almost black, like a nail driven into her forehead from which the rest of her face was sagging down loosely, as if the muscles had collapsed.

"Em, what is it?" Tom, seeing her expression too, gave her a hug. "Now don't you worry about the ice cream! It's all my fault anyway, I should never have asked the kids what they wanted. Janine's quite right. You wait, they'll be settled down up there in no time."

"It's really kind of you to have us all round," Janine added, looking embarrassed.

"Yes, it is. You're a star." Tom hugged Emma again. "We'll be down in a jiffy. Make sure you save some ice cream for us!"

"Aaah, Tom's so sweet, isn't he? If you ask me, Jan ought to snap him up!" Tamsin said tipsily, bare seconds after Janine and Tom had disappeared upstairs.

"Jan can do better than that," her husband snapped back.

"Better than that? A nice bloke who helps out with the kids?" Tamsin said rather pointedly. "He's got a good job, too. He'll never be out of work. They always need teachers, don't they?"

"He's not a real teacher, is he?" Andy said. "He just wipes their bums and teaches them the ABC."

"More than you do," Tamsin muttered.

Andy ignored this.

"My sister can do better than him," he insisted.

It had the sound of an old argument, worn down along familiar lines, and embarrassing for everyone else around the table—particularly the friends of Tom. Emma was stiffening in his defence. Still, it scarcely seemed worth defending Tom's honour to Andy.

"Do you have a headache?" I asked Emma, partly as a distraction. "I've got some pills in my bag."

That wasn't all I had in my bag; at the imminent prospect of dessert, Hugo and I had retired, one after another, to the toilet to do a line of coke each. Emma was welcome to some coke if she wanted it; she was our hostess, after all. And it was probably just what she needed, after being at the stove all day. Still, I had actually meant codeine pills. I started fishing in my bag, but Emma held up her hand to stop me.

"No, dear, it's not a headache," she assured me, "just a bit of a twinge in my back. Don't worry, though, it's gone now. I've probably been on my feet too much today. The doctor warned me it could start playing up if I overdid things. I've got my pills right here." She fished in the pocket of her cords and brought out a little bottle, popping out a couple of pills and swallowing them with a gulp of water.

"You know you have to be careful, Emma," Sheila said unexpectedly, with what almost sounded like gruffly expressed concern in her voice. "You're not supposed to overdo it with those painkillers. And you wouldn't need to take them if you hadn't been to all this trouble cooking a ridiculous amount of food."

"Oh, New Year's Eve only comes once a year," Emma said. "And I wanted to make a good dinner. It's nice to have so many guests, for a change. Right!" she said firmly. "Let's clear the table, and then we can have the ice cream!"

The ice cream turned out to be honey flavoured, tasting almost like molasses, dark and rich and nutty. And it went superbly with the treacle and lemon-curd tarts that Emma had baked as an accompaniment. I pushed my plate away finally, feeling as if I would never be hungry again, and proposed a toast to Emma. Glasses were duly raised. Tamsin, revived by pudding and coffee, insisted that it was bad luck unless everyone clinked with everyone else. So there was much leaning over the table and consequent groaning as bloated waistbands and trouser zips were tested to their limits. Emma, looking much better, was flushed and happy, beaming around the table at her weirdly assorted group of guests. There was a moment of utter, satiated content, broken only by the occasional squeak as people pushed back their chairs to lessen the pressure on their stomachs.

Laura's exclamation made everyone start.

"Oh! My pie!" she cried suddenly, jumping up from her chair. "It must be done by now!"

Glances of desperation were exchanged around the table.

"We're all pretty full now," Tom, speaking for the entire group, said to her back as she squatted down in front of the Aga.

"Oh, just a little bit, it's very light. I made it specially!"

Triumphantly, she produced the ceramic dish from the oven and brought it over to the table, setting it down on a heat-resistant tile.

"Maybe we could save it for tomorrow," Emma suggested tactfully.

"But it's fresh out of the oven, that's when it's best—"

Laura sliced into the pie, which was pleasantly shiny and golden-brown. As soon as the knife cut through the pastry lid, though, it deflated like a punctured balloon, collapsing on to the filling. Laura, undaunted, slid a cake slice underneath the first piece and tried to lift it out. Liquid poured everywhere, though fortunately only back down into the dish. I was beginning to feel nauseous.

"Jeez," she said. "It's kind of runny."

She probed under the pastry lid, lifting it to reveal a mass of sodden apple pulp woven with tangles of pinkish peel, which had fallen away from the apple flesh in the cooking process. The pastry base was soaked through with apple juice, crumpling to pieces as soon as she attempted to lift it.

"I guess I should have drained those apples off before I put 'em in, right?" she said cheerfully. "Never mind, it'll still taste good. I'll get some bowls."

Despite the studious lack of encouragement from everyone around the table—someone went so far as to groan—she reached down a large stack of bowls from a corner cupboard and produced a serving ladle with which to serve the pie. The cake slice was clearly unable to cope.

"I'm full, actually," Tom said firmly. This was a surprise; Tom always had room for a bit more.

"So am I," I chimed in. Even if it had been the best apple pie in the world—one made, preferably, by Emma—I would have barely been able to force down a bite. Pulpy pastry and apple mush, with the prospect of peel getting caught in my teeth, were all too easy to refuse.

This set off a chorus of polite rejections. The only people besides Laura and Ethan who sampled the pie were Andy, who had the stomach capacity of a starving carthorse, and Emma, whom Laura had bullied into accepting a piece against her express wishes.

"But I made it especially for you!" Laura wailed. "Like a house present! You have to try a little bit!"

So poor Emma gamely forced some down. From the careful way she masticated, it was plain that the pie tasted even worse than it looked. Sheila stared at her pityingly the entire time, her expression making it clear that no amount of pressure could have made Sheila eat something she didn't want to.

"So you're staying here?" I said to Laura.

"Yeah, that's right. Emma's been great! My dad was good friends with Walter—Emma's husband—and when Ethan and I were planning this trip Dad suggested we look up Emma. We've been here, what, a couple of months now?" she said, looking at Ethan. He nodded.

"We gotta tear ourselves away sooner or later, but it's just so lovely here," she beamed. "And really good for our work. So quiet."

"What do you do?" I asked. It seemed to be the next question.

"Oh, I paint, and Ethan's writing a screenplay. I've set up a little studio in the shed out back."

"Do you sell anything?" I asked, which was bad of me. I used to hate that question myself. Still, when I hadn't been making my living—such as it was—as a sculptor, I had always said, when people asked me what I did, that I was a weights teacher at a gym, or whatever I was currently doing to earn money. Announcing yourself as a painter if it didn't afford you any income was rather asking for it.

"Just a little, here and there," Laura said casually. "I do a few odd jobs to get by. But the least possible. I really want to spend as much time as I can painting."

Ethan, sitting listening to this, was smiling as easily as ever, without volunteering what he did to bring in money.

"And Ethan's working really hard on his screenplay. He's on to the third draft," Laura added.

I didn't feel up to enquiring of Ethan what the screenplay was about. It's always a meaningless question at the best of times.

"I thought I heard the front door go," Sheila said, interrupting Laura as she started to say something else and not even acknowledging that she had done it. "Are we expecting anyone? Emma?"

But her sister looked extremely tired. Perhaps the painkillers, combined with the wine she had drunk, were knocking her out. She was leaning back in her chair and hardly raised her head to answer Sheila. Footsteps sounded on the stone flags overhead; two long thin black-clad legs appeared around the corner of the staircase, black overcoat flapping around them. Then a body, its shoulders hunched forward, black hair falling over the face. It looked like a crow in urgent need of anti-depressants. The newcomer paused halfway down, rather like Pitt, but without standing on one foot and scratching his head.

The dark hair fell back from his face. Immediately, I sat up straight in my chair. The sight of him had had much the same effect on me as the idea of ice cream had produced on the children.

"Hi, Emma," he said tentatively. "You did say I could drop in after dinner, didn't you?"

4

IN MENTIONING ALAN, LESSER SWINFOLD'S RESIDENT Angry Young Man, it was inexplicable that no-one had bothered to add that he was also the closest thing to a male model that the village could ever have seen in the flesh. Not the kind of beef-cake underwear model with improbably bulging pecs and a bright white smile. Alan's thin frame was made to be filmed in black and white, stretched across a sofa in a semi-transparent shirt, pouting moodily, while an equally skinny girl with equally full lips languished at his feet. His was by no means the kind of handsomeness I fancied generally. I wasn't even sure if I felt any sexual attraction to him. It was impossible to tell while his sheer, drop-dead beauty was taking my breath away.

Emma offered Alan a glass of wine, and he came forward to take it, one bony white hand extending from the heavy sleeve of his coat. He slumped down into a chair and fumbled for a cigarette. He looked profoundly uneasy with his own body, as if he mistrusted its every move. The hunch of his shoulders was clearly protective, but also perhaps designed to conceal his thinness by bulking out his upper body artificially under the coat.

"Did you have a nice dinner?" Emma asked him maternally.

He shrugged. "I just ate loads of mince pies."

Emma looked very concerned.

"But what about your mother? Isn't she well? Didn't she cook?"

Alan looked surprised.

"No, she and Dad went to Paris," he informed us. "They decided at the last moment. Didn't you know?"

Emma clucked like a broody hen.

"Oh, I would have invited you for dinner if I'd known! You poor thing, all alone for New Year's dinner!"

Alan looked horribly uncomfortable at being thus cast as a lonely adolescent. He had to be in his early twenties and I suspected, from my own memories of being that age, had been much happier mooching around the house on his own, watching bad TV and working his way through a packet of microwaved mince pies, than having to make conversation with a load of people over dinner.

"Ooh, that's romantic, isn't it?" Tamsin was saying cosily. "Paris at New Year. We should do that one year, Andy, when the kids have grown!" She nudged her husband, who looked distinctly underenthused by the idea of a romantic break. "I'm surprised you didn't get some friends in, though," she added to Alan in a confidential tone. "Have a bit of a party while they're away."

"Orgies all over the house," Hugo contributed.

Alan looked revolted by the idea of orgies. Still, he couldn't help blushing, a pale rose, which turned his white skin translucent as fine china. He really was exquisite.

"Oh, Alan's parents are always away," Sheila said unpleasantly. "I expect he's too used to it by now to even bother."

"Do you see anything of Priscilla up in London, Sheila?" Emma asked.

"Not really," Sheila said shortly. "I'm too busy working."

Sheila had already told us she was a textile dealer, announcing this with an air of importance. I assumed that her comment was a dig at Alan's mother; Sheila was implying that the absent

Priscilla was a lady who lunched. Still, Alan didn't seem nettled on his mother's behalf. Probably, like most tortured young men in their early twenties, he was far too obsessed by the fascinating state of his own psyche to pay much attention to anything else.

I was still staring at Alan. His skin was as white as the under-belly of a fish, with the imposing bone structure of a young Roman emperor. High-bridged nose, strong cheekbones, smooth white forehead. It was the kind of face it would take him ten years to grow into. His colouring was Snow White's: coal-black hair and eyes, a full red mouth, which probably embarrassed him severely, and that pale, pale skin. And he was thin, his flesh barely covering his bones. Where trendier boys would make a feature of their gauntness, strutting down the street in skintight jeans hanging precariously off their hipbones, shrunken T-shirts stopping above the waist to reveal their cadaverous, pierced stomachs, Alan had so far refused to take off even his overcoat. He huddled into it as if it were a safety blanket.

"Darling," Hugo muttered to me crossly, "your mouth is hanging open. Could you shut it, please? You look like a dull-witted country bumpkin."

Alan caught some of this and misunderstood.

"You're visiting for the holidays, aren't you? It must be pretty boring for you down here," he said. A flush still touched his cheekbones.

Tempted as I was to reply that no village which contained a young man as handsome as Alan could possibly be boring, I restrained myself. Not just for Hugo's sake. Alan would have crumpled up and died on the spot of embarrassment if I had said anything like that.

"I mean, the people here," he continued, impassioned. "They're so fossilised. No-one ever gets out. Most people here have never been to London. They've never even been to *Birmingham*."

"I would have thought it was a good thing never to have been to Birmingham," Hugo observed, perplexed.

"It's nearer than London," Sheila explained.

"I'm so sorry," Hugo said sympathetically. He really was awful.

"D'you know," Alan informed us, "there used to be forty-five shops here and thirteen pubs? Now everyone's moved away. It's only the rejects that are left. And the townies who own houses bring all their own food down with them."

"You see them unloading their Range Rovers," Tamsin chipped in. Clearly, she was used to Alan, enough not to be offended by being classed as a reject. Or maybe, being a sensible woman, she was just used to ignoring the rantings of insecure young men. "Bags and bags from Marks & Spencer in the back. They'd drop dead before they'd buy anything here."

"You can't blame them, though," Alan said. "Have you seen our grocer's?"

This was for us. We shook our heads.

"Disgusting. Like something out of the Fifties: rancid cheese and old bread."

"There's just the one food shop?" I asked.

Everyone nodded.

"It's a bit sad, really," Emma said. "I do try to buy something there every so often, but it is a bit . . . well, Alan exaggerates, but it's not that nice. We all go to the big out-of-town supermarket. It's a bit of a drive, but it's worth it."

Alan muttered a protest and tossed back his hair indignantly at the mere suggestion that he might be exaggerating. Every gesture he made had an odd, angular elegance. I couldn't take my eyes off him.

"Are you still hungry, Alan?" Hugo said evilly. "There's plenty of apple pie left if you'd like some."

"Really?" Alan looked interested.

"Yeah, I made it specially!" Laura said proudly. "Shall I get you some?"

"Oh." Alan looked from Emma to Laura. "Uh, no. Thanks. It's OK. I'm really full."

"So where do your contemporaries hang out?" Hugo asked, foiled. "The local pub?"

Alan made a humphing noise.

"Not really. They all go to Campden."

"But I thought you said they hadn't been to London?" I said, confused. Since I considered Camden Town the centre of the known universe, they could scarcely do better as far as I was concerned; no need for Alan to sound so dismissive.

"No," he said, looking at me as if I had taken leave of my senses. "Chipping Campden."

Hugo and I burst out laughing. We couldn't help it. A faint smile touched Alan's full lips. He didn't seem to mind us finding the whole Lesser Swinford experience amusing in the extreme.

"It must be very exciting, Chipping Campden," Hugo said gravely. "The name alone conjures up a panorama of exciting possibilities."

Alan humphed again.

"It's no bigger than here, really," he said dismissively.

"Come on, Alan, it's bigger than Swinford," Emma protested.

Alan shrugged. "It's just one long strip of road," he explained. "Really boring. It just goes on and on."

"Like Sunset Strip," I said happily.

"Casinos, strip joints, hookers hanging out on the side-walks—" Hugo added.

"Gunfights, drive-by shootings—" I contributed.

"Bank robberies every two minutes—"

"Rival Hell's Angels gangs having punch-ups along the strip—"

Everyone was laughing, but it was Alan I was watching. His face was flushed, his mouth curved and he actually emitted something that might have been a chuckle. His dark eyes were shiny with excitement.

"Chipping Campden," Hugo intoned in a deep American accent. He was imitating a voice-over for an action film. "Where the Uzi makes its own law."

Alan finally laughed. His whole face lit up, the lines around his mouth and eyes creasing into a perfect geometry. I reached for the bottle of red wine. I needed another drink. He was too beautiful to be real.

"Actually, it's more hand-knitted sweaters and expensive souvenir shops," Emma said prosaically.

"What?" I said. We had been howling with drunken laughter for so long I had forgotten what the initial source of the joke had been.

"Chipping Campden," Tamsin clarified.

"Maybe I should apply for the job of sheriff," Hugo said. "Clean up that dirty town once and for all. I could wear my leather trousers," he added, getting increasingly enthusiastic. "The older ones."

"I thought you were going to throw those away," I said. "The knees were getting baggy."

"But that's very lawman, isn't it? You know, lived in. Knocked around the world a bit and now he's coming home. The law's come back to town."

"You ought to drag them behind a horse a bit," Alan suggested unexpectedly. "Scuff them up."

"Good idea," Hugo said cordially. "Do you want to be my deputy?"

Alan went pink.

"Why can't I be the deputy?" I said, offended.

"Because you'd be terrible at it. You'd never follow orders. And don't say, 'Why can't I be sheriff?' instead. I don't see myself as a sidekick. You can run the local saloon."

"Oh, OK," I said happily.

"See?" Hugo said smugly. "I have a gift for diplomacy. I'd make a fabulous sheriff."

"You'd probably have to cut down on using words like 'fabulous,'" Ethan said.

"Yes, it would be the whole laconic aspect of the job that would be most difficult," Hugo said reflectively. "Sam would be better at that. Grunting insults and kicking people out of town."

Everyone looked at me. I smiled modestly.

"Ever played an American?" Ethan asked Hugo.

"Only in drama school. And somehow I don't see anyone casting me in a David Mamet any time soon. Thank God. All those men rampaging around shouting at each other. Acres of testosterone with nowhere to go. So exhausting. I just wish they'd drag each other off to bed and have done with it."

"I think David Mamet's a genius," Ethan said defiantly.

"Someone has to," Hugo said, quite unfazed.

"So no chance of you being in a Western, then?" Ethan said.

"Alas, no. Not unless there's a part for an effete English baddie. I wouldn't get to ride around lassoing things, though. I'd be lounging in my saloon toying with the working girls."

"Not if you're supposed to be effete," Ethan pointed out.

"Oh, does effete mean homosexual?" Hugo said. "I hadn't realised. Perhaps in American it does."

Hugo was definitely winning on points.

"Are you going to come out and see the fireworks?" Alan asked, looking at me. Was this deliberate? Maybe I was just flattering myself. Still, I said, "Yes," enthusiastically.

Emma was consulting her watch.

"We should start clearing up, really," she said. "We want to be at the church in good time."

"The church?" I echoed nervously. I hadn't been on consecrated ground since I could remember, and I wasn't sure if it was such a good idea for me to start trying now.

"For the bell-ringing, idiot," Hugo reassured me. "Don't worry, you don't have to go in. We don't want you spontaneously combusting, do we?"

"Or shrinking back hissing at the crucifix," I said happily.

"What happens when you touch holy water?" Alan was entering into the spirit of things.

"Terrible burns," Hugo assured him. "And she screams like a soul in torment. Which is odd," he added reflectively, "because, on all the evidence to date, she hasn't got one."

Hugo knew me much too well. No wonder our relationship was having problems.

· · · · · · ·

"God, these bells are loud!"

"What?" Hugo cupped a hand to his ear. Since his black furry hat was pulled down over it, this didn't help much.

"I said, these bells are *loud!*" I yelled.

Hugo made a gesture indicating that we should stand a bit further back. We were in the cemetery surrounding the church, leaning against a large tombstone. The church loomed in front of us, orange footlights playing eerily up its façade. We were right below the bell tower. The big double doors to the church were open, and through them you could see excess church furniture—old, dark pews, equally ancient wooden chairs, various bits and pieces of lumber—propped precariously against the stone walls. A staircase led up to the first floor, or whatever the first floor of a church was called. This was the bell-ringers' room. The window was open and the respites from the chimes were filled with their peals of drunken laughter and shouts of what were probably obscene suggestions. We had seen them going up earlier, and they had all looked as if they had been doing some intensive oesophageal lubrication. A lot of the peals sounded distinctly shambolic.

On the top of the bell tower was an enormous Christmas tree, lit up as if it were on fire by strings of powerful white lights. Emma had told us that the tree was fifty feet high and had been hauled up there by a carefully engineered series of winches and hoists. It glittered spectacularly against the black night sky.

"Ooooooooh!" everyone in the churchyard chorused in unison. More fireworks were going off. Three Catherine wheels flamed into life, hissing and spitting like angry cats, throwing out long trails of sparks, spattering into the air. Dogs barked in the distance. Most of the kids present whooped with excitement. The others started crying. Every time the latest sequence of fireworks whirred itself down, the sound of sobbing toddlers throwing themselves against their mothers' legs in fear was all too audible.

I removed the bottle of champagne from Hugo's hand and raised it to my lips. Bubbles poured up my nose. I snorted, drank some more and passed it on to Tom, wiping my mouth. Without even drinking himself, he promptly trotted away to the far wall of the churchyard where Janine was standing. Pitt, her little boy, was burrowed into the small nook between the stone wall and her legs, nervous of the noise. Janine was bending over him, stroking his hair and trying to coax him out, but he just shook his head vigorously and clung to one of her legs. She looked up at Tom, laughing, as he reached her, and shrugged in a what-can-I-do? way. Tom offered her the bottle. She shook her head. He insisted. Finally, reluctantly, she took it, drank some and immediately had a violent sneezing fit. Tom, meanwhile, was crouched down in front of Pitt, persuading him to come out of hiding. The negotiations didn't take long; after a few minutes he reached in and extracted the little boy, standing up and swinging Pitt on to his shoulders. Janine, tilting her head back and still rubbing her nose from the sneezes, caught one of Pitt's hands and seemed to be asking him if he was all right. The nod he gave was tentative but brave.

Janine and Tom looked like a perfect couple; Tom, with his light-brown hair and blue eyes, could easily have been Pitt's father. His expression, as he looked down at Janine, was blissful. God, I hoped things worked out for him. She seemed a pleasant contrast to his usual girlfriends, too. Either that or she was a superb actress. I hadn't seen a trace of flakiness or neuroticism yet, and after Tom's series of twitchy annoying blondes, I knew exactly how to spot the signs.

I noticed Sheila, leaning on a tombstone near us and watching Tom and Janine play happy families too. Her expression was very odd. I wondered if she was jealous; no children of hers had been mentioned, and I had the feeling from what Tom had told me in gossipy conversations that she had never married. Had she wanted kids? Still, I couldn't read anything quite as simple as envy on Sheila's face. Whatever the emotion was, it looked a lot more complicated than that.

"Want some champagne?" Alan said to me.

"Yeah, that would be lovely! Have you got another bottle?"

He held up his hand, mouthing, "Hang on!" and crossed the lawn to where Tom and Janine were standing. The nearly full bottle had been put behind them on the wall; responsible parents did not keep swigging champagne when in charge of small children made nervous by firework displays. Alan slapped Janine on the shoulder familiarly as he retrieved the bottle and said something to her that made her laugh and tug on the ends of his scarf, pretending to strangle him. They must be pretty good friends, judging by the ease with which they touched each other. I was horrified to realise that I was actually jealous of Janine for being able to pull at Alan's scarf and laugh into his face. This was ridiculous. I needed to get a grip. Preferably on a champagne bottle.

Alan, returning with the spoils, swigged at the champagne while walking, never a good idea. Especially since the grassy surface of the green was full of bumps and dips. He tripped, nearly took his front teeth out with the lip of the bottle, and staggered back to me, coughing on champagne.

Clusters of fireworks shot overhead and opened up like overlapping chrysanthemums, violet over gold over green, spectacular against the black velvet sky. Oohs and aahs rose from the spectators. The bell-ringers essayed another peal. Metal briefly clanged against metal in ill-timed disharmony, but no-one cared. The main thing right now was to make a lot of noise.

"Oi!" shouted someone from the door of the church. The bells had ceased, the fireworks had temporarily abated, and we heard him clearly enough. He was in shadow against the bare light bulb, and all I could make out was a big shape wearing what looked like a loose robe, his huge shadow thrown behind him, flickering over the stacked-up church pews like some Gothic apparition. I wondered briefly if this could be the vicar and promptly dismissed the idea. Vicars, in my admittedly limited experience, did not attempt to attract attention by yelling "Oi!" at people while wearing their cassocks.

The man moved out from the church, and I could see him more clearly. He waved his arms back and forth like a drunken semaphorist who has forgotten his flags.

"More drink!" he yelled. "Thirsty work up here, ennit! Georgie, get us a case of beer!"

Someone, presumably Georgie, detached himself from the crowd and disappeared down the main street. A woman in a long padded duvet coat went over to the man, who gave her a rib-breaking hug.

"All right, my duck?" he shouted. "Nice night for it, eh?"

She said something to him of which I only caught the words "more beer."

"Of course we do!" he yelled cheerfully, his voice so much louder than hers that I was beginning to wonder whether he talked at that pitch all the time.

"That's Norman," Alan said to me and Hugo. "He runs the Cow. That's our main local."

"Ah, mine jovial host," Hugo said.

"They've closed it up now for midnight," Alan explained. "Then they'll all go back there for a lock-in."

"I imagine Norman'll be drinking till dawn," I said.

"Yeah, Norman's amazing. He can put it away till four and be up next day at eight," said Alan admiringly. The more Alan drank, I noticed, the more he forgot to be bitter and cynical.

Norman had bent the woman back over his arm and was giving her a long, cinematic kiss, like Rudolph Valentino in *The Sheik*. His white bell-ringer's robe billowed around him, adding to the effect. Hoots and cheers rose from the crowd.

"Go on, Norm!" shouted various men. "Give 'er one!"

The woman, bent over backwards as she was, managed to get one hand loose and give the finger to the mob. They loved it. The women in the crowd cheered her wildly.

"That's his wife," Alan explained. "Chrissie."

"They're too good to be true," Hugo said appreciatively. "Country publican and his rollicking lady wife."

Just then a series of fireworks exploded. They were the kind that sounded as if the village was under attack from a massed rank of mortars on the next hill: a deafening succession of very loud bangs accompanied by flashes of blinding white flame. Their only real purpose was to shock, and that they achieved to the utmost. We all jumped and screamed, and Norm stumbled, tripped over a molehill and fell heavily on top of Chrissie.

"Wey-hey!" bawled a man behind me. "See in the New Year with a bang!"

We all howled with laughter. Norm and Chrissie lay on the ground, laughing as hard as anyone else. Finally, as the explosions died away, leaving a strong reek of smoke and gunpowder in the air, Norm rolled off Chrissie, who heaved herself to her feet.

"Fair took my breath away, he did!" she yelled to her appreciative audience.

"Here, Chris, give me a hand up!" Norman called. He was still laughing, lying flat on his back, arms out at his sides, his big chest heaving up and down under the white robe.

"You must be joking! I'd do my back in. He weighs a ton," she said.

"Come on, lads, give us a hand!" Norman yelled.

Five or six men went over to haul Norman to his feet. There was an attempt to give him the bumps, swinging him up and down by hands and feet, but his sheer bulk and their advanced state of inebriety prevailed before they could get too carried away and accidentally fling him on to a tombstone.

"Aah! God!" Norman, vertical again, held on to the church wall for support. "I need a *beer*!" he shouted. "Where's that Georgie!"

Just on cue, a perspiring youth, the sheen on his forehead clearly to be seen in the livid glow of the orange lights, staggered back through the gate in the churchyard wall, a case of beer clutched to his chest.

"Took your time, didn't you!" Norman said jovially. There was an attack on the beer case, which Norman defended valiantly.

"This is for the lads up there!" he bellowed, hoisting up the case on one shoulder as if it were filled with feathers and heading back inside the church. He ascended the staircase. Moments afterward a ragged cheer rose up from the bell-ringers' room.

I heard some women's voices in there too. Bottles were clinked and a brief silence fell, instantly filled with the explosion of more fireworks.

Hugo was removing the foil from another bottle.

"They put on a good show, eh?" he said, untwisting the wire.

"The fireworks?" I said.

"No, Lesser Swinford. You certainly know how to party," he said to Alan, his tone almost friendly. Large quantities of champagne had mellowed Hugo too.

"Oi!" Norman, the ringleader of the festivities, appeared in the window once more. "It's nearly midnight!"

Everyone looked at their watches. The bells were mute; the tails of fireworks dripped down the sky, fading away. Norman remained in the window, looming in the embrasure like an enormous gargoyle. He began to count out loud from twenty. It was quickly taken up by the crowd.

"Ten! Nine! Eight! Seven! Six! Five! Four! Three! Two! ONE!" we yelled.

On "One!" Norman waved his arms in a gesture to the bell-ringers. It sounded as if everyone was tugging at their bell-ropes simultaneously. An enormous peal of bells clanged out, and a great mass of chrysanthemum fireworks exploded into the air, followed almost immediately by a fusillade of white light. We hooted and whooped with excitement.

"Happy New Year!"

"Happy New Year!"

Everyone was hugging everyone else. I found myself embracing Emma.

"Happy New Year!"

The crowd was a mass of bodies. Alan hugged me shyly, so thin that I could feel his skeleton even through the layers of clothing. He smelt of cigarettes and soap.

"Alan, darling!" Emma said, hugging him. She had had large quantities of champagne and was maudlin by now. "Happy New Year!"

Hugo's arm came around my shoulders.

"Happy New Year, monster," he said affectionately.

I reached up to kiss him. Our hats bumped uncomfortably.

"Wasn't such a bad idea after all, coming down here, was it?" I said.

I hardly caught his answer, the noise was so loud. As we disengaged I looked for Tom. He had put down Pitt and was hugging Janine. As I watched, he tried, tentatively, for a kiss, dabbing a quick one on her lips and pulling back to see her reaction. She put a hand up to his cheek and said something. I held my breath. Would he get lucky? Was a snog in the offing? No, dammit. They hugged again briefly and then Janine disengaged to bend down and embrace her son. Maybe she just hadn't wanted to kiss Tom in front of Pitt. I crossed my fingers. Tamsin's kids ran across the green and into Janine's arms, one after the other. Tamsin followed close behind. Andy, I noticed, was nowhere to be seen. I knew it couldn't be easy being a single mother, but Janine's lot at that moment seemed to me preferable to Tamsin's. At least she wasn't tied to a lazy, unromantic couch potato who couldn't even be bothered to give her a kiss at New Year.

Chrissie was crossing the green, and now she disappeared into the church, presumably going up to celebrate with her husband. The fireworks were a riot of clashing colours. I was reminded of those old-fashioned paintings on black velvet, flowers in hideously bright fuchsia and gold, which could still be found occasionally in second-hand shops. In the night sky the fireworks were breathtaking; painted on velvet, they were embarrassingly kitsch. Context was all.

"There's going to be a lock-in at the Cow in a bit," Alan said to me and Hugo. "Do you want to come?"

I knew perfectly well that once we got to a lock-in we wouldn't emerge till dawn, hopelessly drunk. But hell, it was New Year's Day! What better way to see it in?

"Sure!" I said, without even looking at Hugo.

In retrospect it was a mistake. But then, so are most of my decisions.

"WHAT D'YOU THINK OF THIS ONE?"

I held it out so Lurch could see. While not heavy, it was big and cumbersome enough for me to need two hands. I balanced it on my palms, extending it to him as if it were a tray.

"I dunno," he said dubiously. "The wings are a bit big, in't they?"

"It's not supposed to be totally accurate," I said defensively. "I have artistic licence. It's my interpretation of a cockroach."

Lurch scratched the back of his head. In Lurch-speak, this meant that he thought I was talking bollocks but was too polite to tell me.

"It looks like it's about to take off," he said, searching for a diplomatic way to phrase his objections. "Know what I mean? It don't make you think of a cockroach. Looks like a flying beetle or something."

"Cockroaches are flying beetles," I muttered. "More or less."

But I knew he was right. He nodded discreetly at the enormous colour drawing of a cockroach I had copied from a book on insects. I had never known before how many books on insects there were, or how lovingly and with such precise detail so many artists had sought to render their grisly bodies. It was rather unnerving. Lurch and I had flicked through the pages when I first took the book out of the library, trying to out-gross each other with the pictures, but I think we were both grateful when I had taken it back. We were both horror-film veterans, but this was much worse than any amount of gore: all those hairy legs and probosces.

"OK," I said. "I'll cut down the wings."

I picked up the industrial scissors and started snipping. The prototypes, as the final versions would be, were made out of aluminium foil, thicker than the domestic kind but still easily cuttable with the right scissors.

"Also 'cos they might get caught," Lurch said sensibly. "The wings, I mean. When they're moving round and bumping into each other."

"Good point."

Lurch leaned over me, giving suggestions as I trimmed the wings. It was so much fun. I had been making enormous sculptures for so many years that a cockroach, even one half a metre long, seemed a toy. Lurch and I were sitting in the middle of my studio, aluminium foil cuttings discarded in a huge circle around us, a pair of industrial scissors each, music blaring out from my stereo. I felt like a kid cutting out strings of paper dolls.

"Then there'll be the legs coming down," I said, holding it up again. "Three on each side."

"They don't walk on 'em, right?"

"No, they're just for show. We're going to hinge them so it looks like they're walking. We put the wheels underneath."

I turned it over. The superstructure, the actual cockroach shape, was built on top of a rectangular box of the same foil. The wheels would be attached to the inside corners of the box, and the carapace of the cockroach would extend over, almost to the floor, like a concealing skirt.

"Bit of a change from mobiles, innit?" Lurch said, echoing my thoughts with unnerving accuracy.

Lurch had been my on–off assistant for a long time now, ever since I had made a group of mobiles for a theatre production and he had been the carpenter's charge hand. I had broken him out of captivity to help me on a TV drama of Hugo's, and after that he had decided to apply to art college. He had got in, much to my surprise. Not that Lurch was untalented—that was precisely the point. Nowadays the more meretricious your ability, the higher the likelihood of being taken seriously. Maybe that was just my jealousy talking. No-one was paying me vast sums to expose my unmade bed, littered with the debris of my sordid life—including used Tampax and pants with skidmarks—as one of the Emperor's New Clothes school had done recently to vast acclaim.

Lurch had made a beautiful series of surreal theatre sets for his portfolio, cut with painstaking care out of balsa wood, models for productions that would be deliberately impossible to stage but which were exquisitely detailed. The more you looked at them, the richer they became. Again, this experience was so much the opposite of what was currently fashionable (where instant impact was everything and an entire exhibition could be viewed in a quarter of an hour) that I had held out small hopes of him being accepted anywhere decent.

I had been wrong, luckily for Lurch. Art school could be a pretty dodgy experience nowadays, as far as any actual learning went, but it was vital for making contacts. More and more collectors and gallery owners were scouting out end-of-year shows, hoping to pick up the latest fifteen-minute sensation on the cheap.

"I'm not supposed to call them mobiles anymore," I said, bending the foil back and forth to hear the whoopy metal noise it made. Though it was called foil, it was actually more of a sheet: smooth and unrippled, light as a feather—the perfect material for fooling around with.

"Why?" Lurch said.

"They're hung sculptures. That's what they told me in the States. Mobiles are more Calder-ish. Like things you hang over cots."

"Oh, right. Makes sense."

"That's what the review in *Sculpture* said."

Lurch rolled his eyes.

"You're never going to stop mentioning that bloody review, are you?"

"Hey," I snapped, "when a highly respected art magazine tells you that your pieces 'easily overwhelmed the other works in the show—'"

"'Both conceptually and physically—'" Lurch cut in. "I know, I know."

"—and that they had 'a genuine emotional impact and'"—I waggled my finger at him—"'considerable craft.'" I said this last part quickly so Lurch couldn't chime in too. He thought that craft part hilarious.

"I can't believe you know this all by heart."

"You wait," I said coldly. "You wait till you get a whacking great review in *Sculpture*. We'll see how funny you think it all is then, Mr. Sarcastic."

Sometimes I worried that I sounded like Lurch's mum. I was glad he didn't point out that, despite my brilliant review, everyone else in the show—whom I had so easily overwhelmed—had still sold far more pieces than I had. I was just ahead of my time. Or lacking the "teenage prank quality of young British art," to quote *Sculpture* yet again.

"Anyway, do you think I'm nearly there?" I said, putting the cockroach down on the ground and looking at it hopefully. Maybe the cockroaches would count as teenage pranks and sell for vast sums of money. A girl could dream. "Does it have a genuine emotional impact and considerable craft?"

"No," Lurch said frankly.

"What's the point of keeping you around if you don't think everything I do's wonderful?" I complained. "You used to be in awe of me. I loved that."

"Yeah, but I was young and impressionable then, wasn't I? I'm an artist myself now. I've got a critical eye."

This was too much to bear.

"Ah, piss off, you poncy cunt."

I picked up the cockroach and flew it at him, making what was supposed to be a threatening whirring noise. Lurch promptly grabbed an earlier prototype and countered with a deep buzz like an enraged bumblebee. We chased each other around the studio, swooping and diving our cockroaches at each other, tripping over all my tools and making emergency landings.

"Boom!" Lurch knocked his cockroach into mine. "Explosion! Total roach meltdown!"

We collapsed on to the floor, roaring with laughter.

"I need a fag," Lurch said, fumbling in the pocket of his disgusting old donkey jacket.

"I need a beer."

"Me too."

I pulled a couple of Budvars out of the fridge and chucked him one. He caught it one-handed.

"So. Back to the drawing board," I said, putting down my cockroach, now rather beaten up around the nose area where I had repeatedly rammed it into Lurch's.

"You know what? They look really good in the air," he said, rolling up. "Maybe you should think about—"

"No way. No more sodding hung sculptures for quite a while."

"They'd be mobiles, though, wouldn't they?" Lurch said smartly. " 'Cos they're smaller. Things to hang over kiddies' cots."

"Think of the nightmares. I had a bad enough time after we looked at that insect book."

Lurch shuddered. I uncapped the beers on my soldering iron with a skilled backhanded twist.

"That was worse than anything," he said fervently. "Even than *Hellraiser II*."

He picked up a roach and held it suspended in midair to show me what he meant.

"See? Looks good, dunnit? I mean, floating in the air like that."

"No, I'm over static art," I said firmly. "I'm working in more dimensions now."

Lurch looked at me blankly. He had only been at art school for a term, and so far his tasks had mainly consisted of making found art pieces out of what he could scavenge from garbage bags. All the students had had to do it. I was deeply grateful that my school hadn't been so cutting edge.

"Static art stands still," I explained. "More dimensions means it's kinetic. It moves. I can't believe you haven't learnt that yet, now you're an artist with a critical eye."

Lurch ignored the last part.

"Well, why can't you just say that, then? It moves?"

"You'll never make it," I said sadly. "No grasp of technical terms."

"Piss off. You didn't use to know that either."

"It was the guy who made me the circuits for the roaches," I explained.

"Up himself, was he?"

"Nah, he was OK. But he does a lot of work for this artist who makes enormous pieces."

"Kinetic ones?" Lurch deduced.

"Yup. So he's picked up all the right words."

Lurch reached over to the cardboard box in which were lying the circuits, or kits, as the computer guy had called them.

"Hey, guess what?" I knew Lurch would be amused by this. "He warned me not to let anyone else touch those."

Lurch sniggered. "Yeah, right. Like I'm not a million times more careful than you."

Lurch was much, much better at soldering than me—he had a steadier hand, doubtless due to the fact that I was older than him and therefore had many more years of alcohol abuse of which to boast—and he never lost an opportunity to rub it in.

"Apparently, this artist's really paranoid about his kits," I explained. "He designs them all himself. He won't let any would-be artists work for him in case they steal his schematics. That's like, um, the plans, the ideas that generate the kits. Well, not generate. Um, it's like the whole programming inside."

Lurch looked cynical. "Right, so he'd just hire the working classes, people like me, what don't know anything, and then we go to art school two years later and end up ripping him off right, left and centre."

"Ooh, you've got a nasty mind," I said appreciatively. "Hands off my schematics."

"Come off it," Lurch said, inspecting the kit. "This's got to be the most basic thing there is, right? I mean, what's it have to do? Tell them roaches to keep moving till they hit something? It's not exactly rocket science, is it?"

"They don't hit something," I corrected, "they bump into each other's motion sensors and turn before they actually hit. That's the sophisticated part. Or people. They sense your body heat and turn before they can hit you."

"Urgh," Lurch said appreciatively. "Fancy walking into a room full of them. It'll be really creepy."

"Oh, d'you really think so?" I said happily.

"Definitely. You gotta make 'em a bit scarier, though."

"The red eyes'll help," I said, picking the cockroach up again and contemplating it thoughtfully. "And I think it should have bigger claws. Probosces."

"So this bloke designs much more complicated stuff, right?"

"Yeah. Things that take themselves to pieces and then put themselves back together again."

"Could be a laugh," Lurch said imperturbably.

"Yup. Much more high-tech. He used to be an engineer. He does these big public-sculpture commissions too, with lots of light displays. Fun stuff. Lots of money there, too."

I put down the cockroach and gave it a little shove across the floor to see what it would look like in motion. It definitely needed work.

"I'll give you a ring when I've messed around with it a bit more," I said. "Maybe you can come back and see what you think."

"Yeah, I'd like that. It's funny this, innit? It's like, I dunno, playing with toy cars or something. I mean, it doesn't feel like, well, work."

"I know. I was just thinking that."

"I mean, when I 'elped you with that one—" Lurch tilted his head back. We both looked up at Organism 1, which, despite being described in *Sculpture* as "part suggestive abstraction and part science fiction," had mysteriously so far failed to find a buyer. It was an exploded pod, weird science-fiction tendrils and creepers exuding from the opening, hanging down as if trying to reach the ground.

"—it was much harder work, y'know?" Lurch continued. "Maybe because it was bigger. This is just a laugh, innit?"

"I know. It's like we're having too much fun," I said. "Still, I've got a commission for it."

"Yeah, but people can write up anything so it sounds good, can't they?"

I wasn't at all offended by this.

"Stuff about the artist's personal life goes down really well too," I agreed amicably.

Lurch knew what I meant. I had been kidnapped last year

and kept in a cellar where my only companions had been an extended family of cockroaches. It was that life-broadening experience which had provided the idea for the Cockroach Room. I think Islington Arts Centre would have gone for it anyway—as Hugo had said when I first told him my idea, the concept was certainly cheap and exploitative enough to qualify for a decent chunk of the council's Lottery-funded grant—but the added bonus of all the publicity deriving from my kidnap had made them fall over each other in excitement. They couldn't say yes quick enough.

"That's what Hugo thought," I added. "He told me to put all that stuff into my grant application."

"How's Hugo?" Lurch said enthusiastically. Despite, or perhaps because of, their having absolutely nothing in common, he was very attached to Hugo. Hugo was also fond of Lurch, probably due at least in part to the fact that there was nothing remotely pretentious about Lurch. Hugo had enough of that quality himself to make it superfluous in his chosen companions.

"Oh." I fiddled unnecessarily with a bit of silver foil, whipping it back and forth through the air to make a ripping sound. "OK."

"You had a fight?" Lurch wasn't an idiot.

"Yeah," I mumbled.

"Sam." Lurch sounded very disappointed. "What about?"

I shrugged. I knew exactly what it had been about; I just didn't want to talk about it. New Year in bloody Lesser Swinfold. If I never saw it again that wouldn't be long enough. Though it did have its attractions; if I was being more honest, I would say attraction. Which, of course, had been the whole problem.

· · · · · · ·

We had gone to the lock-in despite all Hugo's sensible arguments for avoiding it. Once we got in, he pointed out, it would be hard to leave. There would be no decent wine and certainly no champagne, so we would end up drinking spirits and giving ourselves horrendous hangovers. I mentioned our supply of coke, which was guaranteed to deal with the hangover question; Hugo looked dubious and said that too much coke was just as bad as too much drink in the end. Displaying my well-known sensitivity to other people's opinions, I sneered at him and called him a wuss.

If we'd gone back to the cottage, we would have probably had excellent sex, fallen happily asleep and got up to go riding the next day. A charming picture. It was exactly what Hugo was imagining, though I knew he wasn't going to say it. Too great a risk that I would make a drunken speech about tomorrow being another day and living for the moment. I was in that hyped-up state when going home is anathema; I needed to be surrounded by raucous people. Alan might not be that, but he was beautiful enough to make up for it. And Hugo was quite aware of that too.

The Cow was precisely what I would have imagined, all red carpets and shiny brass-fitted tables, Christmas decorations swagged everywhere and an enormous tree in the one room big enough for it. It was a rambling warren of a pub, just the way I liked them—a succession of cosy snugs around a central bar. There was money here. That was immediately obvious. The carpets were newish, the furniture polished, the sofas comfortable without being at all worn. I imagined Norman and Chrissie did very well out of the townies and their house guests. And in the summer the village must be full of tourists. There was a big garden out the back, with a palm tree, of all things, growing in the centre of a sheltered courtyard. I could just see the sturdy wooden benches jammed with pink sweaty bodies calling for more beer and sandwiches. They probably did a roaring trade.

"Do you want another G and T?" Alan said.

"God no, thanks, I just started this one," I said.

The whole team of bell-ringers, still in the white robes they had worn over their clothes—I had no idea whether this was common practice or if they had just done it for a laugh—were gathered at the bar, too hyped up from their recent exertions to sit down, and making almost as much noise as their bells had done. Norman was the rowdiest of all, as was only to be expected. Chrissie and the youth Georgie, who had previously ferried over the case of beer, were serving behind the bar. Chrissie seemed the perfect pub landlady, laughing and joking as much as anyone while dealing more than competently with the stream of orders coming her way. She was a nice-looking, sturdy woman with a mass of fair curls pinned on top of her head, which softened her rather heavy features and resolute jawline. No prettiness there, but she had a lovely smile, which cracked open and animated a face that in repose was not particularly attractive.

"Look at those two," Alan said to me confidentially. He was sitting next to me, his thigh brushing against mine. The bar was packed and this kind of contact was normal enough, but I was enjoying it more than I should have done.

"Who?"

He tilted his head in the direction of Ethan and Laura. They were sitting at the next table with Emma and Sheila. Ethan was rolling a cigarette, and they both looked, as they usually did, slightly spaced out, perfectly happy but a little removed from the rest of the proceedings. Their pale-blue eyes, the skin lined with exposure to the sun, took in everything without participating in it. You might have thought they were stoned, but I hadn't seen either of them with a joint in their hands all evening, and I didn't think they indulged. Their floating, hippy quality was an essential characteristic of theirs, as if real life was too intense and complicated for them to engage with.

Washing powder was probably too intense and complicated for them too. I had already noticed the musty smell that emanated from both of them, like old sweaters left in a dusty trunk in the attic for a couple of decades.

"Half a pint each," Alan said, nodding at the table. Barely-touched glasses of lager stood in front of them. "They'll make that last all night. They're famous for it."

"Not big drinkers?" Hugo said, catching this.

"Nah, it's not that." Alan made a derisive rubbing gesture with his thumb and first two fingers. "They're just mean. Been here for months now, and I've never seen 'em buy a drink for anyone. When they first got here people were really friendly to them. It's winter, you know? Everyone's keen to have new faces round. In the summer no-one can be arsed that much, but right now it's all locals, and fresh blood's more than welcome. Still, it didn't last long. They'd smile and say thank you when people bought them drinks, but they'd never reach in their pocket and get one back. Everyone notices that kind of thing."

"I'd better take the hint, then, hadn't I?" said Hugo with an unpleasant edge to his voice. "What can I get you?"

I cast a reproving glance at Hugo. Alan was reddening along his cheekbones, that translucent white skin suffused with a hectic pink, like blood in milk. Stammering out confused apologies and demurrals, he was more beautiful than ever, his dark eyes wide with mortification.

"No, really," Hugo insisted cruelly. "Same again?"

He was threading his way through the crowd to the bar before Alan could manage a coherent sentence.

"I didn't mean—" he finally managed to say to me.

"No, I know. Don't worry about it. He's been in a foul mood most of the evening."

I caught Sheila's eye. She was sitting at the next table to us, talking to some people I didn't know. She sounded as if the champagne was going to her head too; she was pronouncing her words with tremendous care, as if she had just finished an elocution course at the Henry Higgins School and the lessons were still sinking in.

"Have you seen Tom?" she asked, looking around her.

"He was walking Janine home," I said. "She had to put Pitt to bed."

Sheila raised her eyebrows superciliously and turned back to her table again.

"Tom's a nice guy, isn't he?" Alan said. "I like him."

"He's my oldest friend," I said, "so I'm probably prejudiced."

He nodded.

"Well, Jan's an old friend of mine. We used to hang out a lot when we were younger. My parents would come down here for the holidays a lot then. They don't so much now, I don't know why. But Jan and I spent a lot of time together."

"So do you think—" I was careful how to put this. "I mean, I can see that Tom's pretty keen on her, that must be obvious to the meanest intelligence. But do you think—"

"Does she like him? I dunno." Alan drank some more wine. "Jan doesn't really talk about stuff like that, or not much." He looked a little furtive. "But, you know, she's spending a lot of time with him, isn't she? That must count for something."

Alan wasn't going to tell me anything I couldn't see for myself. I abandoned the subject of Tom and his perpetually troubled love life to embark on one that interested me far more: Alan himself.

"So what about you, Alan?" I said. "What are you doing in Lesser Swinfold? You look like you'd be much happier in London."

Walking down Camden High Street or Shoreditch with his black overcoat flapping in the wind, arguing about modern art with a group of similarly clad young urban would-be intellectuals, was what I meant. Alan seemed to understand.

"Yeah, well . . ." he said uncomfortably.

"Your parents have a house in London, don't they?"

"Yeah, Regent's Park. It's really nice."

"Couldn't you stay there till you get a place of your own?"

God, I was sounding like an older sister. Ironic, since my feelings for Alan were scarcely sororal—unless I took the ancient Egyptian royal families as my model.

Alan wriggled self-consciously in his chair.

"I couldn't stay with them," he said. "Not for long. So I thought I'd come down here when I finished college. They come at the weekends sometimes but not much in the winter, it's too damp for Mum."

I still didn't understand what he was doing buried alive in the country, so far from everything that he—and I—would consider civilisation. He could see I was still baffled.

"I'm writing a book," he muttered finally. "A novel. I thought this would be a good place to do it. No distractions. It's too busy at Mum and Dad's, I never get any peace. There's the cleaner fussing round me, and the gardener starting up at the crack of dawn with the strimmer . . . I just can't concentrate."

I was so glad that he hadn't said he wanted to be an artist that I probably overdid the enthusiasm. Young would-be artists or sculptors usually wanted you to come and look at what they were working on, and it was always a no-win situation. If you hated it, you had to lie, and if you liked it, there was precious little you could do to help them.

"How's it going?" I asked.

"Dunno really. I've nearly finished the first draft. I thought I'd have a bit of a break when I'd done that and see what I thought."

He looked as uncomfortable as if someone had dropped a bag of worms down the small of his back. Mentioning his book had brought back with a vengeance all that earlier awkwardness which a couple of bottles of wine and—I hoped—the pleasures of my company had managed to dispel.

"Sam!" Hugo put the drinks down on the table. "I got you red wine, Alan, though God knows what it'll be like. You're a braver man than me. What have you been saying to abash the poor boy, Sam? He looks desperate to get away from you."

That was vintage Hugo: first the implication that he had a much better palate than the unsophisticated Alan, then proceeding to nail Alan to the cross of his own embarrassment. Alan was unable to open his mouth. He ducked his head and hunched over, looking more than ever like a bird of prey with a bad headache.

"Alan's been telling me he's writing a book," I said. I didn't bother to glare at Hugo as it was perfectly obvious that it wouldn't have had any effect.

"Really? How fascinating," Hugo said smoothly. "Do tell us what it's about." He pulled back his chair and sat down with every indication that he was revelling in the prospect of the next few minutes' conversation. He might have been a gourmet, in front of whom has just been placed a dish of *tournedos Rossini* with *pommes vapeur* on the side.

It was a difficult choice. Side with Hugo— which meant allowing him to wreak havoc with Alan's self-esteem—or try to protect Alan, which would simply provoke Hugo to further excesses. I suspected that Alan's novel was highly autobiographical, as all first novels are, which would add more fuel to Hugo's fire. There are a few young male authors who take pride in setting their first books in rural American prisons with grotesquely high violence counts, where all the characters are known only by a series of terrifyingly anatomical nicknames, but somehow I doubted this was the case with Alan. He was too sensitive. You really needed a shaved head and a penetrating stare to carry off that option.

"It's historical, actually," Alan mumbled. "It's set in eighteenth-century Venice."

"Let me guess—young man's social and sentimental education?" Hugo speculated. "With a gorgeous Venetian prostitute madly in love with him, who dies a tragic death, and a pretty little heroine he finally marries at the end? You want to be careful with Sam. She hates those madonna/whore type of books, don't you, darling? She ripped *Lemprière's Dictionary* in half and nailed it to her studio wall."

Alan was speechless. I wasn't sure whether this was because Hugo had summarised his book too accurately or just reduced him to hopeless silence at the thought of being expected to provide a streamlined summary of his plot.

"Hugo's one of those rare actors whose dialogue is actually better off-screen than on," I said, hoping thus to please both parties and calm matters down somewhat.

"Do you write, Hugo?" came Sheila's voice.

She must have been listening in to the last part of our conversation. Turning around in her chair, she propped her arms along the top of it and rested her head coquettishly on her wrists. This proved more difficult that she had anticipated; all her bangles got in the way and she had to burrow through them inelegantly with her chin to find a square inch of naked skin.

"Do I write?" Hugo was completely taken aback. This didn't happen to him often, and I relished the moment. "God, no. Far too much like hard work. And I think my style would be far too mannered and Wildean for modern tastes, don't you?"

Sheila's only response was a sagacious, woman-of-the-world nod. She had probably drunk too much to be able to understand everything he had said. There, of course, the coke was helping us out tremendously.

"Well, we've already got a writer here, haven't we?" she said with scorn. For a moment I thought she meant Alan, and was surprised at the venom in her voice. She hadn't shown any trace of hostility towards Alan that evening. "A *screenwriter*," she added, italicising the word for ironic emphasis, and I realised she was referring to Ethan. "Or that's what he says he's doing in Emma's shed all day. Don't believe a word of it myself."

She couldn't gesture at Ethan because her arms were both under her chin, but she tried to jerk her head backwards to indicate him. It was a mistake. Most gestures made when you are drunk should be carefully planned out. She caught her hair on one of her bracelets, and Hugo had to disentangle it for her.

Sheila was definitely in that state of advanced inebriety where she needed to be taken home while she could still walk—albeit with a little guidance. Having decided to interpret Hugo's chivalrous gesture as rampant flirtation, she fixed him throughout the entire detangling procedure with a deep, meaningful stare, modelled on the lines of the kind of thing Marlene Dietrich might have directed at some dewy innocent German officer in *Mata Hari*. Hugo, being neither innocent nor dewy, was adopting instead a matter-of-fact, strictly practical air, which he must have patented to deal with lecherous older actresses who thought he looked good in tights.

"There you go!" he said, as close to jovial as it was possible for Hugo to get. "All done."

Sheila continued to stare at him. Her chin sagged even further into her hands and her head began to tilt at an ominous angle.

"Um, Emma?" I said, looking around for her.

Emma was sitting at a table near us. The last I had seen her she was chatting to a couple who, by the newness of their country clothes and the wife's gold jewellery, were clearly townies visiting their country house for the festivities. But they had gone, and she was alone, staring off into space with an odd look on her face, her thoughts many miles away. Unlike Laura and Ethan, who gave the impression that they were seeing only wide-open empty spaces, Emma looked as if she was thinking of something specific and not entirely pleasant. I wondered why she hadn't just joined us when her friends had gone.

She caught my eye. I nodded to Sheila. Emma took in the situation with one quick glance.

"Sheila?" she said, rising to her feet. "I'm really tired. I think I'll be going home, it's way past my bedtime. Shall we walk back together?"

Sheila made a snorting noise and flapped one hand at Emma dismissively. This caused her to wobble dangerously. She caught at the chairback for support.

"No, really," Emma persisted. "It's past midnight. Time to be getting back."

"'Time to be getting back.' 'Past my bedtime,'" Sheila parroted. "You were always the killjoy, Em." She looked around her vaguely, the glassy sheen of her eyes indicating how hard she was finding it to focus. "Wish Walter was here. He and I always had a laugh. None of this 'past my bedtime' stuff for Walter."

Emma looked stricken at the mention of her late husband's name.

"Sheila," she said softly. "Please . . ."

"He thought you were a killjoy too, Em," Sheila said loudly, ignoring this. "He'd've stayed on with me. Know what Walter would've said to you? Do you know? He'd've said: 'Em, we're just getting started. The night is young.'"

That did it. Emma exploded.

"Don't you *dare* tell me what my husband would have said! Or done! Don't you *dare!* Walter and I were married for nearly fifty years! I knew everything about him! How *dare* you think you can tell me what Walter would have said!"

She must have had quite a bit to drink, too. It was impossible to imagine Emma making a public scene without the stresses and strains of cooking New Year's Eve dinner, plus a good deal of alcohol to loosen the social inhibitions. Her eyes were flashing with anger.

Sheila was positively abashed, curling up on herself in a mime of humility.

"I'm sorry, Em," she muttered. "I didn't mean—"

"Just get your coat and we'll be off," Emma snapped.

Sheila got clumsily to her feet, averting her face from her sister like a whipped dog. I suddenly had a sense of their relationship: Sheila the loud flamboyant one, Emma the quiet sister who, however, kept Sheila in line whenever she went too far. Emma was the kind of woman who raised her voice rarely, but when she did, everyone listened.

Sheila, reaching for her coat, stumbled and nearly tripped over her own feet. Hugo caught and steadied her. It was a measure of how dizzy Sheila was that she didn't even reward him with a flirtatious glance, just mumbled something, looking dazed.

It was clear that she couldn't make it home on her own, or even with Emma's support. She was weaving like a drunk on the post-iceberg *Titanic*. Hugo rose to the occasion. I would have been more impressed with his gentlemanly manners if I hadn't thought that Sheila's drunkenness provided a perfect excuse for him to get both of us back to the cottage.

"Well, I'm rather tired as well," he said smoothly. "It's certainly past *my* bedtime. Sam, why don't we walk Sheila and Emma home on our way back to our bijou little love-nest?"

I should have gone. I knew I should have gone. And yet I caught Alan's eye at that precise moment and heard myself saying, "Oh, I don't know. I'm not that tired yet. I might hang around here for one more drink."

"Fine, darling," Hugo said with exquisite politeness. That was always a bad sign. "Whatever your heart desires. I'll see you later, shall I? Here's the spare key."

And, putting it on the table, he pulled on his coat and hat. He looked so striking that I almost yielded. But by now, having said that I would stay, I felt it would be ridiculous to change my mind. Stubbornness is one of my major characteristics. I told myself I would have just one more drink and then follow him.

Hugo had got an arm around Sheila's back and was half-guiding, half-lifting her along in a slow progress across the pub. Emma held the door open for them. It would have been easier if I'd helped too. I brushed that thought swiftly from my mind.

"Well," I said to Alan. "One more drink?"

Of course it was many more than one, and of course day was breaking by the time I staggered home. Alan insisted on escorting me and maybe it was my overladen fantasy, but I had the strong impression that he wanted to kiss me at the door. There was one of those charged moments where you both look at each other in an awkward silence, your faces shadowed in the grey light of dawn, and mumble a few incoherent words. I broke the moment. Even I wasn't so far gone as to kiss Alan below the window where my boyfriend was presumably fast asleep. I wasn't so far gone as to kiss Alan at all, in fact. I had no idea what I was doing, but that at least I knew. I was in a state of extreme confusion, unable to distinguish between the effects of the drink and the coke and Alan's perfect features, his huge dark eyes, the sweetness of his expression . . .

Alan finally landed a kiss on my cheek, muttered something about hopefully seeing me tomorrow, and turned away, as reluctant to go as I was to see him leave. I fumbled the key into the door and made my way upstairs.

Hugo was in bed, his back pointedly turned to me. I couldn't sleep; the coke had too much speed in it. I lay there for what felt like hours, my teeth grinding, disparate thoughts scurrying through my mind. I must have slept in the end, but it didn't feel as if I had. I couldn't tell what had been dreams or waking fantasies, and by the time I regained consciousness it was eleven. I was exhausted, only having slept, or whatever I wanted to call it, for a few hours. Hugo was already up and in the foullest of tempers. We had an enormous fight, halfway through which Hugo announced his intention of leaving immediately for London, with or without me. I was tempted to stay for many reasons: I still had hardly spent any time with Tom; awful though it was to admit it, I wanted to see Alan again; and—just as powerful as either of those—whenever someone presented me with an ultimatum, my perversity immediately made me want to tell them what they could do with it.

But even I, the relationship moron, knew that to stay without Hugo would be one of those make-or-break decisions, and I was in too weakened a condition to contemplate one of those. We drove back to London in total silence, melancholy hip-hop playing on the car stereo. Hugo dropped me at my studio and drove away without a single word having been exchanged. We hadn't spoken since.

"It was New Year," I finally said to Lurch, not willing to give even a précis of events. "We went down to see Tom in the country and had a bit of a bust-up."

I wondered in passing why you always said "down" for going to the country when in fact, as far as the map was concerned, we had gone up.

"Oh, New Year," he said, looking relieved. "That happens a lot, dunnit? My sister was reading in one of her gossip mags how all these celebrity couples broke up over New Year 'cos there was all this pressure on them, know what I mean?"

"How is that supposed to reassure me?"

"Oh, you know." Lurch picked up the cockroach again by its carapace and flew it slowly in a series of circles in front of him.

"Big parties, right, everyone expecting you to be all happy and everything, you get really pissed and maybe it all feels a bit much. But it'll all sort itself out, you'll see."

"What about the celebrity couples?" I said rather snappishly.

"Oh, I bet some of them'll patch it up. Wait and see. Just give it a bit of time."

"Buy the gossip mags in a few weeks to see how it's going?"

"That was just, y'know, an example," Lurch said reprovingly. "To show that it happens to everyone, right?"

"Great." I wasn't sure whether I liked reassurance coming in the form of being told that I was simply going through an experience that was all too common. I wanted to be unique.

"Unless of course you two've got other problems," Lurch said, his eyes still fixed on the cockroach.

I took a deep breath. At that point, mercifully, the phone rang. I scrambled to answer it, half-wondering whether, with perfect timing, it would be Hugo.

It wasn't. It was Tom. The conversation was short and highly strained. I put down the phone and stood staring at it in disbelief.

"What is it?" Lurch said, obviously dying with curiosity. My part of the conversation must have been riveting.

"It's Tom," I said. "Someone's been killed in his village, and apparently they think he did it. He says he's going to be arrested any minute."

6

TOM HADN'T BEEN ABLE TO TALK FOR LONG; HE WAS ON morning break and assigned to playground duty. His voice had been muffled, presumably to avoid the information scaring the screaming toddlers I could hear in the background. (I made a mental note once again never to have children.) Still, he had managed to convey the basic facts.

My fingers twitched over the receiver. Eventually, I picked it up again and dialled Hugo's number. If ever there was a good excuse to resume communication with him, this was it.

The answering machine picked up.

"Hugo," I said to it, "it's me. Look, this is going to sound completely surreal, but Tom just rang me. Apparently he's—do you remember Janine? Well, she's been found dead—killed—and the police seem to think he did it. I know it's ridiculous but—"

The line clicked. Hugo had picked up the phone.

"Sam?" he said in tones of utter disbelief. "What was that you just said?"

"Hugo!" I found myself very happy to hear his voice.

"You're not seriously saying what I thought you just said, are you? Tell me it's just a twisted excuse to get back in touch with me."

"No, really. Tom just rang me. It's true."

There was a long pause.

"Tell me," he said, "that you're not thinking about going anywhere near that place."

"Hugo, Tom says he's about to be arrested!"

"He's probably just exaggerating," Hugo said hopefully. "You know what he's like."

"He doesn't exaggerate that much! If he says he's the main suspect—"

Hugo sighed.

"So I expect you're saddling up your horse and riding to his rescue?"

I hadn't even got that far. Still, Hugo was perfectly right. Of course I would have to go down there and check out the situation. He took my silence for assent.

"Sam, as far as I—not to mention the rest of humanity—am concerned, you've already had enough murders to last you a lifetime," he said coldly. "Six lifetimes. Even cats only get nine."

"I'm not exactly a suspect," I protested.

"There's still a murderer down there!" Hugo pointed out acerbically. "It's a tiny village, and I know exactly what you're like. You'll go down there and stick your nose into everything, and sooner or later someone'll try to bump you off too. God knows it wouldn't be the first time. Not," he added coldly, "that I personally would mind that much. Still, I feel it incumbent on me to warn you of a very likely possibility."

Maybe by now I considered myself indestructible. Or maybe it was the challenge. Either way, I rose to the bait.

"You don't know me very well if you think that'd stop me," I retorted.

"Hmn. Well, perhaps I'm simply being devious. Perhaps I'm egging you on to go down there and get yourself killed too. Has that thought crossed your mind? I could conceivably see that as the perfect solution to our current situation."

I knew he was joking—mainly—but I wasn't that amused.

"Fine," I snapped. "If that's the way you want it."

"Sam—"

I slammed down the phone. I knew exactly what Hugo was thinking. The last thing he wanted was for me to return to Lesser Swinfold and the society of the divinely beautiful Alan. I couldn't decide whether he was testing me, or if clumsiness had led him to push me in entirely the wrong direction. Whichever it was, the result had turned out to be the same.

"Lurch," I said, turning to face him. "How long have you got before term starts again?"

"About a week," he said warily.

"Fancy a trip down to see Tom?"

It was the perfect solution. If Lurch came, I would be providing myself with a sort of chaperone against temptation. And if he refused . . . well, at least I could tell Hugo I had asked him along.

Lurch was staring at me incredulously. He had only just recovered from the injuries he had received last time I had asked him to get mixed up in a murder hunt.

"How's your back?" I said, struck suddenly by a wave of guilt.

"Fine." He rolled his shoulders back reflexively. "Hardly notice it."

Driven by much the same impulse, I flexed my fingers. Two of them had been broken when I was kidnapped, and the wrist badly sprained. I noticed them aching more than the broken ribs, but then I hadn't been working out much recently, while I used my hands all the time. The doctor had warned me that the breaks, even when healed, would hurt in cold weather as I got older. But since, according to Hugo, I was running out of lives, that was scarcely something which concerned me overmuch. Maybe Lesser Swinfold would prove to be my nemesis.

"How's your hands?" Lurch asked, seeing the gesture.

"Oh, fine. Had all the movement back months ago."

"Well, then, that's OK, innit?" He looked up at me. "When d'you want to leave?"

· · · · · · ·

The traffic out of London had been negligible—it was well before commuter hour—and I remembered the route fairly well. Besides, my van was a Golf and went like the wind when the English speeding laws allowed. We got lost trying to find Dunster Magna, the location of Tom's primary school, but Lurch was an unflappable navigator. In this he was unlike Hugo, who became pettish when under pressure. Queries of a few inbred-looking locals provided directions that took us through a series of stone-walled back roads and into the scenic delights of Dunster Magna well before three-thirty, the time when Tom unleashed his charges back into the reluctant care of their parents.

Dunster Magna was no bigger than Lesser Swinfold. Like the legendary Chipping Campden, it was basically one long road, with a parade of shops in a long, paved recess in front of which you were technically allowed to park your car only if you were a resident of Dunster Magna with the regulation 2.4 children, an unendorsed driving licence and probably a clean AIDS test to boot. I didn't spend too much time reading the sign; I was more concerned with reaching the pub and getting a pint down me before we went to collect Tom. The parade, which looked prom-ising from a distance, resolved itself on clearer viewing into a dingy post office, a general store, a butcher's, a pub and a craft shop with special offers on crewel wool and crochet hooks writ-ten laboriously on cards propped in the window.

"Hope you haven't brought a lot of money down with you," I said to Lurch as we passed this last. "I don't want you blowing your student grant on knitting wool again."

I had known I would need to fortify myself with alcohol against the massed onslaught of overstimulated small children, and so it proved. We waited outside the school gates with the assembled mothers. Some were in trophy-wife Range Rovers, but there were more with a selection of beaten-up old bangers, which looked like the by-products of the UK equivalent of demolition derbies. Or perhaps they had simply collided too often with the trophy wives' jeeps. Many curious, and downright suspicious, glances were cast at us. I had never been taken for a child molester before. I could add it now to my range of life experiences. Lurch—male, spotty and dressed in a disgusting old donkey jacket—came in for much more of the barrage of accusing stares than I did, but, being Lurch, he didn't even notice them.

I kept an eye out for Tamsin, whose children I imagined came here to have the alphabet thrashed into them by Tom, but there was no sign of her. I wondered why.

A bell rang twice inside the school building, its sound horribly familiar. There was a rustle of movement all around me, and I realised that the mothers had drawn their shoulders back, in unison, like a platoon of soldiers bracing themselves against the latest enemy onslaught. Several of them pushed back the sleeves of their Barbours to consult their watches, as if hoping against hope that they had made a mistake. A muffled roar rose from the building, suddenly amplified tenfold as the doors burst open and the first children, laden down with fluorescent rucksacks and bundled up in winter coats, hove into view. Every single one of the mothers groaned in unison. It was an extraordinary noise, half sigh, half clearly audible whimper, an admission of total exhaustion. I guessed that this was the only moment that they really let themselves feel, in sympathetic company, the full horror of the responsibility they had so foolishly undertaken.

"Ah," Lurch said with appalling timing, staring at the groups of small people stumping across the playground on their short little legs, slapping, pinching and generally abusing each other as they came. "In't they sweet?"

Every mother's head turned to stare at him. I couldn't decide whether they were still suspicious or simply incredulous. Some of them looked almost wistful, as if they were longing for me and Lurch to bundle their offspring into the back of our van and return them a few days later, considerably subdued.

Tom appeared at the door of the school. It might have been my imagination but I thought I noticed some of the mothers putting their heads together on his appearance, whispering among themselves. Even from this distance he looked beaten down by life.

"Jackie!" he called. "Don't hit Jamie with your bag, it's heavy! Kimberley, don't do that! Shereen, pull your skirt down— Shereen, stop flashing your knickers—no, Brittany, it's not funny, it's very silly, Shereen's being very silly—Robby, get off Shereen right now—Shereen! Well, Robby, you shouldn't have grabbed her, should you? Shereen doesn't like that—no, she didn't break your arm, Robby, it's fine. Well, of course it hurts a bit, she hit you very hard—naughty Shereen—go and find your mummy to make it better, Robby . . ."

Tom's voice was becoming increasingly pleading. He flapped the tots away across the playground, towards their waiting mothers, with large, clumsy gestures like an incompetent shepherd whose dog had failed to show up for work that morning. I waved at him, but he didn't see me in the chaos. He stood waiting in the doorway, clearly to make sure that all the children were safely reunited with their adult of choice. I wiggled past the throng, Lurch at my heels, and crossed the courtyard towards him. Mutters rose behind us.

Tom looked first amazed and then, flatteringly, overjoyed to see me.

"Sammy!" He embraced me. "You came so fast!"

I disengaged myself.

"That sounds like you were counting on me to come," I said rather suspiciously.

"Of course I was! I knew as soon as I said someone was dead you'd be down here like a shot. You're worse than a buzzard."

"Gosh, thanks, Tom. I can always count on you for reinforcement of my positive self-image."

"And Lurch! All right, mate!"

Lurch and Tom slapped each other on the shoulders in a manly way. A small dust cloud of coloured chalk puffed up from Tom's sweater. This was multi-coloured and pleasantly chunky, with nicely set-in raglan sleeves; it had evidently been hand-knitted by someone who could tell one grade of knitting needle from another in the dark, blindfolded. Emma, I presumed.

"Tom," I said firmly, "I think we should go for a drink and you can tell us all about—um—it."

I had been meaning to say something jocular about Tom's exciting new prime-suspect status, but the words had crumbled into dust on my tongue. All those kids running to their mothers across the playground had made me think of Janine's little boy, Pill, coming out of school every day with no waiting parent to scoop him up and take him home. I remembered Pill at the fireworks, crouching between his mother's legs, clinging on to her, and imagined him now bereft of that security for ever. I had hardly got to know Janine, but I had seen how she looked after her son, and I thought that her worst nightmare would have been to die young and leave him alone.

Tom's face fell into jowls of misery. Maybe I should have allowed him a few more minutes of relative content. But if he was going to be arrested any minute, there was no time to waste.

"I've got a lot of stuff to do still," he said. "I'll be finished in about an hour."

Lurch looked incredulous.

"You mean you don't go home when they do?" he said, gesturing backwards with one bony thumb at the horde of children. "That's criminal, that is!"

"Clearing up," Tom made a weary list, "paperwork, staff meetings—not that anyone's particularly keen on having meetings with me at the moment. They're having them about me instead. I'm sure I'm going to get the sack."

"They can't sack you yet," I said, desperately trying to scrape up the only encouraging thing I could think of.

"Not till I've been arrested."

"Is that grounds for getting the sack?" I asked.

Tom shrugged. "Bringing the school into moral disrepute?" he suggested gloomily.

"You should get in touch with your union official, mate," Lurch said firmly. "Ring 'em up right now and tell them what's going on. See what they say."

Tom was visibly struck by this idea.

"Actually, Lurch, that's not bad," he said. "Not bad at all. I'll get on to it straight away."

"Nice one." Lurch puffed up his chest, pleased to have been of help. "So we'll see you in the pub then?"

"Yes. I mean, you could come in and wait, but it's not exactly a good time for me to be having people in," Tom said with a good deal of euphemism.

Besides, as his disparaging gaze made plain, we were scarcely respectable enough to be good character witnesses. Lurch, as usual, looked as if he had just spent months working on a building site while living on an endless diet of chocolate bars and fry-ups, while I was still in my work clothes with my leopardskin second-hand coat over the top. Tom would do a lot better with a couple of friends with blonde hair, velvet headbands, discreet pearl jewellery and nice red overcoats from Country Casuals.

"They might think we were your next victims," I offered.

Tom managed to sketch a smile, but it was more like a rictus. I had never seen him this bad, not even after Lee died or his girl-friend had left him for a hippy American would-be guru. Poor Tom. He had really cared about Janine. I wondered how far things between them had actually gone.

And that wasn't just prurient curiosity. It must have been the first thing the police had asked him.

- - - - - -

Tom disappeared back inside, the school doors slamming behind him. I recognised the sound they made as if it were a deep primal memory. In a way it was, even though this was a school for small people, not the adolescent hell that I was remembering. The smell of lockers, stinky gym shoes and unwashed teenage youth, industrial-yellow paint on the walls and scratched old Formica tiles underfoot, the toilets with their heavily-graffiti'd walls and double line of sinks, the open drains below perpetually clogged with wadded-up toilet paper . . . And the bells. I had had enough bells in the last few days to last me an eternity.

"Let's get out of here," I said to Lurch. "I'm getting school flashbacks."

"Yeah, me too. Want to go behind the bike sheds?"

I stared at him incredulously, unable to believe that Lurch was propositioning me. Realising the trend of my thoughts, he turned bright red. When Lurch blushed it was the opposite to Alan, whose beauty was only enhanced by a touch of colour. Lurch went crimson. Usually, he was pallid white, his pasty skin enlivened only by the acne outbreaks. With a crimson back-ground, these didn't fade, as one might have expected, but stood out in relief instead. He looked like a map of craters on Mars.

"I meant to have a fag," he said in an agony of embarrassment, "not—oh, you know—"

I took pity on him.

"Anyway, we can't. It's a primary school, Lurch. The kids don't have bikes."

"Oh yeah." He cleared his throat. "Right."

We returned to the pub, where our corner table was still unoccupied. As was the pub. It must be early yet. As had been the case before, it was overlit. Apart from being a waste of electricity, this only showed up the dingy upholstery and tatty carpets still more. I remembered the Cow with affection.

"They should have a happy hour, get the punters in that way," I observed to Lurch, carrying our drinks over to the table. Every time I did this I longed for New York, where table service was automatic even in the seediest dive bars. Of course you had to tip for it, but who wouldn't willingly pay not to have to spill their beer all over themselves?

"Yeah, right. Theme nights. Karaoke Saturdays. Tropical cocktails with umbrellas in. This isn't Essex, y'know," Lurch said with contempt. "This is the countryside."

So true. I kept expecting poachers to walk in with their pockets full of dead rabbits. I had very sentimental ideas about country life.

"So why's old Tom number-one suspect for this girl getting topped?" Lurch said sensitively.

I glanced over at the bar. The wizened old man who had served me had disappeared somewhere. Perhaps the poacher was already in the back room and they were busy skinning ferrets together.

"He was really keen on her. And they had a big fight the night she got killed."

"They got anyone else looks like a suspect?"

"I have no idea. I don't know anything at all," I confessed. "Tom didn't really have a chance to tell me much over the phone."

Lurch looked thoughtful.

"Well, couldn't you ask your ex on the force to find out what the coppers are thinking?"

Lurch put a lot of spin on this question. Despite having been rescued by the police from imminent death (with not inconsiderable help from me) fairly recently, he had an inbred distrust of them which no amount of life-saving could abate. The fact that I had actually had an affair with a policeman was an enormous mark against me. I wasn't that proud of it myself, but Lurch looked as disapproving every time he mentioned it as if it had been a threesome with a Conservative MP and a vivisectionist.

"I haven't seen Hawkins in ages," I explained. "He's on this big police-corruption task force. Whoops, I wasn't supposed to tell anyone."

"Yeah," Lurch said. "I really look like a nark, don't I? Hang on a minute, I'll just ring up 999 and tell 'em all about it."

"You know what I mean. It's supposed to be a secret."

"One finger wet, one finger dry, cut me throat if I tell a lie," Lurch said, licking his index finger and drawing his hand over his protruding Adam's apple. If he ever decided to have a sex change, they'd have a bad time digging that monster out. "Or, y'know, tell a secret," he added. "I couldn't remember that one."

"Good enough for me," I said. "So, yeah, he's doing this really important top-secret assignment that you have no idea about—"

"You could tell me," Lurch interrupted, "but then you'd have to kill me."

"Exactly. Anyway, I don't think he'd be much help even if I could get hold of him. In all the TV series nowadays, country coppers are really hostile to the Met."

"I thought they were always calling in Scotland Yard."

"That's Agatha Christie," I corrected. "Now they're much more keen on defending their turf. If Hawkins tried to find out what was going on, it'd probably make it all the worse for Tom."

"Fair enough," Lurch said. "You don't want to ring him anyway, do you?"

"Not really. How'd you know?"

"Way you talk about him. Like you was keeping him at arm's length."

Damn, Lurch was good at this.

"He's having lots of fights with his wife," I explained reluctantly. When I had first met Hawkins, he had been living with his girlfriend, Daphne, whom he had subsequently married; from that time on our affair, such as it was, had been put on hold. Hawkins wanted to be virtuous, and I refused to be, even technically, the mistress of a married police inspector. It would have been too ludicrous. I had my standards, such as they were.

Besides, I had met Hugo at about the same time, and since then he had fully absorbed all of my sexual energy. Until now. I wondered what the hell was happening to me.

"Why d'you keep looking towards the door?" Lurch said observantly. "Tom won't be done for another half-hour yet."

"Just wanting to see if anyone we met at New Year comes in," I said. It was no more than the truth. I didn't really expect Alan, drawn by my presence like a needle to the north, to find himself strangely impelled to sink a pint in the irresistible atmosphere of the Four Jolly Coachmen at Dunster Magna, but I was looking forward to seeing him more than any girl in my situation should. Doubtless I would find him sitting on a bench on the village green of Lesser Swinfold, looking moody and existentialist, contemplating his novel of eighteenth-century Venice as the wind blew his black hair over his face and he slowly shivered himself into hypothermia. The fact that I actually found this image alluring rather than snigger-worthy demonstrated what a powerful impression he had made on me.

"You think one of them might have done it?" Lurch asked.

"I have no idea, Lurch." I drank some more beer. "But some-one must've. And we start by presuming it wasn't Tom."

"Yeah," Lurch said. "I don't exactly see old Tom as a murderer. Which at least gives us a start on the coppers, right? I mean, we're ruling Tom out straight away."

"Of course."

The door opened, bringing a gust of cold air with it. The Four Jolly Coachmen was about as welcoming as an undertaker's back room halfway through an embalming procedure, but at least it was warmer than outside. I glanced out of the window. It was already getting dark and the street looked utterly deserted. I imagined London at this time of day, bustling with life, Oxford Street heaving with shoppers shoving their way from one January sale to another, the double-decker buses bright oases of light against the dark sky, Tube trains thundering underground, com-fortably warm and packed with people. How could anyone bear this isolation?

The new arrival was Tom, looking as depressed as if we were in exile in Siberia rather than—I reminded myself so I didn't panic—under two hours' drive from London, with a good tail-wind and no speed cameras. He went over to the bar. After a mere half-hour or so, the ancient bartender appeared. His man-ner with us had scarcely been friendly, but he treated Tom with as much suspicion and hostility as if Tom was the local poaching inspector come to root every illegally caught stoat and rabbit out of the kitchen stockpot.

"You see what it's like?" Tom said, bringing the drinks over to our table. "Before, I wasn't exactly everyone's new best friend, but at least they all said hello to me—though I had to take a lot of crap for being a bloke who taught primary school."

"Did you explain to them that you did it to meet single moth-ers keen to have sex?" I said flippantly. "I'd have thought all the blokes would have clapped you on the back and bought you drinks."

This had in fact been Tom's main admitted motivation for training as a teacher. He was a poet; he had had various sonnets, odes, villanelles and so on published in anthologies, and his first (and only) book had come out a couple of years ago. It had failed to earn back even its minimal advance. Tom had always supplemented the infinitesimal income poetry provided with the occasional grant or poet-in-residence stint, and, more often, a few months' labouring work here and there, but in his middle thirties he had decided that he wanted something more than a room in a co-op house and suppurating blisters on his palms. Tom actually, inexplicably, liked small children. And primary schools were apparently crying out for male teachers to give small boys positive role models. How the description applied to Tom was a matter of debate, but the possibility of frequent sex with lonely, grateful single mothers, who couldn't afford babysitters and therefore had to invite him around to theirs and cook him dinner, had clinched it.

Tom's face had sunk into deep lines of misery. Raising the whole topic of single mothers had been a mistake. A complete lack of tact was one of my defining characteristics. Probably a curse from the bad fairy at my christening.

I decided I had nothing to lose at this point by being blunt.

"Were you actually seeing Janine? I mean, were you two actually, um, doing it?" I asked.

He shook his head.

"Well, what were you doing?" I persisted. *"Anything?"*

I felt like some awful medieval village gossip, clacking my tongue at the sheets hung out of the window after the bridal night and commenting with gusto about the amount of blood on them. "Ooh, look at that, Goody Trueshanks! Not much spotting there! Well, you know, with all the horse-riding that girl does, it's a wonder there's any at all . . . probably had a little help from a chicken, come to think of it . . ."

It was very ironic. I usually derived enjoyment from question-ing my friends about their sex lives and—hopefully—hearing all the juicy details. Lesser Swinfold had turned things upside down in more ways than one.

"I really loved her," Tom said hopelessly. "She was so strong, she'd been through so much—"

"The pregnancy?"

"Yeah, that. Her parents died when she was young and Andy brought her up, more or less. What a bastard that guy is," he added in parentheses. "He's—he was—always trying to do the older brother thing on her. Boss her around. He wouldn't let her alone to run her own life."

"The feeling's mutual," I informed him. "Andy's very fond of you too."

"Yeah, and that was another thing." Tom finished his pint. "He was always trying to put Jan off me. I mean, for fuck's sake, the guy's a bank manager! They're the scum of the earth! Send you a letter telling you they're going to foreclose on your house and add ten quid to your mortgage for writing the sodding letter! At least I'm doing some good for the community. Wiping snot off the noses of his horrible little brats."

I remembered Andy's hostile comment about Tom's choice of profession.

"So did Andy manage to prejudice Janine against you?" I said, sounding more inquisitorial than I liked.

"No. She didn't give a shit what he said. God, I need another drink."

He made to get up, but Lurch was already on his feet, collect-ing the empties.

"Thanks, mate," Tom said gratefully.

"*So were you actually having an affair with Janine?*" I said, willing my voice not to rise into a shout of frustration. Lurch, heading to the bar, looked over his shoulder at me reprovingly, so I couldn't quite have succeeded.

Tom looked utterly despondent.

"Not exactly," he said. "Well, not really. Um. No. We weren't—"

"—doing it," I finished.

"Yeah."

"But were you—"

"I don't know, OK? I don't know what the fuck we were doing!" Tom looked as angry now as I had just felt. His face was growing red, matching the bloodshot veins in his blue eyes. "It was like I was her boyfriend, but I wasn't! We talked on the phone almost every day, I'd see her at school when she picked up Pitt, we'd hang out at hers—I'd help her get his dinner and put him to bed, and then we'd watch a video or something—sometimes Tamsin would babysit and we'd go for a drink in the Cow—"

He ran a hand through his hair. I didn't really want to hear what was coming next. I could feel my forehead creasing in apprehension.

"Oh God, Sam, this isn't the first time this has happened to me, you know?" Tom said hopelessly. "I meet someone and things are going really well, we start to see a lot of each other, and after a while I realise I've got it all wrong and they only want me to be their friend—what's wrong with me? Am I sending out all the wrong signals? God, it's the most fucking frustrating thing! Do I just come across as a nice guy with no balls or something?"

"Tom, we really don't have time to do this now," I said as gently as I could. "I need to know about what happened with Janine."

"She did it deliberately too," he said, only half-listening to me. "I mean, she let me into her life, as if we were going to have, you know, a relationship. She couldn't have thought I was spending so much time with her just because I wanted to be friends, I made it perfectly clear—I thought I made it clear— well, yeah, I know I did. She knew I wanted to go out with her all along. She admitted it."

"What do you mean, 'admitted it'?" I said, trying not to jump to conclusions.

Lurch had come back with the drinks. I reached for my pint and took a deep draught without taking my eyes off Tom's face.

"The night she—died! It all came to a head. I was getting so frustrated—and angry—with myself," he added. "I thought I'd got it all wrong again. I was so furious that I could have been so stupid. Then Jan told me that it wasn't my fault. She said she really liked me, and she'd been hoping we could—you know— that it would lead to us getting together. But she'd realised that she couldn't, and she was really sorry if she'd hurt me, she hadn't meant to, she was so confused herself about what she wanted, and Pitt liked me so much she'd thought it would be a great idea, but she couldn't bring herself to do it. That was how she put it, bring herself to do it. Can you imagine?"

The bitterness in his voice would have turned milk sour.

"And then—oh, this is awful—I accused her of leading me on. God, like the worst kind of old-fashioned male bastard. As if she owed me something. I know it sounded as if I was saying that she owed me a shag, but I didn't mean it like that. Well, maybe I sort of did—some ancient caveman impulse—but I didn't—I wouldn't ever have really expected it—oh God, it was terrible. I've been beating myself up about it ever since. And then she got angry too, which was sort of a relief. I mean, it was worse for me when she was sitting there looking all concerned, with her head on one side, saying she was sorry that she'd hurt me. I'd rather she was showing some real emotion—that I could make her feel something real . . . But when she got angry, she stormed out of the pub, and—"

"She *what?*"

"She stormed out of the pub, and I—"

"Tom!" I wanted to beat my head against the wall till the blood ran. "You had this fight with her in a *pub*? In public?" I grasped at straws. "In here?" I said optimistically.

"No," Tom said, dashing my hopes. He looked at me as if I was mad. "What would we be doing in here? We always went to the Cow."

"So everyone in the village knows you had a massive fight with Janine the night she was killed," I summarised bleakly.

Tom finished off his pint in a gulp. He didn't say anything, which worried me still more.

"What d'you do after she stormed out?" Lurch asked.

"Finished my drink in a hurry and went for a long tramp around the village."

"Could anyone have seen you?" I said.

He shook his head.

"The moon was full. There was lots of light, so I went right out. When I said around the village," he clarified, "I mean literally around it. Through the woods. I was in a bit of a bad way. You know, Dante. In the middle of a man's life he finds himself in a dark wood. So did I."

This wasn't any help at all. I could just imagine how well the Dante part, in particular, would go down in cross-examination. Lurch hadn't asked Tom what the hell he meant. He always asked Hugo if he didn't understand, because Hugo was capable of a succinct explanation. Tom would try to press volumes of poetry on Lurch instead, which drove him crazy.

"Didn't you see anyone?" I said in desperation. "Would anyone in the house have seen you when you came in?"

He shook his head. "They were all in bed. Apart from Ethan.

He writes late in the shed out back. He's set it up with a heater so he can work in it. But he wouldn't have heard me. He's always got his music going anyway. That's why we made him use the shed," he added vindictively. "I wasn't getting any sleep because he was playing his music so late. Says he needs it to write. Wanker. Oh, Emma saw me," he added.

"Did she?" I perked up. It might be no help, but some grasp at an alibi was better than none.

"When I was going out. I came back to get my—" He looked shamefaced. "Well, I told Emma it was to get my hat, but actually I wanted to get a bottle. I had a half of whisky in my room, and I thought I'd take it with me."

"That Dante bloke drinking whisky in the dark wood, was he?" Lurch said, deadpan.

"So she saw me going out," Tom clarified.

Looking like death, I was willing to bet.

"She was really sympathetic," Tom said. "She sort of guessed what it was about. She gave me a hug and told me there were plenty more fish in the sea."

Great, I thought. Emma's reluctant testimony that Tom had been visibly upset by the fight with Janine would be the final nail in his coffin.

"How did this Janine bird actually die?" Lurch asked. "Sorry to be a bit brutal, mate, but we need to know."

"She was in her kitchen," Tom said. "On the floor. Someone hit her and knocked her over, and she hit her head on the table. There was blood on the corner of the table, where she went down."

He saw that we were a little taken aback by this detail and hastened to assure us, "It was in the local paper. They've been writing about nothing else. You can imagine."

"So it could have been an accident?" I said tentatively. "I mean, manslaughter? If someone were really angry at her but didn't mean to kill her—"

But Tom was shaking his head again.

"That's the thing. Once she was on the floor, they—they—she had a toolbox by the back door. She'd been fixing the hinges on a cupboard door—I was showing her how—and she hadn't put the toolbox away yet. Whoever hit her picked up the box and smashed it on to her head. It was really heavy."

"Oh, Jesus," I said. The image before my eyes was all too clear. I knew Janine had been murdered; I could have imagined any conceivable way it could have happened, and this certainly wasn't as bad as some. And yet the horrible reality was a stunned, probably unconscious woman lying on her kitchen floor as her murderer heaved up a toolbox and let it smash into her unprotected face. I couldn't help raising a hand to my own, as if to ward off the same fate. Lurch was similarly affected.

"Who found her?" I realised I didn't even want to know.

"Tamsin. She came round the next morning because Jan hadn't picked up Pitt. He was sleeping over at Tamsin's because Jan was out with me. She brought in Pitt to get his school clothes."

"So he was there?"

I was horrified.

"I think so."

"Poor little mite," Lurch said, looking really upset.

"And everyone thinks I did it," Tom groaned. "I know they do. Tamsin hasn't even sent Courtney or Marc, let alone Pitt, to school since it happened. It's like she thinks I'll try to kill them too."

"Tom—" I said in protest.

"Or at least she doesn't want Pitt around me because I killed his mother! Oh God, as if I could have laid a finger on Jan . . . I loved her so much . . ."

Tom was crying now. He sunk his head into his hands and wept, his shoulders rising and falling with the strength of his sobs. A movement behind the bar caught my eye. The old man had emerged from the back room and was leaning on the bar, watching Tom, his wrinkled ancient face one creased knot, his mouth puckered up as tight as a drawstring purse. A tiny, contemptuous putt of air escaped from it. He thought Tom was putting on an act, or possibly that he was sobbing with remorse.

My eyes met his. He shook his head in scorn and started wiping down the bar. If he was any guide, the sympathy Tom could expect from the locals was as scarce as that which the murderer had extended to Janine.

7

"AH GOD, IT WAS HORRIBLE," TAMSIN SAID. "IT'S THE KIND of thing you see on the telly all the time, you know? Horrible murders. And I used to like that kind of thing. Police series, with a string of people being killed, one worse than the next. God, I can't watch them now. I don't think I'll ever be able to do that again. Your boyfriend's in something like that, isn't he? I was looking forward to that—see someone you've actually met on the telly. Makes me feel sick to my stomach to see something like that now. Dead bodies. Even if you know it's not real. That's the thing, you see. When I found her, it was so—unreal. It was like being in a film. I was sort of thinking it was a set-up, or something. It was so—she was just lying there, on the floor, with the lights on, and—I mean, I knew it was Jan, because I recognised her body, her clothes, but she had this red toolbox covering her face, bright red it was—and then I started to see all the blood underneath. It was dark, not bright like the toolbox, and for a moment I didn't realise what it was. That was like being in a film too. That pool of blood . . . all over her nice clean floor . . . God, I can see it now. I see it every time I close my eyes."

"What about Pitt?" I said. "Did he—was he—"

"Oh, that was the one good thing." Tamsin breathed a deep sigh. "That's what keeps me going, I can tell you. Knowing at least that he didn't see his mum that way. I'd sent him straight upstairs. I told him to get changed, but actually I wanted to give Jan a piece of my mind for not picking him up and not answering the phone. I could see the kitchen light on, so I knew she was in there, and I just thought I'd tell her what I thought of her without him being around. I don't like to have words in front of the kids if I can help it. I was really cross with her, I'd been ringing and ringing . . . and then to find her like that, I was so upset and angry with myself for being cross, when all the time she was lying there, poor thing . . . oh, I still can't believe it . . ."

She got up and went over to the stove.

"Don't think I'm being heartless, will you? I've just got to get the kids' tea ready. And, you know, this isn't the first time I've told people about it. Everyone here's been asking, you can imagine. I've got a bit used to telling it. That helps a bit, actually. Talking about it. It makes it almost like a story, gives me a bit of distance. That's why I don't mind telling you about it."

She dumped a family-sized tin of baked beans into a saucepan and put it on the cooker.

"I can't say a word about it to Andy, you see," she added. "He bites my head off when I try. It's bad enough for him that Jan's dead. The thought of someone killing her just sends him over the edge."

The toaster pinged. Four slices of bread popped out. Tamsin put them on a plate, slid it into the oven to keep warm and filled up the toaster once again.

"I thought it was an accident at first," she said. "Can you believe that? As if someone could fall over with a toolbox on their face. But I was trying so hard not to imagine what really happened. That someone could have done that to her."

I could tell that Tamsin had related the story of finding Janine before. She sounded wearily practised. I had heard people breaking the news of a death before, and I knew that after a while they fell back into repeating the same phrases again and again, partly for ease of communication, and partly, as she herself had said, almost to distance themselves from the shock.

"She was so good with Pitt," Tamsin said sadly. "That's almost what hurts the most. She taught him to read, ages before mine knew what the alphabet was. And she loved him to death."

Tamsin removed a sweaty, plastic-wrapped slab of Cheddar from the fridge and started grating it into a bowl. The cheese was enormous, an economy-sized value pack as big as a house brick. I imagined a monster that big sitting in my fridge, the mould it would gather before I finally got round to throwing it away. Families were a different world. The enormous tin of beans, the extra-long sliced loaf . . . to me they looked like industrial catering ingredients. I lived on individual meals from Sainsbury's and Marks & Sparks, though admittedly the portions were so small I usually needed to eat two at a sitting. Anyway, food took second place in my fridge, which was mostly filled with beer, wine and the extra vodka bottle I kept in there as a back-up for when the one in the freezer ran out.

Tamsin's fridge, however, was stacked with Tupperware containers and plastic tubs the size of flower-pots full of peanut butter and hummus and margarine. She caught my fascinated stare and misinterpreted it. Or maybe, actually, she read me perfectly.

"You hungry?" she said in a friendly tone. She had been friendly all the way through the conversation, from the moment she opened her front door to find us on the step; it had been a relief. I had been worried that she would slam the door in our faces. But now she sounded more comfortable with us, almost cosy, as if the act of feeding us would reassure her in a way.

"I'm just doing beans on toast for the kids' tea," she said almost apologetically, "but you're welcome to some if you want.

Probably didn't have any lunch, did you, coming straight down from London like that?"

Lurch's stomach rumbled audibly at the mere thought of beans on toast.

"That'd be lovely," I said. "Thanks."

"I'll just put in some more toast. They're always starving, my two. And Pitt . . ."

Her voice trailed off. I kept quiet and waited for her to finish.

Tamsin, slathering margarine on to slices of toast, sighed and brushed her hair back with her forearm, her hands too greasy to use.

"Oh, he's been really quiet since his mum . . . well . . ." she said finally, as if answering an unspoken question of mine. "It's been a lot to take on. And Andy doesn't help. He can't bear to hear Jan talked about, like I said. The last thing he'd want to do is give Pitt a cuddle. Reminds him too much of Jan, you see."

"What about Pitt's dad?" I asked. "Couldn't he lend a hand?"

"Don't get me started," Tamsin said shortly. But this was obviously rhetorical. Almost immediately she continued, "Jan never told anyone who he was. Never breathed a word. Social Services were all over her about it—you know, there's this law or something now, you've got to say who the dad is if you want your benefits, so they can get something back from him. But she wouldn't. She strung them along with this story about his being violent and being too scared to tell."

She caught my eye.

"Oh, I'm sure it was all a pack of lies," she added, seeing my expression. "It's just the only thing you can say that lets you get away with not telling."

"She could've said that she didn't know who he was," I offered. "Just a one-night stand."

"Oh, she wouldn't have done that, even if it was true," Tamsin said. She sprinkled grated cheese on the beans. "Do you want some on yours?" she asked.

Lurch and I both nodded in unison like a pair of eager children.

"Andy would've gone ballistic if she'd said that," Tamsin explained. "And it's a small place, Swinford. It would've been a lot to live down."

"So you think this story of a violent ex was total, um, rubbish?"

I had been going to say bullshit, but bit it back at the last minute, in case Tamsin objected to it. She ran a pretty orderly house: everything modern and shiny, surfaces cleaned, a big bottle of Dettol sitting on the windowsill. It wasn't quite the gleaming, spotless kitchen of the super-housewives in advertisements—real life had intruded in the form of kids' drawings pinned up everywhere, a snoring old dog in a basket in the corner, and piles of plastic toys, red and yellow and blue and green, stacked in a crate against one wall. Still, it was a pretty impressive display of housewifely skills, particularly since Tamsin hadn't expected visitors. I had the notion that in her nice yellow disinfected kitchen, with the descent of the children imminent, Tamsin might prefer her guests to omit the profanities.

"Courtney! Marc!" Tamsin called up the stairs. "Pitt! Come down straight away, food's on the table!"

Tamsin pulled milk, water and apple juice out of the fridge and set them on the table.

"I'm going to make myself a cuppa," she said. "Do you two fancy some tea? I could make a pot."

"Ooh, lovely," Lurch said, speaking for practically the first time. "Beans on toast and a nice cup of tea. It's like being back at home."

Tamsin was inordinately pleased by this. It surprised me: I would have thought that being compared by association to

Lurch's mother might have annoyed her, since she could only be in her early thirties. But clearly she took it as a compliment to her hospitality.

"It's not much tonight," she said self-deprecatingly. "Usually I try to make them pasta or something, with some veggies, or an egg in it. But things are all a bit at sixes and sevens at the moment . . ."

The kids tumbled down the stairs and piled around the table, climbing up on to the chairs and settling themselves on the cushions Tamsin had put there to give some height. Pitt was smaller than the other two and looked unbelievably forlorn. He ran to Tamsin and hugged her legs for a while before she gently removed him and plonked him on to his chair.

"You all eat up now. And good manners in front of the guests," she admonished. "You don't want them to think you're a pack of pigs, do you?"

Courtney made honking noises, at which both Marc and Pitt collapsed in fits of giggles. I thought Tamsin might have done better to tell me and Lurch to eat properly in front of the children: Lurch had tilted his plate up and was shovelling down his beans as if barely restraining the impulse to lift the plate to the level of his mouth and scrape them in directly.

I stared at Pitt as he bent over his plate, trying to see any traits of his unknown father. It was a hopeless enterprise; the village must have played this game from the day he was born, and if they had not succeeded, knowing all the possible local candidates as well as they did, I didn't have a chance in hell. He had Janine's colouring, the fair skin, blue eyes and hair the same ash-blond as hers. But Pitt's hair, curling into the ducked crown of his head, was natural. Janine must have been this fair in childhood. Though he was young still, Pitt looked as if he would have a sturdier build than his delicately boned mother. His arms were solid and his legs stumpy as a rugby player's. Even his head was big in proportion to his body. Hopefully everything would balance itself out as he grew, but right now that large head looked almost like a birth defect.

"No ice cream till everyone finishes what's on their plates!" Tamsin said firmly. It was hardly necessary, as we were all busy filling our faces, but the forks and knives clanked even faster on the china. I noticed that Lurch had automatically doubled his eating pace, determined to earn his ice cream with the rest.

"Courtney and Marc, did you say hello to Sam? Do you remember her from New Year?" Tamsin said, pulling up a chair at the table.

Damn. I had really hoped we wouldn't have to enter into conversation with the children. Fortunately, they both had their mouths full; they lifted their heads to give me and Lurch totally incurious glances before reaching once again for the ketchup bottle.

The sound of keys in the front door signalled Andy's return home from the bank. He sloughed off his coat in the hall and stuck his head around the kitchen door.

"All right, everyone?" he said.

"Daddy's home!" Tamsin said to the kids.

Andy came in, ruffling the kids' hair absent-mindedly, his gaze fixed on us. In his pale-grey suit, crumpled by a day's wear, and badly knotted tie, he looked so much the stereotype of a bank manager that I immediately felt as if every single lie I had told mine to prolong my overdraft was tattooed on my forehead.

"You remember Sam from New Year's Eve, don't you, Andy?" Tamsin said. She used exactly the same tone with him as she did for their children, jolly and encouraging, like a kindergarten teacher.

"Oh yeah. Tom's mate from London," Andy said, unknotting his tie and shoving it in his pocket. He pronounced Tom's name—well, as if he was convinced that Tom had murdered his only sister. Clearly, Andy had no doubt about Tom's guilt.

Andy, on closer examination, looked worn out. His eyes were sunk into dark circles like twin bruises, and his neck was red and chafed, as if he had a persistent rash. He and Pitt seemed the only members of the household who were visibly showing their distress at Janine's death.

"This is Kevin," I said, introducing Lurch, who preferred to be called by his real name by people he didn't know well. I couldn't understand why. I would have thought that "Lurch" would be infinitely preferable to "Kevin."

Andy barely acknowledged Lurch.

"Come down to hold Tom's hand, have you?" he said to me.

"More or less."

He made a sound of disgust.

"Well, he'll need it," he said ominously. "They'll have him banged up pretty soon, and about time too. Should be behind bars right now."

"Andy." Tamsin tried not to gesture too obviously at Pitt but her very attempt made it all too obvious who she meant. "Little pitchers have big ears."

"Mum! Pictures don't have ears! I don't know why you keep saying that!" objected Courtney, a precocious child.

Marc sniggered. Pitt, sensitive to the distress in the air, however, kept his head down even though his plate was empty.

"Sam and Kevin just dropped in to say hello," Tamsin said valiantly. "I thought it was very nice of them."

"You staying with Tom?" Andy said, still hostile.

"I don't know," I said. I had thought Lurch and I could stay at the Cow for a couple of nights.

"Might as well go to Emma's. There'll be a room free there soon," he said nastily. "Or maybe she'll get round to kicking out those American spongers."

Tamsin looked as if she wanted to protest again, but settled for standing up to clear the plates, making an excess of noise while stacking them as if to distract us from what was being said. Andy leaned on the back of Courtney's chair, watching her dourly without making any effort to help. Lurch, politer than Andy, half-stood up but Tamsin indicated firmly that he should sit down again.

"Right," she said brightly, "what about some ice cream? You've all earned it, haven't you? Talk about the clean-plate club!"

"I'm off to the Cow," Andy said. "Quick drink with the lads."

"Oh, Andy . . ." Tamsin protested. "I've still got so much to do . . ."

Her husband set his jaw stubbornly. Suddenly, I realised where Pitt's solidity came from: family genes. His stocky frame and potato head could have been modelled on his uncle's. He looked more like Andy than Marc, Andy's own son. If Pitt was lucky, though—or Janine had picked his real father well—he would miss out on Andy's baldness. Already Andy's hair was so thin that the light shone through it, making it seem as insubstantial as a spider's web. He looked like a pugnacious foetus.

"Won't be long," he said. "See you for dinner."

He turned and left the kitchen. A moment later the front door slammed. Tamsin stood for a moment with the stack of plates in her hand, staring towards the open door of the kitchen. Then, finally, she set them down in the sink. A small sigh escaped her lips.

"He's under a lot of stress at the moment," she said to us. "I wanted him to take time off work—they'd have given him it, no problem—but he said it'd help take his mind off things. I don't know. Seems to me it's just making him worse."

"It's because of Aunty Janine, isn't it?" Courtney chirped up. " 'Cos she's gone, and she isn't coming back."

Pitt pushed back his chair, levered himself clumsily off it and ran out of the room.

"Oh, Courtney, look what you've gone and done now!" Tamsin said hopelessly. "You kids go and get Pitt and bring him back to the table. Courtney, you say sorry to him like a good girl."

"But it's true," Courtney said stubbornly. She was an unprepossessing child, with bulging blue eyes like a Hapsburg monarch, but I admired her insistence on the fundamental verities. "I don't want to say sorry for saying something true."

"You're saying sorry," Tamsin said, raising her voice into command mode, "because you upset your cousin, OK? You know perfectly well you both have to be really, really nice to him right now! And you know why! Now go and get him back, both of you, or there won't be any ice cream for anyone."

Lurch looked horrified enough to pack the kids off himself if they didn't obey. Fortunately, the threat of withheld ice cream was more than enough. Though moaning in protest, they lost no time in taking off after Pitt.

"I've tried explaining things to him," Tamsin said, "but kids that age, what do they understand? And having those reporters ringing up all the time didn't help. One of them even waited outside for me, can you believe it?"

"Reporters?" I echoed apprehensively.

"It's settled down a bit now. Or at least they've stopped ringing me to get me to say how lovely Jan was and how much we miss her," Tamsin said rather dryly. "But they're still snooping around the village."

I could see how much of a story this was; murdered photogenic blonde single mother, the father of whose child was a mystery. I wondered with a sinking heart whether Tom would feature in all the papers as the sinister would-be boyfriend with nefarious intentions. Thank God he did at least look the part of the cuddly primary-school teacher in hand-knitted sweaters. The fact that he wasn't shaven-headed and mad-eyed with prison tattoos on his hands could only help. Tom, when he put on weight, tended to resemble a teddy bear. He had always reminded me of those big Paddington Bear dolls you used to see in shops, with duffle coats and wellingtons and a sign around their necks saying: "Please Look After This Bear."

"And Pitt, poor little thing, he doesn't know about his mum—I mean, what happened to her," Tamsin was saying. "I thought I'd keep the kids away from school for a couple of days. Maybe when they go back the gossip'll have died down a bit."

So that was the reason the kids hadn't been to school. Still, everyone in the village, and Dunster Magna too, would think, like Tom, that Tamsin hadn't sent them to school because she didn't want them taught by Janine's presumed murderer.

"He cries himself to sleep every night. And wets the bed."

"Must be a lake in there every morning," Lurch muttered.

Tamsin by now was pulling five-litre cartons of ice cream out of the giant freezer and luckily didn't hear him.

"I really liked Tom," she said rather sadly. "I thought Jan was on to a really good thing there. At last. He was a lovely bloke. Really good with the kids. All the mums were a bit funny about having a man teaching at the primary school at first, but we came round fast. The kids loved him."

I noticed, with a sinking in my stomach, that she was talking about Tom in the past tense. It was as if he had already been found guilty.

Lurch, however, failed to spot that. He was too busy goggling at the ice-cream cartons.

"Is that raspberry ripple?" he said excitedly. "I haven't had that in years."

"Coming right up," Tamsin said, slightly cheered by Lurch's wholehearted appreciation. "Sam? Ice cream?"

"No thanks," I said absently. My mind was elsewhere. I was imagining Andy in the Cow, convinced of Tom's guilt, stirring up the other drinkers with the story of how his sister had been killed. If the police didn't arrest Tom, I could only hope that the men of Lesser Swinford didn't decide to take the law into their own hands. This wasn't Chipping Campden; we could rule out a lynching party—though several of the big trees in the church-yard would have made perfect gallows. Still, there was nothing to stop them duffing Tom up a bit.

I thought of Paddington Bear again. "Please Look After This Tom." Well, someone was going to have to.

I just wished he hadn't lost his temper with Janine.

REPLETE WITH BAKED BEANS AND TEA, LURCH AND I BADE
goodbye to Tamsin. I had said that I would drop in on Tom, who
had gone home, before going around to the Cow and sorting out
our accommodation. I didn't doubt they would have rooms free.
The first week in January people make New Year's resolutions,
not hotel bookings.

Tamsin and Andy lived in a new development just outside
Lesser Swinford. It should have been a mere five-minute drive to
Emma's, but the complicated village one-way system ate us up
and spat us out several times before we mastered its convolu-
tions. It was Lurch who finally worked out that we needed to
loop around and, perversely, come at the village from the opposite
side. I was even more grateful that I had brought him along.

After Tamsin's house, where everything matched and had its
place, Emma's seemed positively chaotic. I couldn't help remembering a favourite saying of a friend of mine: the further you
went up the social scale, the dirtier people's houses got. He had
been brought up in a working-class household, where his mother
had been determined to prove that though they were poor, that
didn't mean they were filthy. She scrubbed all the surfaces with
disinfectant three times a day and the only reason they couldn't
eat their dinners off the kitchen floor was that it was so drenched

in bleach it would have been like picnicking in the middle of a swimming pool. He made this observation when we were invited to the country home of a violently aristocratic fellow student at art college. We spent most of the time picking wet dog hairs out of our food and trying not to touch anything in the house we didn't absolutely have to. All the furniture was covered in a layer of greasy, dirty dust to which our hostess seemed blissfully oblivious.

Still, it was too much of a generalisation. It broke down as soon as you factored in the house-proud *petits bourgeois*, the *nouveaux riches* and, more than anything, the merciful collapse of some of the nastier British class distinctions. There had to be more than a grain of truth in it, though. I thought of it at once as Emma opened the front door and, instead of Tamsin's bright painted hallway with its Monet prints and co-ordinating coat-stand, we saw scuffed dusty wooden floors, old white plastered walls, a huge antique coat cupboard which looked as if it had taken decades of abuse from carelessly wielded hockey sticks and cricket bats, and the wreaths of dried flowers, slightly dulled as if they needed dusting. Emma was house-proud, and I would never have noticed these imperfections if we hadn't come straight from Showhome Tamsin. Maybe it was the sense, too, that the decor had not been planned but had rather evolved over decades, perhaps even generations, till the house was a palimpsest of the family that had inhabited it for so many years.

"Have you had this house a long time?" I found myself asking Emma as I took off my coat.

"Oh yes," Emma said. "Or rather, my husband. It was his family home. Nearly a century now." She looked wistful. "We didn't have any children, so there's no-one to pass it on to. I don't know what I should do about it. I'd like it to go to a Warwick—that's my husband's family—for continuity, but there are hardly any left."

I made clucking sounds of sympathy. This must be why Emma liked to fill the house with guests; without any children of her own, they created a sort of substitute family.

"I assume you're not going back tonight," she said as she led the way through to the living room. "I wouldn't like to have to do that drive twice in one day. Or do you have urgent things in London to get back to?"

"No, I wanted to stay for a few days, keep Tom company," I said. "I thought we'd get a room at the Cow."

"Oh no!" Emma sounded horrified. "I mean, there's nothing wrong with the Cow—but you must stay here. I've got a spare room—I can make up the beds in a moment."

She looked rather doubtfully at Lurch.

"There are two single beds," she said, clearing her throat. "Ethan and Laura are in the guest double bedroom. I assume that's—I mean, Sam, I know you're—um—that is, I know Hugo isn't here, but—"

"Oh God, yes," I assured her hastily. "Single beds."

Lurch looked as if he wanted to die. I hoped this was from embarrassment rather than revulsion at the mere idea of having sex with me.

"But it's a nice room," Emma was assuring us. "Sheila had it when she stayed over New Year's. Actually, she usually has the double bedroom. She didn't like it being taken very much."

For a moment Emma was a naughty little girl, confiding some mischief she had done to her older sister. It made her look thirty years younger. Her eyes sparkled and her crow's-feet crinkled up delightfully into laughter lines.

"I thought Sheila seemed unfriendly to Ethan and Laura," I observed.

"Oh, that's just her way," Emma said quickly, reverting to the staid middle-aged matron. I watched the naughty little girl vanish with disappointment. "She's very protective of me. She thinks they should pay me some rent, but I won't hear of it. After all, Laura's the child of an old friend of mine, and they're struggling artists! I'm only too happy to let them stay here for a while. Laura's doing some very pretty paintings of the village. And, you know, I can afford it. I never went out to work, but my husband was a stockbroker, and he left me very well off, frankly. Sheila has to work for her living, so of course she's more aware of that kind of thing."

I heard this naïve explanation with amusement. I was willing to bet that Sheila resented Emma having married Mr. Pots-of-Money, and her hostility to Laura and Ethan was much less protectiveness of Emma than seeing them getting a free ride out of her wealthy sister. It would explain Sheila's odd antagonism to Emma, the kind of town mouse versus country mouse one-upmanship I had noticed at New Year; she was simultaneously patronising, in the way a career woman is to someone who has always been a housewife, and jealous that Emma had gained financial security so easily when she still had to work for it.

"I'll see about making up the beds straight away," Emma said, looking positively pleased that we had created extra work for her.

"I'll come and give you a hand," Lurch offered.

"Oh, how kind of you!" Emma surveyed Lurch a little doubtfully. Gangly and awkward, he always looked as if he would be all fingers and thumbs until you actually saw him engaged on a task. "But I can manage, really."

"I used to help my mum a lot around the house," Lurch assured her, quite unoffended. "I know what I'm doing."

"He's very handy," I confirmed. "Appearances can be deceptive."

Lurch and Emma went through the usual routine of good-guest-insists-while-good-hostess-refuses for a few minutes before she gave in and consented to let him help her.

"Why don't you go on down to the kitchen, Sam?" she said.

"Tom's there, and I'm sure he wants to see you." She pressed my hand. "Do try to cheer him up, poor boy. This is so awful for him. I mean, I feel terribly sorry for Janine, of course, but there's nothing to be done for her now, and poor Tom is having a terrible time. The police have already questioned him twice. I'm so worried about him."

That third-eye crease was deepening again. I had the impression that half Lesser Swinfold could have been murdered and Emma wouldn't care as long as Tom wasn't suspected. She had spoken quite briskly about Janine's death, but her voice softened whenever she mentioned Tom's name. It was easy to see where her sympathies lay.

Tom was indeed there with a cup of tea, which he was engaged in doctoring with a lavish shot of whisky. I observed this procedure with apprehension. In the emotional state Tom was in, he really shouldn't be drinking this much.

"Another step down the long road to oblivion?" I said, trying to keep the disapproval out of my voice.

"Helps to forget that I'm Public Enemy Number One," he said dourly.

"Oh, it'll be OK, Tom. You worry too much," said Laura, who was sitting at the kitchen table with a big bowl of pasta in front of her.

She made this observation overbrightly. I wondered how everyone else felt about sharing a house with a man whom the entire village—if the inhabitants I had met already were anything to go by—suspected of the brutal murder of the woman he had been in love with. Actually, I amended this. Only Ethan and Laura would have any doubts. Emma was obviously a hundred per cent behind Tom.

Tom shot Laura a look of intense dislike.

"Hi, Sam," she said cheerfully. "Want some pasta? Ethan's still got to eat, but I made a bit extra."

Remembering Laura's apple pie, I declined politely, pleading the baked beans at Tamsin's.

"Oh, are you sure?" she said. "It's veggie. Soy macaroni with tofu cubes. I make it all the time, it's very nice in winter. And cheap."

"Uh, no, thanks," I said, wondering why all hippie vegetarian food was the same pale, unappetising shade of brown.

"Oh well, if we don't finish it, it'll be tomorrow's lunch," she said pragmatically. "I can fry it up with an egg."

"How was Tamsin?" Tom asked me.

"OK. Very nice to us. Even gave us dinner."

I didn't want to talk too much in front of Laura.

"Andy came in towards the end," I added. "He went off to the Cow."

Tom gave me a sharp look, hearing the words I wasn't saying: Andy's full-out conviction that Tom had killed his sister.

"That bastard," Tom muttered. "He's such a weirdo. I always thought there was something funny about the way he treated Jan. He was much too fucking possessive of her. It wasn't normal."

"Hey!" said Ethan, clattering down the stairs. "Where's my dinner? Oh, hi, Sam. I hear you're coming to join our merry band here."

Tom looked at me hopefully.

"Emma's asked me and Lurch to stay for a few days," I confirmed.

"Oh, that's great! It'll be so nice having you round!" Tom said, sounding as happy as possible under the circumstances. "Sammy to the rescue!"

My heart fell. I didn't have a good feeling about this whole situation. I wished Tom was less blindly confident in me.

And I wished I was a little more confident of Tom.

"Exciting times, eh?" Ethan said conversationally, reaching for a bowl and ladling some macaroni into it. "Though I mean," he added quickly, as Tom bristled, "it's terrible about Janine being killed. It's just that you don't expect this kind of thing in a quiet English country village."

"According to the detective novels, it's exactly what you'd expect," I said rather dryly. "Especially the ones written by Americans."

I was trying to distract Tom, who was a crime-fiction buff, and it worked.

"Not enough titled nobility for the Yanks round here," Tom said, perking up somewhat. "All the American detective stories have loads of aristocratic detectives and stately homes."

"Yeah, this is a bit downmarket," I agreed.

"Did you know this house was once the butler's retirement house?" Ethan said unexpectedly. "Isn't that weird? There's a big, uh, stately home a few miles away, and this was where they'd let their old butler live when he was past heaving the silver tray down the corridors."

"Jesus," I said, stunned, looking around me at the enormous kitchen. "Four bedrooms, three storeys, a huge lawn out the front . . . nowadays it's prime real estate."

"I know," Ethan agreed. "Freaky, huh? To think that to them this was just a little cottage you put the old retainers in. I mean, I'd kill for a house like this."

He sat down at the table.

"We have any beer?" he said to Laura.

"Oh." She looked apologetic. "I meant to get a six-pack, but I forgot."

"Too busy buying tofu," Ethan said to us. He sounded jocular enough, but it was clear that he was annoyed.

"Shame," Tom said pointedly, throwing fuel on the flames. "A beer would've been great."

"The beds are made up," Emma announced, coming down the stairs into the kitchen. "Kevin was very helpful."

"Oh, he's a treasure," I said to embarrass him.

"Lurch!"

"Tom!"

Despite having only seen each other a few hours ago, they clapped each other on the shoulders. Lurch and Tom were very fond of one another.

"Want a swig?" Tom said, offering Lurch the bottle, which he had pointedly not pushed in Ethan and Laura's direction.

"Don't mind if I do."

"Oh Tom, not that awful blended stuff," Emma protested. "I can't believe you're still buying that."

"Emma, me darling." Tom stood up and gave Emma a bear hug. Stocky as she was, she disappeared for a moment inside the folds of his sweater. "I keep on telling you, it's no use putting good malt whisky into tea. Will you be listening to me now, woman?"

Tom, whose mother was Irish, had the occasional tendency to slip into bad Oirish when drunk, but I hadn't heard him do it for ages. And besides, he wasn't even that tipsy. Emma must bring it out in him.

Her eyes were shining brightly when he finally released her.

"Well, you know where the Laphroaig is if you want some," she said, patting his cheek.

"That I do. Now pull up a chair and come and have a crack with us."

Tom was trying much too hard to sound relaxed. It was painful to watch.

"Emma, do you want some macaroni?" Laura offered enthusiastically. "There's loads left. I made extra."

"Oh, no thank you, dear," Emma said. "I'm not that fond of pasta."

Laura tilted her head on one side, her reddish curls tumbling over her shoulder, and stared at Emma wistfully.

"Are you sure? I was hoping you'd have some."

"No, really, dear. Thank you so much."

Laura looked deeply disappointed. Over the coming days I was to learn that this was a regular pattern. Laura and Ethan made a big point of buying food and drink for themselves, the most basic foodstuffs, as their funds were limited; then they would offer it to everyone in a great show of generosity. Since it was all too easy to refuse most of their cooking, the offers were very rarely accepted, and thus they could consider that they had behaved properly without having to share overmuch in practice. I realised too why Tom had made that snide remark about the beer; though they were always talking about buying some, it actually appeared extremely rarely. That it would have been much more considerate for Laura—or Ethan, come to that—to offer to shop for and cook something that their hostess actually liked to eat had obviously never entered either of their heads.

"I was meaning to ask you about all that stale bread," Emma said to Laura, sitting down. Tom held her chair courteously for her, and she smiled happily up at him over her shoulder.

"The stale bread?" Laura echoed.

"In the paper bags in the larder."

"Oh, yeah! Well, it seemed such a shame to throw it away, you know? I was looking for a recipe and I found this one where you grate breadcrumbs over pasta, so I thought I'd try it—oh, no, I meant to do that tonight and I forgot."

"That sucks," Ethan said sympathetically.

"Stale breadcrumbs?" Tom said in disgust.

"Oh, you toast them first. Or fry them, in a little oil. It's Italian peasant food."

No matter how obviously Tom expressed his antipathy, Laura never seemed to take offence. If genuine, it was an impressive display of hippy tolerance.

Tom made a noise that was halfway between a cough and a laugh. "Sounds more like what Italian peasants feed to their pigs," he said brutally.

"Oh, you wait! I'll make it tomorrow, and you can see!" Laura promised. "The picture looked real pretty."

"Still, Laura, you're never going to get through all that bread just grating a little on pasta," Emma said, a faint note of desperation creeping into her voice.

"Oh, I'm looking up other recipes too. Besides, you can put breadcrumbs on lots of things, can't you?"

"As long as it doesn't get all mouldy," Emma said with unusual firmness. "Because if you don't want it, I could always take it to Mrs. Harbright for her hens."

"Tell her to fry it first in a little oil," Tom recommended. "I bet the hens'll like that."

Lurch spluttered with laughter.

"This is Kevin, by the way," Emma said, realising that there were still introductions to be performed. "He's a friend of Sam's. Kevin, these are Ethan and Laura, who are staying with me too."

"Didn't Tom call you something else?" Ethan said.

Lurch was capable of being embarrassed by his nickname, but not by an American called Ethan whose girlfriend hoarded dried crusts of bread to grate on soy macaroni.

"Yeah," he said nonchalantly, "Lurch. It's a nickname what they give me at this theatre I used to work at, 'cos they said I looked like the butler from the Addams family. It sort of stuck. You could call me that too, if you like," he said to Emma. "Sam just said Kevin 'cos with people who don't know me well she knows I'd rather. But all me theatre mates, and all Sam's lot, call me Lurch." He turned to Ethan and Laura. "You two going out, then?" he asked. "I almost thought you was brother and sister when I seen you."

"Yeah, people often say that," Laura said equably. "We do look pretty alike, I guess."

They looked at us from identical washed-out blue eyes. The colour could have been cold, like an Alaskan husky's, but the effect was more like faded denim, or far-off blue hills: friendly but distant.

"That often happens, doesn't it?" Emma observed. "Like meeting like."

"Did you look like your husband, Emma?" I asked.

"Oh goodness, I don't think so," she said, laughing. "At least, I hope not. Walter was very, well, craggy. There he is, you can see for yourself."

She gestured to a group of photographs hung on the wall behind her. They were mostly of Emma and Walter. The word "craggy" did him a disservice; Walter had been a good-looking man, with a shock of silver hair and a distinguished expression. Certainly, in the later photos he was increasingly wrinkly, but that was only to be expected. Emma hung on his arm and looked up at him adoringly in best wifely fashion, like the cover of a romantic novel. They must have been taken by someone who knew what they were doing because the quality was excellent. The only blurry one was of Walter by himself, sitting on the bench on the front lawn, cocking his head as he read some papers with great concentration, scratching behind his ear as he squinted into the sunlight. I assumed that Emma had taken it herself. It looked like one of those photographs that is precious because of its associations, rather than its quality. Gradually, examining them, I noticed that Sheila featured in quite a few of the photographs too, hanging on Walter's other arm as possessively as if she were trying to stake a claim to him. That was interesting.

"He been dead long?" Lurch said.

It sounded rude—or at least overabrupt—but it wasn't meant that way, and Emma turned to him with delight. I imagined that people didn't ask about a dead husband much, not wanting to stir sad memories, and Emma had little chance to talk about him.

"Only a couple of years," she said. "It was very sudden—we knew his heart wasn't good, but we didn't expect it. Of course we all have to go some time, but I thought Walter had many more years left to him. He was only sixty-five. I could hardly believe it. He dropped dead of a heart attack on the train coming down here. I was picking him up at the station, and I saw the ambulance waiting, but of course I had no idea who it was for . . . Still, the people in the carriage he was travelling in said it was very quick. Just grabbed his chest and keeled over. It was a good way to go, really. I know he'd have hated to have had a stroke and be a cripple. He was always so independent."

We murmured words of sympathy, but Emma seemed perfectly sanguine.

"Oh, it's something you think about a lot as you get older," she assured us. "I'm just grateful it was so fast. Of course, you don't expect it, not when you're only sixty-five—"

Blank faces. The concept of considering oneself a mere sixty-five sat oddly with the rest of the people around the table, including me.

"—but, you know, we all have to go some time."

This must be a phrase Emma repeated often to herself; it sounded as if it were her mantra.

"Like Janine," Laura said with a marked lack of tact. "But, I mean, who'd have thought that that was her time? I wonder if she ever had her horoscope done?"

"What, you think it would have predicted being killed with her own toolbox?" Tom snapped.

"Well, I didn't exactly mean that—"

"I should bloody well think not!"

Emma put her hand on his.

"Sorry," he said at once. But he didn't look at her; he was still staring furiously at Laura.

"Hey, buddy, hang on a minute," Ethan said pugnaciously. "Laura was just saying—"

"I know what she was saying, OK, *buddy*?" Tom said aggressively.

"Tom, please." Emma patted his hand. "Laura was a little thoughtless, but—"

"Well, that makes a fucking change!"

Tom pushed his chair back from the table, the wooden legs scraping on the tiled floor. Standing up, he shook his head like a horse irritated beyond bearing by a swarm of flies.

"I'm going upstairs, Emma," he said shortly. "Sorry again."

Grabbing the whisky bottle, he slammed up the wooden stairs without another word. I wished he hadn't taken the bottle with him. It boded ill.

"Oh, dear," Laura sighed.

"Talk about overreaction," Ethan said unwisely.

Emma frowned. She might have been about to say something, but I got in first.

"Tom's upset," I said coldly, "because the woman he was keen on has been murdered, and he's worried the police will think he did it. Under the circumstances I would say he's doing rather well. How would you like it if Laura'd been killed and you were the prime suspect?"

Both of them looked as if I had been unacceptably blunt. Even Emma gave a little murmur of protest.

"Though I'm sure it would make a good premise for a screenplay," I added nastily.

That was the hippies duly silenced. Mentally dusting off my hands, I turned to Emma and Lurch.

"I thought I'd go down to the Cow for a drink," I said. "Either of you want to come along?"

Actually, I was glad that Tom had stormed out. Otherwise I would have had to ask him too, and that was definitely best avoided. Tom, in his current state of sensitivity, might well have been provoked by a casual remark, and the last thing I wanted at the moment was Tom showing his temper around a group of people who were only too ready to accuse him of a crime of passion.

9

"PRETTY LITTLE PLACE, INNIT?" LURCH SAID PATRONIS-
ingly. He had all the attitude of a born-and-bred Londoner to
whom anything outside the M25 was the provinces. "Bit of a
one-horse town, though."

"Twenty-Range-Rover town," I corrected.

But all the Range Rovers were already stabled for the night.
Lesser Swinfold, at ten in the evening, was of a peace that passeth
all understanding. The shops were shut, naturally, but without any
of the graffiti-daubed metal shutters that we were so used to seeing
in London we took them for granted. It was odd, in fact, to see
shops whose owners could simply lock the door and leave at the
end of the day; they looked somehow naked, their glass frontages
strangely unprotected. Not much ram-raiding here, obviously.

And the shops, in any case, were few and far between. We
had already passed the village grocer's, which had, even in this
dim light, fully justified the description that Emma and Alan
had provided at New Year. Tins of baked beans and frying oil
were stacked precariously in the dirty window. The brands—
which were hard to make out, since most of the labels were dry
and peeling off—were ones that I had never seen before and
probably never would again. The designs were unnervingly old-
fashioned, as if they had been remaindered from the 1970s.

"It *is* pretty, though," I said almost despite myself.

The pavement was a few feet above the cobbled road, an iron railing running along the edge of the wall. The houses, all Cotswold stone, were almost as small as cottages, clustered together, net curtains at the windows, through which shone golden light and the flickering bluish glow of the television, and because the pavement was narrow we passed very close to their front windows, keeping our voices low, as if in church. In a way villages like these were the new seats of worship, these and the huge out-of-town shopping centres; tourists made pilgrimages here to see Old England in all its authentic quaintness. That was exactly what made me uncomfortable about Lesser Swinfold. I reminded myself that a very nasty murder had just taken place here and, as I had known it would, the thought cheered me up considerably. It helped to cancel out the English Heritage—approved atmosphere: shops selling oven mitts and tea towels printed with a twee pen-and-ink drawing of the village green.

The Cow was well insulated for sound; its presence announced itself, not by any noise, but the light pouring out through its windows. It looked like an ocean liner moored incongruously next to a series of tiny little skiffs.

"What do we do in the pub?" Lurch said. "Are you going to ask questions?"

I shook my head, then reconsidered.

"Well, you might be able to. It's easier when you're a bloke. Don't tell them you're an art student, eh? Or they'll think you're a poncy twat."

Lurch shrugged. "All me mates do already," he said phlegmatically, "but I know what you mean."

"But actually I think we should shut up as much as possible and just get a feel for the atmosphere, OK? And people might start talking to us. If Andy's still in there, it might be a problem though. He wasn't exactly friendly before."

"He should be home for his dinner by now."

"He might have come back afterwards."

"Yeah, that's true. OK, keep shtum. Seen and not heard. Like good little kiddies. Be a change for you, eh, Sam, keeping quiet?"

I ignored this in the spirit of maturity. We went in through the front entrance and were immediately greeted by a girl in an enveloping white apron who told us sympathetically that they were closed.

"At ten o'clock?" I said incredulously.

She bristled.

"The kitchen closes at nine," she said, affronted at the criticism.

I looked around me. I had forgotten that the Cow was a restaurant as well as a pub. There were a handful of diners at white-draped tables, and the music playing in the background was the jazz-lite much favoured by traditional restaurants as an aid to digestion. The fact that the interior was a series of small interconnecting rooms made the restaurant cosy, rather than pointing out the paucity of dinner guests.

"We were actually just after a drink," I said hopefully.

"Oh." Her brow cleared. "You want the pub. Up those stairs at the back. Sorry if I confused you, but most people go in at the back."

"We're not from round here," Lurch said gravely.

She giggled.

"No, I can tell that just by looking at you. Where're you from, then?"

"London," said Lurch with quiet pride, as, in the days of the Caesars, a freeborn Roman might have announced his origins while visiting one of the more Godforsaken outposts of the empire.

"I've been there a couple of times. Leicester Square and Piccadilly Circus—we had a real laugh. I'd love to live there."

"Lots of waitressing jobs there," Lurch said affably. "You should give it a try."

"Do you think—" she started flirtatiously, only to be interrupted by a call from a nearby table.

"Sorry," she said to us, looking wistful.

"No problem. We'll go and have that drink," I said. "You can always come and pick his brains later when you get off work."

She flashed us a quick smile and went over to the table in question.

"Lurch, you raving tart," I said *sotto voce*.

"Thought you wanted me to get friendly with the locals," he said, slightly offended.

"No, you go for it. I won't tell Di if you don't."

Di was Lurch's girlfriend, a dropout from a posh background whom he had met hunt sabbing. The jury, i.e., me, was still out on whether Di would eventually decide that she had annoyed her wealthy family sufficiently by doing a degree in political theory, going out with a working-class skilled labourer and living in a squat with a collection of animal-rights activists and would return to the fold. I rather thought she wouldn't. Di seemed to have enough principles for an entire Greenpeace local chapter, and I couldn't imagine her tamely discarding them all for a nice City job and a flat in Putney. Still, I was keeping an eye on the situation. Lurch aroused all my elder-sisterly protective instincts.

My surrogate younger brother shot me a reproving glance, intended to convey that no amount of waitresses ready to idolise him for his London origins could shake his love for Di. I wished I were still that young and pure of heart.

As if to emphasise the relative corruption of my heart, I heard my name called. Turning around I saw, just rising from a corner table, my personal nemesis in the struggle to stay as true to Hugo as Lurch was to Di. Alan was dressed formally in a dark jacket with a white shirt underneath, open at the neck as if to show off the fragile hollow between his collarbones. He looked like a young Victorian poet doomed to an early death of consumption. Having just called to me, his full red lips were still slightly parted. I had to give myself a good hard mental slap around the head to stop me from staring at them too lasciviously.

"Sam!" he said again, taking a couple of steps towards me. His obvious pleasure in seeing me would have been seductive in itself, even without his world-class beauty. Those big dark eyes, that mass of dark curls clustering around the perfect bone structure of his pale face—I managed to get a grip on my more lurid imaginings before I started ripping off his trousers in the middle of the restaurant.

"Hi, Alan! I didn't expect to see you here."

Perhaps it was fitting that my first sentence to him should be a lie, or at very best a distortion of the truth. If I hadn't expected to see him, I had certainly been hoping for it.

"Oh, yeah." He gestured deprecatingly back towards the table. "Well, I'm here with, um, my *parents*."

Alan was clearly still suffering from an adolescent embarrassment about the fact that he actually had parents. He almost blushed as he pronounced the last word.

"Alan," called his mother, "why don't you bring your friends over here and introduce us?"

Now Alan did blush. I watched the delicate colour rise in his face with a fascination that showed no signs of wearing off. Perhaps after years of knowing Alan, one would become blasé about his beauty and weary even of his tendency to flush when under stress, but that prospect was a mere hypothesis, bearing no relation to the state of my feelings right now. He stood paralysed in the middle of the restaurant. Obviously, the last thing he wanted to do was bring us over to his parents' table. I, however, had other ideas. The more people I met in this village, the better. I needed lots of background information if I was ever to dredge up another potential suspect for Janine's murder.

"Hi," I said, approaching it with my best social smile. "I'm Sam Jones. I met Alan over the New Year."

"Oh, the artist girl?" said Alan's father, rising politely to shake my hand. "I remember he talked about you a lot."

If Alan didn't actually plead "*Dad*," like a tortured schoolboy, he was not far off.

"I didn't really . . ." he said to me, writhing in mortification. "I mean, I did say I'd met you, but . . ."

"Do join us," said Alan's father convivially. "We were just about to order coffee."

With the restaurant half-empty, it was easy to locate a couple of chairs. Alan and Lurch pulled them up to the table, and we settled ourselves in.

"John Fitzwilliam," said Alan's father, shaking Lurch's hand. "And this is my wife Priscilla."

John Fitzwilliam was a tall, grey-haired businessman type in a blazer, extremely well maintained. He was a very good-looking man, if you liked them older, which I didn't. I noticed that he still had a thick head of silver hair, which boded well for Alan. The thought of Alan going bald was too awful to contemplate.

Priscilla Fitzwilliam, however, took my breath away. I would have assumed Alan had handsome parents, given his looks, but she was a knock-out, one of those rare women who manage to make me feel scruffy and clumsy. It's easy to despise the women who are overgroomed, whose hair is carefully styled and whose make-up co-ordinates perfectly with their nail polish, but she wasn't one of those. She was simply perfect. She looked as if she had spent years evolving her style and now knew it so well that all she needed was the minimal amount of care to achieve it. Her dark hair was beautifully cut, her face barely made-up. She wore a simple beige cashmere sweater and a pair of dark trousers, with a single, doubtless genuine, diamond on a slender chain at her neck. Her skin was smooth and showed hardly any signs of ageing, and the large dark eyes, which Alan had inherited, were outlined with just a trace of eyeshadow and mascara.

In short, she was the popular conception of a *Vogue* style editor, who in practice are rarely that beautiful and often look as if they are straining too hard after an effect. Priscilla Fitzwilliam probably spent most of her life in a series of expensive spas and gyms, and she was a walking advertisement for what natural beauty can become when given an unlimited budget to enhance it. She was terrifying. I became immediately conscious of my shiny forehead and my baggy layers of work clothes, which usually I wear like a badge of pride.

"I can see where Alan gets his good looks from," I said, unable to help myself.

"Oh, thank you," she said, smiling at me. Her teeth were flawless without being suspiciously uniform. It was like sitting opposite a model, but worse; she wasn't a vapid or ignorant twenty-year-old but the kind of woman those twenty-year-olds wanted to become. I remembered Sheila's catty remark about her and understood exactly why she felt hostile to Priscilla. I was more in awe of her than envious, but then I wasn't Sheila's age and confronted by the kind of looks and grooming that a skin-care manufacturer would have killed to use in an advertisement for anti-ageing cream.

"Are you staying down here?" Alan's father asked.

I nodded. "For a few days. We came down to see Tom."

"Oh yes," Priscilla said. It was clear from her intonation that the Fitzwilliams knew all about the current crisis in Lesser Swin-fold. "Poor Janine," she added. "It's just incredible."

"You knew her?" I asked.

Alan looked violently uncomfortable.

"She used to work in the local shop," she explained. "That was a while ago, wasn't it, Alan? When you were younger. She was a very pretty girl. I always thought she should have left here for London or Birmingham. Most of the young people do, you know."

"I was wondering where they all were," I admitted. "It's a bit like the *Village of the Damned*. As if all the kids were culled, or kept in bunkers till they're thirty."

Alan barked with rather nervous laughter.

"I don't know why she stayed on," Priscilla said. "Mind you, I scarcely knew her. But it must have been so dull for her here. I mean, for us, it's a country refuge, really. Peace and quiet after London. But she must have been terribly bored."

"Turned out to be more dangerous than boring, didn't it?" said her husband.

She shivered.

"I expect, when she had the little boy, it made more sense to stay," she said. "Family here and a flat. It must be awful to be a single mother in a big city."

"Did she have a job?" I asked.

"Yeah," Alan said. "She was a lab assistant at the comprehensive." He fidgeted, and said to me quickly, "How's Tom doing?"

"Not too good."

Everyone nodded understandingly.

"It must be difficult for him," said John Fitzwilliam. "This is such a small place. The temptation is always to blame the outsider, isn't it?"

"Well, what do you guys think?" I said, testing them. "Who do you blame? You've been here for years, haven't you?"

"Nearly fifteen years," said Priscilla Fitzwilliam, nodding. Then the other part of my question struck her, and she looked shocked. "Oh, I really don't know . . ."

"Oh, we couldn't possibly hazard a guess," said her husband bluffly. "We hardly know the locals well enough to speculate about that sort of thing."

Alan, beside me, shifted uncomfortably in his chair. I bet they had all been doing exactly that before our arrival.

"Well, I was friends with Jan," he said rather defiantly.

"Oh, you weren't really friends, were you?" said his father. "You'd just bump into each other in here every now and then."

"No, Dad, we were friends," Alan said resentfully. "I mean, since she had Pitt she didn't hang out in here so much, but we still talked a lot."

His father gave him a reproving stare, which Alan ignored. I wondered why John Fitzwilliam minded Alan having been friends with Janine. Was it a class thing? Had Janine not been the kind of person he had thought his son should know?

"What did you talk about?" I asked, turning to face Alan and taking the full power of his handsomeness full on, only a foot or so away. It was like sitting next to a film star.

He shrugged uncomfortably.

"She'd ask me about college, stuff like that. I told her she ought to do a degree. She was definitely brighter than a lot of the morons I was at uni with."

Just then the waitress arrived with a tray of coffee and the drinks Lurch and I had ordered.

"Didn't have to go all the way to the pub after all, did you?" she said amiably, setting Lurch's pint down in front of him.

The huge apron made her seem more like a cook than a waitress. After London, where the waiting staff were more and more New York–style model-clones dressed in tight black Lycra T-shirts, this nineteenth-century Mrs. Beeton look, which showed less of her figure than a hemp sack would have done, was positively refreshing. I realised too that its bulk meant that she couldn't move as fast or nippily as the stripped-down Londoners who had to manoeuvre between tables packed in tighter than airline seats. Here in the countryside things went at a slower pace. It should have been a welcome change, but I was such a die-hard townie that instead it made me long for a Red Bull and vodka with a line of coke as a chaser.

"The police were doing interviews all round the green today," Alan volunteered. "They wanted to see if anyone had noticed anything."

His father frowned, indicating the waitress with a glance. As she moved away, Alan said impatiently, "Oh, come on, Dad. As if anyone's talking about anything else right now."

"I'm sure that's true, John," said Priscilla Fitzwilliam, playing with the only other ring she wore besides the gold wedding band. It was another large diamond. I couldn't imagine what it must feel like to wear countless thousands of pounds on your finger. For a moment I found myself calculating up the amount of power tools I could buy with that kind of money.

"Nevertheless, that doesn't mean we shouldn't show a little discretion," John Fitzwilliam said, with the air of a man who is used to having the last word at board meetings. His family duly subsided, but I saw a glance of mutual comprehension exchanged between Alan and his mother, which I had the feeling was a long-established ritual; buckle under to Dad in public and ignore him in private. John cleared his throat and looked at his wife, clearly giving her some sort of signal.

"And what do you do, Kevin?" said Priscilla, dutifully taking her cue from her husband. "Are you an artist too?"

"Yeah, I am, actually," said Lurch, beaming with pride. "Well, I'm at art school. I used to help Sam out with her sculptures, and it sort of gave me the taste for it."

"He saw how easy it was and thought he might as well have a stab at it too," I contributed.

"Oh, I'm sure it's not that easy," she said politely. Yawn. I liked Priscilla much more when she wasn't being the perfect wife; this kind of routine conversation was boring for everyone. "If it were, everyone would be an artist, wouldn't they? It must be such an interesting life."

"Practically everyone *is* an artist nowadays," I said rather dryly.

"Like that woman who put her filthy bed on show in a gallery," John Fitzwilliam said with disgust. "Dirty knickers and God knows what. Things I won't mention in company."

Alan groaned and pushed back his chair a fraction.

"Yes, that was complete rubbish," I agreed, much to Alan's confusion.

His father was warming to his subject.

"Is that the same woman who made a bit of material with the names of everyone she'd gone to bed with written on it? And had the audacity to call it art?"

"It was a tent," I corrected. "But yeah, that's right."

This wasn't the first time that the excesses of modern art led me to agree with a died-in-the-wool conservative, but I always found the experience surreal.

John Fitzwilliam snorted.

"I'm not a philistine," he said expansively, "but one has to draw the line somewhere."

"Dad . . ." Alan moaned.

"And what do you make, Sam?" Priscilla asked, fixing her large dark eyes on me. Seeing Alan's eyes in his mother's face was oddly jolting. They had the same nose, too, high and slightly arched, like a pair of beautiful falcons. "Not tents, I hope," she added with a nice dry humour.

"No, I'm a sculptor," I explained. "I used to make mobiles. I did that one in the atrium of Mowbray Steiner, the bank," I said to John. "I don't know if you've seen it."

Fortunately, he did not seem to have heard, or remember, the publicity surrounding it a few years ago when it fell on someone's head.

"Can't say I have, I'm afraid," he apologised. "I've been through there plenty of times, of course, but I expect I wasn't looking up."

I sighed inwardly. Probably ninety-nine per cent of the people who walked under my mobile never actually bloody noticed the thing. It was very frustrating. Still, no-one would be able to ignore the sodding cockroaches. That was a considerable consolation.

"Oh John," said Priscilla, pushing back her smooth dark hair, which immediately fell into a perfect configuration behind one ear. "That's terrible."

"I'll keep my eye out for it next time," he assured me. "Very impressive, though. Congratulations."

He looked as if he wanted to shake my hand. Making a piece of sculpture for a bank he had heard of had definitely sent me up in John Fitzwilliam's estimation.

"And what are you doing now?" Priscilla asked me. "You said you used to do the mobiles. Have you changed direction?"

"Yeah," I said with satisfaction. "I'm working on a new project for Islington Arts Centre. It's a room full of giant motorised cockroaches made out of aluminium."

I watched happily as this piece of information struck everyone dumb. Priscilla, despite her highly polished social skills, had no idea what to say to this. John clearly did, but was biting it back out of politeness. I bet he'd have a few things to say about it being funded partly by Islington Council, too. And Alan was staring at me in awe. Giant cockroaches must be his idea of modern art.

I wished I had done them years before; apart from causing beautiful young men to stare at me worshipfully, it was such a useful way of making my auditors do a double-take. Mobiles simply didn't have the same shock value.

10

CHRISSIE, THE LANDLADY OF THE COW, NEVER ASKED ME
what I was currently working on, which was a shame. I think
that she would have found the idea of giant motorised cockroaches a blast. She had a very broad sense of humour. Still,
since she was more than happy to discuss the village murder with
me instead, I could only be grateful. I had thought all the locals
would be tighter than uneatable clams on the subject. Well, that
was proving to be a misapprehension. I was gradually working
out that they were more than glad to have someone to talk to
who couldn't have been directly involved.

"It's a bloody mystery, that's what it is," she said, refilling my
glass.

I was sitting at the bar while Alan and Lurch were off playing
darts. Since one of my gifts is the ability to throw straight, I
regretted not being able to join them, but Chrissie had been
so friendly when Alan had introduced me that I had sensed
it might be worthwhile to play the girls-together card with her
instead. There were very few women in the pub this evening,
and Chrissie had struck up a conversation with me almost
immediately.

"I remember you from New Year," she said convivially. "You
and that tall bloke in those big black hats. Very striking, you

looked. You're friends of that poor Tom's, aren't you? Poor sod. He's getting it in the neck right now."

Talk about an icebreaker. I had pulled up a stool immediately and played the worried friend for all I was worth.

"He's really upset," I said confidingly. "I mean, he liked Janine a lot—though there was nothing between them, you know—and it's bad enough what happened, and being questioned by the police, without thinking that everyone's looking at him funnily."

"Oh, they probably are," she said, plonking her elbows on the bar and sighing. "It's like that round here. Mind you, I can't blame 'em in a way. It's always easier to blame someone from outside, isn't it?"

This was the leitmotif of every single conversation I had with a Lesser Swinfordite.

"Still, it's so stupid," she continued. "Like I was saying to Norm only this morning, you've only got to take one look at Tom to see he wouldn't hurt a fly. He's a lovely guy, really. Not like some of our regulars."

She shot a long-suffering look at a rowdy group of men in the corner. I noticed Andy was one of them, sitting slightly back from his boisterous friends, cradling his pint as if it were a comfort blanket.

"They can get really out of control sometimes," she said. "Lucky Norm knows how to deal with them. He's thrown a couple out from time to time, shakes 'em up a bit. Don't bear any grudges, though. I think they actually like him the more for it. That's men for you. Weird bastards, en't they?"

I finished my gin and tonic and said, "Same again. And why don't you join me?"

"Well, that's very kind of you. Don't mind if I do."

She poured our drinks, saying, "And, you know, he works with little kids, doesn't he? Tom, I mean. You're never going to tell me a bloke who teaches little kids to read's going to turn round and do—that—to one of their mums. Doesn't make sense."

While dubious about Chrissie's reasoning, I was more than happy to concur with her conclusions.

"He needs a good woman to take care of him if you ask me. Always looks a bit frayed around the edges." She sighed. "Lots of women round here were all excited when they heard there was a bloke coming in to teach at the primary school. And when they clapped eyes on him—and realised he wasn't a homo"—she leaned over the bar and whacked me on the shoulder, roaring with laughter—"that would've been a big disappointment, eh? Don't reckon he'd've lasted long, either!"

I plastered a smile to my face, mentally apologising to all my gay friends. Right now Tom's crisis took priority over political correctness. I would have to atone later: offer up sacrifices to the appropriate gods, maybe lay some flowers on Oscar Wilde's grave.

"Anyway," Chrissie was saying, "there were a lot of girls after him, I can tell you. But he goes all moony over that Janine. Last person in the world he should've picked. Mind you, there's some who never learn."

"Why do you think Janine was such a bad bet?" I said.

Chrissie was a gift; all I needed to do was prompt her, and it would come spilling out. Pub landladies, like hairdressers, were used to telling the same story again and again, with equal enjoyment the hundredth time as the first. And, like hairdressers, they were superb collectors and spreaders of gossip.

"Oh, she was an odd one. Always was. Never satisfied. And my God, she could keep a secret. I mean, fancy getting pregnant so young and not telling anyone who the father was! Nearly drove her brother crazy. He went on and on at her, but she wouldn't tell. Ooh, that was a nine-day wonder, I can tell you. No-one talked about anything else. What's that, my duck?" she said to a customer. "OK, two Guinnesses coming right up."

She started pulling pints, still looking at me as she talked. Chrissie was so experienced behind a bar that she could probably have served blindfold the whole evening without spilling a drop. "What Tom needs is some nice woman who wants to settle down and darn his socks. Not that anyone darns socks any more, now you can get five pairs from Woolies for fifty pee, but you know what I mean."

She had hit the nail on the head. Tom always went for the frail blondes who looked as if they needed protection; he was a knight errant centuries too late, trying to sweep a series of ungrateful damsels on to the pommel of his white charger and ride away with them to Happy-Ever-After land. Meanwhile the damsels wanted bad-boy types who would drink too much, cheat on them, refuse to commit and generally provide them with an endless supply of material for dramatic late-night phone calls to their long-suffering friends. And Tom's eyes passed right over the sensible ones who didn't want to live in a perpetual soap opera and were looking for a nice bloke to breed with. Emma-types, a good thirty years younger.

"Did Janine have other boyfriends?" I asked Chrissie when she had finished with the Guinness drinker.

She shrugged.

"That girl was a complete mystery to me. I couldn't make her out, and I've known her since she was a little thing no higher than Pitt is now. He's a lovely little boy," she said wistfully. "I could never have kids. We tried for ages, but there was something wrong with my tubes. It was awful. I went right off sex for a while, there didn't seem to be any point, you know? But I turned forty last year and that was a bit of a help, in a way. I just said, Oh well, it's over now, no point crying about it if it can be helped, and things got better."

A waitress clearing glasses to the bar reached over it and squeezed Chrissie's hand briefly in sympathy. Chrissie smiled at her and patted hers back. This must be a familiar story to everyone. I sensed that Chrissie used the bar as her personal broadcasting station.

"Funny," she mused. "I've often thought I must be the only person that actually didn't mind forty, because of that. Norm hated it."

She glanced over at her husband fondly. He was clearing glasses, wandering around the pub, a jocular word for everyone. Mine Jovial Host of the Red Cow.

"Still, he was OK about the kids. He didn't really want them. The Cow's his baby. That's what he said to me one day when I was crying my eyes out. Don't you worry, love, I don't need kids, I got you next to me and the Cow's my baby."

"Did it help much?" I said sceptically.

She burst out laughing.

"Not really! I mean, I always knew Norm wasn't as bothered about kids as I was. Still, we're very happy, and that's the main thing."

Further down the bar a couple of drinkers clinked their glasses together in agreement. Chrissie raised hers to them.

"To happiness," she said cheerfully.

It really was like a public broadcast. I wondered how Norm felt about having his marital life, or lack of, discussed with the entire village on a nightly basis. Still, Chrissie radiated good sense and competence. Norm was very lucky to have her. Though, as I had noticed before, she had no claims to prettiness—her features were too solid and her jawline too square—there was such warmth in her eyes and smile that after a while you forgot that she was homely. The blonde curls helped, too, counteracting her sturdiness. Though she had a stocky figure, her bosom was magnificent, which I bet Norm appreciated. He looked like a tit man to me.

"God," she said, lining up full pint glasses on the bar for Norm to take over to the table of rowdies, "here I go chattering away about myself. I didn't mean to go on about my troubles. Not that they're troubles, really, just life, you know? Things that happen. What was I talking about?"

"Janine," I said, glad that I hadn't had to draw her back to the subject myself. "And Pitt."

"Oh yes, that's right. Norm? Can you take these over to the boys? They wanted another round. And clear that table. They must have half the glasses in the pub on there! Anyway, every time I look at Pitt I think how lucky she was. Such a pretty little boy. Poor Tamsin'll be taking him on now, I imagine. As if she doesn't have enough to cope with as it is."

"The two kids?"

"And her job. Mind you, it's quieter now, but in the summer she's working all the hours God sends. She does cleaning for summer rentals and bed-and-breakfasts. Busy morning to night. And Andy always wanting the house spick and span and his dinner ready on the table when he actually manages to come home of an evening."

She looked contemptuously over at Andy.

"You don't like him much?"

"He's a bit of a dinosaur, love. You know what I'm talking about. One of those old-fashioned blokes who think a woman's place is in the home." She snorted, wringing out the bar cloth as if it was Andy's neck. "They've got a big mortgage on that house, and he should know better than anyone they can't manage on the one income—he works in a bank, for Christ's sake! Those days are over now. Everyone's got to work, men and women

alike. But he still makes a fuss when Tamsin's rushing around trying to earn some money. I tell you. Ridiculous. And besides,
even if they didn't need it, everyone should have a bit of money
of their own. It's humiliating having to go cap in hand to your
husband. Ooh, I'd hate it."

"Didn't Andy think Janine should stay at home with Pitt,
then?" I prompted.

"Oh, Janine could always twist Andy round her little finger,"
Chrissie said dismissively. "Well, up to a point," she added more
thoughtfully. "He could be really odd with her. He was much too
possessive. Still is, really. Their mum and dad died when she was
small, you see, and he was left with bringing her up. But she
could still go out to work, or come out for a drink with friends,
and he wouldn't give her a hard time about it. Not like poor
Tamsin. If she wants to come out for a drink instead of him,
you can bet there's a nuclear meltdown in that household." She
grimaced. "Me and Norm, we've always worked side by side,
none of this chauvinist nonsense, I'm glad to say."

It seemed like a good opportunity for a toast. I had noticed
Chrissie's fondness for them.

"Let's drink to that!" I said, clinking my glass with hers.

We chugged the rest of our drinks.

"Another G and T?" Chrissie suggested immediately. "This
time it's on me."

"I won't say no."

"I like a woman that can hold her drink," Chrissie observed
with approval.

"Me too."

We clinked glasses yet again. It was a positive love-fest.

"Tell me something," she said confidentially. "I don't want
to be nosy, but is Tom OK? We haven't seen him in here since,
you know, since poor Jan was killed. And he used to be in here
every night. I've been a bit worried, frankly. Thought he might

be staying away because he got the idea that we've all turned against him."

I grimaced.

"There is a bit of that," I admitted. "And, you know, the last time he was in here, he was with Janine. It's probably got bad memories for him."

I really wanted to ask Chrissie about her impression of Tom and Janine's fight, without being too blatant about it. It sounded as if she was here every night; she must have seen it. I hoped this was enough prompting.

"Ooooh, yeah," she said immediately. "Talk about a lovers' tiff. Well, it was a bit more than that, to be honest. Tom was furious with her. They were trying to keep their voices low, of course, but everyone could tell that. He got her all worked up, too. She slammed out of here in a real strop. We didn't think anything of it—I mean, it wouldn't be the first row like that we've had in here, and it won't be the last, either. I thought Tom was going to go after her, but he just sat there and finished his drink with a face like thunder. We all left him alone. It's much better that way, give him a bit of time to cool down. I thought he'd be going after her—you know, kiss and make up—when he'd had a chance to catch his breath."

Clearly, no-one had heard the substance of the conversation, then. That was at least something to be thankful for.

"Well, he didn't," I said. "He went for a long walk instead."

I left out the Dante in a dark wood part. I didn't think it would help matters much.

Chrissie pulled a face.

"Out walking, in this cold?" she said incredulously. "God, he must have had it bad. That's a shame, though. No alibi."

"Exactly."

I tried to read on Chrissie's face what she thought of Tom as a suspect, but she forestalled me.

"It's a nasty situation," she admitted, "but I know one thing. Tom's a sweet, caring bloke. You see him with the little kiddies, he's really"—she reached for a word—"tender with them. No-one's going to get me to think he could have killed Janine."

For one horrible moment, I wished I could be as sure as Chrissie.

"You girls are getting thick as thieves," Norman observed, coming back to the bar with two enormous fistfuls of glasses. "Hi, I'm Norm," he said to me. "You must be that friend of Tom's from London."

"She was here New Year, Norm," Chrissie said. "With her boyfriend. Remember we were wondering who those two in the hats were?"

"Oh, right. Real London types, we said. All that black."

It could have been a sarcastic comment, but he sounded friendly enough.

"I'm Sam," I said, shaking his outstretched hand. "Sam Jones."

"Nice to meet you, Sam. What do you think of our little village, then? Bit of a change after London, I bet."

"Pubs are a hell of a lot friendlier down here," I said ingratiatingly.

He roared with laughter. "Only the Cow, my duck. You want to try the George. Put you off country pubs for life."

"I thought Alan said there were three pubs."

Chrissie and Norm rolled their eyes.

"Yeah, there's the Arrow, too," Norm said. "Three old geriatrics and a bloke with Alzheimer's behind the bar. He owns the freehold, see. That's how he can keep it going. Still, won't be long now before it's just us and the George."

"Run the opposition out of town?" I suggested.

Norm laughed again. "Wait for them to die off," he said. "Easier that way."

Norm was a big man, solid rather than fat, with the muscular, village-blacksmith build that can pile on weight over the years and still take all comers in a bar brawl. His back was as wide and brawny as a side of beef. Like his wife, though not actually good-looking. Norm had charisma to spare. With his fleshy features and easy manner, I recognised his type: he was the kind of man who would walk into a pub or a club and immediately start chatting up the prettiest girls, while guys who were technically more handsome and better built would watch his prowess enviously from the sidelines.

"So you're down here to give Tom some moral support?" he said to me.

"More or less."

"Staying with Emma?"

"How did you know?" The village grapevine was very impressive.

"Oh, it wasn't even a guess. Emma's like that. Open house. Very nice of her, but there's some that take advantage."

"Norm!" Chrissie snapped.

"Oh, I didn't mean you, my duck!" he said quickly. "You've come to see your friend, what could be more natural? No, it's those Yanks I'm thinking of. Got nothing against Yanks in general," he clarified, realising that he had pronounced the word with a good deal of contempt. "Far from it. Some of our best customers come the summer. Tip like there was no tomorrow, bless 'em."

Chrissie humphed.

"Those two're cut from a different cloth," she said. "Never seen 'em put their hands in their pocket for anyone. The nerve of them. And always with those smiles on their faces."

"Watch it, love, you'll make Sam think you're a grumpy cow," Norm said agreeably. "Objecting to our customers looking cheerful."

"Oh, I bet Sam knows what I mean. Smiling in that nothing-bothers-me way all the time, those two. I dare say nothing does bother them. Why should it? Emma's giving them a free ride, isn't she? That Ethan mowed the lawn once, and you should've heard him go on about it. So what?"

"It was Laura kept talking about it," Norm corrected. "'Ethan mowed the lawn, isn't that nice of him?'" he said in a passable imitation of Laura's Bostonian drawl. "God, you'd think he'd rebuilt the house or something. We should lay bets on how long they'll last there."

"They'll stay till she throws them out," Chrissie said dryly. "They know when they're on to a cushy number, people like that."

"Do you remember that night when Tom was telling us about her eating all those cheese rinds?" Norm said, laughing. "Emma was going to throw them out and Laura went, 'No, no,' and insisted on eating them all. Hard greasy cheese rinds, if you can believe that. Pig food, that is!"

I told them about Laura hoarding the stale bread. It went down wonderfully. Chrissie was nearly crying with laughter.

"Oh dear," she said, wiping her eyes in reflex. "I needed a good laugh."

"Mmn," Norman said. "I reckon we all do. It's a bad business, this. And bound to get worse."

There was nothing we could say to this. A mutual, gloomy silence was observed, like a mini-period of mourning, which Chrissie finally broke by telling Norm firmly to stop being morbid and go and check there was enough loo roll in the Gents.

"It *is* a bad business, though," she said to me as he went. "Same again?"

"Please. And d'you want one?"

"Oh no, my duck, I'm at my limit." She looked at the gin bottle. "Well, maybe just a little one. Every time I think of that poor girl, lying on her kitchen floor all night, bleeding to death—and Tamsin walking in and finding her like that—ooh, it turns my stomach. It's just a mercy little Pitt didn't see his mum dead. That's the only consolation. Not that the bloke who did it gave a toss," she added angrily. "For all he knew that little boy could have stumbled in on her with that horrible toolbox on her face and been scarred for life by the sight."

"How do you *know* all this?" I said incredulously.

"You've never lived in a village, have you?" she said pityingly.

"I've practically never *been* in a village," I said, trying not to make this sound too self-congratulatory.

"I told you, you want to know anything, you ask the pub landlady," she said. "Norm's sister's married to a local copper at Finchingham. That's where the police station is. But I daresay we'd know anyway."

"Why do you keep saying 'he' when you talk about the killer?" I said, wondering if the investigation had demonstrated somehow that Janine's murderer must have been a man.

"Well, it's obvious, isn't it?" Chrissie said matter-of-factly, filling my glass with tonic. She chucked the empty bottle into the dustbin with a deft flick of her wrist. "I mean, who but a man could've done something like that?"

It wasn't the time to recount my stories of female murderers I had known. The table in the corner had become increasingly noisy over the last few minutes, and now it reached a pitch at which even Chrissie looked over, frowning. Someone was shouting. I swivelled on my stool to see what was going on. Andy was on his feet, swaying like a cut tree that needed just one more gust of wind to send it toppling.

"Bastard!" he slurred. "Bastard!" He took a swing across the table at one of his drinking companions. Everyone grabbed their glasses, but one of them wasn't quick enough; his pint went flying into someone else's lap.

"For fuck's sake!" The man with a lapful of beer jumped up, still holding his own pint high where he had pulled it out of Andy's reach. He was dabbing uselessly at his crotch with the other hand.

"Hey! Jim's wet himself!" yelled one of the other men, cueing uproarious laughter.

"Fuck off!" Jim said furiously. "I'm bloody soaked!"

"At least you've still got your pint, mate!" said the man whose drink had been spilled, laughing as hard as the rest of them.

Andy seemed completely unaware of Jim's mishap. His eyes were as heavily glazed as amateur pottery, and his face was pasty. I wondered if he was about to vomit.

"You're all bastards!" he said, louder now, but his words still as blurred as if his mouth was full of mashed potato.

"Look, Andy, it was just a careless word, mate. No hard feelings. Sit down, why don't you?" said the man who had lost his pint. "Finish your beer, eh?"

This struck me as the worst possible advice, but no-one was asking my opinion. In any case, it was irrelevant. Andy wasn't listening to anything except the voice inside his own head. His shirt was open and plastered to his pink sweaty chest, his balding head shining with beer sweat.

"I'll fucking . . . I'll fucking have you all . . ." he muttered.

It was then that Spilled-Pint Man made his mistake. Pushing back his stool, he stood up and took hold of Andy's arm.

"Why don't we go outside and get some fresh air, eh?" he said.

Perhaps the idea that Andy might be due for a Technicolor yawn all over the carpet had occurred to him by now. But Andy couldn't hear the words, or the good intention behind them. All he saw was a challenge, a hand on his arm. He shook Spilled-Pint Man off so vigorously that he stumbled back on to Jim. The pint Jim was still holding wobbled dangerously, sending droplets of beer on to Spilled-Pint Man's back.

"Fuck!" he said, brushing his shoulders as if trying to get rid of dandruff. He pointed threateningly at Andy.

"You'd better watch it, mate," he said, aggressive now. "You're among friends here, but I'm telling you—"

The pointing finger must have seemed like deliberate provocation. With a bellow of anger, Andy lowered his head and charged. I wouldn't have thought he had it in him. The crown of his head took Spilled-Pint Man smack in the chest and sent him flying. He crashed into Jim, who went down too, heavily. The pint duly followed. Beer and glass crashed on to the carpet. With the dexterity of much experience, I pulled my drink from the bar, slid off my stool and removed myself to a safer distance.

"You fucking cunt!" yelled Spilled-Pint Man, clambering to his feet.

So much for conciliatory tactics. A split second later he and Andy were locked in each other's arms, feet planted on the carpet, heaving each other back and forth with grunts and groans of effort. Andy caught his foot on something and tripped back, pitching Spilled-Pint Man on top of him.

"Go on, Ted!" yelled Jim, still recumbent on the floor, clutching his hand, from which blood was pouring. He must have cut it on the glass.

Ted smashed Andy's head back into the wall. From the crunch with which it landed, it should have been definitive. But Andy was in such a violent rage that the adrenaline was pouring through his veins, making him as impervious to blows as Superman. He came back off the wall with an animal howl, both his hands grabbing around Ted's neck, the thumbs pressing into his Adam's apple as if he was trying to pop it right through Ted's throat and out the other side. Andy's eyes were glazed with fury, so bloodshot that I wondered if he knew who he was attacking, if he could even see Ted through the red mist clouding his irises. He had almost lifted Ted clear off the ground. I was impressed, in a perverse kind of way. Not bad for a bank manager. My money was definitely on Andy. I wondered if any of his friends would take my bet.

Just then, however, the referree intervened. Striding masterfully through the throng of spectators, who fell aside to let him pass as if they had been a group of mime artists representing the Red Sea, Norm arrived on the scene. By now I had climbed on to a barstool, and I had a bird's-eye view of the whole proceedings. Norm took one look at Andy—who now had his fingers firmly wrapped around Ted's neck and was shaking him like a terrier with a rat—and grabbed a couple of pint glasses from the frozen hands of the onlookers. He threw first half a pint of beer, then a hefty spray of Guinness, into Andy's convulsed face. Having gained the advantage of surprise, Norm then slammed one sledgehammer fist down on Andy's wrists, missing Ted's nose by a millimetre. Andy's grip was broken. Ted, who by now was bright red and looked about to suffer a congestion, fell back, gulping for breath and clutching his bruised throat. Andy stood dazedly, looking down at his hands, which must have been hurting him badly. Beer ran down his head, dripping on to his collar. He seemed oblivious to it. Raising his face finally, he managed to draw enough of a focus on Norm to recognise him.

"Oi!" Norm said loudly. "Enough's enough!"

"Norm, you bastard . . ." Andy slurred, taking a last, blurry swing at Norm. The boy was game, I had to give him that. He missed by a mile, though. By now he must be seeing at least four Norms, spinning around each other in blurred circles, and he had made the classic mistake of punching at one of the multiple figures rather than aiming for the voice.

Norm shrugged.

"Ah, fuck it," he said, and let fly with his left. I had no idea what precise kind of punch a haymaker was, but this, in broad terms, was how I had always imagined it. It took Andy squarely on the point of the jaw. His ass, as the Americans say, was grass. He swivelled around ninety degrees and hung on tiptoes in a dizzy poise for a moment, like a ballerina who has just done thirty pirouettes across the stage but forgotten to keep whipping her head round. Remembering Audrey Hepburn in *Breakfast at Tiffany's*, I put my hands to my mouth and hollered, "Tim—berrrrr!"

Andy hit the ground face forward. No-one even winced. (Though one of his drinking companions thoughtfully removed a stool from his landing path.) Norm blew on his fist.

"Bloody bank managers," he said. "Eh, boys? Nothing but trouble from first to last."

11

JIM'S HAND, FORTUNATELY, TURNED OUT NOT TO BE BADLY cut. Chrissie gave him a brandy and bandaged him up, producing a much-battered first-aid box from under the bar. Jim, a big stocky man with a shock of red hair, had protested that he didn't need medical attention; Chrissie had said firmly that the brandy was only on the house if he agreed to let her look at his hand. Having gauze wrapped around his palm by one woman while another looked on was proving too much for his masculinity, however. He was wriggling on his barstool like an enormous, recalcitrant tadpole.

"So what was the fight about?" I asked curiously.

Jim bubbled air through his pursed lips. It was intended to sound dismissive, but it reminded me instead of an outboard motor trying to start up. Maybe I had had enough gin for the night.

"Andy," he said in weary tones. "He's always had a bit of a temper, and he's on a hair trigger these days. Ow."

"Got to make it tight or there's no point," Chrissie said unapologetically. "So what set him off this time?"

I was glad that Chrissie had asked: Jim would be much more likely to tell her than me.

"Just a bit of joshing," Jim said, doing the tadpole impression again. This time, however, it was out of embarrassment, which was quickly explained when he added, "We might've gone a bit far, but it was all in fun. I mean, we all take the piss out of each other, don't we?"

"Don't tell me you started on Janine," Chrissie said, giving him a long, hard stare. "Not after what's happened. Tell me you didn't start on Janine."

"It wasn't starting on her," Jim pleaded. "It was just—"

"You didn't go on about Pitt's dad, did you?" Chrissie sounded almost angry. "You know that always drives Andy up the wall. Can't say's I blame him, either."

"No . . . well . . . not exactly . . ." Jim hung his head. "It all got a bit out of hand, you know?"

"You'd better tell me, Jim," Chrissie said grimly. "Norm's planning to bar the poor bastard, and that don't seem fair if you lot were taking the mickey. Not after . . . what's happened."

I had noticed before, in my encounters with sudden death, how reluctant the survivors were to use words like "killed," or "murdered," or even "smashed on the head with her own tool-box and left for dead."

Jim wouldn't meet her eyes. She was still holding his hand, and it lay on the bar between them like a hostage. His fingers curled up briefly, touching the gauze bandaging, as if trying to pull away. But he must have known that was impossible. Chrissie was determined to have the full story.

"It started off all right," he said, his voice muffled. "We were all saying how sorry we were, you know. And he said he was just waiting for the cops to arrest that teacher bloke, the one who was always hanging round her. But Ted said he didn't reckon it was the teacher."

I cheered up at this.

"He said he thought that'd be too obvious," Jim went on, deflating my bubble of optimism almost immediately. "He said,

'You know, Andy, your Janine was a real woman of mystery, and I reckon it'll turn out to be a bloody mystery what happened to her.'"

"Oh God," Chrissie sighed. "That'd be more than enough. He'll've taken 'woman of mystery' to mean 'village slut.' Which she wasn't," she said for my benefit. "Not like some I could mention. When she got up the duff with Pitt, all the blokes round here thought she was fair game. Single mum, bit of a goer, lonely for a bit of male company. Bet you all tried, didn't you?" she said to Jim.

He looked horrified. His mumbled denials were so vigorous that both Chrissie and I took them for an involuntary assent.

"Andy'd've killed you if he'd known," she said. "But I bet she wasn't having any, was she?"

This put Jim in a quandary.

"I wouldn't know," he said finally, without much of a ring of truth behind it.

"Hmn."

"I don't know what she was after," Jim said, choosing his words carefully. "But it wasn't that. I don't think it was anything here. Don't know what she was doing in Swinford, really. She was a bright girl, she could have got a job somewhere, made a bit of a life for herself."

"Ah, God, we'll never know now, will we?" Chrissie reached for an elastic bandage. "Let's talk about something else. Poor girl, she was hardly into her twenties. And that poor little mite without a mum or a dad now, or one he knows, anyway. It doesn't bear thinking about."

Clearly, we had to change the conversation, but I didn't want it to drift away completely from the events surrounding Janine's murder.

"I didn't see Andy as the type to start a fight," I reflected. "Shows how good I am at sussing people out."

"You should see him in the rugby scrum," Jim informed me. "Good man to have on your side, I can tell you."

"How many times is it now, Jim?" Chrissie said, nodding to something behind her. I followed her gesture. It was a large trophy, bulbous and ugly but shining like the Star of Bethlehem.

"Third," he said proudly.

"Lesser Swinfold Irregulars," Chrissie explained to me. "That's our rugby team. They're the terror of the district."

"Norm play for them too?" I asked.

"You bet," Jim said. "He's our prop forward."

"John Fitzwilliam's the coach," Chrissie said to me. "He used to play for Oxford, didn't he, Jim?"

"Yeah, one of them posh unis. Public school boys. You can take the piss as much as you want out of their accents, but ever since Mr. Fitzwilliam started coaching us we've been demons," Jim boasted. "He got us organised, you know? Took a lot of ribbing from the boys at first, but he knocked us into shape, I can tell you."

"Does Alan play?" I asked, glancing over to where he stood in the group of men around Andy's recumbent body.

Jim snorted. "Nah, not him. Too skinny. And his ma wouldn't like it much. Ruin his pretty face, wouldn't he?"

He said this without malice, however, and I realised why when he added, "He's a cricketer. We don't have a village team exactly, but the vicar gets a match together sometimes. Got a good eye, that boy, and he's a fast runner. You should see him when he gets going."

"I'd love to," I said with enthusiasm. "When exactly does the cricket season start?"

Chrissie wrapped an elastic bandage around Jim's palm and taped it up neatly.

"There you go," she said. "Try not to get it wet for a couple of days, eh?"

"Word of honour," Jim beamed, getting to his feet. He regarded his bandaged hand with a newly affectionate gaze. "I'm not much of a one for soaking in the bath anyway."

I was close enough to him to know that this was no more than the truth.

"Sam!" Alan said, making his way through the crowd of onlookers, Lurch at his side. "Did you see the fight?"

I nodded. "Short and decisive, but not without its moments of tension. All upper-body work though. A few nice Bruce Lee kicks would have added extra interest."

"And broken a lot more," Chrissie said dryly.

"Yes, there is that," I agreed. "I bet you and Norm'll be the first people to picket any tae kwon do school that tries to start up a branch in Lesser Swinfold."

Alan, as always, thought everything I said was the height of wit. Despite myself, I was beginning to feel more sympathetic to those wrinkled old men one saw in expensive restaurants with fresh-faced babes, appendages in every sense, clinging to their arms and hanging on their every word. Of course, the case with Alan and me was quite different. He was genuinely charmed by my intellect, and I also flattered myself that I was, if not a fresh-faced babe, not yet that far down the road which led inexorably to Wrinkled Old Woman. Still, the sensation of being looked up to was intoxicating. By his appreciation of my bons mots, Alan even egged me on to further heights of achievement. What a change from Hugo, who was so competitive he immediately tried to top them.

Thinking about Hugo, however, made my head swim as if I had drunk too much. Which, of course, I hadn't. I grabbed the thought of him with both hands and shoved it as far back inside my head as I could manage.

"I didn't have Andy pegged for a bruiser," Lurch said, echoing my earlier observation.

"Apparently, he's a vicious rugby player," I explained.

"They're psychopaths," Alan said with disdain. "Tearing around in a bog of mud, smashing each other's faces into each other's boots. It's like some ancient British ritual. Like tying people to logs and throwing them into the river to watch them drown. Or burning them in cages."

"Weren't those fertility rituals?" I asked, noticing Chrissie's little smile. Clearly, the village was a lot more tolerant of Alan's posturing than one would expect. Or Chrissie, too, was not immune to hollow-chested male beauty of the Consumptive Hero school.

"Hard to imagine rugby players being that fertile, what with all that kicking each other in the balls," Lurch volunteered. "Can't be good for the family jewels, can it? Mind you, so's wearing tight jeans. No wonder the Italians have the lowest birth rate in the world."

I stared at him in disbelief.

"The things you pick up, Lurch," I said. "You've got the mind of a magpie."

"It's called making conversation, Sam," he said with hauteur. "Drop in a few facts, contribute to the debate."

Sometimes I thought I didn't know Lurch at all.

The comment on fertility, however, had had a depressive effect on Chrissie. I had caught her eye for a moment, instinctively, but she had looked away at once and started rearranging some bottles, her back to the bar, perhaps giving herself time to reset her features into the traditional landlady's smile of bonhomie. Even despite that, I had been thinking that it was time to hit the sack. Emma had given us a key to the door, but I didn't want to stagger back too late, drunk and shaky on our feet—well, my feet. Lurch could put away enough beer to fill an empty barrel and then stay as steady as the full keg.

"We should be getting back," I announced.

Lurch looked disappointed. I reminded him about the Emma situation, however, and he understood immediately. We didn't want to prejudice our welcome by waking up the household at three in the morning on our first night there.

"I'll walk you back," Alan offered. "I go that way myself."

Chrissie shot him an incredulous glance, which fortunately he didn't catch; he was already pulling on his overcoat.

"Come back any time," she said to me. "We've usually got a lock-in, most nights anyway. Alan can show you the back door if you come along late. You just ring the bell. You won't mind showing Sam, will you, Alan?"

This time there was no mistaking her implication. She was teasing Alan.

Alan, halfway through the act of winding a long woollen scarf around his neck, blushed furiously. Chrissie winked at me; clearly, she considered Alan too youthful, not to mention callow, to be capable of interesting me. There, for all her worldly wisdom, she was making a big mistake. I was at that very moment busy imagining a wide range of things I could do to Alan that would be pretty much guaranteed to call up that blush.

* * *

"She was a good friend of mine, Jan. A really good friend. We spent a lot of time just hanging out."

Alan's face, in the flickering light of the candle, was nothing but bone structure: the hollows under his cheekbones, the deep sockets of his eyes, so darkly shadowed he looked like a hero from a silent film. He reached for the bottle of wine and took a long swig. I lost myself in watching him; the scarf, student-style, was wrapped several times around his neck, so I couldn't see his white throat, but as he set the bottle down again and wiped the droplets of red wine from his mouth his full, beautifully shaped lips were so erotic I had to clench my hands to stop myself reaching over the table and licking them clean.

I cleared my throat and dragged my thoughts back to the subject under discussion. It was as hard as walking through a pool filled with treacle in thigh-high waders. Not that I had ever done that myself; but there was bound to be a site on the Web catering for people who did.

"She was so quiet that evening," I said at random.

"Yeah, that was a bit odd," Alan agreed. "I mean, she was always more forthcoming when there were just the two of us, you know? She tended to be quieter in company. But still, she hardly said a word to anyone, at least when I was there. I thought she might have been upset about something. I meant to ask her, but somehow I never did. I must have been distracted."

He looked straight at me for a moment to make his meaning clear; then, losing courage, he ducked his head and started fiddling with the end of his scarf.

I filed the observation about Janine away for future consideration, wondering if there had been something—or someone—upsetting her that night.

"So what did you guys talk about?" I said, reaching for the bottle. I was wearing woollen gloves, and the glass, moist with wine, was slippery in my hands. I had to use both to make sure I didn't drop it.

"Everything, really," Alan said. "Life, you know. What we wanted to do. How claustrophobic Swinfold is."

He shot a glance, which I assumed was contemptuous, down the slope of Emma's lawn in the direction of the village green. Alan and I were sitting at a stone table a little way from the house, having decided that we weren't quite ready to call it a night, but thinking it more tactful to keep drinking outside rather than make too much noise in the kitchen. Lurch, mercifully, had decided to go to bed. We had protested briefly and then shot outside with a bottle of Emma's wine before he could change his mind. Actually, I had suggested the lawn as a rendezvous because somehow it had seemed much easier to sit opposite Alan in the sheltering dark than in the comparatively bright light of the kitchen. Out here we were lost in our own little circle of night, the fat white candle planted in a saucer on the table flickering medievally between us. The fact that it was so cold we were both shivering constantly was something we had mutually, silently, agreed not to mention, for fear of breaking the spell.

Trying not to let my teeth chatter too obviously, I wedged my hat down still further on my head.

"She used to ask me loads of questions about London," Alan said.

"Had she never been?"

"No, I think she had. But not for long. Just a couple of days here and there. She was really secretive, actually. I'd only realise, after we'd had a long conversation, that she never talked much about actual facts, if you know what I mean. It was all very abstract."

"So what did she want to do?" I said curiously. Maybe Alan could provide some clues to the Janine enigma.

"She really wanted to go to college and do a chemistry degree," Alan said unexpectedly, until I remembered that Janine had been a lab assistant. "That's what she'd always planned. Then she got pregnant when she was only eighteen. I didn't see that much of her then because I was just off at college. But she said she'd wanted to go on to college, and Andy put his foot down, talked her out of it. She really regretted it. She had a place all ready."

"Why didn't he want her to go?"

"Oh." Alan shrugged. "It's so old-fashioned here. I think he thought a mother should spend all the time with her kid, you know, not go off to college and leave him in a crèche. And Andy wouldn't've wanted her to go anyway. He liked having his baby sister under his wing."

"Doesn't sound like he was very successful," I observed.

"No. He really got up her nose. She said it wasn't good for Tamsin, either."

"How come?"

"Oh, Andy was always dropping in at Janine's to see how she was doing. She said she thought he ought to ask Tamsin how *she* was doing more, because it'd be better for the marriage. And she—Janine, that is—was fine, except for Andy getting on her nerves."

"You seem to have known Janine very well," I observed.

"Yeah, she was OK," he said, leaning back in his chair. It tilted dangerously on the grassy slope, and he scrabbled to settle it straight. "We knew each other when we were small, you know? Used to play together in the summer. Then we didn't come here so much—when I was older my mum got really keen on holidaying abroad—but when we started coming back again Jan was working in the local shop on Saturdays—" He coughed and cleared his throat, sounding almost embarrassed. "So anyway, we caught up straight away. We must have been about sixteen then. When I heard she was pregnant, I couldn't believe it. I mean, she seemed too intelligent to do something like that."

"Did she never think about having an abortion?" I said rather bluntly.

It embarrassed Alan. He started fiddling with his scarf again.

"I did sort of ask her that once. I mean, not so directly. She said everyone had been on at her to do it, but she wouldn't. She really loved the father, and she wanted his baby."

"Who was it?" I said, unable to resist the question. "Did she ever tell you?"

"No way! She never told anyone!"

The candle spat and guttered, the wind tilting the wick sideways to spatter wax over the table. My back was aching with cold; I really would have to go in soon.

"Why was it such a big secret?" I asked, not so much because I lacked theories of my own, as to hear what Alan would say.

"Oh, he was married," Alan informed me, trying to sound worldly-wise and cynical. He didn't succeed, but the attempt was utterly charming. "Must've been. She hinted at that a couple of times."

I nodded.

"He was older, you know," he added, almost challengingly, as if annoyed by my lack of response.

"Did she tell you that?"

He shook his head.

"Didn't have to. Janine only ever went for older guys. She was really pretty—well, you know that, you met her. Practically all the boys our age round here asked her out, but she'd never even look at them. Oh, not me," he added hurriedly. The candlelight made it impossible to see the flush I knew would be there. "She wasn't my type. I don't like girls my own age either. I prefer, you know, *women*."

Was I a woman? I supposed so. But I wasn't a hundred per cent sure I liked it.

Disconcerted by my lack of response to this ploy, Alan continued, "She had pictures of Clint Eastwood and Paul Newman stuck up everywhere."

"Good taste."

"Yeah, but them as they are now, you know? Not when they were younger. Well, OK, maybe not as they are now, but definitely . . ."

"Mature."

"Yeah. Mature. Well, middle-aged."

He stared at me significantly. I was very cold now, and I had just enough maturity to decide that this was probably a good point to terminate the conversation, before we started discussing Alan's sexual tastes in more detail. Besides, I was also nervous that he was about to announce that he, too, preferred not only women but mature ones to boot. I didn't relish the idea of being described in those terms by a mere stripling.

I stood up.

"I'm freezing," I announced. "I've got to go inside."

"OK," he said eagerly, jumping to his feet. "I'll bring the bottle."

"No," I said with reluctance. "I meant I really should go to bed."

"Oh." His voice went flat. "OK. Yeah, it must be late."

I glanced at my watch.

"It's past two."

So much, I thought, for not staggering in late on my first night at Emma's.

"Right. Well . . ." He tailed off.

"I'll take this lot in," I said, gesturing at the debris on the table.

"Oh, I could give you a hand—"

"No, it's fine. Really."

Neither of us had moved. Nervously, Alan wound his scarf yet again around his neck. By now it was as thick as a neck brace. I was surprised he could move his head at all.

"Well, good night, then," he said hesitantly.

"Good night."

We were still rooted to our respective places. Alan came around the table towards me; the little gravel path that led down to the gate was at my back. But as he drew level with me he stopped, looking down at me with great seriousness, and bent over. I was expecting at most a kiss on the cheek, and was taken aback to realise that he had had the nerve to aim for my mouth.

His lips were cold as a corpse's on a mortuary slab. Then they parted, and I felt his breath, warm and moist and scented with red wine. I put my hand behind his head—just to get my balance, I told myself, the slope was quite steep here—and the next thing I knew he was kissing me passionately, his icy-cold hands on my cheeks, awkward and yet delicate, as if he was frightened of bruising me. He wasn't very good at kissing; he went at it almost desperately, as if, sure that I would inevitably pull away, he was trying to cram in all he could before then. I twined my arms around his neck and kissed him back, slowly at first, trying to show him how to take his time, to play with it, teasing him with the tip of my tongue till he moaned in frustration, then kissing him so deeply his hands left my face and wrapped around my waist, grinding me to him. His skin was as smooth as a boy's, hardly a trace of beard on his jaw. I unwrapped his scarf, one turn after another, refusing to be rushed, and finally bared his neck to the cold night air. Nuzzling my face into it, I breathed in the scent of soap and water. On a man any older than him it would have been incongruous; on Alan it had a schoolboy touch I found very erotic. I licked his throat and then breathed warm air where my tongue had traced.

He was shaking, and I flattered myself that it wasn't the cold. I had forgotten what being twenty-two was like, and being a boy of that age was probably much worse; though still a seething mass of undisciplined hormones, they were expected to be the seducers, and how they were supposed to manage that without any experience was a particularly nasty Catch-22. I could feel Alan in my arms, trembling, holding me clumsily, torn between his natural shyness and a wish to appear knowing, to sweep me off my feet without much idea beyond the most basic of what he'd do with me if he got me. It was such a world away from Hugo. Not just the boniness of Alan's body, the width and lushness of his mouth, but his every movement, the tentativeness and—simultaneously—the urgency with which he was kissing me. Hugo hated to be rushed. It was one of the many things that made him so good in bed.

My thoughts were making me too uncomfortable. I pushed Alan, just a little, and immediately he let go of me and jumped back, looking horrified and mumbling apologies. I had to reassure him over and over again before he stopped making excuses.

"It's OK, really," I repeated patiently, seeing that my words were finally getting through. I reached up and kissed him briefly on the lips, one hand flat against his right pectoral, so he couldn't embrace me again. "It's just—I should really go to bed now."

"Yes. Right. Of course. I'm sorry, I just—"

"Alan."

"Yes?"

"Shut up. Stop apologising. It's fine."

"Right, OK. Sorry. I mean—yeah, fine. OK."

Finally, he located the path and made his way down it, shoes crunching on the gravel. At the garden gate he looked back and gave me a little wave before going through it. I waved back, feeling ridiculous. In his big overcoat and flapping scarf he looked like an eighteen-year-old public schoolboy going back for his last term at school. As an object of lust, he was most bizarre. Or at least unexpected. I closed my eyes briefly, but when I opened them the scene was just the same. I still had to clear up the table and then manoeuvre my way through a darkened house and find the right bedroom without falling over any tables and waking anyone. I would have slept on the sofa if it wasn't for having to explain myself to Emma when she found me the next morning. Sighing, I reached out for the bottle. There was a little trickle of wine still left. I upended it into my mouth. All I wanted right now was artificially induced oblivion.

That was a lie, of course. What I really wanted was to lock myself inside a bedroom with a naked Alan and a couple of bottles of champagne. Artificially induced oblivion was only a poor runner-up.

12

I HAD SWORN TO MYSELF, BEFORE FALLING ASLEEP OR
passing out or whatever I preferred to call it, that the next morning I would sit down and really reflect on what was happening
to my love life. Actually, I woke up at five, parched with thirst
and too terrified of stumbling into the wrong room to go to the
bathroom for a long drink of water. I lay awake, deeply unhappy,
in the paranoid state that overconsumption of alcohol produces
when you wake up in the wee small hours. Between fantasising
about two-litre bottles of water, cold from the fridge, beads of
moisture clinging to their blue plastic sides, plus terrible guilt
feelings about Hugo and confused lustful ones about Alan, I flag-
ellated myself thoroughly. Sam's virtual cat o'nine tails with extra-
nasty barbs on the tips. I reminded myself sternly that Alan, for
all I knew, had first knocked Janine down and then smashed a
toolbox on her head—I had to suspect absolutely everyone at this
stage. Hugo, at least, was definitely innocent of having killed
Janine. This reflection made my existential panic even worse.
Only Lurch's breathing, the deep, regular, slow exhalations of a
young man leading a virtuous and healthy life, calmed me down
at all. When I fell asleep again dawn was breaking, and I was
maudlin with self-pity. Lurch was still fast asleep, damn him.

The plan for the morning—cup of coffee, the location of

some quiet place where I could sit down and work out what the hell was going on with me—was put on hold. I was woken by Lurch grabbing my shoulders and shaking me back and forth like a vicious toddler with their least favourite doll.

"Sam! Wake up!" he was saying.

"Whaa? Burgh. Lurch. Fuck off."

I tried to pull a pillow over my head, but Lurch was still shaking me. I was beginning to feel like a piece of laundry in the spin cycle.

"It's Tom! The Bill just come and took him away! You got to do something!"

"What, put on my Wonder Woman outfit and bust him out from prison?" I said crossly. "Catching all the bullets on my special arm cuffs?"

"No," Lurch said impatiently. "He needs a solicitor, don't he?"

That rather shut me up. I sat up, shoving Lurch's hands off my shoulders.

"Emma probably knows someone local," I said, thinking aloud. "But they might not be used to representing murder suspects."

"He ain't been arrested," Lurch offered.

"Down the station to help them with their enquiries? Come on, Lurch, it's as good as. You know that."

"He ain't been charged yet."

I shuddered.

"I can't think what they're waiting for. If they've bothered to come and haul him off to the station, when they've questioned him twice already, it must only be a matter of time."

I pushed back the covers.

"I'm going to have a shower. And then I've got to make some phone calls," I announced. "Is there any coffee going?"

There was coffee, and it was better than anything I had at home. Emma, naturally enough, ground her own beans. The noise was shatteringly loud for someone in my delicate condition, but the resulting coffee was good enough to compensate. I needed it, and not just because of Tom's plight. Emma was in such a state of distress that she had somehow managed to convince herself that she was entirely to blame for the entire situation.

"It's all my fault," she wailed, fishing the milk carton out of the fridge and putting it on the table next to the full cafetière. This was a clear indication of her emotional misery. Emma had always decanted the milk into a jug before. Being reduced to pouring it straight out of the packet was near-degradation, her equivalent of scraping the mould off Indian takeaway leftovers and eating the rest.

I really didn't want to know why Emma was taking the blame on herself. In my experience, there was a breed of middle-aged women, usually the ones who had hardly ever worked outside the home, who compensated for their shortage of professional achievement by considering themselves responsible for absolutely everything that happened to their extended family. It was a kind of Napoleon complex in reverse; a fantasy of total power, bred of its lack. My Aunt Louise had exemplified this perfectly, and I had had enough of it in my teenage years to last me a lifetime.

Emma brushed back her grey-streaked hair impatiently, but it kept falling forward. Her failure to even do something as simple as keep her hair off her face seemed suddenly to depress her beyond measure. She sank down into a chair with a deep sigh. I thought that if Lurch and I hadn't been there she would have buried her face in her hands. But she was the kind of woman who put great value on keeping a stiff upper lip, if at all possible.

"Emma," I said, as gently as I could manage, "Tom needs a solicitor right away. God knows what he's telling the police. Do you know anyone?"

She shook her head. Her face looked worn and tired.

"I tried mine, but he said he's never done anything like this and doesn't want to start now. And he was very unhelpful about suggesting anyone else."

I frowned. If the idea that Tom was Janine's murderer had circulated to the point that even the local lawyers didn't want to touch him, we were in big trouble.

"I could ring up people I know in London," I said, "but I have the feeling that someone local'd be a lot better. Maybe I should try the London lot anyway and see if they can put me on to someone in the area."

"What if they don't know anyone?" Emma said hopelessly.

I bit my lip in thought.

"OK," I announced. "I have another idea. It may not come off, but fuck it, anything's worth a try at this stage, right?"

Emma was so glad I had thought of something that she didn't even flinch at my bad language. I reached for the kitchen phone.

"Oh, you'll have to wait," Laura chirped up. "Ethan's making a call right now."

She was sitting at the far end of the table, eating what looked like baby rusks. I had been doing my best to ignore the annoyingly loud crunching sounds—like a beaver eating bark—up till now, but on this I cracked. I could almost hear the fracture.

"What?" I said, in my most dangerously quiet voice. Strong men had blanched when I had used this voice on them. But Laura was too much of an idiot to realise its significance.

"I said, he's making a call right now," she said through a mouthful of tree shavings. She smiled at me and Emma. "It's very exciting, he's talking to this agent in London—"

I made a noise that caused Emma to back away from me and even Laura to pause in her mastications. Grabbing the phone, I said into the receiver, "Ethan? It's Sam. We need this phone for important things. Like getting the arrested member of this household a solicitor."

"But I'm in the middle of—" Ethan started.

"Hang up now," I said. "Or I'll come upstairs and shove it so far up your arse your stomach will be ringing for the rest of your life."

"Probably better to call me back later, Ethan, what do you say?" an urbane agent's voice drawled. "I'd do what she says if I were you. She sounds awfully like she means it."

"Well, I—" Ethan protested.

"Hang the fuck up!" I yelled into the phone. A click, then merciful silence. I almost regretted Ethan's having obeyed me. I was in exactly the right mood for kicking some hippy loafer all around the village green.

I ended up making the call. I would have preferred Emma to do it, but she said that she couldn't face talking to anyone. I was devoutly hoping that Alan wouldn't answer the phone; I didn't want him to think I was trying to get in touch with him and using this as an excuse. But, fortunately, it was his mother who answered.

I explained the situation and Priscilla Fitzwilliam was very understanding. She kept saying, "Of course, of course," in such deeply empathetic tones that it occurred to me that she would make a damn fine grief counsellor.

"Let me just have a word with John," she finally said. "It's lucky you caught us—we're leaving for London in a couple of hours. John has a board meeting this afternoon."

"I thought he was retired," I couldn't help saying, even though it was totally irrelevant. My nosiness is no respecter of time and place.

"Oh, he is," she said, seeming to think my implied question was perfectly natural, "but he has a few non-executive directorships. It's nice for him, gives him something to do, you know? And it's very flattering, of course, that they still want his advice."

Jobs for the boys, I thought cynically. John Fitzwilliam was at the level of big business where, even if you had made a complete mess of one company after another, your friends rallied around to make sure you got a golden handshake, a huge yearly income and a nice little collection of seats on various boards so you could continue to make a mess of everyone else's companies in turn. Just as long as you played a good game of golf. Oh, and were skilled at thinking up ever-new justifications for sacking large sections of your workforce while simultaneously plundering their pension fund.

"John?" Priscilla was saying. "It's Sam Jones on the phone. You know, Alan's friend. The artist. It's about her friend Tom— she wants to know if we can recommend a solicitor—I said we'd do what we could to help—"

I couldn't hear what John Fitzwilliam said in reply, but it didn't sound friendly. I was glad I had managed to talk to Priscilla first.

"Sam?" she said into the receiver. "Can you hold on a moment?"

She put her hand over the mouthpiece. I could hear a muffled dialogue, which sounded unpromising. I had doubted that John Fitzwilliam would want to get himself involved in a messy murder case, but at the same time I had been counting on his involvement with the village. Someone who bothered to put a large amount of time into coaching the Lesser Swinfold rugby team must have some sort of investment in local issues.

When Priscilla finally came back on the line, she was much more subdued. Previously, she had sounded almost excited; there was a guilty thrill to a murder which made most people want to be involved, at least from the sidelines. And maybe Priscilla didn't get asked for her advice and help very much. I imagined everyone went straight to her husband. Now, however, he must have read her the riot act. Her tone had become that of the perfect politician's wife: discreet, and much less promising.

"Sam?" she said. "John suggests you try a firm of solicitors in Chipping Campden. They're not actually the ones we use down here, but he's heard they're good, and they'd be better for, you know, a criminal case."

She read off the name of the firm, a contact there and the phone number. I took them down gratefully. When I rang the man John had named, I would cite the Fitzwilliams as a reference and ensure the police knew about their involvement too. Anything to make Tom look as respectable as possible.

"Thanks very much," I said appreciatively. "I know this can't be easy for you, but you were the only people I could think of to ask."

"How's Emma?" said Priscilla, concerned. She had put her finger on it; Emma would indeed have been the right person to deal with this, and Priscilla knew that as well as I did.

"Oh, not too good," I said carefully. Emma was sitting right next to me, her nice homely face a mask of anxiety.

There was a pause, and then Priscilla said, in a lower voice, "We're going to be in London for the whole week. I'm not sure if we're coming down for the weekend. I was wondering—I don't know what your plans are—but maybe if you're coming back to London at all you'd like to come round for a drink? John's got a very busy schedule, and he'll be out during the day all this week."

Clearly, John was not overhearing her side of the conversation. I assumed that he had given her the name of the solicitor, reluctantly, and then made an exit telling her to wash her hands of the whole business in those dictatorial tones which probably went down so well at his rounds of board meetings.

"That would be great," I said, my curiosity aroused. "I don't know what my plans are—I'm probably going to want to be round here as much as possible for Tom—"

"Oh, of course. Well, don't worry about it, then." She said this so quickly that it made me want still more to hear why she was inviting me over for a drink.

"No, no," I said. "I'm going to have to go back to London at some stage. I've got a hell of a lot of work to do still."

I said this as an excuse, so she wouldn't think I was making a trip up just to see her, but as soon as I heard the words I realised it was true. I had a couple of people from the arts centre coming around next Monday to see how the cockroaches were getting on, and practically nothing to show them. Bugger. I suddenly felt as if I had the weight of the world on my shoulders.

"Of course," she said sympathetically. "Your exhibition. You must be very busy."

What a boon Priscilla must be as a businessman's wife; she recollected even the snippets of conversation she had had with a sculptor who couldn't possibly be of any use to her husband's career. I bet she was superb at remembering the names and hobbies of people she had met at cocktail parties, not to mention all the birthdays of John's non-executive directors' wives. God, what a life. I'd be a screaming, tranquilliser-addicted wreck in twenty-four hours.

I promised to give her a ring later in the week and took down the London number. She sounded genuinely happy at the prospect of my call, which was an experience I don't have that often.

Then I drank some more coffee, braced myself and dialled the number of the solicitor. I had been expecting a brush-off, but I wasn't sure how to interpret the response I got. The man John had recommended listened attentively to what I had to say and then passed me on to someone he described as a junior partner, a woman called Gail Christie, who was as sharp as a whip. She promised that she would head off to the police station immediately, which I found reassuring.

That didn't last long. Just until she told me that Tom had been charged with Janine's murder.

· · · · · · ·

When I met Gail Christie later that evening, I was reassured, at least to some degree. She had come straight from the police station, and she looked tired, the kind of weariness that comes from spending the day arguing with obstinate people in poorly ventilated rooms lit by strips of artificial light. I had been in enough police stations to remember all too vividly the claustrophobia they induced. But then I felt the same in most office buildings, though they didn't have the locks on the doors and young recruits practising their intimidating stares on every passer-by.

If we had been in America, there would have been a diner somewhere on the edge of town where we could have sat in a booth, drunk filter coffee and eaten home fries. The United States hasn't contributed much to world cuisine but the all-night diner has to rank up there as one of their proudest moments. As it was, we had to settle for a pub in Dunster Magna, where Gail Christie lived. It wasn't the one where Tom, Lurch and I had met for a drink; it was slightly more civilised, by which I meant welcoming, but unfortunately had pretensions to being a London-style gastro-pub. This involved serving everything with sun-dried tomatoes and tasteless out-of-season avocado and describing a sauce inaccurately as a coulis. The chef, on the evidence of my dinner, would have been much better suited to cooking bangers and mash.

Gail Christie, however, was a revelation. I recognised her at once as I entered the pub; she looked so urban that she was as out of place as I was. Small and squarely built, she was dressed in a well-cut black trouser suit with a close-fitting grey silk shirt: classic New York–style power dressing. The grey didn't suit her—it hardly suits anyone—but it was very fashionable, and the whole outfit had clearly been expensive. Her dark hair was bobbed, and her brown lipstick was still shiny after her long day of work. She looked considerably smarter than most of the young London solicitors I had met, who were desperate to present themselves as urban trendies despite the conventionality of their job; they wanted to convey that they went clubbing at weekends at least as hard as the rest of us.

"You must be Sam," she said, shaking my hand. Hers was cool and firm. "Tom described you pretty accurately."

"Well, no-one described you at all," I said, sitting down opposite her on a rickety wooden settle. The pub was a queasy combination of would-be fashionable menu and olde-worlde decor—brasses everywhere and beams low enough to knock out anyone over five feet eight. For once I was grateful for my lack of height. I tried to make myself comfortable, but the cushion was meagre and kept slipping along the highly polished boards. At least my bottom had its own built-in padding. Another rare cause for gratitude.

"I wasn't expecting you to look so—" I began. "So big-city, I expect."

"You thought I'd be wearing a twinset and pearls?" she said quizzically.

I wasn't going to put up with this kind of thing. Admittedly, I might be guilty of stereotyping country people, but not quite as badly as she was implying.

"More a badly cut chainstore designer knock-off," I retorted. "I didn't know country solicitors made enough money to buy the real thing."

"We don't. Not at my level, anyway," she said, deliberately not answering the rest of my implied question.

I raised my eyebrows.

"Rich parents?" I suggested. "Rich husband? Or paybacks for putting through dodgy land deals to build out-of-town super-markets?"

Gail Christie burst out laughing. She wasn't pretty, but her features were good, particularly her wide-set grey eyes. She had a snub nose, like a little girl's, sprinkled with a couple of freckles. I bet she hated it; it didn't go with her hard-edged lawyer persona. But it added a touch of cuteness to her face, and when she laughed, her eyes crinkled very attractively at the corners.

"I asked for that, didn't I?" she said. "Tom really did describe you accurately."

"Said I was a stroppy cow?" I suggested hopefully.

"He said you didn't let anyone mess with you."

"Oooh," I cooed. "He's always paying me compliments."

She grinned.

"My suit," she said, "is a relic from my time spent being a career-crazed London solicitor. I burnt out a couple of years ago. Got completely sick of the rat race. I was working ridiculous hours and spending all my spare time and a large part of my income on alter-native therapists. I had every stress symptom known to humanity. So, finally, I decided to jack it in and move to the country."

"God," I said respectfully, "that was brave of you."

It was her turn to raise her eyebrows. She beat me, though; she had the trick of lifting one much higher than the other. It looked superbly quizzical. I was highly jealous. I couldn't even wiggle my ears.

"From the brief sketch Tom gave me of you, it sounds like you've done some pretty dangerous stuff," she said dryly.

"Believe me," I said with great sincerity, "I would infinitely rather be chained in a cellar for a few days than have to move to Dunster Magna indefinitely. No offence," I added hastily.

"None taken. I read about that, by the way. I remembered it when Tom mentioned your name."

"Me being kidnapped?" I shrugged. "The cellar wasn't too hot, but the gallery that represents me was really happy about it. Sold a couple of sculptures on the publicity, anyway."

She did the raising-one-eyebrow thing again.

"So what's it like living down here?" I said. I hated talking about my lurid past.

She shrugged. "Let's put it this way. My shoulders don't go into stress-related spasm, and my digestion is back to normal, so I don't need to spend a fortune on Shiatsu massages and herbal medications any more. The main risk is boredom. Which is why," she continued, "I was so happy to be given Tom's case."

"Is it a bit of a hot potato?" I asked. "I thought the guy I spoke to at your firm was keen to wash his hands of it."

"Oh no, it's not that bad. I mean, Tom's respectable enough. Male primary school teacher: what could be better! We're not defending a druggie who killed a local pillar of society." A note of cynicism had crept into her voice. "If Andrew sounded funny, it's just because the whole mention of murder scared him out of his mind. He's Mr. Conveyancing."

"So what's up with Tom?" I said, leaning forward.

Gail Christie looked serious.

"It's not too good right now. Previously good character aside. They've arrested him."

"Oh, God." I had been expecting the news, but it was still a nasty shock.

"They found his fingerprints on the toolbox."

"Of course they were! He was in her house all the time! He was showing her how to rehang her door!"

"Yes, he told them that. He's a real handyman, by his account. Very useful to have around the house."

Though her words were measured enough, I noticed with much relief the tone of amused protectiveness creeping into her voice. Tom aroused that instinct in most women over twenty-five. Look at Chrissie. We would have to hope for an all-woman jury.

"How good is the case against him?" I asked.

"They're not exactly spilling the beans to me," she pointed out. "But, between you and me, I don't think they're a hundred per cent convinced."

I knew enough about the workings of the police mind to be aware that this wasn't as good as it sounded. They needed to clear up a high-profile murder like this one as quickly as possible: even if the case against Tom wasn't watertight, they would forge ahead with it in the absence of any other plausible-looking suspects. I said as much to Gail as our food arrived. The chef had made a pathetically overambitious attempt to pile it up in the middle of the big white plates, Pacific Rim–style. The hand that had constructed the tower had been inexpert and the waitress was much too slack to have bothered to keep the plates steady. The pile of rubbery mozzarella and shredded grilled chicken had skidded all over the plate, slopping into the circle of grated carrot garnish around the edge. The inevitable avocado slices were already starting to brown, and the sun-dried tomato pieces were as dark and chewy as jerked beef. I picked at the food in disbelief.

"God," I said. "We should have gone to McDonald's. At least there they don't put sodding grated carrot round the bottom of the hamburger carton."

"There's not much choice round here," Gail said ruefully.

"Something you miss?" I suggested.

"Oh, I miss a lot about London. But I don't want to go back," she said firmly. "So. Tom said you'd be full of helpful suggestions about ways to get him off."

"That boy's an eternal optimist," I complained. "Do you know he decided to teach primary school because of the opportunities of meeting single mothers desperate for a shag?"

Gail wrinkled her nose.

"I think we'll forget you said that," she suggested.

"Oh yeah." I winced, thinking of Janine. "Not that she seems to have been desperate."

"Yes, that's what I've heard. We're not going to be able to play the she-was-a-slut card."

I pulled a face in disgust. She looked apologetic.

"I know, I know," she said. "But let's face it, it would have helped a lot."

I had always loathed the concept of post-feminism, but sometimes, reluctantly, I had to admit its existence.

"I can't help feeling that finding out who Pitt's father was might help," I suggested.

"Pitt?" She looked baffled for a moment. "Oh yes, her son. Jesus, what a name."

"Brad would scarcely have been an improvement."

She shrugged and took a mouthful of food.

"Any ideas?" she said. "About the father, I mean."

"She seems to have preferred older guys."

"No shortage of those round here," Gail said dryly, looking round the pub. Like the Cow, there wasn't anyone in here under forty; we were the youngest customers by a long stretch. That should have cheered me up, but instead I found it depressing.

"Her brother's a bit of a psycho," I suggested. "Very overprotective."

"Then he's more likely to have killed whoever he was protecting her from."

She was right. I grimaced.

"I know Tom doesn't have an alibi," I said, "but he didn't do it."

"How do you know?"

It was a very good question. Feebly, I said:

"Because . . . because he didn't."

"No offence," Gail said, "but we're going round in circles here."

"God," I said in irritation, more at myself than her. "I hate the trained legal mind."

She grinned at me.

"Let me keep digging, OK?" I said. "Maybe now Tom's been arrested, everyone will relax a bit and more stuff will come out."

She took another bite. She had ordered veal. I noticed that she had to chew every mouthful so thoroughly that it must have been as rubbery as my mozzarella, which tasted like the kind of vacuum-packed stuff they use on cheap pizzas.

"I hope you're right," she said. "I really do. Because right now I've got nothing to go on at all. I don't want to panic you, but unless we come up with something good, Tom's going down for this. They'll take that fight he had with Janine and throw it at the jury so hard they'll convict on that. And the toolbox stuff, of course. He knew where it was—he'd been helping her—it would be natural for him to think of it . . ."

I felt like the star of one of those TV shows where you have to build a thirteenth-century Roman church by teatime, with only a spade, two incompetent sidekicks and a box of children's toys: Challenge Sam. I sighed. A wave of depression rolled over me. I was feeling very tired. And I was still scared that Tom wasn't telling the truth.

13

GAIL CHRISTIE'S COMPETENCE WASN'T ENOUGH ON ITS
own, not without extra evidence of Tom's innocence. But it was
enough to make me feel that I could leave Lesser Swinfold for a
couple of days without panicking at what might happen in my
absence. I wanted to go up to London for my drink with Priscilla
Fitzwilliam. The more I contemplated it, the more curious I
became about why she had invited me.

I had plenty of other good reasons too. I needed to get at least
one electronic prototype ready for the Islington Arts Centre
cockroach inspectors. If I threw myself into work for a couple of
days and thought about nothing else, maybe when I emerged on
the other side I'd have cleared my mind and come up with better
ideas for saving Tom's increasingly lardy arse. And getting away
from Lesser Swinfold meant having a break from Alan, which I
needed too. I didn't have the faintest notion what to do about
him, except the all too obvious.

The only problem with London was Hugo. I didn't really
want to see him either. I felt guilty, which was a state of mind
almost totally unfamiliar to me, and distinctly unwelcome. I
knew that if things were going wrong between me and Hugo
then I was the one to blame. I hadn't told Lurch this, but Hugo
had recently been suggesting that I move in with him. Not to

give up my studio—that I would keep on, but purely as a studio. I would sleep, live and generally bring my slobbish uncivilised existence over to his charming bachelor flat in Spitalfields.

I couldn't do it. The idea had sent me into such a spiral of panic that, as Hugo bitterly pointed out, I was incapable of appreciating even the huge compliment he was paying me by offering to share his exquisite flat with someone who had the hygiene standards of a subway rat and the musical tastes of a clinically depressed eighteen-year-old dropout. I thought his summary of the latter was rather harsh. No arguing with the hygiene part, though.

But I had lived alone, ever since I left my Aunt Louise and Uncle Harold's house at sixteen for the local squat. My God, the fuss. Aunt Louise haunted the entrance of my sixth-form college sobbing—God knew why, I was as much trouble to her as she was to me—till I agreed at least to come back for meals. It was a bloody good deal. My fellow squattees took the piss relentlessly, but I knew it was just because they were jealous. In revenge, I would come back after hefty helpings of shepherd's pie and baked alaska to find them dining off lentils with tinned tomatoes for the umpteenth time and take great pleasure in describing the contents of my stomach till their mouths practically ran with drool.

At eighteen I came into my parents' money—the insurance payments they had posthumously received when their house blew up due to a faulty gas main—and immediately bought my studio. I gave a hefty whack to Aunt Louise and Uncle Harold too for the expenses of bringing me up. I was big on paying my debts. That way I never had to feel . . . guilty.

Since then I had been by myself in my big echoing studio, and I liked it that way. It had never occurred to me to invite any of my gentleman callers to move in with me. The only one with whom it might have been possible was Nat. I hadn't known him long, but I had had the instinct that his opinions on hygiene and music would have accorded with mine. And he wouldn't have cramped my space, as the Americans so elegantly put it. Nat, like me, had been a cat that walked by himself.

No, that wasn't true. I remembered a jealous fit he had once thrown. Despite his cool, Nat would have done that where-are-you-going-and-when-will-you-be-back thing that so many boyfriends had tried to pull on me in the past. Unsuccessfully. Jesus, why was I thinking of Nat now, when I had managed to blot his memory out for years? I must have been having a deeper existential crisis than I had realised.

I put a Pixies tape into the car stereo and turned it up high enough to make my ears bleed. At least that would stop my current train of thought.

⋯ ⋯ ⋯

Lurch had stayed behind in Lesser Swinfold. It wasn't some lightning-quick conversion to the joys of country life, such as they were. But he didn't have to be back at college for another week, and his investigative blood was up. As I had thought, he had managed to insinuate himself into the blokey atmosphere of the village almost immediately. He had all the crucial requirements: he was a good darts player, well informed about football and could hold his drink. It probably wasn't necessary, on consideration, to have all three. The regulars in the Cow would have welcomed a mangy badger as a new recruit if it could play darts and keep downing pints with everyone else.

Of course, everyone knew that Lurch was a friend of Tom's. But I had the feeling that after a few days that would fade into the background. Lurch was so likeable, so easy-going, that he would almost immediately be accepted for himself. People would start to forget the Tom connection and start to talk freely. I had seen the Lurch Effect in practice again and again: on the set of a

TV show, where Hugo had been filming and I had been working as a stand-in, Lurch had melted into the notoriously insular group of techies so fast that I had hardly seen him go. Later I had got him to infiltrate a hunt-sab group with the same result. Within a couple of days he was everyone's best mate. He still went out with the sabs when he could.

I had told Lurch to concentrate on two things in particular: the first was Andy, whom I couldn't stop speculating about. Everyone said that his attachment to his sister had been unnaturally intense. I had seen Andy's tendency to violence at firsthand. It didn't seem at all unlikely to me that Janine had made a bid for more independence than he wanted to allow her, and that he had reacted badly. Maybe even the idea that she was involved with Tom had done it. As far as I knew, Janine hadn't been seeing anyone since her affair with Pitt's mystery father.

And that was the other point. We had, if possible, to work out who that had been. I remembered Alan telling me that she had really loved Pitt's father. Had he been local? And if so, had they ever managed to let him see his son in secret, to play with him, to have time alone together? It was hard to imagine how that could have been arranged in a small village where everyone knew everyone else's business better than the backs of their own hands.

・ ・ ・ ・ ・ ・

God, I had missed London. My spirits rose as I started threading my way through the surrounding suburbs. I was even happy to see the nasty little mock-Tudor semis with their carefully tended patches of lawn outside—on an A road, no less, how bizarre was that? As if you could ever sit on that lawn with a constant stream of lorries rolling past, trailing diesel fumes. I always found this experience real cultural tourism. To see people actually living in these endless rows of streets with no shops or restaurants within walking distance, just suburbia stretching out for ever like an open prison, Brent Cross shopping centre at the end like the Holy Grail of the North Circular. How could they bear it? I would start having panic attacks if I just stopped the van here for a quarter of an hour.

What was the point of technically being part of London if you were cut off from everything that made it special? What chance did you have to get to know it? You would visit London like a tourist. I bet the kids here all went up to Leicester Square on a Friday night to get drunk and eat crappy Mexican food before they had to catch their last train home and vomit barely digested burritos over their friends. And they'd think that was a great night out in the big city.

I kept going straight down the Finchley Road until I reached Swiss Cottage, the bad-architecture capital of north London. A bizarre pub, timbered and gabled to look like a monstrous Swiss chalet, sat incongruously on a promontory where the roads from Edgware and Hampstead and Camden flowed together like a series of mighty rivers. The pub was a rare haven of old-fashioned British bad taste in a London that was rapidly becoming far too trendy and expensive for its own good; no martinis or DJs here, just average beer, games machines and scampi in a basket.

Making a mental note to sink a pint at the Swiss Cottage next time I was passing, out of solidarity for old-school pubs everywhere, I headed down towards Regent's Park and the enviable streets of Primrose Hill. It had everything, Primrose Hill. Pretty parks, good pubs, nice little local restaurants. And if you started to miss the filth and mess and confusion of urban life too much, Camden Town was a mere five minutes' walk away, willing to provide you with that quintessential inner-London experience any time you wanted. I wasn't ready for the more sheltered delights of Primrose Hill yet, even if I could have afforded to live there. I felt perfectly comfortable in Holloway, shouldering past the drunks and kicking rubbish out of my way as I went about my daily business. But it was impossible not to be charmed by Primrose Hill. It was one of the few rich corners of London that had so far managed to hold on to a certain individuality.

The Fitzwilliams turned out, damn them, to live in one of my favourite houses on Regent's Park Road: overlooking the park, narrow, with round windows up the staircases like portholes and a kind of tower at the top that always made me think of a crow's nest. It could have been an illustration from a children's book for the house where the retired sea captain lived, a parrot in the tower cawing, "Avast there, ye swabs!" whenever the doorbell rang. I didn't have any particular fantasies about parrots, let alone retired sea captains—though I wouldn't have minded a couple of cabin boys—but there was something about the house that stirred my fancy. I liked the idea that you could live in the centre of London in a house that resembled, even a little, a ship, so that you could imagine casting off and sailing away at any time, over the grass of the park, heading for adventure once you were tired of settling down.

I noticed this escape fantasy rather grimly. So much for thoughts of moving in with Hugo. The mere idea was rapidly making me turn into Peter Pan. No, I was worse than Peter Pan. At least he hadn't been a cradle snatcher.

I rang the doorbell of the woman whose cradle, metaphorically at least, I was hoping to snatch, trying to wrench my brain back to thinking about Janine's murder and not Alan naked. The latter image was obsessing me right now. In my confusion the two ideas blurred together and for some reason produced a flash of Alan tied to a tree, rather like St. Sebastian, a few arrows in his chest, trickles of blood dripping erotically down his pale flesh. I was getting dangerously into gay-porn territory. I shook my head so vigorously in a desperate attempt to clear it that when Priscilla Fitzwilliam opened the door I must have looked like a wet dog in a tumble dryer.

"Hi, Sam," she said with a nervous edge to her voice. That didn't worry me. I was used to people talking to me as if I were a psychopath with a big grin and the pin of a grenade clamped between my teeth.

"Hi," I said. "Hey, do you like blonde jokes?"

One had suddenly popped into my head.

"Um, yes, I think so," she said, even more nervous.

"What do you do if a blonde throws a pin at you?" I said.

She shook her head.

"Run like hell—she's got a grenade in her mouth!"

To do her credit, Priscilla's laughter sounded genuine, rather than as if she were humouring me out of fear. She stood back from the door and said:

"Won't you come in? I give free coffee with every blonde joke."

I had forgotten how beautiful she was. Or maybe I had blocked it out because the younger and more attractive Alan's mother looked, the more he seemed, by comparison, barely out of his teens. Her dark hair was caught at the back of her head in one of those fashionable loose ponytails with the ends twisted around in a single clip. She wore a tight black polo neck and butterscotch suede boot-cut trousers with embroidered Chinese house slippers. Her figure was better than mine; she looked as if she worked out—which I did too—but managed not to eat much the rest of the time, which is always my fatal flaw. Still, she had nice breasts, and they were in proportion to the rest of her, rather than looking as if Sophia Loren's bosom had been grafted on to Twiggy, which was the current fashion in supermodels right now. Rip out those lower ribs, liposuction the bum and slap some soya implants into the non-existent breasts. Voilà, one boy with tits. It was the Brazilian transvestite look. I bet the plastic surgeons were in ecstasy.

Bare floorboards, white walls, fresh flowers everywhere in those up-to-the-minute, New York–style arrangements, where you take a big bunch of identical blooms, trim their stems short and put them in a low round vase, so they look like topiary. Lushness and minimalism combined. Three vases filled with dark red roses lined the hallway, and the living room, into which she led me, was filled with carnations done in the same way, pale orange with dark-green frilled edges, set into silver vases as big and round as bowling balls. In the cast-iron grate a fire was burning and the gold-orange flames were bright against the black background, flaring like the carnations on the mantelpiece above. A huge antique gold-framed mirror hung over the fireplace, tilted slightly into the room. I sank into a huge navy-blue leather armchair and looked around me with admiration.

"This is really beautiful," I said.

The rugs were modern, abstracts in dark-blue and green, flowing into the dark-stained floorboards as gracefully as water over stone. The furniture was simple: glass and chrome and a few antique pieces in dark wood. It was usually easy to scoff at rich people's houses: more money than taste, and a panicked attempt to copy the latest fashion in interior design. But whoever had done up this house had avoided all such traps. I felt very immature. I would have loved to live somewhere like this—eventually, when I was grown-up enough to do it justice. I imagined the squalor of my studio seen through Priscilla's eyes and squirmed. Suddenly, my insistence on living in the most basic conditions felt like a wilful clinging to adolescence, rather than the untrammelled existence of a wild, free, artistic spirit. Which had always been my excuse for not cleaning the bathroom.

"Coffee?" she was saying. "Or would you rather have tea?"

"No, coffee'd be great, thanks."

She went into the kitchen, which I could just make out from my seat in the armchair. It was open plan to the living room, which was the long stroke of an L to the kitchen's short one. Both rooms looked out on to a back garden, but the kitchen had been extended into a high-vaulted conservatory from which trailing plants hung over a large and beautiful oak dining table. The kitchen itself was chrome and blue and green. Priscilla was operating a chrome Gaggia machine, which was gurgling louder than the one at Bar Italia.

"Do you want a cappuccino?" she called to me.

"Lovely," I yelled back over the noise of water reaching a level of pressure that sounded like the Boulder Dam in the middle of a heavy storm.

She emerged with a tray containing two perfect, chocolate-dusted cappuccinos and a plate of glazed almond biscuits with chocolate bottoms.

"I always feel as if I'm showing off with that machine," she said, a little apologetically, "but I'm madly in love with it right now. John bought it for me for my birthday, and I can't stop playing with it. It's a total indulgence. They told us in the shop it wasn't worth getting unless you were going to make coffee all day long, because it's really a bar machine. But I couldn't resist it. And I do drink a lot of coffee."

"What about Alan?" I said, unable to resist bringing his name into the conversation. "He looks like a coffee drinker to me."

"Oh, he won't use it," she said regretfully. "He says it's too complicated. He insists on making instant instead. I'm sure it's just to annoy me."

"Yeah, he looks like he's going through a bit of a rebellious stage."

"Oh, you think so?" Her beautiful dark eyes brightened. "I'm so glad you said that, it was what I really wanted to talk to you about . . . if you don't mind . . . Have a biscuit?"

She handed me the plate. I took one. Its surface was as shiny as glass; the almonds were glazed with what tasted like apricot jam.

"Mmn," I said through my first mouthful, "these are wonderful."

"I get them from a little deli in St. John's Wood. They cost a fortune, but they're worth it."

"Makes a nice change from chocolate Hobnobs."

"Oh, I love chocolate Hobnobs too," she said enthusiastically. Still, I noticed that she took a little nibble of her biscuit, then put it on her saucer, obviously meaning to spin it out. I was already on my second. I envied her self-control. Add that to a long list of things I envied Priscilla Fitzwilliam.

I was taken aback by my own feelings. What the hell was I doing, sitting here wishing I were this woman, who was clearly a banker's trophy wife?

"Do you mind my talking to you about Alan?" she was saying cautiously. "It's just that he seems so taken with you—he was talking about you a lot after we met you in the Cow. And, you know, all his other friends are his own age, and I can't really ask them about him. I know you haven't known him long, but as I said, he seemed really struck with you. It almost felt like a bit of hero-worship, you know—you're a successful artist, I expect you're doing in a way what Alan would love to do . . . I think, if you don't mind my saying so, that he has a bit of a crush on you."

"*Really*," I said, trying to look mildly surprised and a little amused.

Priscilla nodded and took a sip of her cappuccino. So that was what she wanted to talk to me about. People did confide in me. Tom said it was because they sensed that I wouldn't overwhelm them with too much sympathy or try to empathise, that my detachment made them feel safer. And here he was being proved right again. I had the feeling that Priscilla was going to ask me for some nice disinterested advice about what to do with her problem son. I braced myself for a bout of lying through my teeth. I couldn't imagine explaining to Priscilla what I really wanted to do with Alan for more than thirty seconds before she threw me out on my possibly over-padded arse.

"Ever since he left university he's just been drifting," she said, her smooth brow creasing slightly in two pretty little pinches of skin. I thought of that deep dent between Emma's eyebrows, a brand of worry clear as the mark of Cain, and didn't imagine that Priscilla Fitzwilliam had ever had to bother her lovely head about anything too serious.

"I thought he wanted to write," I said.

"Oh." She waved her hand dismissively. "I mean, that's all very well, but isn't he too young? I mean, don't you have to have done things before you write about them?"

"He's writing the classic first novel," I said casually. "You know, coming of age. But in a historical setting."

"Historical?" She looked surprised. "You see, he hasn't even told me that!"

"Well," I pointed out as delicately as I could, "you *are* his mother. And people don't usually talk about what they're writing. Tom's a poet, and he doesn't like talking about his poetry at all."

"Oh, I didn't realise that Tom was a poet!" Priscilla looked impressed.

I shrugged. "I'm sure he's still writing. But it only pays enough for a diet of tinned dog food and a cardboard box under a railway arch."

"So he decided to teach? And ended up in Lesser Swinfold," Priscilla said, deftly bringing the subject right back to where I wanted it. I sensed that she was as eager to talk about Janine's murder as I was. "And in quite a lot of trouble, from what I hear."

I sighed and put down my cup. I wanted to lick out the last trace of foam, but that wasn't the kind of thing you could do around a woman as chic as Priscilla Fitzwilliam.

"Yes. It's looking pretty bad. I don't believe for a moment that Tom killed Janine—even his solicitor doesn't think he did it, and she'd only talked to him for a couple of hours. But they don't seem to have any other suspects. Or they don't want to look for them."

Priscilla pulled a face.

"I imagine everyone in the village is clamming up," she said.

"I don't know. But you must be part of the village now, mustn't you?" I said hopefully. "In a way. I mean, John coaches the rugby team. They were singing his praises in the Cow the other night."

"Oh yes." Priscilla smiled. "That was my idea. I rather went off Lesser Swinfold for a while, and when I changed my mind it was hard to persuade John to go back there. I'd been giving him a line about how boring it was, and when I decided I wanted to start going back more regularly—my garden was getting terribly neglected—it wasn't that easy to make him change his mind again. So I suggested the rugby team. It was a stroke of genius. He used to play for his university, and he was thrilled at the idea of doing some coaching."

She gestured behind me. I turned and squinted over the back of the armchair. On a table by the far window was a large group of photographs in silver frames.

"Can I have a look?" I said, levering myself out of the armchair. I wasn't that big on family photographs generally, but they could be very telling when you were scavenging around desperately trying to pick up any clues you could.

"Of course."

The ones she must have meant were John's team photographs from when he had played for Oxford. I spotted him immediately. John Fitzwilliam was the only one who didn't look as if his features had been systematically ground into pulp by a series of hobnailed boots that could have done double duty as industrial potato mashers.

"God, he was handsome," I said involuntarily. Then I apologised: "I didn't mean to say that he isn't now, but—"

"Oh, I know." Priscilla came over to stand beside me. "I didn't know him then—well, I couldn't have. He's nearly fifteen years older than me."

"Wrong way round," I said absently. "Women last longer. You ought to pick someone fifteen years younger than you . . . God, he looks like a young Harrison Ford, doesn't he?"

Great legs, I noticed too. Muscley but not ridiculously swollen. I remembered a description of Arnold Schwarzenegger as looking like a condom full of walnuts. Some of the men sitting on the bench next to John Fitzwilliam had thighs as big as both of mine put together—no mean achievement. And that had been pre-steroids, too.

"Look at our wedding photographs," Priscilla said, breaking into my reverie.

She indicated the biggest one of all: she and John emerging from a church, a cloud of confetti filling the air above them. Both of them were laughing, their arms linked tightly, their faces creased by two of the happiest smiles I had ever seen. It could have been a film still. Priscilla was wearing a dress rather like Audrey Hepburn's in *Funny Face*, a ballerina-style puff of tulle, which was saved from being too twee by its absence of any excess decoration. She looked very beautiful. There was something about the picture that nagged me, however.

"Oh, you had curly hair then," I said rather vaguely, trying to pin down what it was that had caught my attention.

She put up one hand to the knot of hair at the back of her head.

"Yes, I straighten it now. I always wanted straight hair. It's an obsession, really. I hate going out in the rain because it curls up straight away when it's wet. I mean, I look at yours and think how pretty it is, but I wanted straight hair all my life, and so I have to spend half an hour every morning blowdrying it like that . . . stupid, I know."

She gave a little self-deprecating laugh, the one women always use for telling people how much money they spend on anti-cellulite massage or moisturiser invented by NASA scientists or Brazilian bikini waxes with the St. Tropez fake tan to follow. I hardly heard it. I was too busy staring anew at the photograph in a kind of controlled horror. I had realised what had been nagging me about it. Priscilla Fitzwilliam was younger than me in the photograph, and at least a stone thinner; I had never dreamed of getting married, let alone in a frock that looked like a designer version of the Sugar Plum Fairy; and yet the resemblance was unmistakable.

I wasn't hallucinating. She saw it too.

"My God," she said, bending over to look at the photograph more closely, then turning to me. "You know, I thought you reminded me of someone when I first saw you, but of course I didn't think—I mean, who would?"

She was laughing. I found it considerably less amusing.

"You look like me when I was younger!" she said. "Isn't that funny!"

It was the first time, to my knowledge, that someone had fancied me because I looked like a younger version of his mother. Maybe it was going on all the time, and I had just been unlucky to be confronted with the evidence. But I didn't like it one little bit. If I wanted to be called Jocasta, I would have already changed my name by deed poll.

I was teetering on the edge of a sulk so massive that it would have made all my previous tantrums look like mere love-bites. I wanted to stamp my foot and scream and scream and scream till I was sick. Mercifully, Priscilla happened to say exactly the right thing to defuse the stormclouds before Hurricane Sam could start whirling into action.

"Oh, this is so nice! I always wondered what a daughter of mine would look like," she was saying. "Of course it's not quite the same thing, but still—"

I cheered up at once. Picturing myself as Alan's older sister was a sexy kind of incest without the Oedipal implications. Immediately, I started imagining us in our formative years having pillowfights that gradually shaded into something much more suggestive . . . bouts of mock-wrestling in our pyjamas, one of us pinning the other down challengingly . . . brother–sister incest. God, that was sexy. I could just see Alan in stripy pyjamas, or maybe just the bottoms, held up by a perilously loose cord, which threatened to come undone as we rolled about on one of our beds, pretending that we weren't both getting dangerously excited—

"Sam?" Priscilla said.

I jumped. A wave of guilt swept through me.

"Would you like another coffee?"

I looked dubious. I was thinking that coffee might stimulate me even more than I was already.

"Or, I know! Let's have a drink. It's past six. What about a gin and tonic?"

"Lovely," I said with enthusiasm.

Maybe Priscilla could adopt me. The only catch was that the Fitzwilliams were far too rich for Alan and me to have to share a bedroom. Still, we could sneak into each other's rooms after lights out to play Strip Poker and Naked Hide and Seek—

Tom, I chanted to myself. Tom Is in Trouble. Tom Is Under Arrest. Get Your Mind Out of Alan's Knickers Now. Then I just concentrated on the first two slogans. The last one was giving me ideas again.

14

"IT'S THIS WHOLE INSISTENCE ON STAYING DOWN IN LESSER Swinfold that worries me," Priscilla continued as she topped up our gin and tonics. The Americans called this "refreshing" a drink. I liked that expression. The Americans were full of useful euphemisms. "What *is* he doing there?"

"It's probably a really good place to write," I said reasonably. "Nice and quiet and absolutely no distractions. Unless you count the fleshpots of Chipping Campden, of course."

Priscilla hadn't been in on the Chipping Campden joke, but it was scarcely too arcane for her to understand. She laughed and said, "Yes, I doubt those are much of a long-term lure . . . No, do you know, for a while I thought it might be Janine. They always liked each other—they used to hang out together when they were younger, and John was worried—I mean, we both were worried, well, that something might happen. I expect he—we, that is—were rather overdoing it. After all, even if he did have a boy-and-girl thing with her when they were both sixteen or so, that's all part of growing up, isn't it?"

Here were plenty of bones to pick over. I noticed the way Priscilla was protecting her husband; it sounded as if he had really been the one to object to Alan hanging out with Janine. Village girls with little education and fewer prospects were doubtless not considered to be good enough for John Fitzwilliam's son. I felt a twinge of jealousy at the image of Alan with Janine, even in a youthful, clumsy, schoolboyish embrace. Then I remembered the conversation he and I had had about her.

"I don't think anything like that happened," I assured her. "The way Alan talks about her is more, well, brotherly. It doesn't sound like they were each other's types."

Alan, after all, preferred sophisticated women of the world, who looked not unlike his mother when her hair had been naturally curly. And Janine had gone for the truly mature type. Men who looked like they could have been her father. No wonder they had been friends: they had had plenty in common.

"I never really liked her," Priscilla said confidingly. "I shouldn't say that, I suppose. But I didn't. I thought there was something sly about her."

That jarred a little. Janine, in my brief acquaintance with her, had been composed; she had, as Tamsin put it, kept herself to herself, but I hadn't seen a trace of slyness in her manner. Perhaps Priscilla, knowing that Janine was secretive, was confusing that with a trait which to me was quite different.

"Sly," I repeated, trying not to put any weight on it. "She seemed quiet, but . . ."

Priscilla retreated at once.

"Oh, maybe I'm just exaggerating. Like I said, I really didn't know her that well. It was just a sort of instinct."

She took another long sip of her gin and tonic. I noticed that she was slurring some of her words, so slightly that it was hardly noticeable, and I wondered why. She wasn't a secret drinker; she didn't have that artificial brightness to the eyes, and she wasn't holding her glass in that alcoholic's way, the grip a little too tight, each pull at the drink tinged with an eagerness which was impossible to hide. No, it was something else. I listed possibilities in my head as she continued.

"John's tried to set Alan up with a job at a publisher. He knows one of the directors, and apparently they're always looking for male editors' assistants." She laughed again. "John said the director told him he had Katies and Sophies and Camillas coming out of his ears, and if he didn't get some testosterone into the office, he was going to go insane."

"Alan isn't exactly macho," I pointed out.

"No, but you know what he means."

"But Alan wouldn't take the job?" I deduced.

"No. He says he wants to do things under his own steam, and anyway it would be fatal for him to work for a publisher if what he wants to do is write."

"That's all very well, I suppose," I said dubiously, not knowing a great deal about it. "But there's no point saying you're going to do things for yourself if you keep on living in your parents' country house."

"Exactly," Priscilla said. "I think that John should buy him a flat."

This wasn't precisely the point I had been making, but I let it go.

"What does John think about that?" I asked.

She shrugged. "He feels Alan should be earning some money first. I don't know, I take his point, but it's a bit of a Catch-22, isn't it? Especially if he wants to be a writer. I mean, we have the money, so why not use it to help our son? It's not as if he'd spend it all on drugs. He's always been very serious. I was worried about sending him to public school—I thought he'd get in with a really bad group of boys. You know, too much money and very bad habits. But he came through that all fine. I was very proud of him."

I couldn't help reflecting on the irony that now rich parents were concerned about the dangers to their children's morals at public schools rather than comprehensives. Mind you, they were probably right. Certainly there was an endless supply of rich titled junkies prepared to make spectacles of themselves all over the tabloid newspapers.

Just then the phone rang. Priscilla got up to answer it.

"Hello?" she said. "Oh, hi, darling. Hold on a second."

She put her hand over the receiver and said to me, "It's John. Sorry, it might take a little time."

"I might just go to the toilet," I said, standing up.

"Oh, it's upstairs," she said, "first door on the left."

As I left the room I heard her say, "No, darling, it's Sam Jones, that sculptor friend of Alan's . . . no, I told you she was coming over this afternoon . . . so, how's Vienna? Everything going smoothly?"

I tripped up the lushly carpeted stairs and found the bathroom straight away. I didn't use it, though. If Priscilla was going to be on the phone for a while, I had time for a little snoop around.

Their bedroom was at the back of the house, a huge, beautiful room dominated by an oak bed with twisted, carved two-foot-high posts at each corner and an antique embroidered bedspread, which had probably cost a fortune. The bed was striking, but every time I see posts like that I wonder about the dangers of falling on them when you come home worse for wear and putting an eye out. I couldn't see Priscilla getting roaring drunk on too many margaritas, but there was that slight slurring of her speech that had made me wonder about prescription drugs instead.

I headed swiftly through the bedroom and into the en-suite bathroom, wanting to check out the medicine cabinet. For all I knew she had one of a whole range of diseases whose medication produced that kind of side effect, and I wouldn't recognise any of those drugs. Still, I was curious enough to want to have a snoop.

Paydirt. The bathroom was exquisite—a violet bathroom suite and cherrywood cupboards. And in the one over the toilet

I found a range of pill bottles that took even me aback. Prozac was the best known: but next to it were ones labelled Effexor, Paxil, Desyrel, Klonopin and Risperdal. Jesus. I was pretty sure that the first two were anti-depressants, but the others were new to me. I committed their names to memory and closed the cupboard door, wondering what the hell lay behind Priscilla Fitzwilliam's perfect façade. They were all hers: the cupboard was so full of feminine evidence—Tampax boxes, douches and a plastic case containing her cap—that I couldn't imagine John Fitzwilliam storing his pills in here. He was the kind of man who would definitely not relish looking at his wife's douches every time he reached for his Prozac.

Lying on a long upholstered bench at the foot of the bed was her handbag, half-open. I cocked my ears and heard her voice downstairs, talking on the phone. I had some time still. Yielding to my worst impulses, I rummaged through the bag, looking for further pill bottles. In an inner compartment were mini-containers of Prozac and Paxil, besides a few phials of homeo-pathic pills. I couldn't imagine the last standing a chance against all the prescription drugs raging through her bloodstream, but perhaps they made her feel a little less guilty about stuffing her-self full of all that artificial happiness.

Three devoré scarves, the shop labels still on them, were loose at the bottom of the bag. I couldn't help taking one out and running it through my fingers. It was soft and silky and so airy it felt as if you could pull it through a wedding ring; hadn't that been one of the tests for the delicacy of material, centuries ago? This kind of thing made one realise how shoddy the high-street knock-offs I bought were by comparison. Still, without a banker husband to supply me with a whole series of charge accounts, I would have to make do. I'd already turned down one banker husband, and I didn't imagine others would be crawling out of the woodwork any time soon.

I had been in here long enough. Casting a longing glance at the huge, silk-embroidered tapestry that hung over the bed—she really did have incredible taste—I arranged the handbag as I had found it and nipped into the toilet. I flushed the loo and emerged on to the landing to hear Priscilla saying, "No, no, it's a lovely surprise! Yes . . . yes, I'll book Odette's right now . . . oh, I'm sure we'll get in, John, we go there all the time . . . all right, darling . . ."

She was putting down the phone as I came back into the living room.

"John just called me from the car. He's about ten minutes' away," she said, sounding so unnaturally cheerful at the news that it was obvious his proximity was not as welcome as she had made it seem to him.

"I thought you said he was in Vienna," I said, picking up my glass. Imminent arrival of her husband or not, I was finishing my G and T.

"Yes, well . . ." She sighed. "He hates to be away from me for long. I think he must have cancelled some meetings to rush back."

"Wow," I said politely. "After all these years of marriage, that's pretty flattering."

"Yes . . ." she said automatically. "It's just . . . oh, I don't know, he's always been like this. And ever since he's retired he's been around the whole time. It's lovely, of course, and I feel so guilty even complaining . . . all my friends have to struggle to get their husbands to spend any time with them at all. They can't believe how keen John is to spend time with me. I know I'm very lucky. But I do like my space—and having him round the *whole* time is a big adjustment . . ."

Her voice trailed off. I bet she wouldn't have talked to me like this if she hadn't had two gin and tonics.

"I should ring the restaurant to book for dinner," she said. "Do you mind? And we were having such a nice time . . . I was thinking maybe you and I could just have strolled up the road and have dinner at that little Greek place on Regent's Park Road, I was going to ask if you were free . . . Oh well."

She picked up the phone again. Clearly, the number of the restaurant was on speed-dial because she just pressed one button and waited, the phone to her ear. As she charmed the restaurant into letting her make the reservation at such short notice, I heard her husband's key in the door. He came in, wearing a cashmere overcoat and unwinding a scarf from his neck, which, though very far from Alan's big stripy knitted one, made me think of his son with a renewed rush of attraction. Now that I had seen the photographs of John as a younger man I could see his resemblance to Alan much more strongly. Alan had had a lot of luck with his gene pool. Two better-looking parents would be hard to imagine.

"Sam!" he said, shaking my hand. "How nice to see you again. And very nice of you to keep Priscilla company while I'm away. I always worry that she'll be lonely while I'm off on these trips."

His grey hair was brushed back from his forehead, thick and gleaming silver. His shoulders were wide and his rugby-playing frame had not been overindulged after his years as a sportsman; his stomach still looked reasonably flat, his pectorals trim. The ideal City husband in late middle age, the wet dream of a million women married to corpulent stockbrokers who had eaten so many corporate meals that they had bellies down to their knees and saggier breasts than a mother of six. He crossed the room to embrace his wife, who was just finishing her phone call.

"Darling," he said, with such love in his voice that I couldn't help but be touched, even while I noticed how Priscilla, while not actually avoiding his hug, looked considerably less enthusiastic about it. She patted one of his hands rather as if it were the head of an overaffectionate Labrador whose excesses she was trying to restrain.

"I should be going," I said, putting down my glass.

"Well, thank you again for dropping by," John Fitzwilliam said, smiling at me, his arms still around his wife. "Do come and see us again."

I noticed how he had immediately taken over the social niceties, even though I was Priscilla's guest. Doubtless he did this all the time, without realising it. There wasn't anything truly proprietorial about his treatment of her; I had seen enough possessive husbands and boyfriends to recognise the signs. He just adored the hell out of her and wanted to look after her. Which was lovely, of course, but in a way it could be even more oppressive than overt jealousy because it gave Priscilla nothing to complain about. Just an overprotectiveness, which, if she didn't welcome it, probably made her feel as suffocated as if he was holding a pillow over her face.

I made my goodbyes to her and left. She led me into the hall, finally managing to detach herself from the circle of her husband's arms, and said as she opened the door, "It was so nice seeing you, Sam. You must come round again. Maybe when Alan's back in London."

"That's what I just said, darling!" John echoed, following her down the corridor and kissing her forehead before he took off his overcoat.

"Maybe we could have lunch," she suggested.

"I'll ring you," I said, waving goodbye and heading down the front steps.

As I drove away I felt a huge wave of identification with her which I knew, even as I recognised it, was completely unfair. Hugo didn't cling; he didn't hang on my every word and echo everything I said; he was away for long periods of time on location and didn't pester me with phone calls and unexpected returns that interfered with any plans I might have made. I had nothing to complain about, compared to Priscilla. And I still felt panicky at the thought of a relationship. Poor Priscilla. She had the perfect husband. And clearly it was such a strain that she was drowning in a sea of anti-depressants.

· · · · · · ·

My studio looked even more scummy by contrast with Priscilla Fitzwilliam's beautiful house. Jesus, even my skin, which was one of my primary assets, looked sallow next to hers. Whatever those pills were she was taking, they clearly didn't have the kind of side-effects that made you break out or put on weight. Rich women wouldn't pay through the nose for them if they did.

I had been so looking forward to getting back home. And now it was an anti-climax. The studio was actually relatively clean. I wasn't in the middle of a big work-cycle yet, which was always the worst time for my personal and domestic hygiene standards. The fridge wasn't too stained, the cooker wasn't thick with dried blobs of food, my tools were stored reasonably neatly instead of being strewn over the floor as if a giant hand had picked them up and dropped everything from a great height. My cockroach proto-type sat on the slab of wood I used as a coffee table, reminding me very much of a smaller version of the Thing, my first-ever suc-cessful sculpture, before I had realised that it was really a mobile. The Thing had squatted on the floor for months, loathing every minute of it; as soon as I had hoisted it up on a chain it came into its own and became positively benign. The cockroach was radiat-ing exactly the same negative energy the earthbound Thing had projected. I hate it here, it was saying. I want to move, god-dammit. Charge me up and let me race around the room.

I picked it up and stared it straight in its nasty buggy eyes. It looked just as sulky close up. Lifting it up wasn't enough; it wanted to shoot off under its own steam. I put it down again and gave it a push. It slithered along on its base for a few feet and then slid to a halt. Perhaps it was my imagination, but I thought it had a slightly less hostile attitude now.

Well, it was too late to do anything about it tonight. I was tired. I had all tomorrow and the morning of the next day before the cockroach inspectors came to call. And no Lurch. On my own with the creative process.

Weirdly enough, the thought steadied me. This was how I'd started, all alone in this studio. It was my base. Maybe, in the middle of all this horrible mess—best friend arrested, love life a shambles—getting back to work was exactly what I needed to ground me.

I knew I should ring Hugo. He had called Emma's a couple of times, and I had avoided him, not knowing what to say. I felt as if I was in limbo at the moment; talking to Hugo would force me to tell him what the current state of my emotions was and, since currently I had no idea what this might be, I knew it would only get me into even more trouble. The single, strong, clear desire I had right now was a fervent wish to bed Alan and sharing that with Hugo scarcely seemed the best tactic in the world.

Though he probably suspected my designs on Alan already. Hugo knew me too well. That was part of the problem. I wasn't used to being known, and as far as I was concerned the disadvantages outweighed the benefits. Everything seemed to be conspiring at the moment to make me feel trapped, and yet now I was back in my studio, the home I had fiercely defended against Hugo's wish to have me move in with him, it wasn't satisfying me as much as I had expected. I had thought I would come home, sink into my utterly tasteless vinyl sofa suite with smoked-glass corner tables, get a takeaway and crash out in front of the TV in utter, solitary bliss. But it wasn't working out that way. I stood in the middle of the huge room and turned around slowly, taking it in, feeling restless and unsatisfied.

A pressing need was squeezing at my bladder. All that coffee and gin at the Fitzwilliams', plus not really having been to the toilet there, was making itself felt. I crossed the studio and went into the bathroom, which I had lovingly installed with my own hands and a hell of a lot of trial and error. It too seemed shabby. There was a ring around the bath; there was always a ring around the bath, about which Hugo complained incessantly, and for the first time I took his point. It did look pretty sordid. The grouting was dirty and the mirror stained with a myriad droplets of spattered toothpaste and water, where I had washed my face in a hurry, or brushed my teeth while talking to Hugo and spat everywhere while making a particularly telling point. The memory of those moments called up a powerful, complicated nostalgia. I liked and hated the intimacy with equal force. Flushing the toilet, I noticed that it too, inevitably, needed a good going over with a toilet brush—which of course I didn't have—and a large quantity of bleach. I sighed, remembering Priscilla's pristine violet bathtub. Maybe I should get a cleaning lady. Then I couldn't believe I had thought that. What was I turning into, some bourgeois career girl who couldn't even be bothered to clean her own toilet?

I was utterly depressed and confused by now. I wandered back into the studio, zipping up my jeans, my head spinning unhappily. There was only one solution to this kind of mood: an Indian takeaway and a couple of ultra-violent Hong Kong–inspired action films. I went down to the Holloway Road and stocked up on both. But even Jet Li in *Romeo Must Die*—even his co-star, the godlike Russell Wong, an Asian Gregory Peck with an even better body—didn't manage to console me. Nor did the vodka. I had had plenty of bad crises before, but this one went deeper than I had ever known, and I hated it with every fibre of my being. Eventually, I fell asleep on the sofa, but even unconsciousness didn't help much. I dreamed confused, endlessly cutting film moments where Alan and Hugo and Priscilla jumped in and out of shot, none of us ever quite meeting, and for some reason I dreamed too that I was trying to pack my suitcases but kept remembering extra things I needed to fit in and couldn't find. It was about as comforting as being headbutted by Andy with the rest of the Lesser Swinfold rugby team following close behind.

15

IF YOU WANT TO KNOW ABOUT DRUGS, ASK AN ADDICT.
Ginny was actually what she would term a recovering one, but
her knowledge and contacts were still unrivalled. They had probably even been heightened by rehab; nothing like a group of
addicts sharing horror stories to expand your drug information
still further.

I used to score coke and speed off Ginny before her boyfriend
staged an intervention and packed her off to the country to
clean up. The boyfriend hadn't lasted—they usually don't, you
come out of rehab a very different person—and neither, sadly for
me, had her job as friendly local drug dealer. Now she was a legal
secretary, of all things.

Still, we had kept in touch, or rather bumped into each other
down the Holloway Road every so often. She lived not far
from me, and we kept making those vague promises about getting together, on which we never followed up. Ginny had
been clean for three years now and so was relatively relaxed
about meeting up with people she had known in her fast-living,
dealing days. I sensed that it would be OK to ring her with a
query about Priscilla Fitzwilliam's row of pill bottles, and so it
proved.

"Klonopin's anti-anxiety," she said immediately. "Lots of

junkies take it. Effexor and Paxil are anti-depressants. I don't know the others, but I can ask my shrink."

"Will she know?" I said dubiously.

"Oh yeah. It's a him, actually, but he's OK. And he's a psychiatrist, so he knows all about this kind of thing," she assured me. "It's really useful, actually. When I get prescribed something by the doctor I can always double-check with him in case it's got any narcotics. You know. I have to be really careful."

Ginny was hyper-alert to the dangers of getting hooked on any form of prescription drug. She was paranoid about ever having to have an operation; she had told me stories about ex-junkies who had cleaned up successfully but, after experiencing opiates again in the form of a general—or even local—anaesthetic, had promptly gone back on to smack. I knew that she made her GP check out the precise constituents of anything she was prescribed, but she had told me before she didn't think the GP took her seriously enough.

"Which is bloody ridiculous, considering we're in sodding *Holloway*," she had said at the time. "Every second person in the surgery has to be on something. I mean, how else could you live in this shit-hole?"

"Maybe you could ask him something," I suggested now. "Your shrink, I mean."

"Sure. What?"

"Just if he has any idea what someone might be taking this combination of stuff for."

Ginny sighed.

"Sam, you know, I think you should just bite on the bullet and ask your friend what's wrong with her," she said.

"I just want to get a better idea of what I'm dealing with first," I lied. "She's so nervous anyway. She used to have panic attacks for years. I don't want just to walk into a bad situation without any information."

"OK, that makes sense," she conceded. "Your friend's really lucky to have you."

I felt bad. Nothing new there.

"Do you want me to drop you in some NA information leaflets for her?" Ginny suggested. She was one of the prime movers in the local Narcotics Anonymous group and was always eager to spot new potential candidates.

"Uh, let me wait and see what the situation is first, OK? I don't want to spring everything on her at once."

"Sometimes that's the best way," Ginny said wisely. "Look at me. I woke up to find my entire family and my boyfriend standing round my bed. Did I tell you about that? I'd actually passed out with a needle in my arm and the blood had run down my forearm and into my hand. It was sort of pooled in there, like a cup. And I actually laughed when I saw it. It seemed like a perfect metaphor for something. I was still really out of it, and I hadn't even noticed all the people yet. God, it was rough. But it was exactly what I needed."

I had heard this story what felt like a million times before, and I hadn't even seen that much of Ginny. I wondered whether St. Paul had been this much of a bore about his own epiphany. "So, did I tell you yet about the revelation I had on the road, to Damascus? It was really amazing. I was just walking down the road, and suddenly I saw this blinding light and fell to my knees . . ."

You could just imagine all the Corinthians and Ephesians looking at their watches and muttering timeworn excuses: "Sounds fascinating, mate. Tell me all about it another time, OK? Got to run now. It's my turn to, um, pick up the kids from school."

"Well, I'll definitely bear that in mind," I said, just hoping that she wouldn't decide to drop off the NA leaflets. The last thing I needed in my emotionally debilitated state was a load of anti-drug propaganda asking me probing questions about my life. Drugs were about the only thing keeping me going right now.

"I'll call you as soon as I can," she promised. "Things don't sound too good for your friend. All these happy pills we take nowadays make me shiver, you know? I mean, that was never my thing, but I see a lot of people in meetings who were hooked on the anti-depressants for years, and it's one of the hardest things to get off. Society is totally fucked. They're just busy inventing more and more ways for us to lose touch with our own emotions. God, I should know. I lost myself for ten whole years."

I got off the phone as fast as I could. I agreed with everything Ginny said, but it was still boring as hell to have to hear her repeat it that earnestly. Nothing as heavy-going as a reformed sinner. Mind you, she never lectured me on my own drug use, for which I was heartily grateful. I always assumed it was because she knew I wasn't that much of a serious case—who better than your dealer to know that kind of thing?—but maybe it was just that she didn't think me worth saving.

I spent the rest of the day with my cockroach. As usual with work, the hardest part was getting myself started. I would do anything to put it off—apart from cleaning the studio. Still, once I was going it was pure fun. I turned the answering machine's volume control down to nil so I couldn't hear anyone leaving me messages and lost myself completely for hours. When I finally emerged some time that evening, I had one working prototype, plugged into its charger. I imagined a whole line of them, sucking on their electronic teats like a series of genetically mutated puppies, and felt a huge swell of pride. I really liked the little fucker. I hadn't felt like this about anything I'd made since the first Thing. It still needed work on its legs; they dangled down over its wheels, covering them successfully enough, but they moved too slackly. I knew that people wouldn't be bending down to examine them closely, but I still wanted them to look plausible enough to suspend disbelief. However, that was fine-tuning. And they made exactly the right clicketing noise on the floor, which I remembered all too well from my incarceration. That was what had given me the idea to make the cockroaches in the first place; I had been kidnapped and chained in a cellar with a group of the little monsters as my only regular companions.

I certainly had led a rich, full life. My friend and ex-lover Hawkins (the detective inspector I had met when someone was killed in the gym I'd been working in) kept suggesting stress counselling to me after every lurid episode in my increasingly violent progress through life, and I had always refused contemptuously. It was just possible, though, on contemplation of everything I had been through, that Hawkins might have a point. The very unworthy thought occurred to me that if I told Hugo I was going into some sort of delayed shock from the kidnap and needed counselling, he might cut me some slack while I, well, while I shagged Alan.

This was really bad. I was plumbing the moral depths, and I doubted I was anywhere near hitting bottom. And I pitied any therapist who got the short straw and had to attempt to untangle my twisted psyche. I had the instinct that by now it was such a Gordian knot that the only thing to do was cut through it and start all over again.

That, of course, was flattering myself. What I really couldn't bear to contemplate was that I might be a lot more obvious than I liked to think. The idea that I was more complex than one of those Raymond Chandler plots, where even the author doesn't know who committed all the murders, was the spar I clung to in my current emotional shipwreck. If a shrink tried to tell me that actually I was fucked up in a comparatively straightforward manner, I would go into so much denial that I would probably have to kill them.

That wouldn't be too much of a problem. I had seen enough dead bodies to have a pretty good idea of most of the effective methods.

Reluctantly, I checked the answering-machine messages. There were two hang-ups. I wondered if those were Hugo. I was so ambivalent about Hugo; I didn't want to talk to him, and yet I wanted him to want to talk to me. Classic dog-in-the-manger syndrome. I looked longingly over at my power tools. I felt under so much pressure that the temptation to drill a hole in the top of my head and let some air in was almost overpowering. Fortunately, the next message was from Tom, which proved a useful distraction.

"Sammy! It's me! I'm out on bail! Gail's been a genius! I feel so much better! You know, she actually doesn't believe I did it, which is such a relief—I mean, OK, she'd probably have done a good job anyway, but just knowing that my brief thinks I'm innocent is brilliant—I can't thank you enough for finding her. The coppers are taking her really seriously too—I think they were a bit funny at first, you know, her being a woman, we really are in the sticks down here, but then she put the fear of God into 'em and they really respect her now—I feel so much better! Anyway, ring me. I'm walking on Cloud Nine right now."

The last message was from Gail Christie herself. Solicitor as guardian angel.

"Sam? It's Gail Christie. Give me a ring. Tom's out on bail, as he's doubtless rung to tell you. I've got some good news and some bad news, but things are looking a little better than we thought. I'm still trying to remind Tom that he's under arrest for murder, though. I think being out is making him overoptimistic. Still, it's nice to see him in better spirits."

I noticed that her voice had softened perceptibly on the last sentence. Good. The more sympathy she had for Tom, the harder she'd work to get him off. Not that I had any doubts about her professionalism, but there was nothing like a personal motive to get someone to go that extra mile.

I looked at my watch. It was just past eleven. I tried Emma's number, but it was engaged. It was probably too late to ring Gail, who would have to be up for work at an unfeasibly early hour. I called her anyway. She sounded a little groggy.

"Oh, sorry," I said, "did I wake you up?"

"Yes. But since I'd fallen asleep on the sofa, that's all to the good. I'd have had a terrible crick in my neck tomorrow morning."

She yawned.

"You know what I really miss about London?" she said. "Good fast food. Or at least a Tesco Metro nearby. If I were still in London, my fridge would be stocked with sushi and taramosalata and vine leaves and ready-made salads and those baked potatoes with grated cheese you just bung into the microwave for thirty seconds. I can't bear cooking. I've just had toast and Marmite for dinner and even that was more time in the kitchen than I like to spend."

"Tom's a really good cook," I said, in an admittedly feeble attempt to prejudice her even more strongly towards her client. "You should get him to make dinner for you when this is all over."

"I should get him to do it for me now," Gail said. "This is when I need it. When I'm on a case like this, I can't think about anything else."

She yawned again.

"Right, I just gulped down the cold coffee I went to sleep in front of an hour ago," she said. "Lovely. Not. But at least I'm a bit more awake."

"You said you had good and bad news," I prompted.

"Oh yeah. It all comes together so I can't ask you which you'd rather hear first. I went and talked to Tamsin, Janine's sister-in-law. She's nice, isn't she? And she seems to have been practically the only one who was close to Janine. No real girl-friends, not even the other mothers at the primary school. Janine must have been a pretty unusual person. It's not easy to keep to yourself in a small village. Round here you're really expected to mix in, you know? Everyone knows your business, and you know theirs. If you don't play along with that, it doesn't go down too well."

"I'm shuddering."

"Yes, I know. But, speaking personally, I don't mind it that much. One of the things I wanted to get away from in London was the anonymity. Besides, the locals cut me more slack for being from London. They think I just don't know their ways. And my job gives me a bit of status, sets me aside. I know that's bizarre. It's a country thing, really. The doctor, the lawyer, the vet—no-one quite expects them to mingle in the same kind of way. But Janine was a local girl, so her being a bit aloof would've made them think she was giving herself airs. Anyway, I wasted a lot of time trudging round trying to find people who Janine might have confided in and drew a big blank. Apart from Tam-sin. But, finally, guess what popped out of the woodwork? A bloke who was after Janine last year. Young guy, about her age. Apparently, he was really pestering her."

"Like Tom. She seems to have attracted that," I said. "No, I don't actually mean attracted, that's really sexist. But—"

"I know what you mean. *Men*," she said with contempt. "When a woman just doesn't seem that interested they go crazy. Run after her with their tongues hanging out."

"Women do that too," I said to be fair.

"Yes, that's true." She sighed. "Sorry, bit of personal bitterness creeping in . . . Where was I? Oh yes, this guy. He's called Jamie Rickson. I got all excited by the idea of him as a nice juicy sus-pect. Unfortunately, it turns out he was on holiday with his mates. Club 18–30, shagging by the sea in Eilat over New Year. Rock-solid alibi. Probably put his crush on Janine right out of his head, though."

"Too busy being tied in a bag with some girl and thrown into the swimming pool with thirty seconds to get their swimsuits off to win a round of drinks."

"My God, is that what they do on those holidays? Thank God I'm too old to qualify. But, here's the good part, he told the coppers about the guy Janine was involved with."

I sat up straight.

"Janine was seeing someone?"

"Apparently. No names, no pack drill. But he was married, and she didn't want anyone to find out about him."

My heart was beating fast.

"Is this Pitt's father?" I asked.

"We don't know. But it's a good lead, isn't it? Or it will be, if we can track him down."

"Did the police take it seriously?"

She sighed again.

"I hope so. You know how it is. They've got Tom in the frame, and it's much more work for them to chase around digging up the mystery man. Still, it's a start. I mean, they'd have given him bail anyway, eventually, but that helped a lot. Emma did too, actually. Talk about middle-class respectability. She came tearing down to the station to swear blind Tom couldn't have had anything to do with killing Janine and made all kinds of threats about going to her local MP and raising a stink unless they released him at once. Social status is so important—well, I don't imagine I need to tell you that. If Tom'd been this bloke Jamie Rickson—bit of a loser, part-time labouring jobs, that kind of thing, heavy local accent—they'd have banged him up till kingdom come."

"How on earth did he know about Janine's boyfriend?" I said curiously. "I can't imagine she'd have told anyone about him, let alone some guy who was pestering her."

"Oh, that was really charming of him. He got Pitt on his side—bought the kid some of those nasty electronic games that go peep all the time and drive you crazy. Won the kid's confidence a bit. He wormed out of him that Pitt had heard Janine talking on the phone to someone. You know what kids are like, they can be pretty sharp about this kind of thing. Pitt'd never met the guy, never heard his name. But he could tell that Mummy liked him and he heard her making arrangements to meet him. There was a bit of 'Will you be able to get away from the wife?,' that kind of thing. Pitt didn't know what it meant, of course. But Jamie did."

"What a bugger that Jamie was on holiday," I said wistfully. "No chance that he hopped a plane back from Eilat when no-one was looking?"

"Nope. He was with some local boys. They confirmed he was with them all the time. Well, not all the time, of course, they were busy passing out in pools of their own vomit on the beach. But he wasn't missing for a whole day and night, which is what it'd've taken. Nowhere near it."

"And how d'you know all this?" I said. "I can't imagine Jamie confided in you as well as the coppers."

"Ways and means, darling," she said cheerfully. "I've been here long enough to have made some friends at the station. Naming no names, but there are a couple of ambitious girls working there who need to make a name for themselves to get out of Hicksville. It's not just I'll-scratch-your-back-you-scratch-mine, though that'd be good enough. But I was pretty well connected in London too, and I still know a lot of people. I haven't actually promised them good jobs at the Met, or anything like that, but I could put in a good word with some people I know. Every little helps."

"Nice one," I said approvingly.

"Thank you."

"I'm surprised Tamsin told you about this Jamie guy at all. I thought Lesser Swinfold had quite a big *omertà* thing going."

She laughed.

"She didn't. I really put the emotional screws on, and I could see she wanted to tell me something. She doesn't think Tom did it either. She couldn't say that in front of her nightmare husband, but she doesn't. Then, a couple of hours later, the nick gets an anonymous phone call from the payphone outside the primary school. Very sensible of Tamsin. If she'd told me herself, it would have got back to someone, and the Rickson family'd probably have been on her doorstep that evening with a can of petrol. They're nasty pieces of work, by all accounts."

"Tamsin's no fool," I observed.

"Absolutely."

"So are you anywhere near working out who Janine's married man was?"

A last, gusty sigh. Gail sounded more tired by the moment.

"Not even close. But, and this is a good lead, even if it's a bit tenuous—Jamie thought it was a local guy. His theory was that Janine wouldn't have been so careful not to name names on the phone, even if there was only Pitt in the house, if it was someone Pitt might have known. Or whose name he might have recognised."

"That's pretty perspicacious of Jamie."

"Not really. It's just basic local rules. You or I might not have thought of that. But down here, like I said, everyone knows each other's business. You've got to be tighter than—"

"A chorister's arse."

"Yeah. Tighter than a chorister's arse not to let something slip."

I wondered if Janine had said anything to Alan, anything more than he had told me. It sounded as if he had been her only confidant, if there had been no close women friends. I decided to make the drive back to Lesser Swinfold tomorrow, after my appointment with the cockroach inspectors. I could make sure no-one lynched Tom, try to nose around on the scent of Janine's mystery boyfriend and pump Alan. Jesus, that was an unfortunate turn of phrase

16

THE FIRST PEOPLE I SAW AS I DROVE INTO LESSER SWIN-
fold were Lurch and Alan, sitting on the latter's favourite bench
on the village green. They were unmistakable: both tall and
thin, Alan in his black overcoat and the stripy scarf, which for
some reason tore at my heart with tremendous tenderness, Lurch
in his signature donkey jacket, the fluorescent panels at the
shoulders smudged with black marker-pen graffiti. They both
waved at me. Perhaps it was just my fantasy, but Alan's wave
looked particularly eager. I parked the car at the edge of the
green—how nice to be in the country and find a space to park
straight away—and vaulted over the low stone wall in what I
knew perfectly well was a pathetic attempt to impress Alan with
my strength and agility. Actually, I landed in a bush on the other
side and had to drag my coat free in a swift tug to stop myself
looking like a complete prat. I heard something rip. Even though
it was my favourite leopard-skin Fifties coat, I didn't pause to
examine the damage. I just gritted my teeth and kept walking.

They were smoking a spliff. I was worried for a moment about
the safety of this—they couldn't have been in more public a
space—before reminding myself that any representatives of the
law in the vicinity would be hot on the trail of a killer right now,
with no time left to spare for rounding up any small-time pot-

smoking degenerates. Besides, Alan came from Lesser Swinfold, or at least was currently a resident, and must know what the limits of local tolerance would be.

"Hey!" Lurch said enthusiastically. "Sam! How'd it go with the Islington Arts people?"

"Oh, fine."

I thought it was sweet of him to even remember that my appointment had been this morning.

"They liked the roach?"

"Yup. I think I might have been overconcerned for their approval. I mean, I promised them a giant metal cockroach, and that's what they got. There wasn't much to say, actually. They went 'Oooh, Aaah, It's a Giant Metal Cockroach' a lot, and then we ran out of conversation about it."

Lurch grinned. His skin looked better, I noticed. Usually, when he smiled, all the acne joined up into large pink patches. Maybe Emma's healthy cooking was having a good effect. That and the clean country air.

"They freaked when it got close to them," I added, justifiably proud. "It was very satisfying. I've still got to do some work on the legs, but they didn't even notice that they weren't quite right yet."

"Heat sensors working, then?"

"Perfectly. I was really pleased. I can't wait to fill a room with them. That's the only test left, really, whether they'll bump into each other or not."

"They shouldn't," Lurch said reassuringly. "If the sensors're working, it should be OK."

"I know. But even if they do, it won't take that much sorting out."

I wrapped my coat around my bottom and sat on the bench between the two boys. Alan looked at me shyly for a moment and then ducked his head. Ah, bless.

"So what are you two up to?" I asked. "Having a good gossip? If you're dealing, Lurch, I have to tell you that a park bench on an otherwise deserted village green could scarcely be more conspicuous."

Alan laughed a little too loudly at my feeble joke.

"You're joking," Lurch said, handing Alan the joint. He knew I didn't smoke. I followed the movements of Alan's long white fingers as he grasped the spliff and raised it to his mouth.

"I've barely got enough for myself," he added. "Lucky Alan had a bit too."

"Oh, I'm sorry, did you want this?" Alan said to me, proffering the joint. He almost stuttered in his concern that he might have seemed rude.

"No thanks," I said. "Not my drug of choice."

Our eyes met, and for a moment I felt as if my gaze was physically locked to his. Twin electric shocks ran through me. I was definitely going to have to shag him, if only to get some perspective on what was happening between us.

"So what else d'you get up to in London?" Lurch said.

Uh, I went to nose around Alan's mum's house and snooped through her bag and medicine cabinet. I discarded this as an answer, opting for a simple, "Nothing much," instead.

"See Hugo?"

Beside me I felt Alan's whole body tense up, the spliff pausing on its journey to his mouth, ash dripping on to his coat, delicate dirty-white flakes sprinkling on to his lap like snow. He didn't even notice.

"No," I said shortly.

Now it was Lurch who stiffened up. Clearly, however, he made the decision not to discuss this with me in public. I was more grateful than I could say.

"How's Tom?" I asked, determined to change the subject.

"Oh, not too bad," Lurch said. "Pulling a bit of a hermit thing, though. He's not going out much except for work."

"They've let him back at the school?"

"Yeah. He got the union on to it. I don't think they was actually going to sack him, but the local shop steward had a word with the school and made sure it was OK. For now. Funny, though. Now he's out of the nick I think he'd've been grateful not to go back to work. He don't really want to see no-one, he's just holing up at Emma's."

"Well, I can understand that."

"I think he's doing the right thing," Alan volunteered. "Better to keep his head down till all this gets sorted out. If he was going out to the pub, being seen around like nothing was wrong, people might get worked up," he elaborated. "It's better just to keep out of sight for the moment. Otherwise well, you know what Andy's like. He's itching for a fight, and he's convinced Tom did it. If he sees Tom out drinking, it'd be like a red rag to a bull."

Lurch and I nodded understandingly.

"There's nothing much to do down here, you know," Alan continued, emboldened. "So it doesn't take much to set people off. You don't want Andy convincing everyone that Tom's getting off scot-free and getting up a posse of guys to administer a bit of rough justice."

This was exactly what I had been afraid of. In a perverse way it was gratifying to know that my lurid imaginings hadn't been that far off the mark.

"Yeah, we had that down my mum's estate," Lurch chipped in. "Bunch of mums got it into their heads that this bloke was a paedophile 'cos he hung out around the school playground a couple of times. They got a group together and stood outside his flat with banners, shouting, 'Pervo Out!' and stuff like that. Then they got the kids worked up, and some of 'em went round at night and chucked some burning rags through his letterbox. Whole place nearly went up. Charming, eh? I mean, this was a tower block. Whole place could've gone down. They was too young to work it out. Council had to rehouse him in the end."

"And was he?" I asked.

Lurch shook his head.

"Turned out he was a divorced dad just moved into the area so he could be closer to the kid. Wife wouldn't let him near the little girl 'cos she'd got a new bloke and didn't want the new one getting jealous."

"God," Alan said.

"I know. Worst thing was the kids. All them little faces screwed up with hate, shouting things they didn't even understand. Awful, it was."

"So the poor dad didn't even get to see his daughter?" I said.

"Nope. And you know the worst thing? Well, two worst things. First, they re'oused him, right, but everyone on the new place knew what'd happened and went, 'No smoke without fire.' So everyone thought he was a pervo and gave him the cold shoulder. And secondly, the wife's new bloke was a bit dodgy himself with the little ones. Reckon 'e was going out with her because he could get close to the little girl, y'know? Irony is, everyone knew that, really. But they picked on the husband 'cos he wasn't a local bloke. Easier target."

We sat in silence for a while. Lurch and Alan finished the joint, and Lurch concealed the roach in the thick grass under the bench.

"Tom should be getting back from school soon," Lurch said.

"I'll take my bag into Emma's and wait for him," I said. "I'm getting pretty cold."

"Yeah, I'll come in with you. Make a cup of tea. You want to come, mate?" Lurch said to Alan.

"I should really be getting some work done," he said reluctantly.

"See you in the Cow later?"

"OK."

Alan looked at me, obviously wanting to ask me along, but too shy to get the words out.

"I'll see you in the pub, then," I said, getting up.

He flushed with pleasure.

"OK," he mumbled.

"I think Alan's got a bit of a crush on you," Lurch said as we heaved my bag out of the van.

"Oh, really?" I said, trying to sound as if this was news to me.

"Yeah. He's really chatty when you're not around, but when you turn up, he shuts up like a clam and goes all pink when you say anything to him."

"Oh, you know," I said, aiming for light and airy. "Teenage boys."

"Oi, watch it. Alan's a year older than me."

"Yeah, but you're a man of the world, Lurch. Wise beyond your years."

He aimed a mock-punch at me.

"Watch it with the sarcasm, you. Just for that you can carry your own bag."

"I brought posh biscuits," I said.

"Oh, in that case—"

He hauled the bag off my shoulder and lifted it with one hand. Lurch was thin as a rake, but incredibly strong considering he smoked like a chimney and never did a stroke of exercise.

Emma's house was as warm and cosy as a cottage from a fairy tale after the cold outside. There was a fire burning in the living room, and Emma and Laura were curled up on the sofas in tranquil domesticity. Emma was embroidering what looked like a cushion cover in the tinest of cross-stitches, bifocals clamped to her nose. She looked genuinely pleased to see me, for which I was grateful. At least she didn't seem to think that I was treating her house like a hotel.

"Sam! Welcome back!" she said, smiling at me over the riot of colour on her lap. "How was London?"

"Good. Very productive. I stopped off at a deli and brought loads of biscuits and things."

"Oh, how nice. You didn't have to, though."

I shrugged, embarrassed as always by the niceties of social intercourse.

"That looks very pretty," I said of the embroidery.

She giggled like a naughty schoolgirl.

"I know. I found this site on the Internet that pirates crewel-work designs. Isn't it bad of me? I think it's a group of American women who've been swapping embroidery patterns between themselves for ages, and now they've put it on the Net. They cost an awful lot to buy, you know."

"Emma," I said in mock-disapproval. "That's totally illegal."

"Isn't it neat?" Laura chimed in. "I really like the idea of all these rebel housewives taking control of technology and doing down big business."

It wasn't that I disagreed with Laura; there was just something in the way she phrased things that got on my nerves. Or maybe it was Laura herself who got on my nerves. She was wearing a frayed old towelling dressing gown with the name of a hotel stitched in blue on the right breast, the lettering much faded. She or Ethan must have nicked it at least ten years ago for it to have reached such a state of shabbiness. Clearly, they had commenced their ligging careers comparatively early in life.

"We're going to have a cup of tea," I said. "Anyone want one?"

Just then the phone rang. Laura, to my surprise, dashed over to it, rather than leaving it for her hostess to answer.

"Hello?" she said eagerly. "Oh, hi, honey!"

The pleasure in her voice was unmistakable. It had to be Ethan.

"Yeah . . . Did it? It really went well? Oh, that's great!"

I raised my eyebrows at Emma.

"Ethan's in London, meeting that agent," she whispered. "It's very exciting."

"Has he sold his screenplay?"

Emma looked blank.

"Oh, great! So I'll see you later!" Laura was saying. "Love you, honey!"

She hung up and looked at us proudly.

"Ethan's meeting went really well!" she announced.

"Great!" Lurch said in a parody of her accent, which sailed right over her head.

"Oh." Her face fell. "Sam, you just drove here from London, right? What a shame Ethan didn't have your number! He could have kept you company and saved the train fare."

Fortunately for the serenity of the household, a distraction was provided just then by the front door opening, followed by the unmistakable noise of Tom entering a house. Crash, bang, big boots on the paved floor, large overcoat thudding on to a clothes hook. I ran out into the corridor to give him a hug.

"Hey, Sammy," he said into the top of my head.

I raised it to look at him. He wasn't at his best. Despite the cheerful message he had left on my machine, his eyes were lacklustre and his jowls heavy. His hair was sticking up in clumps and had lost its usual reddish tinge; it was dull and looked uncared for. I reached up and pinched his cheeks.

"You don't look great," I said familiarly.

"I'm out on bail," he said gloomily. "I was so excited to be out, at first it didn't really sink in. I was just going, 'Wey-hey, I'm free!' Gail kept telling me there'd be a come-down, and she was right. I feel like shit."

"How was school?"

"The teachers are treating me like a bit of a pariah, but I'll tell you what—no problems keeping discipline. All the kids are giving me huge amounts of respect. Apart from those nightmare brats of Andy's."

"Is Pitt in your class?"

"No. But I was on playground duty today, and he freaked every time he saw me. God knows what Andy's been telling those kids. I tell you, it won't be enough if they just drop the charges against me. I mean, they need to finger someone else or I'm dead in this town."

I thought this was being overoptimistic. Gail seemed pretty sure that if the police didn't have any other strong suspects, Tom was going to trial. Still, this was hardly the moment to bring that up.

"Cup of tea?" I said winningly. "And I brought really expensive chocolate biccies."

Even this prospect didn't abate Tom's bad mood. He mumbled something incoherent about not wanting company and went off upstairs to brood. I watched him go, feeling a frown crease into my forehead. I didn't like any of this, and Tom's reaction in particular was worrying me more than anything. There was a furtiveness about him that I had never seen before. I would have followed him up and shaken him ruthlessly if I hadn't been so worried about whatever it was he was hiding from me. I knew Tom too well not to be aware that he wasn't telling me the whole truth.

· · · · · · ·

"So look," I said to Alan, plonking the drinks on the table—G and T for me and a red wine for him—"we need to talk."

We had some privacy: Lurch had gone off to play darts with the local youth. A raucous game was in progress. I looked over briefly to see Ethan was hanging around by the dartboard. As I came in he had caught my eye and tipped an imaginary hat brim to me. It was a corny gesture, but he carried it off. When Laura wasn't around, he was definitely more flirtatious. I hadn't thought Ethan that attractive before, or maybe it had just been that he wasn't my type. But the cowboyish hat tipping and the crinkling up of those blue eyes were undeniably sexy.

Still, I had an example of my type sitting right in front of me, and right now he was looking petrified with fear.

"It's about Janine," I added quickly, in case the poor boy thought I was going to attempt a conversation about our snog in the middle of a crowded pub.

Probably he had. He seemed hugely relieved at the mention of Janine.

"What about her?" he said, picking up his wine glass.

"I can't believe you drink wine in a pub," I said irrelevantly.

"Oh, it's actually OK here," he said seriously. "Chrissie and Norman try to keep some decent wine because of the restaurant. And, you know, I come in here a lot. They've given up taking the piss out of me by now."

"Regular's privileges."

"Exactly."

"Ahem." I cleared my throat. "Janine."

"Oh, yeah."

He set down his glass and looked at me expectantly.

"This local guy who was after her—Jamie Rickson—"

"How did you know that?" He looked suitably impressed.

"Tom's solicitor ferreted it out."

"That's Jamie over there."

Alan indicated a young man in the group of dart players. He was tanned, in the classic British-man-on-holiday style, which was to say that his face was bright red and the skin around his eyes, which had been covered with sunglasses, considerably whiter. His nose and the back of his neck were peeling, which he doubtless exhibited as badges of pride along with his panda eyes. Involuntarily, I imagined him naked, the colour of a boiled lobster apart from his white, spotty behind. It was deeply unappealing. Jamie Rickson would have been unattractive in any circumstances, though. While not actually bad-looking, he was one of those young men who fancy themselves so much that their self-love sends out a force field as repellent as bad body odour.

"I can see why Janine didn't go for him," I observed.

"Yeah, she wouldn't touch him with a bargepole. The trouble was, the more she told him to piss off, the more he came after her. I think he thought she was playing hard to get."

"Very exhausting," I said, reaching for my glass.

"Yeah, she said it was pretty heavy going."

"Why didn't you tell me about Jamie Rickson before?" I said, trying and failing not to sound exasperated.

He looked blank.

"Well, I knew *Jamie* was away on holiday, so he couldn't have done it," he said fairly. "He's been showing everyone the photos. God, you should see them. It looked like a Roman orgy. Bodies piled up everywhere, bad wine, vomiting, the lot."

"Yes, but you never know what's going to turn out to be important," I said, still hearing that note of exasperation in my voice.

"How could *Jamie* be important?" Alan said incredulously.

I looked over at Jamie again. He was relating an anecdote to a group of his peers, who were listening eagerly. It wasn't hard to work out what was being described. Jamie's gestures, like those of any Englishman, were considerably more limited than any Italian or Frenchman in similiar circumstances, but there are some which are pretty much universal. Clearly, he was sharing with the boys a moment of romance under the stars—or possibly,

knowing Club 18–30's reputation—in broad daylight on a hotel balcony.

"I see he got laid in Eilat," I said.

Alan turned to glance at the knot of young men. Jamie was in the middle of a particularly graphic piece of pantomime. Either he had had sex with a porn star or he was exaggerating his lady love's dimensions somewhat. Alan, to his credit, didn't blush. He turned his back pointedly on the merry group of revellers, doing his best to look world-weary instead.

"So why should I have told you about Jamie?" he said, returning to the main subject under discussion.

"Because," I said patiently, "Jamie told the police that although he wasn't having an affair with Janine, someone else was. A married man." I stared at him narrowly. "You don't happen to have any idea who that could have been?"

Now he did blush. Gone was the Byronic cynicism. He ducked his head and stared at the floor and started playing with the ends of his scarf.

"Alan," I said earnestly, "you've got to tell me everything. Please. This helps, but it isn't enough. If we don't track this guy down, Tom's still in enormous trouble."

"I don't know who it was," he mumbled. "I'm sorry, I know I should have told someone. But I didn't want everyone to think—Jan wasn't a slut, you know? And because of Pitt, everyone was already so down on her. I thought if people knew she was seeing a married bloke that would be the last straw."

"But she's dead, Alan. Nothing you can say can affect her now. And what if it was this guy who killed her?"

He glanced up at me, his dark eyes wide and luminous.

"I don't know who it was," he said. "I really don't." Seeing how unsatisfied I was with this answer, he added, as if throwing me a bone, "But I'm pretty sure he was local."

"Didn't she give you any hint at all?" I said fretfully.

He shook his head.

"Well, think about it, OK?" I said crossly. "Maybe something else will pop out that you didn't tell me because you didn't think it was important."

I put a twist of sarcasm on these last few words, which wounded Alan to the quick.

"I'm sorry," he said rather hopelessly, finishing his wine. "I'm really sorry, Sam."

Guilt washed over me. Here I was putting pressure on Alan in the name of moral righteousness when just the day before yesterday I had been rifling through his mother's most private possessions. That wasn't even an exaggeration; I had handled her douche box. And I had rung Ginny before coming out to the pub. What she had told me had sent all manner of speculations about Priscilla Fitzwilliam spinning through my mind. I looked again at Priscilla's son. Would he still want to have sex with me if he knew how much I had been digging into his mother's private life?

The question was moot. I certainly wasn't going to tell him.

"Hey guys, how's it going?"

I looked up to see Ethan at my shoulder.

"Didn't want to interrupt you," he drawled knowingly. "Looked like you two were having a heavyish conversation."

He put a lot of spin on to this comment. I opened my mouth, but Alan got there first.

"We were talking about Janine," he said with hauteur.

"Oh. Yeah, right."

This didn't take Ethan down a peg; instead he smiled slightly, as if remembering a private joke.

"Tom still in the frame?" he said. "I hear you got him this hot-shot lawyer, Sam."

For some reason I didn't want to tell Ethan anything beyond the most basic information that he could have picked up in the pub from the local gossip.

"It's early days yet," I said primly. "The police are pursuing lots of lines of enquiry."

This had the intended, conversation-deadening effect, and we all fell silent.

"Hey, you just got back from London, yeah?" Ethan said.

"That's right."

Ethan hooked his thumbs into the belt loops of his jeans.

"I was there too today," he said nonchalantly. "For a meeting with my new agent. He's a bit of a hotshot too."

"Congratulations," said Alan enviously. "Did you sell your screenplay?"

"Oh, I've got lots of exciting projects in the works," Ethan said noncommittally, with the same little smile. God, he was annoying. He would have made a mystery out of what he had for breakfast.

"So if you're going back at all, let me know," Ethan said. "I'll be back in London for more meetings, and it'd be nice to have a lift."

"Great!" I said, not missing a beat. "The van's overdue for an oil change, and I need a couple of new tyres—how nice of you to offer!"

Ethan blinked. I thought this would be the last I would hear about giving either him or Laura a lift.

"Well, I'll catch you later," he said finally.

"Oh, are you going?" I said, hamming up the regret for Alan's benefit.

"Yeah," he said. "I have a date with my computer. It's writing time. Getting on for the witching hour. I always start work around midnight. Cup of coffee, couple of cigarettes, fire up the laptop and start creating."

He sketched a salute at us and ambled out of the pub.

"What a *wanker*," I said.

"He likes to make out he's more important than anyone else." Alan, owing to writerly rivalry, was more resentful. "That's another reason why nobody likes him much. All that cowboy posing. I mean, he and Laura come from New England. That's not exactly the wide-open plains, is it?"

I looked at Alan thoughtfully.

"Did you get the idea he was nursing some secret?" I said.

"No way." Alan shrugged impatiently. "He was just being enigmatic. Ethan wants everyone to think he's Clint Eastwood, it's all part of his act."

"OK," I said docilely. There was no point in arguing. I had many more things in mind to do with Alan, which would be much more fun than that.

17

"I HAVEN'T SEEN MY SHRINK YET," GINNY HAD SAID. "BUT I don't think I need to. For this, I mean, not generally."

I made a mmm'ing noise to encourage her to keep talking.

"I asked some NA people after yesterday's meeting. There was one woman who'd been on almost exactly the same set of stuff as your friend. I'm sorry, Sam, this isn't going to be brilliant news."

"What?" I said anxiously.

"Well, this woman—I can't give you her name, obviously— but she comes from a pretty posh background. That's one of the things I like about NA, it's such a social leveller. Anyway, she had a terrible marriage. Trophy wife kind of crap. Didn't love the husband, married him for security, unspoken agreement, he'd earn the money, she'd keep the house nice and look pretty, all that kind of thing. But when she hit the menopause, and the kids were at uni, he finally left her for a much younger woman he worked with."

"Trophy wife model number two," I said. "One for childbearing and one to show how modern he is, having a wife that goes out to work."

"Exactly. So this woman—the one in our group—went into total crisis. She was on the Effexor and Prozac anyway, but they didn't help much. She started shoplifting. Her shrink says it was

243

to humiliate the husband through her own humiliation, if that makes sense. And like she was seeing the shop as a sort of image of him, the one in control, with all the stuff, so she was getting one over on him like he got one over on her. Sort of having her revenge, taking back what she felt he'd stolen from her."

"Shoplifting," I echoed.

"Yeah. Does your friend fit that pattern?"

"Actually, no. She's got a trophy husband who's madly in love with her. Pretty possessive, in the nicest way possible."

"Then she's probably rebelling against his perfect image of her. 'Look, I'm not just your little doll, I've got problems too.' That does make sense, actually. This woman was talking about the whole façade-of-perfection thing, and how you can never actually satisfy that. You know, shops take your money but they never really give you what you want, because what you want you can't pay money for. You keep shopping and shopping, but you're never satisfied, so you start stealing to punish them for that. And you want to tear down the façade, but you don't know how, so you're hoping you get caught and someone else will help you do it."

"Wise words, Gin."

She sighed.

"Whatever it is, your friend should get help. And not from the person who's stuffing her full of prescription drugs. Do you know what Risperdal is? An anti-psychotic."

"Oh my God," I said, thinking immediately of Priscilla Fitz-william sitting in her lovely living room, in her black sweater and perfectly cut trousers, imagining her cracking one day and slaughtering her family with an axe.

"That doesn't actually mean that she's psychotic," Ginny said quickly. "Just that there's an awful lot of stuff down there that needs to come out."

"Jesus."

"I know. This woman said she had classic Stepford Wife syndrome. Herself, I mean."

I thought of how squalid my studio had seemed after Priscilla's beautiful house. Maybe I hadn't made such a bad life decision after all. I was shallow enough that this actually cheered me up. Someone else's pain—Sam's gain. I made a note to despise myself when I had time.

- - · · · · ·

"No, don't turn on the light—"

"Why not?"

"I'm shy—aaaah, shit!"

I had just knocked the lamp off the side table while fumbling for the switch. Alan crawled up me and hung off the arm of the sofa, examining the damage.

"Looks OK," he reported.

"Great," I said insincerely.

"But maybe I should just check to see if the shade's—"

"No. Shut up. Come here." I wriggled out from under him and managed, in a manoeuvre successfully executed only due to years of practice in writhing around on sofas, to flip myself on top of him instead without having to set foot to the ground for balance, even momentarily. Heh. Modesty Blaise might be able to break a bloke's neck using only her ankles, but I bet I could take her on a sofa any day. As it were.

I pinned Alan down beneath me and started kissing his neck. His eyes rolled up into his head and he moaned, the lampshade instantly forgotten. Men have such short attention spans. His lips were as full and sweet as cherries. I bit into them to make them redder. Then I had an ever better idea. Reaching down to the floor where he had propped his glass, I stuck my finger in it and moistened his lips with wine. Then I licked it off as slowly as I could bear. Alcohol and a good-looking young man—two of my favorite things. I never understood the priority Julie Andrews gave to schnitzels with noodles and brown paper packages tied up with string.

I started tracing the wine down his throat, following it with my tongue. Alan was bucking beneath me, his hands wound in my hair. Fervently I hoped that he wasn't getting so excited that all of this would be over before it had begun. I slowed myself down to help him out. This was never a problem with Hugo, who had near-tantric levels of self-control. Stop, no thinking about Hugo. Banned, banned, banned.

I consoled myself with the reflection that Alan was practically a teenager. If he did come too soon, I'd just give him five minutes and start him up again.

I had his shirt open now. His chest glimmered in the moonlight, his skin as white as a character from a fairy tale. Snow White's elder brother. Against his pale skin his nipples stood out like two tiny dark bites. I dabbed them with wine and kissed it off. He didn't like that so much. Some guys don't. Cross out one erogenous zone; that still left me a good ninety-nine to try for. I got down to the task with enthusiasm.

Alan had to dash upstairs for condoms after a while, which rather broke the moment.

"Come up too," he said urgently. "There's a spare room with a double bed—"

"No, it's sexier here," I said, sprawling lasciviously all over the sofa, moonlight pouring across my near-naked body. We were using condoms; we weren't going to mess up Priscilla's upholstery. "Hurry back."

Alan looked as if he was going to protest—probably the moonlight was too much illumination for him—but finally yielded reluctantly. He was shy. Oh well, I would just have to break him in a bit. What a debt of gratitude his subsequent women would owe me.

. . . .

I would almost have gone back to Emma's after our first bout if I hadn't been as drunk as a skunk and seriously dubious about my ability to find my way out of a paper bag, let alone across the green and into the right house. Alan was gratifyingly enthusiastic; the sex, once I worked out how to use the sofa to best advantage, had been, if not great, pretty good, and yet afterwards I had lain there, panting, pleasure swirling through me, my head on Alan's shoulder, and all I could think was that he smelt wrong. Not bad, just wrong. I was near enough his armpit to be able to verify my instincts at source. To me his sweat was thin and reedy, like the voice of a chorister in a fourth-rate church choir. Which meant that our chemistry was off. To someone else he might smell as rich as Napoleon brandy in a balloon glass, warmed by hands wrapped around it. Alan was wrong for me. Well, I hadn't needed the scent test to tell me that.

If it had been straightforward bad sex, I would have felt a lot easier. It would have sobered me up enough to reach for my clothes, pour some cold water over my head and head back to Emma's, on my hands and knees if necessary. But this was more complicated. I passed out, overloaded with confused sensations, and awoke a couple of hours later wrapped in Alan's arms, lying on the living-room floor, cold, cramped and with a stinking headache. I detached myself without waking him and managed to locate first the kitchen and then an upstairs bathroom, which contained, if not some Solpadeine, at least some aspirin.

I gazed at myself in the bathroom mirror. Despite the white overhead light, which in my current debilitated condition made me feel as if someone—Priscilla, probably, in revenge for my taking advantage of her son—was piercing my skull with laser beams,

I looked good. Of course I did. I had just had sex with a twenty-two-year-old. That was the irony. What had had such a flattering effect on me was precisely the thing I was now, to be honest, regretting. So if I kept having sex with Alan, I would look great but feel like crap. God, life really was full of tough decisions.

Alan entered the bathroom. He was wearing his boxers and looking a little delicate. Wordlessly, I filled a glass with tap water and handed it, together with two aspirin, to him. He swallowed them, his Adam's apple bobbing.

"Shall we go to bed?" he said. "I mean—"

I was fascinated to see that he was still capable of blushing, even after all the things that we had done to one another. No wonder he hadn't wanted the light on. He must have been the colour of a beetroot all the way through while we were actually doing it.

We tumbled on to the spare room bed, and of course we had sex again. Alan was twenty-two and could probably have kept it up all night, and I had its proven benefits for my complexion as an extra incentive. It was better the second time around; we took more time and spun things out till we were both near screaming with anticipation. We finally collapsed in a tangled heap of limbs, our nerve endings still so sensitive that we jumped as if electrocuted when the other one moved. This time had definitely been good. But the connection just wasn't there. Sometimes the sex takes you by surprise, for better or worse; something can explode between the two of you or, for all the eager anticipation, fizzle out when you're still only halfway through, leaving the two of you to go through the motions as quickly as possible and get the hell out of there. With Alan, there was nothing that dramatic. It was just sex, that was all. And I could get sex anywhere. Besides, we had less to say to each other now that we had bumped bodies than we had had before, which was always a bad sign.

I went to sleep again. I was still doing my best not to think about Hugo, but it was getting harder and harder. Particularly since Alan still smelt wrong.

- - - - - -

He was sleeping as soundly as an innocent child as I rolled myself off the bed, sliding my leg out from under his with the skill of long practice. His long dark lashes lay on his pale cheeks, fluttering slightly as his eyelids twitched, dreaming of God knew what. I watched him for a while, feasting my eyes. I was eager to go, but this would probably be the last time I'd see Alan naked and asleep and, for purely aesthetic reasons, I wanted to make the most of it. Despite his thinness, his belly was slightly rounded—I couldn't imagine Alan doing crunches—and as velvety soft as baby skin. Or, in fact, his penis. I leant down to stroke it. His belly, not his penis. That was curled up and sleeping as soundly as the rest of him. It would have been cruel to disturb it. God knew, it needed its rest.

Naked, and with a stomach considerably more rounded than Alan's, I slipped out of the room, closing the door behind me. I prowled down the corridor, looking for the master bedroom. It was at the far end, with a bow window overlooking the green, and an en-suite bathroom so large and luxurious that it made me reflect yet again on the parlous state of my own. I wasn't here to feel bad about my own life, however. Quite the contrary. I was snooping behind the façade of someone else's.

The bathroom cabinet was filled with the same array of pill bottles that I remembered from the Fitzwilliams' London house. That was only what I had been expecting. When you were on this kind of medication, you kept it well stocked. Priscilla would be very careful not to run out. I went back into the bedroom and, moving very quietly, opened one cupboard door after another.

The first thing that had occurred to me, when Ginny had mentioned shoplifting, had been those exquisite scarves in Priscilla's handbag. Three of them, the price tags still attached, but no bag from some expensive little boutique, and no tissue-paper wrapping. No receipt either, I was willing to bet. The thought should have occurred to me before. One scarf with a price tag might be plausible; she could have snatched it up from her drawer in a hurry, not having worn it yet and thus not having removed the tag and put it in her bag, meaning to wear it later. But three? That was when you stood next to a display table and flicked the top layer of scarves off it and into your open bag, all the while using your other hand to flick through the ones you weren't stealing, to cover what you were really doing. And if you looked like Priscilla Fitzwilliam, nobody would suspect you for a moment, because you obviously had enough money to buy yourself all the scarves your heart could ever desire.

Small items, like the scarves, were perfect. Jewellery, underwear, accessories. No security tags, because they were so heavy they would damage the delicate fabric. I wondered what else she stole. Of course, this was still only a theory; there was no hard-and-fast evidence for assuming that Priscilla was a shoplifter just because Ginny knew one who was taking the same medication. Still, there was no denying that the facts fitted together.

I stood looking at the contents of her cupboards. They lined an entire wall of the bedroom, fitted and built-in, with little overhead lights that came on when you opened the doors. It was like Ali Baba's cave. Shelves and shelves of cashmere sweaters and sequinned tops, racks of shoes that would slide forward if you pulled them lightly, revolving to bring each level forward in turn. Dresses and coats and jackets, many still in transparent rustling bags from the dry cleaner's, the rich fabrics gleaming dully under the lights. Suede and velvet and grosgrain and leather, a treasure trove for a fashion victim. And this was only their country house. Ninety per cent of these clothes were far too glamorous for Priscilla to wear in Lesser Swinfold; even if she and John went out to the occasional dinner with friends at a smart restaurant, most of this was far too London-smart to be appropriate. And Priscilla did dress appropriately. She wasn't a Russian gangster's wife, covered in diamonds and Valentino frills for dinner at home.

There was no actual evidence of shoplifting here, but I had scarcely expected to find that. Professionals had their foil-lined bags, through which the security tags wouldn't work, and their clippers for severing those electronic cords that run through the sleeves of expensive leather jackets. That wasn't Priscilla. If she stole, she did it out of a psychological, rather than financial, need; she would be impulse-driven, not coldly calculating. I remembered Ginny talking about the façade of perfection and how oppressive it could be. Should I have wondered about picture-perfect Priscilla as soon as I had met her? Maybe if she'd been more of a Stepford Wife, I would have done. If she'd had streaky blonde hair and too much carefully applied eye make-up and lots of gold jewellery and a big bright medicated smile . . .

But I was out of date. We weren't in the Eighties any longer; the era of shoulder-pads and gold jewellery was over. Modern Stepford wives wore cashmere lounging trousers and pashminas and carried witty little embroidered bags of the kind that I could see in front of me, stacked on shelf upon shelf, glinting like a pirate's booty. They didn't flaunt their husband's money. On the contrary, they bought clothes that proclaimed how much they had cost only to those in the know, other women who had priced that pashmina at Harvey Nichols and knew it cost enough to keep a family of four living below the poverty line in food for a couple of months. No wonder that the latest trend among the young, rebellious, cutting-edge fashionistas was in-your-face bad taste—cheap spangly tops, glittering 1970s handbags bought in Brick Lane market, tattered old denim skirts and teetering, deliberately vulgar slingbacks.

Poor Priscilla. I wondered if she'd ever worked. John certainly wouldn't have allowed her to after they were married; he needed his wife to be constantly on tap. Her decision, of course, her fault. I still felt sorry for her, though. Maybe I was maturing with age despite myself.

I closed the wardrobe doors, the little lights turning themselves off one by one like fashion fairies going to sleep, and left the bedroom. Whether Priscilla was a shoplifter or not, one thing was clear: she was at least addicted to shopping, well past the point of necessity and into the territory of pure obsession.

My clothes were in the usual sordid, scrunched-up pile in the living room. My bra had somehow ended up right across the room, hanging off an occasional table. I flashed back to its removal and couldn't for the life of me work out how it had got there; I had no memory of whirling it around my head and letting it fly, which would seem the only possible explanation for its location. At least I hadn't been dressed up the night before. Nothing worse than having to put on tights and high heels when your body's aching and all you want to do is pull on a pair of jeans and a comfortingly big sweater and crawl back home to your den.

Of all the walks home at dawn from the houses of one-night stands, this was the easiest. I cut across the green, the morning air damp and cool on my face. More than anything I would have liked to have a head completely clear and empty of anything except a running roll of highlights of last night's activities, but instead my damn brain kept spinning into another groove. Though Alan's inexperience had been completely charming for a one-night stand, it would have driven me mad in the long term. He was not a natural; he was going to have to work at various things, and I was too lazy, and too impatient, to teach him. I was much more likely just to knock his hand away and snarl that I would do it myself.

I had the best sex I had ever had in my life with my boyfriend; so what was I doing messing around with a pretty boy who didn't even have a bottom? This, incidentally, had been a major disappointment to me: Alan's back seemed to go straight down to his legs. He had been too bundled up in big sweaters and overcoats for me to realise this defect until I got his clothes off, and by then it was too late.

I missed Hugo. And not just his bottom, which was round, firm and perfectly formed, giving a girl something she could really get a grip on. I missed the way he smelt and the way he tasted and the way he made love to me, and right at this moment I felt a million miles away from him, as if we were separated by oceans. I didn't want to jump in my van, drive back to London and creep back into bed with him, a penitent returning to the fold. I didn't know what the hell I wanted, apart from all the mists in my head to clear. My main hope right now was that Lurch would be asleep and I wouldn't have to face an interrogation about where I had just been and what I had just done. I longed for my studio, where I could lock the door, unplug the phone and give myself some much-needed space. Instead, I was sharing a room with a stern young moralist who would give me hell if he woke up and caught me sneaking back into it at six in the morning looking, frankly, as if I had just been making the beast with two backs with someone who wasn't my boyfriend.

I never even made it to bed. Just as I was hanging up my coat in the hall, trying to arrange some of its folds behind the other coats so it didn't look too obviously hung on the peg hours later than everyone else's—strange how paranoid a lurking sense of guilt can make you—I heard a slight rustle from the living room. I froze, assuming it was Lurch, who had stayed up in order to confront me as I finally rolled back in from my night of sin. How self-obsessed I was right now.

I looked in, but could see nothing. My instincts immediately went on full alert. Now I was imagining someone lying in wait for me, with motives much worse than moral disapproval. I swivelled to put my back to the coat rack, judging the distance to the door. My hand was already on the lock, the other one reaching out for the torch that hung on a peg beside the rack. My head was screaming with hangover, exhaustion and guilt. I wasn't in a fit state to fight a murderer. At the first sign of trouble I would yell my head off, whack them with the torch and run out of the house as fast as my sex-weakened legs would carry me. One of the reasons I had survived this long through a series of violent encounters with people trying to kill me was my highly evolved sense of self-preservation. No false heroics for me.

The rustle came again. It didn't sound menacing, and it certainly wasn't getting any closer. Warily, grabbing the torch as I went, I stepped through into the living room and surveyed the territory. The noise had come from the back of the room, and as I looked over to the far wall I found its source.

It was Laura. I recognised her from the flaming red hair and the dressing gown she was wearing, the old towelling one so faded by now that its original pale blue was barely noticeable. I couldn't see her face; she was curled up in a ball a few feet from the back door, back to the wall, head buried between her knees, rocking to and fro with such a tiny movement it was almost imperceptible. For one craven moment I wanted to pretend I hadn't noticed her, turn on my heel and go upstairs to bed. I really didn't have the energy to deal with some hippy throwing a crisis at six in the morning.

My better instincts prevailed. No, that's a lie. I was curious.

"Laura?" I said, putting down the torch on the coffee table. "What is it?"

She looked up at the sound of my voice. The pale white light of dawn filtered in through the fanlight over the back door, illuminating her face. Her reddish curls were tangled and matted around her forehead, her eyes blurry and unfocused, shot through with red as if she had just rubbed them. The circles under her eyes were as dark as fresh bruises.

"Sam," she said dully.

I didn't respond. There was something so ominous about the tone of her voice that I just stood there, waiting. A sensation of guilt washed over me so strongly that I almost felt as if I had committed whatever action had reduced Laura to this state. I was feeling bad enough to have taken responsibility for anything right then, up to and including original sin.

Laura stared at me as if she was seeing me for the first time, her eyes actually focusing on me rather than looking past me into the distance as they usually did. It was very uncomfortable. Maybe that was due to my bruised and bleeding conscience. I had already decided that it must be something Ethan had done that had upset her so deeply; nobody else was remotely close enough to her to affect her this way. For a second I had the idea that Ethan hadn't come home last night, and Laura thought I had been shagging him. I was on the verge of blurting out that I had been with Alan instead. I bit back the words, realising that I must still be drunk if I could even have contemplated telling her that.

"Laura," I said, trying to sound gentle. It was an uphill struggle. "What *is* it? Why don't you go to bed?" And finally: "Where's Ethan?"

That did it. Tears started falling from her eyes. She wasn't actively crying; not a muscle on her face moved. But her eyes were overflowing silently, as if someone was pouring water into a pair of blue china bowls till it streamed out over the rims.

She made no move to brush the tears away.

"What's he *done?*" I said impatiently.

She unwrapped her hands from around her knees and pressed them to the floor. It took me a moment to realise that she was

trying to stand up. I reached her in a few strides and hauled
her up.

"Jesus!" I said. "Your hands are freezing! How long have you
been sitting there?"

It must have been a while. She could hardly get to her feet,
her limbs were so cramped and stiff. I steadied her till she got her
balance. Her entire body was cold; there was a draught under the
back door, and she had been sitting right in its path. I was beginning to have a bad feeling about this. Probably I was slow on the
uptake. But six in the morning never finds me at my sharpest, let
alone under these circumstances.

Laura reached up one cold damp hand and shoved the damp,
slightly sweaty red curls back from her forehead. She still hadn't
said a word. It was most unnerving. I had the impulse to go back
to the coffee table and pick up the torch again.

But she was turning away from me now to the back door,
which she was opening. It hadn't even been bolted. That was
very odd.

"Laura?" I said. "What are you doing?"

She didn't look around, just walked out of the door. I followed
her. What else could I do? Outside it was icy cold. My breath
came out in puffs of smoke, white wisps of air testifying to what,
in my debilitated state, felt like a sub-zero temperature. Laura's
slippered feet slid on the cobbles as she crossed to the little outhouse that she used as a studio. It was hardly more than a shack,
used for storing garden furniture, but it had a couple of cob-
webbed windows and a skylight, which gave Laura the minimum
of light to paint by. The door was unlocked. She pushed it open.

The shed boasted a gas heater which ran off a cylinder, but it
wasn't turned on. A faint smell of gas hung in the air, unpleasant, but not strong enough to make my head spin. I couldn't
imagine how anyone could stay in this cold unless they had
fainted from hypothermia. Yet Ethan had gone to sleep on the

table, his arms sprawled over its surface. It looked as if he had been writing; a laptop computer—state of the art, Ethan hadn't skimped on his work necessities—open in front of him. Above his head a screensaver of tropical fish flickered eerily.

Laura went over to him, her slippers padding on the wooden floor. She touched his shoulder, looking at me, as if she were showing me something. Ethan didn't react. She pushed him harder. A strange sound came from her mouth, like a long, stifled moan. She rocked at his body again, and suddenly it fell back into the chair, his head lolling into thin air, his arms coming up grotesquely rigid, maintaining the shape that they had been on the table. It looked as if he were doing a one-man Mexican wave.

A faint little thread of white breath issued from Laura's mouth, as if she had said something so quietly that I had been unable to hear the word. It hung in the air for a moment, then faded. She went absolutely still, staring down at Ethan's body, almost as rigid as he was. I went over to feel for a pulse, but I was going through the motions. We both knew perfectly well that Ethan was dead.

18

IT WILL COME AS NO SURPRISE TO ANYONE WHO KNOWS me that this was not the first time I had stumbled across a dead body. Sometimes I had found them alone, sometimes I had been in company—I like to vary my routine. But in all my encounters with fresh corpses, I had never had a co-discoverer react the way Laura did to Ethan's body. People had screamed or tossed their cookies. Once everyone thought I had caused the death, which I had naturally not taken well. But no-one had ever stood there with tears running down her face and said, in a low quiet voice, "I found him like this. It must have been his time. I just hope he went peacefully."

I did not react with the tact and sensitivity that would have been appropriate under the circumstances. Instead I snapped, "Went peacefully? For God's sake, Laura, he's been murdered!"

She turned to stare at me, her expression more far away than ever.

"How do you know?" she said, her voice no more than faintly puzzled.

Why was I always cast as the crass, obvious one in this kind of situation? Wordlessly, I pointed to Ethan's back. He was wearing a dark, fleecy jacket, and it had taken me a moment to see the huge gaping hole in his back, dense with dark clotted blood. The back

of the chair was low. I assumed that someone had come up on
him from behind and stabbed him over the top as he sat writing.

Why hadn't he turned around, even unsuspiciously, to see
who was coming into the shed? My eye fell on a portable CD
player, a chunky black plastic thing as spattered with paint as if
it had spent its entire life on a series of building sites, and I
thought I had my answer. Ethan had been playing music. If the
heater had been on, hissing gas, and a CD playing, the sound of
the door opening would have been negligible. In rubber-soled
shoes it would have been easy to sneak up on him. And if he had
made any noise, the music might have drowned that too.

That was one solution. The other, of course, was that whoever entered had been so well known to Ethan that he hadn't
even turned around to greet them. Someone who could walk in
saying, "Hey, it's me, don't let me disturb you," and stab him as
he sat there hunched over the computer.

Laura was staring at the stab wound. She made a tiny whim-
pering sound and brought her hands up in a gesture, which could
have been anything: denial, protest, an attempt to hide her face
from the brutal reality of the sight in front of her. Her arms fell
back almost immediately, hanging limply. She just stood there,
staring at Ethan, her expression hardly altering.

"When did you find him?" I said.

"I don't know," she said, her voice whispery. "Maybe an hour
ago. It was getting light."

"And you just—I mean, did you do anything, touch anything—"

She shook her head.

"I woke up and he wasn't there," she said. "He always wrote at
night, but never that late. So that was really weird. I slept like
the dead—I had a glass of wine with Emma and Tom, and it
really knocked me out, so I woke up feeling funny, and I freaked

out that Ethan wasn't in bed. I came downstairs to see if he was still in the shed—I thought he might have watched some late-night TV and fallen asleep on the couch or something. But as soon as I touched him I knew, I knew he was dead—" Her voice broke. "Then I don't remember much of anything. I think I must have run out of there and come back in the house, but I don't even remember that . . ."

I waited, but Laura had told me all she was going to say.

"We've got to call the police," I said finally.

For some reason I didn't want to touch her. Someone more filled with the milk of human kindness would probably have hugged her, or at least put an arm around her and escorted her gently out of the shed. But I couldn't. Something about her reaction had unsettled me too much. I stepped back, indicating the open door, wanting her to precede me out, and as I did so I noticed a pruning knife lying on the wide waist-high toolshelf that ran along one wall of the shed. The rest of the tools were stacked and ordered with the neatness I would expect from Emma, ranked in order of size and function, trowels and clippers and carefully wound balls of twine. But the pruning knife was right on the end, as if thrown down in a hurry, which had attracted my attention to it.

The blade, with a nasty downward curve that must have made it perfect for its most recent task, was thick with Ethan's blood. Oddly enough, it was exactly the colour of my toenail varnish. Only that was called Black Cherry. Coagulated Blood would probably have been too long to fit on the label.

· · ✦ · ✦ ✦ ✦

I would have coped much better with the situation if I had had a full night's sleep, a decent breakfast inside me and no traces of a hangover. Despite my hugely ambivalent feelings about having just shagged the living daylights out of Alan, I still wanted to bask in the afterglow, lie down somewhere quietly and replay the highlights. Instead I had to rouse Emma, Tom and Lurch out of bed, keep an eye on Laura to make sure she didn't go back to the shed and start messing with the crime scene—I didn't know why I had that instinct, but I wouldn't let her out of my sight—and marshal us all down to the living room to wait for the police.

We were not a pretty sight. Tom, in his pyjamas and flannel dressing gown, looked like a teddy bear who had just been informed that Mummy and Daddy Bear, together with all the other bear siblings, had just been wiped out by a freak logging accident. Emma, poor thing, seemed completely unable to believe that this latest horror had actually happened in her house. She had made an attempt to brush her hair and pull on a pair of jeans, the unfashionable peg-legged kind with elasticated waists advertised in the back of the Sunday colour supplements. Over it she had pulled a big hand-knitted sweater whose bright colours gave her by contrast a grey-smudged pallor. Her skin looked the colour and texture of used chewing gum, dirty from much handling. And Lurch, as the crowning touch, was wearing novelty pyjamas adorned with big black arrows and lettering reading "Property of Kansas State Prisons Dept." on the back. We were all too shocked and exhausted to make a single joke about those pyjamas during the interminable wait for the police.

Laura sat in an armchair, slightly apart from the rest of us; she had stopped crying and was rocking back and forth, arms wrapped around her knees, just as she had been when I had found her. Emma had made an effort to comfort her, but she had been unusually clumsy; her normal motherly instincts seemed completely off. Laura had stared right through her with those glassy bloodshot blue eyes and behaved as if Emma wasn't even there.

"What did you do last night?" I said finally, breaking the silence. "Did anyone hear anything?"

I was desperate to find out if Tom had anything resembling an alibi; if he had gone to bed early, with no-one to testify to his whereabouts, I would really feel like taking another pruning knife and sticking it in my eye out of sheer frustration. It was too much to bear. Tom was just out on bail; why couldn't someone have stabbed Ethan while Tom was still in custody and a proud possessor of one of the most air-tight alibis known to humanity?

Various answers to this question, all too unpleasant to contemplate, filled my brain. I realised I still had no idea who had killed Janine, let alone Ethan. A wave of absolute weariness swept over me. I wanted to bury my face in the sofa cushions and howl like a dog.

"Well, we just stayed in, didn't we?" Emma said, looking at Tom. "Tom didn't want to go out, so we watched TV till late."

"Till late?" I said, perking up a bit. Ethan looked as if he had been dead for quite some time. Rigor mortis, blood thoroughly clotted. Of course, the cold in the shed would make it more difficult to determine the time of death. If he had been killed just after he got back from the pub—he must have left about ten— and if when Emma said late, she meant really late—

"What time was that?" I asked. "I mean, just wondering if Ethan had got back before you went to bed."

"Oh yes," she said. "He came in when the film was just starting, didn't he, Tom?"

Tom shook his head slowly. I knew this gesture; it wasn't denial. His brain was still thick with sleep, and he was trying to clear his head.

"I think so," he said slowly. His voice sounded heavy, almost slurred. He must have slept like the dead, his first night back in his own bed. "I don't really remember, though. I was so tired, I dozed off a couple of times, I think. I can hardly even remember watching the film."

"Well, I remember," Emma said, as briskly as someone who has just been pulled out of her bed at six-thirty in the morning can. "Let me check . . ." She reached for yesterday's paper on the coffee table, still open at the TV listings page. "The film started at ten, so Ethan must have come in at about quarter past. He said he was going to do some writing and went straight out of the back door to the shed. Laura, were you there, dear? No, you'd already gone to bed, hadn't you?"

Laura didn't react to the mention of her name. Emma shot a nervous glance at her and decided not to repeat the question.

"Did you two go to bed when the film finished?" I asked. "What was it?"

"A James Bond," she said. "*Moonraker.*"

"That's the one with the chase scene in Venice, innit?" Lurch said. "That boat that goes up into the big square with all the pigeons. Excellent."

Emma nodded absently. "And then we watched the late-night news. Tom wanted to see the football results. We can't have gone to bed before one."

Good, I thought. If Ethan had been killed before then, Tom was in the clear.

"Besides," Emma added, "I stayed up for another hour or so. I'm not sleeping very well these days, with all the . . . well . . . and now this has happened . . ." She cast a sidelong glance at Laura, who seemed oblivious to the subject under discussion. "Tom's room is just below mine and his door creaks terribly. I'm sure I would have heard if he'd left it."

Emma had understood immediately what I had been getting at. I relaxed slightly. At least Tom had some sort of alibi.

I couldn't ask her if Laura's room also had a squeaky door. Would Emma have heard Laura going downstairs? Laura couldn't have had access to the shed before Emma and Tom went to bed; the living room had a view of both the back and front doors. Unless she had shinned down a drainpipe and climbed back up the same way, Laura had an alibi until their bedtime. After that, however, was anyone's guess.

Just then a creaking noise came from upstairs, so on cue that we all jumped. A door was opening. Footsteps padded across the hallway and stopped for a moment at the head of the stairs. The natural thing would have been for one of us to call out and ask who was there, but we all sat paralysed for a moment, staring wildly at each other. Then, in unison, our heads turned to stare at the ceiling, as if we were trying to see through it. Wild speculations ran through my mind. Had the murderer, unable for some reason to escape after killing Ethan, holed up in the house, and were they now trying to make their escape? But how could they have failed to hear the racket I had made waking everyone up? How could they think they could leave the house without being seen?

The footsteps started down the stairs. The feet were unshod; it sounded as if the person was wearing slippers, or was carrying their shoes in their hand to avoid making too much noise. My heart was racing. I imagined a murderer appearing in the hallway, having decided that the only way to escape was—what? I was being ridiculous. To shoot us all with an AK-47? There were four people in the living room; we were far too many witnesses to eliminate easily.

A body hove into view, obscured for a moment by the high banister rail before it rounded the corner and emerged into the living room. The irony was that she seemed just as shocked at the sight of us as we were to see her.

"*Sheila?*" Emma said in utter disbelief. "What are you doing here?"

Sheila's appearance was so incongruous that it momentarily made me forget to speculate about this myself. She was wearing a quilted satin dressing gown with fake fur trim at the wrists. Enormous padded slippers with bunny ears peeked out below the hem. I had never seen her face bare of make-up before; without the heavy eyeliner and foundation, she looked literally wiped out, as if her face was only a rough, smudged, clay model waiting for the features to be sculpted in. Her eyes, without the emphasis, seemed tiny, the lids sagging. She had brushed her hair, however, and the contrast of the comparatively groomed coiffure and her naked face was painful.

"What am I doing here?" she said. "What on earth are you all doing sitting in the living room at dawn looking like the wrath of God?"

I thought the wrath of God crack was pretty rich coming from a woman who didn't have eyes until she painted them in.

"Sheila," Emma said in anguish.

"Well, what's going on?" Sheila was positively accusatory. "I heard everyone shouting upstairs, but it took me ages to wake up."

"I didn't even know we were expecting you!" her sister said more feebly.

Sheila shrugged. "I drove down last night from London on impulse. I felt like a couple of days in the country."

One had to admire the way she didn't even pay lipservice to the idea that she might have wanted to see her sister.

"When I got in," she added, "everyone was asleep, so I just went up to the spare bedroom. Since they're in the room I usually have."

She glared at Laura, who whimpered. We all knew that this was because Sheila had referred to Ethan; all of us except Sheila, who took it as an indication that Laura's conscience was playing up.

"Well, if you feel badly about it, you can always move rooms," she snapped.

"Sheila," Emma said for the third time. She sounded unutterably tired. Partly because of the crisis on her hands, partly because she had barely had five hours' sleep, but mostly, I thought, she was simply weary of her sister's dramatics. "Someone's killed Ethan. We're waiting for the police."

"Tom killed him," Laura said, her voice flat.

We all jumped and turned to look at her.

"What?" Sheila sounded as if she thought we were playing a bizarre practical joke.

"Tom killed Ethan," Laura repeated.

Tom made a convulsive movement. I looked over at him. He had sunk his head in his hands.

"Why do you think that?" I said carefully to Laura.

"Because I know," she said.

"Did you see him?" I asked as neutrally as I could.

"Of course she didn't!" Emma said indignantly. "Because he didn't do it!"

She leant over and stroked Tom's shoulder.

"Everyone will think it was me," he wailed through his hands. "Everyone's going to think it was me!"

"No, they won't," Emma said reassuringly. "You were with me. You couldn't have done it. I'll make sure they know."

"Laura?" I said nervously.

"He killed Janine, and he killed Ethan," Laura repeated, staring into space.

"Oh, *Laura!*" Emma had reached the end of her tether. "Stop saying that! It's not true!"

"Have you got any proof, Laura?" I said, unable to let this alone. "Did Ethan tell you anything? I mean, do you know anything concrete to tell the police?"

"I just know," she said.

"There, you see?" Tom said bitterly, raising his head. "She 'just knows.' The whole of Lesser Swinford is going to 'just know.' I might as well turn myself in right now."

"Tom . . ." Emma pleaded. "Please calm down. Laura's so upset she doesn't know what she's saying—"

Sheila made a humphing noise.

"God knows why you care what *she* says anyway," she said, tilting her head towards Laura. "She's always had one screw loose. I mean, she's scarcely representative of village opinion, is she?"

Though this was callous in the extreme, considering that Laura's boyfriend had just been killed, Sheila's matter-of-factness was very welcome.

"What time did you get in last night?" I asked her.

Sheila turned to look at me.

"About two," she said.

"And you didn't see anything unusual?"

"What, mad murderers creeping through the house? Of course I didn't! I just poured myself a drink and went up to bed! I've hardly had any sleep, and I'm completely exhausted!"

The doorbell rang.

"That'll be the police," I said, identifying all too strongly with Sheila's last sentence. How many times had I had occasion to use those words in my life? I was a magnet for trouble. If I were a mutant superhero, my power would be finding dead bodies.

- - - ⋅ ⋅ ⋅ ⋅ -

The superbly competent Gail Christie made sure that the police didn't immediately lock Tom back up in custody and throw away the key. Emma's testimony helped, as had her efforts on Tom's behalf before. None of this would have sufficed, of course, if the pathologist hadn't given her preliminary opinion that Ethan had been killed well before one in the morning. They hadn't had time to do the autopsy yet, so we were waiting for the results. But Gail's well-placed connections in the local police force had informed her that the pathologist took one look at Ethan's advanced state of rigor and announced her conviction that he must have been killed shortly after his return from the pub. It was always much more difficult to establish a time of death than detective novels, for the purposes of alibi construction, proclaimed it to be. But there was more than enough doubt for Gail to work her magic on a reluctant investigating officer. Tom was still charged with Janine's death, but so far Ethan's had not been added to the tally. So far. I was sure they were champing at the bit to find any evidence they could scrape up that would enable them to pin that on him as well.

A complete lack of any motive was a help too. But only up to a point, since that went for everyone else who could have conceivably been considered a suspect. No-one seemed to have the faintest idea why Ethan should have been murdered. I was thoroughly grateful to Emma for having stayed up to keep Tom company the night before. Particularly as Tom had told me that he had been so exhausted that he had nodded off several times during the film. What if he had been alone, and the murderer had sneaked into the living room to plant the bloody knife on him, for instance? I shuddered at the thought.

I had hated myself for having the least suspicion of Tom. When I thought about it calmly, it was impossible for me to imagine Tom even hitting a woman, let alone smashing her face in with a toolbox. Admittedly, I had seen him get into fights on a couple of occasions, but both those times had been with men at least his own size. And that had been a while ago, in his hellraising, penniless-young-poet-about-town salad days. I didn't really think he might have killed Janine. I just wished he would stop being so damn furtive with me. He was pretty much avoiding me; I had tried to talk to him, but he had withdrawn into a state of depression that was scaring me. He spent most of the time in his bedroom, where he had rigged up a small television. It was very worrying.

Laura, meanwhile, was resisting any attempt by Emma to be seen by a doctor. Sheila thought she needed anti-depressants; Emma favoured counselling. My solution would have been to get her drunk enough so she could have a proper cry, but no-one was listening to me.

Unlike most people, I myself had an alibi of sorts, embarrassing as it was. And so did my partner in crime. I had rung Alan, and, in a highly loaded phone conversation, had informed him of the situation and impressed on him that the official version of last night's events was that we had gone back to his parents' house after the pub and kept drinking till we passed out. Recounting that story to the police made me feel like a badly behaved teenager. I had not enjoyed it.

Still, we were officially in the clear. Technically, neither of us could alibi the other for those post-coital portions of time in which we had been passed out in alcoholic stupors. But, I remembered how debilitated I had been last night. And I was much more used to that kind of thing. If Alan had managed to put his clothes on, cross the green, stab Ethan, return and have sex with me again, he deserved an endurance medal on the level of a triathlon competitor.

It was a relief to have crossed Alan off the suspects list, and not just for the obvious reason. Right now I was suspecting almost everyone; it was nice to narrow the field, even by one. I decided to try talking to Tamsin again. She had known about Jamie Rickson, the sunburnt young man with the panda eyes who had been pestering Janine. Maybe she had some idea about who Janine's married lover had been. It was a tenuous possibility, but it was all I had to go on. And I badly needed to keep busy. The more I threw myself into trying to find out who had killed Janine and Ethan, the less time I had to contemplate how thoroughly I was quite literally fucking up what passed, by my admittedly immature standards, for my love life.

· · · · · · ·

My plan was cunning, but perfect in its simplicity. I hid around the corner of the school lane at an obscenely early hour of the morning—yet another reason never to have children—until the mothers of Dunster Magna, Lesser Swinfold and various other quaintly named villages had dropped off their brightly anoraked and rucksacked brats. Then I came ambling out, past the school gates, and executed what I hoped was a convincing double-take at the sight of Tamsin. Luckily for me she wasn't chewing the fat with a support group of other mothers, most of whom were lighting cigarettes as a reward to themselves for having delivered their children into the custody of others for the day; she was already walking away, her step fast-paced. I hoped she didn't have an urgent appointment.

"Tamsin!" I said. "How's it going?"

For a moment she didn't seem to recognise me. Her eyes flickered over me blankly, seeing me more as an obstruction on the pavement than a human being. Then I came into focus. She stopped in her tracks, her hands shoved into the pockets of her padded coat.

"Sam," she said. "What are you doing here?"

The words could have sounded accusatory, but they didn't. Tamsin was operating on autopilot. She looked exhausted. Her mane of hair was scraped back from her face, and she wore no make-up at all. The Lesser Swinfold murders were scarcely doing wonders for the aesthetic values of the village.

"I just came out for a walk," I said. "It's terrible in the house. You can imagine."

Naturally, I was assuming Tamsin knew all about Ethan's murder. The atrocious atmosphere at Emma's was compounded by the fact that we had had the phone ringing off its casing with calls from journalists, local and national. A couple had come around yesterday, but Sheila had sent them packing. We would probably be besieged today.

I didn't mention the presence of the media, though. I had the strongest of instincts that Tamsin would close up tighter than a clam as soon as she heard the word "newspaper." If I got anything out of her, it would be deep, deep background.

She was nodding.

"I heard that sister of Emma's came down," she said. "That can't help much. Emma's always been OK, but that Sheila's a raving snob. Mrs. High and Mighty, I call her. Thinks all of us who come from round these parts are a bunch of village idiots."

This was promising. Tamsin clearly wasn't including me in the London snob category.

"I shouldn't say Mrs., should I?" Tamsin added. "She's never married. That's why she's so snotty to Emma, I reckon. Can't bear that her sister got the man and she didn't."

There spoke the married woman.

"She used to really flirt with Walter, you know. That was Emma's husband," Tamsin continued. "I wondered how Emma put up with it. Maybe she didn't even notice. She's like that, Emma. In a world of her own."

"I know," I said sycophantically. "I was surprised that she let Laura and Ethan stay for so long."

"D'you know what Andy said when he heard about the American?" Tamsin said. "One down, one to go. Awful, isn't it. I was really angry. He's not himself right now. I can't do anything with him."

"Tom's in a terrible state too," I volunteered. "He's just lying in bed watching American chat shows on daytime TV."

"Well, that'll cheer him up if anything will," Tamsin said. "I watch 'em sometimes to remind myself I don't have it as bad as I think. I mean, at least my mum's not gone off with a twenty-year-old Hell's Angel and my husband's not getting my sister and me pregnant simultaneously. I saw that one last week. I don't know where they find these people."

She sighed. "Still, it doesn't help that much. I've got to keep going. It's all very well for Andy, but I can't afford to have a nervous breakdown—everything would fall to pieces. It's always the women who keep things going, isn't it?"

I nodded hypocritically. The thought of cleaning my own toilet, let alone running a large and complex household, sent me into a spiral of panic. Still, I must have done the woman-to-woman solidarity successfully. Tamsin was looking positively friendly. I chanced my luck.

"Do you want to get a cup of tea?" I suggested. "I've been wandering around for a while. I really want to stay out of that house as long as I can. Is there a café or anything round here we could go to?"

I tried to sound pathetic and needy, so that Tamsin's motherly instincts would come into play. Whatever I did, it worked. She shook her head.

"Tell you what, let's go back to mine, and I'll put the kettle on. I could do with a bit of company. Hope you don't mind the house being all sixes and sevens. It's not just having one more kid—though that's more work than I expected. I mean, I thought, two, three, what's the difference? Meals are all right, but I'm doing all these extra washes. But it's Pitt being so upset about his mum, and the others getting jealous 'cos I'm spending time with him and not them. I tell you, I haven't picked up properly in ages."

Having already seen Tamsin's housekeeping skills, I took this with a pinch of salt. The only difference to the house, apart from the overflowing laundry basket next to the washing machine in the kitchen and the stack of children's clothes on the dryer waiting to be ironed, was the slight diminution in the general shininess of the surfaces. I remembered a prevailing odour of bleach before, as if Tamsin had wiped tabletops and kitchen counters down with disinfectant every hour; now the kitchen smelt of fabric conditioner and starch, like a big laundry. It was much more homely.

Tamsin put on the kettle and set out a plate of ginger nuts.

"So how's Emma taking it?" Tamsin said. "A murder in her house and everything. Ooh, she must be cursing the day she let those Americans move in."

Laura and Ethan were always "the Americans" to the locals, I noticed; people hardly ever called them by name.

"I feel so sorry for Tom," I said, as Tamsin brought the teapot to the table and covered it with a knitted tea cosy, which brought back memories of my Aunt Louise, a fanatic proselytiser about the benefits of tea cosies. "Ethan being killed just as they let Tom out on bail. Everyone'll be pointing the finger. Though Tom didn't do it, you know."

"Not many around here'd blame him if he had," Tamsin said, pouring the tea. It was strong enough to dissolve your stomach lining, just the way I liked it. "I don't mean anyone actually wanted that American dead, but no-one'll be losing any sleep over him."

I nodded with suitable gravity as I reached for the milk carton.

"But Tom has an alibi, you know." I considered it important to stress this crucial fact. "He was watching TV with Emma when Ethan was killed. He couldn't have done it."

"But wouldn't they have heard someone else come in?" Tamsin was dubious.

"Ethan was killed in the shed," I explained. "It's out the back of the house, with a passage through to the car park behind. Anyone could have got in that way without going near the house."

"Oh, I didn't know that," Tamsin said, her hand arrested for a moment in the act of tipping the milk carton. She looked down at it and continued pouring. "I didn't know that," she repeated. "That does make a difference."

"Does it?" I said, blowing on my tea and willing myself not to look at her.

She sounded embarrassed, but clearly felt obliged to explain.

"It's just that Andy's been—well, he's got a real temper on him—you know he thought Tom killed Janine, that's no secret. Mind you, so did the coppers, didn't they? But it must have been the same person killed Janine as that American, musn't it? Stands to reason. I mean, we haven't suddenly got two loony killers running round Swinfold stabbing people. That might happen in the films, but you don't get it in real life. So if Tom didn't kill the American, then he didn't kill Janine. And Andy . . ."

Her voice trailed off.

"Who would Andy think did it, if it wasn't Tom?" I asked. I really wanted a ginger nut, but the plate was in front of Tamsin, and I was scared of distracting her if I reached for it.

She remained mute. I had the instinct that in some way I had asked the wrong question. I sipped my tea, hoping that she wouldn't come out of her silence and change the subject. After what felt like a very long time, I decided to throw something else into the equation. Another x-factor. If Tamsin wasn't talking anyway, I had nothing to lose.

"There was that married man Janine was seeing," I suggested, casting my eyes sideways at Tamsin to see how she would take this.

She looked appalled.

"How do you know about that?" she demanded, her expression hardening. I had never seen Tamsin, usually the soul of friendliness, look so hostile.

I shrugged. "Tom's solicitor's been asking around," I said. "You know how it is, Tamsin. She's not looking for dirt for the sake of it, but neither of us thinks Tom killed Janine. And if he didn't, someone else must have. It might have been this bloke. Someone told her Janine was seeing a married guy."

Tamsin still looked antagonistic.

"What else was she supposed to do?" I demanded. "*You* don't think Tom killed Janine either! But if she doesn't find any other suspects, he's going to prison for something he didn't do."

Tamsin looked horribly worried.

"Now that Ethan's been killed, Tom's in the clear, isn't he?" she said hopelessly.

"Not completely," I said. "Besides, the police are going to start looking around for other suspects now. Everything's going to come out."

Tamsin closed her eyes. I took a ginger nut, deciding that we were deep enough in this conversation now for me to be able to indulge.

"It's terrible," she said, her eyes still closed. "Something like this happens and everything gets stirred up. Stuff that's got nothing to do with it. People's lives could get ruined because of this. Some bloke gets a bit stupid—midlife crisis, whatever you want to call it—doesn't really mean anything by it—and then his wife finds out, they've got the police on their doorstep—oh, it's just terrible."

I finished my biscuit and wiped the crumbs off my mouth.

"You know who he was," I said, not as a question but a statement of fact.

Slowly, she nodded.

"I don't know if I should say," she muttered, sounding hopeless.

"It'll all come out anyway," I reassured her, though I was much less sure of this than I seemed. Still, I sensed that Tamsin was almost looking for an excuse to tell me. Very few people can carry secrets for any length of time; eventually, you explode with frustration, especially if you're not secretive by nature. I remembered Aesop's fable of the barber who, being the only one that knows the king has ears like a donkey, is driven crazy by the weight of the knowledge, and finally goes down to the river to whisper it into the reeds for relief.

Tamsin exhaled, another long sigh. I had a moment's flashback to the night I had first met her, New Year's Eve, when she was vibrant with life, chattering away, full of excitement at Hugo's celebrity. And now she was sitting there looking like a long-suffering matriarch on one of the resolutely unglamorous TV soap operas.

"It was Norm," she said finally, staring into her empty cup of tea. She wouldn't meet my eye; it was as if she was convincing herself that telling the dregs of tea didn't count. They might have been Aesop's reeds. "Janine was seeing Norm."

19

I WAS COMPLETELY TAKEN BY SURPRISE. FINALLY, SHE
lifted her head to look at me, nodding.

"Norm," I said incredulously. "*Really?* Are you sure?"

My prime candidate for Janine's lover had always been John
Fitzgerald, for no other reason than he was by far the most glamorous older man I had met in the village. I had even wondered
uncharitably whether Janine had made friends with Alan
because she had a crush on his father. John's uxoriousness would
seem to rule him out from the suspicion of even looking at a
woman who wasn't his wife, but my nasty cynical mind had considered the possibility that John had put Priscilla up on a
pedestal so high that bringing her down to have sex with her
would be out of the question. That would certainly explain all
Priscilla's prescription medication. And a pretty young thing his
son's age with a taste for older men would be hard for anyone
to resist.

Beefy, brawny Norm was such a far cry from John Fitzwilliam
that I had to readjust my thinking.

"How do you know?" I said. I must have sounded disbelieving
still, because Tamsin reacted badly.

"It's true, OK?" she said crossly. "I wouldn't say anything like
that unless I was sure."

"No, I believe you," I assured her, reaching for the teapot. I thought that if we both had full mugs in front of us the atmosphere might calm down a little. "It's just—I don't know, Norm and Chrissie seem so happy together. I wouldn't have thought it of him."

"Chrissie had this real crisis a few years ago," Tamsin explained. "She'd always wanted kids, and she started going for all these tests. Well, she couldn't have them and no-one really knew why. She was in a terrible state. Put her right off—well, you can imagine. Norm used to joke about it with the boys, but he was frustrated, you could tell."

"She told me something like that," I remembered. "She said once she turned forty she got better because she just decided there wasn't any more hope, and she could come to terms with it."

"Yeah, Chrissie's never made a secret of anything," Tamsin said. "She's a great believer in a trouble shared being a trouble halved."

She sugared her second cup of tea.

"They seem fine now," I said.

"Night and day," she said. "Night and day. Chrissie couldn't even bear him to touch her, used to snap at him when he went past her in the bar. Ooh, it was awful. Real atmosphere you could cut with a knife."

"So now that Chrissie's over the crisis," I said, stirring my tea, "was Norm still seeing Janine?"

Tamsin grimaced. "I don't know." She looked at me. "I put two and two together, you see. I was babysitting for Jan, so I was the only one who knew the times she was out. And gradually I realised that when I was babysitting for Jan, Norm wasn't in the Cow. Andy'd come back and say that Norm was off seeing a film in Chipping Campden or something."

"Wasn't that suspicious? That Norm was taking nights off from the pub?"

Tamsin shook her head. "He and Chrissie were getting on so badly everyone was grateful. She'd have her nights off too, of course. But she'd encourage him to get out as much as he wanted. She felt so guilty, she thought it was the least she could do."

"Do you think she knew he was having an affair?"

This question had obviously already occurred to Tamsin.

"I did wonder," she said. "Mind you, she didn't think it was Jan. Not a local girl. Maybe she thought there was someone he went to see every now and then, far enough away from the village so there wouldn't be a problem. She might even have been glad, you know? Take the pressure off her."

Tamsin made this last observation with considerable cynicism.

"And I'd see the way they looked at each other," Tamsin added. "Norm and Jan, I mean. Once you knew, you could tell. Little things, but really clear."

"Did you ever talk about it with Janine?"

"God, no. More'n my life'd have been worth. I didn't want to stir up anything. Let it run its course, I thought. Norm'd never have left Chrissie, he adores her. And besides, how could they split up? What would happen to the Cow?"

"Did anyone else know, do you think?"

I was pestering Tamsin with questions, but she didn't seem to mind. Again, I sensed that she was hugely relieved to be talking about it. Her muscles had loosened as if a weight had literally been removed from her shoulders. She shoved her hair back from her forehead and relaxed comfortably back in her chair.

"Once I wondered if Alan knew," she said reflectively. "We were in the Cow for Sunday lunch—all the kids running round screaming. Chrissie has a whole lot of toys for them, she's really good that way. It's such a pity she can't have any of her own, she's great with them. Anyway, Norm sat down at our table for a couple of minutes, and he and Jan were joking with each other. There was a bit of tension in the air, not that Andy would have noticed. Thick as a plank about that kind of thing, he is. Not to mention that it'd never occur to him that his precious baby sister'd be having an affair with a married man. God, if he'd ever found out . . . Anyway, Alan was in for a drink, and he came over to say hello to Jan, and I saw him look at Jan and Norm sitting together."

"He guessed?"

Tamsin looked sybillic. "I think he knew already. He looked a bit worried. As if he was thinking—what are they doing sitting together? Isn't it a bit dangerous? He really liked Jan, you know. They got on very well. Funny, 'cos they had nothing in common."

Alan, I thought. If Alan had known about Janine and Norm and not told me, I was going to be livid. What the hell was the point of sleeping with someone if they didn't yield up their secrets about a murder you were trying to solve? Whatever happened to pillow talk?

"Was Janine still getting you to babysit for her," I asked, "now that Norm and Chrissie have made up?"

Tamsin's expression was furtive. Finally she nodded.

"Not so much, though. And don't ask me if Norm was out of the Cow those nights," she added hastily, " 'cos I don't know. I didn't want to know, frankly. It was bad enough as it was."

"You were worried about Andy finding out?" I guessed.

She looked as if she was about to cry.

"He's got such a temper on him," she said. "Norm had to throw him out of the Cow the other week 'cos he got in a fight about Jan. And that was based on nothing, from what the boys told me. Just a few silly comments. If he found out about this, there'd be hell to pay. It's such a small place, too. I don't know what we'd do."

She set down her mug, staring into the distance.

"Poor Jan," she said. "I wonder if she knew what was happening to her. I think about that a lot. And if she was terrified about poor little Pitt being left without his mum. He wets his bed every night and cries for her. He still doesn't believe she's never coming back. It's so sad the way he carries on. And we don't even know who his dad is. I expect we never will, now." Her forehead was creased. "I was reading this article on adopted kids in *Woman's Own*, and it came home to me. I mean, what if he's got some, you know, genetic disease or something, and we don't know about it? Jan didn't even leave him that! She should have left a letter or something in case she died, so Pitt could find his dad."

I hardly dared to broach my next question.

"Do you think—"

She cut me off before I could even get there.

"No," she said, "it wasn't Norm. That's only been going the last two years at most. Pitt's nearly five now. There's no way Norm could be Pitt's dad."

"But what if he and Janine had had a fling five years ago— a one-night stand or something—and picked up again when Chrissie went off sex?" I suggested. "It's possible, isn't it?"

Tamsin went white.

"Oh my God," she said. "It would kill Chrissie. It'd just kill her. And as for Andy . . . he'd go mad. Oh my God. I don't even want to think about what he'd do."

I thought about Andy that night in the Cow, how violently he had reacted to Janine's name being taken in vain. I could see exactly why Tamsin was worried.

"Do you think—" I cleared my throat. There was no good way to phrase this. "Do you think—did you worry—that it might have been Norm who killed Janine? If he was worried she might tell Chrissie about the affair?" There was an even worse possibility. "Chrissie?" I suggested weakly.

Tamsin was horrified. But her reaction was to my suggestion, rather than because I had hit on a secret fear of hers.

"Oh no," she said at once. "No. They'd never do anything like *that*. Chrissie wouldn't hurt a fly. And Norm—well, he's the one who breaks up the fights round here. I've never seen him so much as lift his hand to anyone unless it was to stop something that was getting out of control."

I remembered how Norm had poleaxed Andy with one well-placed blow. And suddenly I realised what Tamsin was really uneasy about. I looked at her forehead, creased with worry lines, her hand, gripping the mug so tightly that the bones shone white at the knuckles. Tamsin was scared that her husband might have killed his sister in a fit of rage.

· · · · · · ·

"Sam!" Alan said.

Though clearly pleased that I had turned up on his doorstep, he also looked a little wary. Since this was the reaction that my boyfriends—or, in the case of Alan, paramours—practically always exhibited on seeing me, I didn't misinterpret it. I pushed past him and through the open front door. Closing it behind me, he turned to face me, the wariness now well to the fore.

"What—are you OK?" he stammered. "I heard about what happened to Ethan. I wanted to come and see you, but there were all the reporters round the house. Is everything all right? I mean, apart from—apart from—"

"No, it isn't," I snapped, my hands on my hips. "Why didn't you tell me Janine was having an affair with Norm?"

He looked stunned.

"I—I—look, do you want to take your coat off?" he said feebly. "I could make us a cup of coffee—"

"No thanks," I said curtly. "I'm swimming in tea."

Actually, what I really needed was to go to the toilet, but that could wait.

"Why didn't you tell me?" I repeated.

"I—" Alan hung his head. "I didn't—well, I wanted—"

"What?" I was beginning to sound like a headmistress inter-rogating an erring member of the Upper Sixth.

"I didn't think it had anything to do with it!" he said feebly.

I clicked my tongue.

"How could it not have anything to do with it?" I said furi-ously. "Or how could you be sure of that? My best friend's been arrested, for God's sake. I need to know everything that's been going on in this Godforsaken little armpit of a village, don't you understand that?"

He raised his head, his dark eyes huge and liquid with pain.

"Is that why you went to bed with me? Because you needed to know everything and thought I could tell you?"

"No, of course not," I said, my voice softening. Damn, now he had distracted me from my objective. "I went to bed with you because I wanted to. I thought I made that perfectly clear at the time."

A vivid crimson blush spread over his high cheekbones. And even though the sex hadn't been up to my usual high standards (spoilt by Hugo. No. Don't think about that), even though he smelt wrong to me, I still wanted him powerfully. It was like a gipsy curse. When I found that gipsy, I'd tear her head off with my bare hands and nail it to my wall.

"So why didn't you tell me?" I said, considerably more gently.

"Because I really didn't think— I mean, I know Norm! I knew he couldn't have killed Janine! He's the nicest guy in the world, really. I mean, I know you saw him knock Andy down that evening, but it was to break up a fight, that's all. And besides, he didn't care about her enough. It was just a bit of fun for him. Look at the way she was killed! That was someone who really hated her!"

This was a very good point.

"But what if she was threatening to tell Chrissie?" I suggested. Alan shook his head vehemently.

"Jan would never have done that. She wasn't that kind of person. She didn't want to break up their marriage."

"Was she keen on him?"

Alan pulled a face.

"Jan never took anything lightly," he admitted. "I think, yeah, she did like him a lot. But she knew what she was getting into. She knew Norm was married. And it's not just that, you know. I mean, he's married to the Cow and Chrissie, it sort of all goes together. He'd never want to do anything to mess that up."

"And what if Chrissie had found out? What would she have done?"

Alan sank on to the arm of the nearest sofa. He was looking more and more deflated by the second, as if my questions were draining him physically. He wore a heavy sweater and jeans, and his body hollowed up inside them, the material sagging around his bones. Under the sweater he wore a shirt with the collar turned up messily around his neck, as if he had pulled it on in a hurry, and the indentation just below his Adam's apple was shadowy and vulnerable.

"I don't know," he admitted, his voice faint.

"And Andy?" I pressed home my advantage. "Andy would have done his nut if he'd found out about Norm and Janine, wouldn't he?"

Alan paled visibly, the fading blush of colour standing out hectically as the blood drained from the rest of his face.

"That's why I needed to know," I said more gently. "You can't see all the factors here, Alan. You're too involved in the situation."

"And you're not?" he retorted. "You're so convinced Tom didn't kill Jan that you won't even consider for a moment the possibility that he did!"

We glared at each other. The moment was broken by a sound upstairs. I jumped, partly from the shock and partly from déjà vu. If Sheila appeared on the stairs in her dressing gown, I would have a heart attack.

"Alan?" called Priscilla from the first-floor landing. "I heard the doorbell. Who is it?"

Alan and I exchanged a panicked look of mutual conspiracy in which awareness of our activities the night before last and talk about village secrets were equally mingled.

"It's Sam, Mum," he called back. "She's just dropped in to— um—see how we're doing."

"Oh, how nice!"

Priscilla came downstairs quickly, eager to greet me.

"Sam!" she said. "How are you! I was so sorry to hear about everything that's been going on! I really can't believe it. Swinfold seems to have turned into the murder capital of Great Britain."

She took my hands and kissed me on the cheek.

"Can we get you something? A cup of coffee?"

"No thanks," I said. "I just had loads of tea."

I knew I sounded ungracious, but I was distracted. Knotted loosely around her neck Priscilla was wearing one of the Whistles' scarves I had come across in her handbag that day in London. I had never had such a strong wish to turn back time and cancel out the knowledge I now had of this lovely, apparently composed woman's true mental state.

"Sam! How nice to see you!"

John Fitzwilliam came down the stairs, in corduroy trousers and a cashmere turtleneck. Perfect country-casual wear for the off-duty banker. His silver hair was brushed straight back from his forehead and as he shook my hand I caught a whiff of expensive aftershave.

Suddenly I felt hugely uncomfortable. The sofa on which

Alan and I had had sex seemed to be lit up with a red neon light and a police-car flasher, whooping an alert to his parents. His *parents*. What was I doing here? How had I got myself into this ridiculous situation? Catching Alan's eye, I could see that he was just as unhappy as I was.

"I really should be going," I said, desperately racking my brains to come up with some sort of an excuse for leaving almost as soon as I had got here. "I just dropped in for a moment. I feel bad about leaving Tom. He's in a terrible state."

Priscilla looked a little puzzled.

"Can't we even offer you something?" she said hopefully. "Would you like a soft drink? Or some biscuits?"

This made it even worse. I felt like Alan's little friend come around to play, to be taken to the kitchen and regaled with fizzy drinks and chocolate digestives.

"I'll walk you back," Alan said, grabbing his coat. His eyes met mine again, full of an unspoken appeal, begging me not to refuse his offer.

"OK," I said ungraciously. I was terrified that he would try to have a talk about what had happened between us, but it seemed impossible to refuse in front of Priscilla and John.

"Do come by again when you have more time, won't you?" Priscilla said to me with a beautiful smile, which was so like Alan's that I gulped in anguish.

Alan grabbed my arm as soon as the door shut behind us. His touch was hard to resist. For a moment I wanted to grab him and kiss him as hard as I could, just to have something concrete and physical, one clear sensation in all the mess of feelings that were ravaging me. I turned to look at him. His eyes were huge.

"I have to tell you something," he said urgently. "Just so—you said you needed to know everything—it doesn't have anything to do with Jan, but, well, I trust you." He stroked my arm clumsily. "And I need to tell someone. I just don't know what to do, and I'm so worried. Jan knew but she's dead now, and I don't have anyone else to tell, I feel so on my own with this, and I don't know what to do about it . . ."

The words were spilling out of him faster than his mouth could articulate them, jumbling up one over another.

"Alan. Calm down." I put my hand over his. Even through both sets of gloves I could feel him so acutely it was as if we were naked flesh to naked flesh. I curled my fingers between his, unable to help myself. His twined around mine in response.

"Do you want to come back to Emma's?" I said.

"No—no—" He looked panicked at the idea. "Someone might overhear. Let's just sit down over there."

We were on the village green. Alan pointed to a bench sheltered on one side by the church and on the other by a thick row of trees. It was the least bad option. I was profoundly grateful for my warm coat and the hat Hugo had given me.

Every time I thought of Hugo now it was as if I was being stabbed. I almost welcomed the pain. It had to be some sort of expiation.

"What is it?" I said, sitting down. At least it hadn't rained recently; the wooden slats were cold but dry.

Alan collapsed his long limbs on to the bench, folding his coat over him like two black wings. He hunched over immediately, dragging up his collar to protect his white exposed neck. Then he looped his scarf around his hands and stared down at them. Whatever he had wanted to tell me was obviously hard to say.

I reached over and took his hand, telling myself it was merely to console him. Instinct instructed me to keep quiet and let him take his time; though, to be honest, what I really wanted to do was slap it out of him. My nerves were all on edge these days.

"It's Mum," he said finally, letting the words out on a defeated exhalation of breath. He was addressing his hands, as if I wasn't there. Still, his fingers curled around my hand, holding it fast between his palms. "I don't know what to do. And I can't talk to Dad about it. He just pretends it isn't happening."

I nodded and tried to look as if I didn't have the faintest idea what he was talking about.

"She's really unhappy," he continued, after a long pause. "She takes all these pills. Anti-depressants. I think she should go and see someone properly—get some therapy—but both she and Dad would hate that. It would be really admitting she had this big problem. As it is she's got some tame doctor in Harley Street who just doles out whatever it takes to keep her quiet."

Now I was honestly baffled.

"But taking pills isn't a sign she has a problem?"

He shook his head.

"Dad's line is that she has a chemical imbalance and the pills just even that out."

He twisted his head to look at me imploringly.

"But that's bollocks, obviously. I think Dad's terrified of her getting therapy. He's scared she might leave him. He's always kept her too close. And now that she's started having problems he keeps her even closer, and that just makes it worse. It's so obvious to me. But I can't tell him that." He shrugged miserably. "Dad's never been happy about her having a life separate from him. I mean, he's not a monster or anything. But any time she's arranged to see friends, he looks disappointed, and says he was planning to do something with her that evening. Or he'll try to come along too, or arrange to pick her up early. I think in the end she decided it wasn't worth upsetting him. And look at her now."

I made a sympathetic noise.

"You said Janine knew," I commented, after he had remained silent for a while. "Did you tell her?"

He gave a short, dry laugh with no humour in it at all.

"Oh no," he said. "She found out."

"Found out?" I echoed.

Alan didn't answer immediately. Instead he squeezed my hand convulsively, as if for support.

"Mum's been—" he started. "She's been—it's because she's so unhappy—"

He ran himself down and sat there in terrible conflict, unable to tell me what I already knew. I searched around for a way to help him along. And then I realised the full magnitude of what Alan was trying to tell me. I remembered that Janine had worked for a while in the local shop. My heart stopped momentarily at the thought of the risks Priscilla had been running.

"Sometimes when people are really unhappy they do things they would never normally do, because they can't think of any other way to let people know," I said as carefully as I could. "It's called a cry for help."

"Yes." He looked up. "That's exactly what it is—was—"

"So how did Janine find out?" I prompted, thinking with great pity of what Priscilla had been reduced to.

"She saw Mum—in the shop—" Alan mumbled, confirming my hypothesis. "Mum was—she was—"

I thought it would be plausible for me to guess now. Even if it seemed a wild leap of deduction, Alan would be so grateful to me for not making him say the words that he wouldn't notice.

"*Oh,*" I said, as if the thought had just struck me. "Do you mean she—she took something from the shop? Your mother?"

Alan nodded frantically, unable to meet my eye.

"It's very common, Alan," I said as reassuringly as I could. "It really is. It's a recognised syndrome."

"Jan was so nice about it," Alan muttered. "She pretended not to notice. It's just 'cos *she* was there. Betty—that's the owner—she'd never pick that up in a million years. She just sits behind the counter smoking all day long and talking on the phone. And she's really in awe of Mum anyway. She'd never believe Mum would do something like that even if she saw her with her own eyes."

"So Janine didn't say anything to your mother?" I asked.

"No. God. No. But she came and found me afterwards. Poor Jan, she was so upset, she was sobbing her eyes out. She was so scared of upsetting me too. And I think she thought I might not believe her." He made a violent shrugging movement with his shoulders. "But I did, almost at once. I knew things hadn't been right with Mum for ages. I was hardly even surprised, which was awful too."

"You didn't tell your mother that Janine had seen her?"

He shuddered.

"Are you joking? I could never do that! We can't even talk about how she's feeling, even when I can see that the pills are knocking her out. She always says she's fine and changes the subject. But then I started to notice things."

He looked shamefaced. "I started to go through her handbag, and I'd find things. You know, with the shop price tags still on, and no bag or wrapping or anything. It was obvious once you knew. I told Jan and she was great. She was researching it. She'd go on the Net and check it out . . . there's a whole . . . syndrome, like you said."

I noticed that Alan couldn't actually say the word "shoplifting." I couldn't blame him.

"I tried to talk to Dad once, but he yelled at me and walked out of the room before I'd got anywhere near it," Alan said hopelessly. "I think he's more fucked up than Mum, in a way."

"I'm so sorry."

I couldn't think what else to say. And, of course, the kind of speculations were running through my mind that must, subconsciously at least, be terrifying Alan. What if Priscilla had somehow found out that Janine knew her secret? Priscilla might even have caught Janine's eye for a moment as she stole something and had a flash of realisation that Janine had seen her and kept quiet. Maybe she had rung Janine and arranged to meet her—no, that wouldn't work, Janine had had a date with Tom the evening she was killed and certainly wouldn't have agreed to meet Priscilla then. Well, Priscilla could have had a mad panic for some reason, brought on by her elaborate cocktail of mood medications, driven down from London to confront Janine, and fought with her . . .

But my thoughts were shifting to John Fitzwilliam. He was far more likely than Priscilla to have killed Janine. Priscilla might have even wanted, despite herself, for her kleptomaniac tendencies to come out; certainly, if she had stolen from the village shop, it would have been—as I had suggested to Alan—a huge, if coded, cry for help. But, remembering John's face, with that set of the jaw which proclaimed his standing in the world, I was sure that he would have done anything in his power to cover up a scandal.

Alan gulped beside me. I sensed that he was trying very hard not to cry. Though it must be a tremendous relief for him to spill out his family secret, the enormity of what he had told me—considering that his last confidant had been murdered—had to be crushing. I reached over and stroked his face. He grabbed my hand, pulled me towards him and kissed me ferociously. With a small detached part of my mind, I noticed how much he had improved since the first time he had kissed me. I had certainly given him confidence.

His lips were deliciously soft, his hands on my face pushing back my hair, tangling in it, the sensation of gloved hands on bare flesh irresistibly erotic. I kissed him back with fervour, grabbing his shoulders and pulling him into me, my fingers closing around that bare white nape of the neck which I found so sexy. He groaned and clutched me even tighter. The sheer naughtiness of this—kissing madly on a bench in the park, like desperate, randy teenagers—swept me away for a few moments. Then I came down to earth with a bang.

Alan's tongue was still in my mouth. Suddenly it felt as intrusive as a speculum. I closed my lips gently, pushing him away and held his shoulders now at a slight distance. He wasn't an idiot; he read almost everything just by looking at my face.

"Sam—" he said in panic. "Don't say it!"

But I had to.

"This is a dead end, Alan," I said. I wanted to mention Hugo, but I couldn't bring myself to say his name in front of Alan.

He looked about to argue with me. I could see him physically biting the words back. I found myself impressed by his sensitivity; my mind was made up and nothing he said would change that. After a short while, he took a deep breath and said, "I hope you change your mind."

"I'm sorry," I said. It was a crappy, crappy thing to say in this context, and I regretted it as soon as the words left my mouth.

"Don't be," he snapped.

It seemed shitty to walk away from him just after he had confided in me. But I couldn't stay here. The tension was unbearable. I stood up, buttoning my coat where Alan had pulled it open.

"You know where I am if you need me," I said awkwardly. "I mean, about your mother."

"Don't worry about it," he said, shrugging and doing his best to sound dismissive.

"But I do." I managed—barely—to avoid apologising again. "It's just difficult for me right now."

"Yeah," he muttered.

I was only making a bad situation worse.

"I'll see you," I said.

"I won't hold my breath," he said, turning away from me and fumbling for his cigarettes.

When I reached the church, I turned to look back, unable to resist. He was staring after me, his black hair blowing in the wind. From this distance he looked like a Marie Laurencin: white face, dark eyes, red lips. Snow White as a boy. My stomach twisted over. But you can't go back to something that isn't there any more.

The cold air blasted me, a gust of wind whipping around the corner of the church and catching me full in the face. It was exactly what I needed. I stood there for a moment, opening my arms and breathing in deeply, letting the wind blow through me and clear out all the mess and confusion. It only helped briefly. I still felt like a leper, bringing disease and unhappiness wherever I went.

20

IT WAS NEARLY ONE O'CLOCK. AND I HAD NO INTENTION OF heading back to the house, running the gamut of journalists, simply in order to sit around the house watching daytime television while Laura drifted around the house like a ghost, or a zombie whose spirit had left its body, her eyes so blank that she seemed to look right through you when you passed her on the stairs. She had stopped accusing Tom; she seemed to have stopped speaking altogether, which should have been more relaxing than it was. Sheila was busy criticising everyone and everything, while Emma vainly tried to make nourishing meals for Tom and hold the entire household together like some parody of a mother in an old-fashioned BBC sitcom.

I wandered across the green, not sure where I was going, but unable to stay still. Maybe I should just keep on walking all day, head out into the countryside and tramp the hills till I was good and tired. I hadn't been to the gym for a couple of weeks, and I was twitchy from lack of proper exercise. Besides, walking was very good for the thought processes. I always had my best ideas for work when I was walking. Somehow the fact that the body was occupied let the mind rove more freely, generating the sorts of connections it was usually too snarled up to make.

Still, the way my luck was going right now I would probably

be shot by some irate farmer for trespassing. It was a measure of my current messed-up mental state that I found the idea strangely comforting. Solve all my dilemmas in one single stroke.

I passed the church and came to the rickety little gate, which opened on to a cobblestoned path to the main street. I had no wish to pass the Cow right then, or see anyone I knew. I was just debating whether to turn on my heels, go back across the green and leave Lesser Swinfold that way, when I noticed the village shop, a little to my left. For lack of anything better to do, I strolled over to it. The window display was still full of Christmas decorations, despite the fact that we had passed Twelfth Night. Great swathes of tinsel were draped over the tins of tomatoes and boxes of cereal, reminding me strangely of the haberdashery shop I loved in Camden, whose window was always hung with artfully arranged feather boas. The boas, however, were always colour co-ordinated and looked luxuriously expensive, whereas the tinsel was horribly tatty, kinked and torn. The straggly red, yellow and green glitter was dulled by a film of greasy dust. I expected the owners of the shop were long past caring about the bad luck conferred by not taking down your Christmas decorations on time.

I pushed open the door. A bell above made an effort to tinkle, but it was so old or so dirty that all it managed was a faint, strangled yelp. The linoleum floor was smeared with mud. A scene-of-crime officer would have had a lot of fun trying to identify all the smeary, overlapping boot marks trodden across the once-white floor. I added my own to the collection. Without a doormat to wipe one's feet on, it was impossible not to.

The two aisles were so narrow and the shelves so crammed that it was hard to see to the end of the shop. I didn't think I had heard of a single brand on the shelves. This was where discontinued products came to die. I checked the sell-by date on a box of cornflakes, out of curiosity, and put it back hurriedly when

I read the label. God knew I was scarcely fastidious, but even I had limits.

The bell yelped briefly again. Someone else had come in. I glanced back to see who it was, but they were already heading up the other aisle towards the back of the shop.

"Pack of Silk Cut, please, Betty," I heard a muffled voice say.

I knew who that was. Chrissie. I edged up the aisle till I had a view of the back counter. It was thick with smoke. Through the mist, I saw Betty reaching behind her for a pack of cigarettes. It was impossible to tell her age; her face looked so battered by the elements, not to mention smoking, that she could have been anything from forty to sixty. Her skin was sallow, with a greyish cast, and her hair a frizzy mop whose texture looked as if it had been singed regularly by the cigarettes.

"Didn't know you were smoking again, Chrissie," she said. "You shouldn't—sounds like you've got a cold coming."

I cringed. How could these people bear to live in a village so small that everyone knew every little habit of their neighbours'?

"Yeah, well. It's one of those days," Chrissie said shortly. Her voice did sound bloggy, as if her nasal cavities were congested.

"Didn't want Norm to know, eh?"

"What makes you think that?"

Chrissie sounded positively hostile now.

"Well, you've got a vending machine in the pub, haven't you? That stocks Silk Cut?" Betty probed. "Unless it's run out, of course."

I couldn't help but be impressed by this woman's deductive skills. Perhaps I should ask her who had killed Janine and Ethan. She was bound to have a better theory than I did.

Chrissie didn't answer. She must have handed over the money, though, because I heard Betty ring up the sale on a till that sounded as if it had been bought in the 1940s.

"I'll keep mum, then, shall I?" she said conspiratorially.

"Do whatever you want, Betty," Chrissie snapped. "I really don't care."

"*Well*," Betty said, tutting at Chrissie's discourtesy. But by then Chrissie was already on her way out, returning this time by the aisle I was standing in. I had had enough warning to remove myself down it far enough so I wouldn't look as if I had been eavesdropping.

"You!" she said, distinctly unhappy to see me.

She couldn't pass me; the aisle was too cramped. I backed up till I was next to the door and held it open for her, following her out myself.

"I was looking for some cornflakes, but they're all past their sell-by date," I said, to explain why I was leaving too.

She sniffed. "I'm not surprised. Betty gets everything from that discount warehouse in Briarfields. You'd have to be pretty bloody desperate to shop there."

Chrissie was trying to light a cigarette, but the wind made it difficult, and her hands were shaking. I took the lighter from her and made a little cup of my hands to shelter the flame.

"Thanks," she said, drawing deeply on the Silk Cut. "Ugh, this tastes disgusting. They say the first one back's always wonderful, but this tastes like an ashtray. I haven't smoked since I—"

She broke off, looking at me. I could see that she couldn't decide whether to talk to me or just walk away. Even the jaunty blonde curls, whipped by the wind, couldn't disguise the fact that her nice, homely face was strained and tired. It wasn't a cold, I realised; she had been crying. Her cheeks were blotchy and her nose red. She looked every year of her age, and more. She was wearing one of those padded coats that always made me think of duvets; it bulked her out still more, but despite her size she looked heartbreakingly vulnerable.

"Tamsin came to see me just now," Chrissie said finally. "She told me she'd been talking to you."

I nodded.

"She told me about Norm and Janine. Said it was bound to come out, and it was best I heard it first."

Looking closer at Chrissie, I could see that her eyes, already small, were shrunk even more by the skin around them, puffy and swollen. She sounded defeated by life.

"Did you have any idea?" I said.

She shook her head and drew deeply on the cigarette.

"Nah. Nothing. Didn't suspect a thing. He used to get me all these little presents. I worshipped the ground he walked on, you know? Thought I had the best husband in the world."

"They say that having an affair makes people be nicer to their partners," I offered. Hah. That was scarcely true in my case.

Chrissie's only reply to this was to blow her nose loudly.

"It was probably just about the sex," I said unhappily, feeling I was making a bad situation worse.

"I never liked Janine," Chrissie said finally. "She thought she was better than the rest of us, you could tell. Well, she wasn't that clever, was she? Got caught out like any stupid little girl that couldn't even use a condom with her boyfriend. I tell you, life's so unfair. Here's me, desperate for a baby, and that Janine just got pregnant like that." She snapped her fingers. "There's no justice in this life."

It was my turn to stay silent.

"You're really nosing around, aren't you? Digging up all our dirty little secrets?" she said, an unpleasant edge to her voice. She sounded as nasty as is possible for a person who can't pronounce their n's and m's. "And all for what? Because you're sure Tom didn't kill them? You can't be sure of anything, you know. I thought I was sure of Norm."

She lit another cigarette from the butt of the first one.

"Gave up smoking when I was trying to get pregnant," she said. "Doesn't matter much now, does it?"

She sighed.

"I don't really blame you," she said grudgingly. "You're looking out for your friend, I suppose. I heard they're not so happy about Tom, now. The coppers. Apparently, Emma said he couldn't have done that American, 'cos he was with her, and you can't help believing Emma, now, can you?"

"What are you going to do?" I said.

"What is there to do?" Her face sagged around the cigarette in her mouth, as if it was deflating her features. "Just keep going. Isn't that what I always do? Just keep going."

She gave me a long hard look, her mouth thinning into a narrow line.

"But you'd better watch out for yourself," she said. "No-one round here likes people who start nosing round things they don't want anyone to know about. I tell you, if Norm finds out it was you that got Tamsin to tell about Janine and him, you're in big trouble. He'll go ape. There's no telling what he might do."

This would have been more menacing if Norm's name hadn't been coming out as "Dorb."

"Someone made sure Janine couldn't tell, didn't they?" I challenged her. "Is that what you're worried about?"

Chrissie stabbed me in the chest with one finger, so hard it felt like being poked with a stick. It was totally unexpected. I took a step back in surprise.

"Don't you go spreading ideas like that!" she said furiously. "You'd better watch yourself, girl. I'm warning you."

She closed the distance between us, stepping so near to me that I could smell the smoke on her breath. Her finger shot out and jabbed me in the breastbone again. It really hurt.

"I won't forget it was you that started all this," she said angrily. "If it hadn't been for you, I'd never have found out about Norm and Janine."

Coupling their names hurt her, I could tell. Her voice trembled on the last words, but kept its fury.

"I thought you just said it wasn't my fault," I said, angry now. Being poked in the breastbone had pissed me off. Chrissie had done it hard enough to leave bruises. And she had nearly burnt me with the cigarette she was holding.

"I don't care what I just bloody said, all right? You keep out of my business. You keep out of everyone's business, or you'll suffer for it."

"What, someone's going to kill me?" I snapped. "Don't you think there've been enough murders already?"

"We're all in the shit now, aren't we?" Chrissie said with tremendous bitterness. "Lives falling apart everywhere you look. What difference is one more murder going to make, eh?"

"Are you threatening me?" I shoved my face up to hers.

This was ridiculous. It was like a standoff from a Western, transferred to an English country village outside a fly-bitten local shop. But the menace emanating from Chrissie made it impossible for me to trivialise the situation so easily.

"If that's the way you want it—yeah! That's right! I bloody am!" she shouted.

She tried to poke me again, but I blocked her hand, knocking it away so hard the cigarette flew out of her hand and into a bush. This enraged her further.

"You go back to London," she yelled, "and mind your own bloody business, you hear me? And don't try showing your face in the Cow again or I'll sling you out on your ear!"

She turned and stormed away, fumbling as she went for another cigarette. I stared after her, feeling the wind icy on the back of my neck. Finally, I went over and ground my heel on the fallen cigarette, squashing out the embers. Enough information was finally coming loose so that for the first time I thought I had the beginnings of a thread in my hand, which, if I kept pulling at it, would finally unravel and lead me to the truth. It was like the ripcord of a parachute, which you have to tug on really hard to finally open it up and sail down to the ground. I had the ripcord in my palm, and thought it would need a couple more good heaves, but at least I wasn't floundering around in freefall any longer, unable to connect with it.

I had forgotten, though, that for the first time I was in a small village where everyone knew what I was doing. When I had investigated murders before, I had been in big cities—London or New York—where, compared with Lesser Swinfold, I was as anonymous as a drop of water in the ocean. Here, by making it so clear to all and sundry that I was digging hard into the truth, I might as well be walking through the woods in hunting season with antlers on my head and a target pinned to my back.

"D'you think she knew already? About Janine and Norm?"

I gave Lurch a disbelieving stare.

"What do you mean? Of course she didn't."

"Well, the way you described it, she didn't sound that surprised, you know what I mean? More like sad about it, but like it wasn't the biggest shock in the world."

I thought about this. Reluctantly, I had to admit it made a certain degree of sense. For someone who had just found out about her husband's affair with a girl who had subsequently been murdered in a particularly nasty way, Chrissie had reacted with a certain amount of sangfroid.

"Maybe she was still in shock," I suggested.

"Yeah. I mean, it's possible, innit?" Lurch was curled up in the armchair, an ungainly heap of bony elbows and knees, like a string puppet that has been dropped from a great height. "All I'm saying is, it's something to think about. That she might've been on to them already."

"If she did know . . ." I considered this. "She was pretty angry with me."

"Well, you can't blame her, can you? I mean, it was your fault she found out hubby was shagging a blonde half her age."

"I thought you just said Chrissie might have known."

He shrugged.

"Then you're the one what brought it out, ain't-cha? And now everyone's going to know, and she'll feel terrible. Either way, she's put the blame on you."

"She was furious with me. Look." I lifted my sweater to reveal the marks where Chrissie had jabbed me with her finger. "I'm going to have bruises."

Lurch unfolded his limbs, hinging his legs out from beneath him to cross his feet on a footstool. He had taken off his Doc Martens, in respect to Emma's upholstery, and one long bony toe poked out through its greyish sock. Emma would doubtless find this deeply endearing. I was revolted by the sight.

"Maybe Chrissie did her. Janine," he clarified. "It's a big motive, innit? Girl shagging your husband?"

"But why would she kill Ethan?"

"He was a toerag?" Lurch suggested.

I made a gesture of frustration.

"*Lurch,*" I wailed, "*please.* I'm trying to think things through here."

"OK. What about if Ethan was shagging Janine too?" Lurch suggested more helpfully. "Norm found out and topped 'em both."

"That's not bad. Or Laura might have done it."

We were keeping our voices low, for fear of being overheard, but I practically whispered this last sentence.

"Yeah, I like that better," Lurch said enthusiastically. "I mean, Norm had a wife and the pub and everything. He probably wouldn't care as much. But Laura, Ethan was all she got. If she found out he was carrying on with Janine, she'd go ballistic."

"Where is she?" I asked, looking around a little nervously.

"In the shed," Lurch informed me.

"What's she doing there?" I said doubtfully. "Just sitting where he was killed? That sounds really morbid."

Lurch shook his head.

"Nah," he said. "She's 'working.'"

The inverted commas were clear as if he had made the gesture that signified them.

"Painting?" I said, confused.

"Nah. Writing. She's finishing his screenplay. I think."

I stared at him.

"But she's not a writer," I pointed out. "Don't you have to know what you're doing to write a screenplay?"

Lurch shrugged.

"She told me she was finishing his work in memory of him. I dunno, it sounds mad to me. The coppers took his laptop so she's sitting in there scribbling away on a big mess of paper."

"I wonder if they found anything on his laptop," I said thoughtfully.

"What, like he typed 'So-and-So just stabbed me' before he died?" Lurch said sarcastically. "Easier than writing it in blood on the wall, I s'pose."

"No," I said, too abstracted to be insulted by this. "I was wondering if he kept a diary or something. I mean, if he knew anything . . . there must have been a reason he was killed—"

"Well, if there was anything, they ain't found it yet. Some copper popped by a few hours ago to talk to Laura. They're pissed off 'cos they can't get into much without a password, and Laura said she didn't know what it was."

"Oh yeah?" I looked at him. "Do you think she was telling the truth?"

Lurch gave a monumental shrug, his bony shoulders rising and falling with Gallic emphasis.

"When it comes to that girl, I got no idea," he said frankly. "She's such a weirdo."

Silence fell as we both contemplated Laura's undeniable weirdo status. This made the huge crash that shattered the living-room window sound even louder. It was like a bomb going off. I jumped to my feet in a panic reflex. Lurch made an effort to do the same, got caught on the footstool and fell clumsily on to the floor.

"Fuck!" he yelled. "Fuck! What was that?"

My senses were on red alert. The window in front of us had a gaping hole in its centre, glass still falling in shards on to the floor below.

"Get back!" I yelled at him and ran to the front door, yanking it open. Emma's lawn, reaching down to the road, was hoary with frost, the sky grey as pewter. I thought I heard the garden gate bang, but the tall hedge at the bottom of the lawn prevented me from seeing anything in the lane below. I sprinted out on to the lawn, scanning the area furiously, but I already knew it was too late. By the time I got down the steps and through the gate, whoever had done this would be well away.

I returned slowly to the door. Emma and Sheila were running up the stairs from the kitchen like lemmings in a panic.

"What *happened?*" Emma said frantically.

I went back through into the living room. The stone that had been thrown at the window had landed on the coffee table. It squatted there like a big grey toad, broken glass strewn around it, exuding menace. Emma screamed and jumped back, clutching at Sheila as if it had been an unexploded grenade. And in a way, it was.

"Oh my God . . ." she was moaning. "Oh my God, what more can happen to us . . ."

Lurch crossed the room and bent over the stone.

"Don't touch it!" I said quickly. "Leave it alone! There might be fingerprints."

I turned to look at Emma.

"Call the police," I said.

I looked over at the broken window. Already it was cold in the room, the icy wind streaming through the hole in the window, all the cosiness of Emma's living room with its roaring fire cancelled out by one violent act of vandalism.

"And a glazier," Sheila added practically. "Don't worry, Em. It'll all be fine," she soothed her sister.

It was the first sign of sororal feeling I had observed in Sheila. Her eyes met mine over Emma's head, and I could tell we were both thinking exactly the same thing. Sheila was lying through her teeth.

. . . .

Worse things had happened to Lurch and me than a stone thrown through a window. One just had to look at the scars on Lurch's back to see that. Mine were less obvious, but any full-body X-ray would have revealed an impressive collection of once-broken bones. Still, no-one gets blasé about random acts of violence, not unless they're a hero in one of those brick-thick international spy thrillers with shiny covers you buy in airports.

The police had been and gone, Sheila was sorting out an emergency glazier and Lurch and I had escaped from the house. Not that it made much difference. If that stone had been aimed at us, we were targets anywhere.

"I want a drink," I confessed.

"Well, we can't go to the Cow, can we?" Lurch said practically. "You've been barred."

"It's amazing to think that I've never actually been barred from a pub before," I said, briefly distracted from the stone incident.

"Can't wait to tell Hugo," Lurch said, laughing, before he remembered our current situation. The smile faded from his face.

"He rang this morning, while you was out," he said. "Just said to tell you he'd called."

"Right," I muttered.

"Sam—"

"Can we not talk about this now, please? We've got a double murderer on the loose, and now they're trying to stone us out of the village, or something. Can we concentrate on that?"

Lurch didn't answer. Glancing over at him, I saw that his face was set into a sullen mask of disagreement.

"Where are we going?" I said finally.

He shrugged sulkily.

"The Arrow, I s'pose. It's that or the George, and they'd probably stone us out of there too. Twice in one day'd be pushing it."

"The Arrow?" I remembered Norm mentioning it. "That's the pub run by the old bloke, right? The one Norm's waiting to die so it'll close down?"

Lurch nodded.

"Don't even know if it'll be open."

The Arrow had once been a cottage very similar to the one Hugo and I had rented over New Year. Lurch had to duck to get through the low doorway and could barely stand up inside without scalping himself on the beams. It was very dark; the windows were tiny and heavily leaded, and it was lit only by a few lamps and a fire burning in the grate. For an instant I had the impression that we had stepped back in time, pitched into one of those films where you suddenly find yourself in the Middle Ages.

I felt the floor with the heel of my boot. No rushes on the stone flags. And the lamps, now I looked at them closer, ran off electricity. Thank God. I really couldn't have dealt with a time-travel experience right now.

Something moved at the far end of the room. I looked over to the bar, squinting through the shadows. Though it was so dark, the Arrow wasn't gloomy; there was a cosiness about the old settles and the low beams. You could curl up in here and lose yourself happily for a few hours.

Lurch coughed and said, "Anyone there?"

A rustling came from behind the bar. We moved in its direction rather cautiously.

"You're the London people, aren't you?"

Eventually, I made out an ancient man, sitting behind the bar, so small that he looked almost gnomeish. His face was a mass of wrinkles, and he was nodding at us, as if confirming a theory of his own.

"Yeah, that's us," Lurch said. "You open?"

"Of course I'm open, young man. The door was open, wasn't it? What would you like?"

"What are you having?" I said, noticing a tankard in front of him, from which was issuing a cloud of steam which smelt delicious.

"Hot buttered rum," he said with considerable satisfaction. "Warms your bones on a day like this."

"We'll have some of that," Lurch and I said in unison.

"A very good choice," he said. "Sit yourselves down, and I'll bring some over."

He levered himself off his high stool and disappeared completely from view. Leaning over the bar, I saw him pop into sight again, making his slow progress to a little kitchen behind the bar. Gas hissed into life as he put a saucepan on the hob.

"Go on," he called. "Sit yourselves down in front of the fire. It'll be a few minutes."

It didn't feel like being in a public bar, more as if we had strayed into someone's house and been invited to have a drink. We dutifully took our seats at an old oak settle in front of the fire, propping our feet on the fender.

"This is nice, innit?" Lurch said with considerable satisfaction.

"Just don't stand up in a hurry, or you'll knock yourself out," I advised.

"Yeah, that makes sense. Seeing as I've just avoided getting hit on the head with a rock, be a bit stupid to do it to myself."

I looked at him.

"What the hell do you think that was about?"

"Buggered if I know."

"If it was meant for me . . ." I speculated. "Or you. After all, we were the ones sitting there."

"I dunno if whoever did it've got close enough to see who we was," Lurch pointed out. "If they'd been near enough, they wouldn't have had time to get away."

"So Emma, Laura or Tom could have been the targets as well."

"Or Sheila."

I shrugged. "Technically. But she hardly seems involved with any of this."

"Most likely to have been for poor old Tom," Lurch said. "Soon as he gets out of the nick, Ethan cops it."

"The village knows Tom's got an alibi," I said feebly.

"Ah, come on, Sam. The police've got to believe Emma, but I bet some people in the village think she's just protecting Tom."

"Do *you* think she is?" I asked suddenly. I had meant to say something completely different and the words had just popped out.

Lurch gave me an odd look.

"What're you saying?"

Lurch would think any nasty, lurking suspicion I had of Tom was abominable. But Lurch had only known Tom for the last couple of years, during which time he had been considerably more tranquil. Lurch had never seen Tom in a mad rage, and so would think I was being unbelievably disloyal in suspecting him even for a moment.

"I don't like this, Lurch," I said, changing the subject deliberately. "Things are getting really nasty. If people are throwing stones in broad daylight, what the hell's going to happen at night?"

"They surround the house, drag us out and burn us on the lawn?"

"Shut up. It's serious."

Lurch responded to the unusually terse note in my voice.

"I know," he said equally sombrely.

"Oughtn't you to be getting back to London?" I said. "When does term start?"

"Day after tomorrow."

He looked at me seriously.

"But I don't want to leave you and Tom like this. You need me around. And Emma," he added. "I'm not going till things are sorted out."

I was deeply touched. I would have hugged him, but I knew he would recoil in horror. We were in a public place.

"Two hot buttered rums," announced the ancient proprietor.

Lurch and I took the tankards out of his hands. He was so tiny and wizened their weight was dragging him perilously off-balance as he struggled to carry them. He stood there, beaming at us, as we sniffed the vapour rapturously, every wrinkle on his tiny face creasing together till I could hardly make out his features.

"Quiet in here, innit?" Lurch said, clearly feeling he should make conversation.

The door slammed back with such a crash that it was lucky Lurch and I had just set down the tankards on the table or we would have dropped them. I looked around wildly, half-expecting to see a stone come flying towards us. Lurch shoved me, trying to get in front of me and protect me from whatever new menace was threatening. We stumbled over each other's feet like a pair of pantomime clowns. Someone came thundering through the door, a large, menacing silhouette. The only thing I had to hand was the tankard. I reached for it. I could always throw a mugful of hot buttered rum in their face and hit them over the head with a settle.

The only one of us unaffected by the commotion was the proprietor. Turning to face the new arrival, he said politely, "Mug of hot buttered rum, young man? And would you kindly shut the door? There's a nasty wind out there."

21

IT WAS ANDY. HE STOOD IN THE MIDDLE OF THE ROOM, swaying on his feet, breathing hard, as if he'd just run a race. The room seemed to shrink around him, his presence filling every nook and cranny. Violence radiated from him almost visibly, like an electricity machine cranking out sparks.

"Andy?" I said tentatively.

He took a step forward. Lurch and I sucked in our breath. In the dim light from the lamp next to him it was suddenly obvious that blood was running down his head. Oblivious, he didn't even reach up a hand to wipe it away.

"I came—" he said, panting out the words. "I came—"

"Why don't you sit down, young man?" said the gnome, pushing a big oak chair towards Andy. It was so heavy, and the gnome so weak, that all he managed was to make the chair squeak on the floor, but Andy received the suggestion with gratitude. He sank into the chair, staring ahead blankly.

"Andy," I said again, gaining courage now that he was sitting down. "You've got blood all over your face."

I scrabbled in my pocket and produced an ancient tissue.

"Here."

I held it out to him. It wasn't enough to do more than smear the blood around a bit, but it was better than nothing.

"Ta," he said automatically, dabbing at his head with it. Then he looked at me closer and realised who I was.

"You!" he said furiously.

It was the second time this had happened to me today. It was like being in a Victorian melodrama. I should be wearing a big cloak I could swirl around me and moustaches I could twirl evilly when recognised.

"Uh, hi," I said. I took a long pull at the buttered rum. It was wonderful. I felt it right down to my toes.

"Who hit you, mate?" Lurch said, trying to distract him.

"That bastard," Andy spat out. "That fucking bastard. Oh, thanks," he added politely.

He accepted a big mug of hot buttered rum from the gnome, looking faintly surprised at its appearance.

"That *fucking bastard*," he continued, his tone immediately returning to full-on menace. "First he does my sister—my little Jan, that *bastard*—then he fucking throws me out of his pub and tells me not to show my face in there again. He can't do that!"

"But how did you know he was—um—" I had seen how Andy reacted when anyone took Janine's name in vain. "I mean—"

"My *wife*," he said angrily. "My *wife* rang me up at work and told me today in the middle of a client meeting. Said it was bound to get out, and she wanted me to know before anyone else told me. I'm sorry, Mr. Blakely, could you run that by me again about the loan for expanding your business premises? What's she think I'm going to do? I couldn't bloody concentrate on work, could I? I had to get out of there and come and find that *bloody bastard*."

I bet that Tamsin had told Andy at the bank in the hope that a few hours at the office would help to take the edge off his fury. Nice try, but it clearly hadn't worked.

"And Norm just told me to piss off. Said it was between him and Janine and nobody else. I said, 'What about your wife, you cunt?' And he went, 'That's none of your business, is it?' and told me to piss off. So I went for him."

He touched his head gingerly.

"He hit you?" I said.

"That was Chrissie," he said. "She got me on the head with a beer mug. I had him on the ground, and I was pounding the shit out of him."

"Jesus," Lurch muttered, "I wish I'd seen that."

"And you!" Andy shouted at me. "This is all your fault!"

Great. Sam Jones, Official Village Scapegoat.

"Oi, wait a minute," Lurch said angrily. "It wasn't Sam what was shagging your sister, mate. And it wasn't Sam who killed her, neither. If you want to get pissed off with someone, I'd concentrate on that."

"My little Jan!" Andy started crying.

The ancient proprietor wisely leant over and removed the tankard from his hand a split second before his whole body crumpled over on itself. He sank his head in his hands and started sobbing.

"My little Jan," he cried. "She didn't deserve that. She was a good girl. That bastard took advantage of her. I'll kill him. I'll kill him."

But now he sounded like a little boy. There was no menace in his voice, just an aching grief. He was wailing like a baby. His bank-manager grey suit was crumpled and bloodstained, and his body rocked back and forth in paroxysms of misery. We watched in silence. There was nothing we could say or do to help him. Lurch handed me my mug, and we drank our rum down, waiting for Andy to drain himself dry of his tears.

· · · · · ·

"And what happened then?" Sheila asked intently.

She had certainly been altered by the latest turn of events.

A dead body in the house, or at least the garden shed, combined with the nervous collapse of her sister, had knocked Sheila out of most of the annoying, world-weary poses she normally assumed. She was not only behaving less affectedly, but she looked much more natural too. Gone, when she threw out her hands, was the heavy clanking of her illegally poached ivory bangles. Batting her eyelids, should she wish to do so, was now considerably easier without the thick coating of make-up and mascara with which they were usually caked.

But the changes in her appearance were merely an indication of the deeper alteration that had taken place. The normal relationship pattern between the sisters had turned on its head with a vengeance; now it was Sheila who was looking after Emma.

Emma's attempts to paste over harsh reality by the compulsive cooking of lavish meals for the dysfunctional household had come to an abrupt end when, this afternoon, practically out of her wits with stress, she had burned her wrist badly on the Aga and dropped an entire tray of jam tarts on the floor. Being Emma, she had been much more concerned for the latter than the former. But to my surprise, Sheila had descended upon the scene with great authority, commanding me to throw away the broken tarts, picking Emma up bodily off the floor, where she had collapsed in tears, and hauling her off to bed with a series of very efficient-looking burn dressings.

(I salvaged most of the tarts and took them up to Tom and Lurch for an afternoon snack. The floor was perfectly clean; Emma swabbed it down every day. The worst we could expect was a faint aftertaste of tile wax with the raspberry jam.)

"Uh."

I collected my thoughts. It was late in the evening, and I was catching Sheila and Tom up on some of today's highlights. The jam-tart incident had occupied a large part of the late afternoon, and then we had had to scrabble together some sort of dinner without Emma's no-longer-capable hands on the kitchen tiller. Actually, with Emma temporarily removed from the roles of domestic goddess and den mother, our disparate household was pulling together much better. Sheila wasn't the only one who had risen to the occasion. Tom had finally got out of bed and made us all a big pot of pasta. Years of communal living had honed his skills at cooking for large groups of people. We didn't tell Laura Tom had cooked it, or she wouldn't have touched it. I took her a plate of pasta in the shed; she was refusing to enter any room in which Tom was present. Lurch had been right. She was writing away on a great sheaf of typing paper, which she tried to shield from my eyes as I entered the shed.

"Supper," I announced, putting it down next to her. "Try to eat something, eh?"

At sight of me Laura had hunched over on herself, and though she turned to see who was entering the shed, her gaze as always was fixed on a point miles away. I felt increasingly uncomfortable in her presence. Her behaviour might be quite plausibly attributed to a violent reaction to her lover's murder, but it could equally be due to extreme guilt and remorse.

"It was awful," Lurch said to Sheila, seeing that my thoughts were momentarily elsewhere. "Andy just kept on crying. We didn't know what to do. I mean, normally you'd say, 'Have a drink, mate,' but you know what he's like when he gets drunk. Could've smashed the whole place up."

"Then, finally, he just got up and staggered out," I contributed. "He was weaving from side to side as though he was concussed."

"Maybe he was," Tom said sensibly.

"I told him he should get that cut stitched up," Lurch said. "It looked pretty nasty. And, y'know, maybe while 'e was in they'd've kept him in for observation or something."

"Instead of the current situation, where for all we know he's wandering round the countryside, blood caked all down his face, like some modern version of the Ancient Mariner," I added. "Grabbing all and sundry and telling them about his wrongs."

"That's the best-case scenario, innit?" Lurch said. "I mean, what if he's hiding out till dark with a petrol can in one hand and an axe in the other?"

"Do you think it was him who threw the stone?" Sheila said suddenly.

"No," I said. "Tamsin hadn't told him by then. He'd have been in his office still."

"I thought it might be Chrissie," Lurch suggested. "You said she got more and more pissed off the more she talked to you, Sam."

"How unusual," Tom muttered. But it was a mere shade of the way we used happily to insult each other.

At least he was out of his room and sitting around the table with the rest of us. That was the only positive aspect of the situation. Misery did not suit Tom. He had the kind of solid, chunky Irish features, which, while not handsome, could be hugely charming in a bear-like way when he was happy. Right now his flesh was the grey of uncooked veal, and his blue eyes had almost disappeared into the swollen puffs of skin beneath them. I toyed with the idea of booking him into one of those all-male spas for a day, when this was all over, and then discarded the idea. He was in such bad shape that any self-respecting beautician would rather pedicure the lifers at a top-security prison than take Tom on as a client.

"I don't understand it," Sheila said helplessly. "I can't believe any of this is happening."

All evening it had been like this; as soon as we had started to speculate about possible murderers, Sheila had descended into a sort of keening. Put a headscarf and clogs on her and she could have been an Irish peasant woman out of a J. M. Synge play, wringing her hands and moaning at every new eventuality.

"If Walter were here, this would never have happened," she added wistfully.

It always annoyed me when women of a certain age referred to their husbands as some kind of supreme authority with the power to sort out everything remotely troublesome. Besides, Walter hadn't even been Sheila's husband, but her sister's. I wondered if Sheila resented Emma, not just because her sister had got married, but because she had wanted Emma's husband for herself.

"He was so capable," she said, in a melancholic voice. "He always knew what to do for the best."

"He could scarcely have stopped people from throwing stones through the window," I said, irritated.

Sheila just pursed her lips and shook her head at me in a manner intended to convey that, not having known Walter, I was unable to appreciate his omnipotence to the full.

"No-one would have dared to throw stones at the house if Walter were still alive," she said firmly.

She looked over at the framed photographs on the wall, the ones at which Emma glanced nostalgically so often. I noticed once again that most of the photographs featured the Emma–Walter–Sheila trio, their arms around each other, Walter always in the middle, beaming at the camera as if showing off his two women. Emma hugged his arm and smiled for the camera too; Sheila, however, looked up at Walter almost possessively, as if she was the wife and Emma the sister. On camera, carefully made-up, her hair groomed, she looked much younger than Emma. I reflected momentarily on the unfairness of the rule that allows men to age gracefully, their wrinkles and grey hairs a sign of the rich full lives they have lived, whereas women are supposed to disguise the signs of ageing by any means necessary.

Something made me frown, and it wasn't that particular injustice. I looked at the photographs more closely.

"Isn't there one missing?" I said.

"One what?" Tom said.

I gestured to the photographs.

"I thought I remembered the shape they made on the wall differently."

"Could we leave the trained artist's eye for now?" Tom suggested. "We're practically under siege and you're mentally rehanging pictures. Talk about violin playing on the *Titanic*."

"Did Laura ring her parents yet?" Sheila said. "Does anyone know?"

Ostensibly this was Sheila sounding concerned, but I knew that her real hope was that Laura's parents would sweep down and carry their dumb-mute daughter back to the United States with them. Ethan's next-of-kin, an older brother, had been contacted but was apparently unable to take time off work to fly over here for the funeral.

"Nah, I don't think so," Lurch said. "She ain't left that shed all day."

"She hasn't *washed* for days," I added. "When I took her dinner, I could smell her. You know how musty she and Ethan smell—smelt—well she still smells . . . Anyway, she smells like a charity shop now. Like stinky, dusty old shoes."

"Erk," Lurch said.

Sheila pulled a face.

"You're going to have to wrestle her into the shower soon," Tom said to me.

"Ugh." I thought of Laura's greasy red curls straggling into the nape of her grimy neck. "She's really not my type."

"And that rocking she was doing before," Tom said. "It's like having Anthony Perkins' mum as a house guest."

I was very grateful to see that Tom was perking up, even if it was only to insult Laura.

"Her parents' number'll be in Emma's address book," I suggested. "She's friends with them, isn't she?"

"So it will!" Sheila said more cheerfully, seeming to brighten up at the prospect of having a task to sink her teeth into. "I'll have a look when we go upstairs."

"Tom," I said. "I was meaning to ask you—"

But what I had been going to ask Tom was forever lost in the mists of time. A resounding crash shattered through the night. It was the unmistakable sound of breaking glass. After the quiet in the kitchen it sounded as if the house was being blown up.

22

"YOU'RE NOT DOING THIS," TOM SAID FURIOUSLY. "I WON'T let you."

I sneered at him.

"Won't let me? Who do you think you are, King Kong? Big hero beat on chest and lock up fainting maiden in house?"

"All right, you two, pack it in," Lurch interrupted quickly, before we came to blows. Tom's chest was indeed swelling up, if not quite to King Kong proportions. Lurch looked at me. "I got to say I think it's a pretty crap idea too, Sam. We got a murderer wandering round the village and some other sod chucking stones at us every two seconds, or maybe it's the same person for all we know, and you want to go outside at midnight and prowl around? You're the one what's always shouting at those heroines in horror films who go down to the cellar all by themselves so the killer can chase 'em around with a carving knife."

"Or that crime novel you tore in half and burnt because the heroine kept going to deserted cemeteries at midnight with a serial killer on the loose," Tom chimed in.

My jaw set sulkily.

"I'm not exactly putting on a negligée and fluffy mules and popping out to the barn to investigate weird screams and chain-saw noises," I pointed out coldly. "I can take care of myself. And may I add that those heroines always survive? It's their friends who get gutted with meat hooks to prove how dangerous the killer is."

"Lovely, Sam," Lurch said with heavy sarcasm. "Really fucking tasteful."

"I'm sorry," I apologised.

"You know what your problem is?" Tom said angrily.

"Which one?"

"You think you're indestructible! And you're not! You're just lucky!"

"How *dare* you!" I was outraged.

"Please!" Lurch yelled. "This in't helping things, is it?"

"We have to do something," I said, calming down. "We've had two stones through the window already today. It makes sense that there might be a third."

"Not much fun throwing stones at a boarded-up window," Tom pointed out. The glazier had refused to turn out at night, and I couldn't say I blamed him.

"There are plenty of other windows," I said. Lurch and Tom were unconvinced.

"Maybe if Lurch came out with you," Tom suggested. "I'd do it myself but—"

"Forget it," I said. "Your reflexes are shot to hell right now."

I wouldn't have asked Tom anyway; he was notoriously clumsy and had always had difficulty telling right from left. Besides, he was so big we would have to find a bush the size of a small field to hide him in. I had already considered bringing Lurch, but rejected the idea. There wasn't that much cover outside the house. And I wanted to be able to prowl around as and when I wanted without having to discuss everything in whispers with a fellow lurker.

I looked from Tom to Lurch. It was clear that neither of them was giving in, and I couldn't be bothered to argue it out any longer.

"OK," I said reluctantly. "I *am* pretty tired. Let's sleep on it and talk about it in the morning. Maybe Lurch and I can stake the house out tomorrow. We could have a sleep in the afternoon so we'll stay awake later on."

"No problem," Lurch said enthusiastically.

Tom sniffed. "Sammy sees sense for once," he said sarcastically. "I must make a note in my diary. This had to be some kind of record."

· · · · · · ·

Two hours later I was easing open the bedroom door with great care. Lurch was fast asleep, as I had known he would be. You practically had to set fire to his clothes to wake him up. I had no intention of going down the stairs; they creaked too badly. I had toyed with sliding down the banister, but discarded it as being too risky. It looked pretty rickety, and the thought of my embarrassment if it gave way under my weight was enough to put the idea right out of my mind. There was only one option left.

I crossed the hallway, padding on socked feet, and slipped into the bathroom. To open the window was the work of a moment. I pulled on my boots, buttoned up my jacket and slithered out on to the sill. P. G. Wodehouse novels made shinning down drainpipes sound as easy as sinking a dry martini. I was about to find out the truth of this for myself.

Actually, the scramble down the drainpipe turned out to be the easy part. I hadn't really anticipated how nasty it would feel to squat in the middle of a bush for hours on end in the icy winter air. Not having been able to go downstairs for my coat, I had bundled up in as many sweaters as I could, and my movements were considerably constricted as a result. But I hadn't done more for my lower half than pull on my jeans, and my bottom was so frozen that it probably had frostbite. This thought was the only consolation keeping me going. If I really did have frostbite, they'd have to slice off some chunks, which would really help with getting into my jeans. Now if I could just get frostbite on my stomach too . . .

I stifled a yawn. I had been out here for over an hour, and nothing was stirring in the village. The last few lights in the houses around the green had flickered out, one by one, leaving only the orange streetlights for illumination. The night was overcast, and though the moon should be waxing, neither it nor any stars could be seen; the night sky was a pall of black. A couple of times a car had circled the green, cruising slowly along; doubtless a responsible citizen who had had a few beers too many at a lock-in and was overcompensating in an effort not to speed. The occasional night bird made faint, too-whoo-ing noises in the trees. Or maybe I just thought it was a too-whoo sound because the only night birds I knew about were owls. A cat darted across the neighbour's hedge, paused for a moment on the lawn, its light paws making no sound on the hard frozen grass, and nipped away around the back of the house.

I was getting increasingly bored and stiff. Only now did it occur to me that a far better place for a stakeout of the house would be a car parked within view, where at least one would have a comfortable seat and more insulation. Tomorrow night I would definitely set that up. Tonight . . . I looked at my watch. It was past three. And the silence could not have been less ominous; it was deeply peaceful, without a hint of menace. Lesser Swinfold was deep in the comforting arms of Morpheus.

I decided to stroll once around the green and then go back to bed. I was having increasingly voluptuous fantasies about my yielding mattress, my crisp sheets and my lovely warm duvet. Straightening up cautiously, more to avoid cutting myself to ribbons on the bush than in case any possible stone-throwers might be lurking in the vicinity, I did another sweeping survey of the area. Nothing had changed: no sudden movements at the corner of my vision. I sneaked through the hedge at the bottom of the garden and jumped down over the wall into the street, to avoid using the garden gate. Again, this was more so that no-one in the house would be woken by the rasping of its rusty iron hinges than because I thought there was anyone out on this cold night, save for one overenthusiastic metal sculptor playing detective.

I slipped across the road, past the concrete pillbox of the public toilet and on to the green. My feet crunched on the icy grass, its texture like gel-coated hair, blow-dried to hard crispy strands. It was a relief to be stretching my legs. I jumped up to grab at a tree branch and hung off it by my gloved hands, straightening out my back till it clicked into place.

At the other side of the green was the Fitzwilliams' house, all its lights off. Alan wasn't burning the midnight oil writing his novel. I stood under his window, fantasising about climbing up to it. I was tired mentally, but not physically. A rousing bout of sex with Alan, made all the more exciting by the need to keep it quiet, would redeem the boredom and disappointment of this evening perfectly. Still, somehow the idea of having to keep quiet because of being caught by his parents was not as sexy as it might have been when I was younger. Maybe I could throw up stones to his window—gravel, rather than the rocks that our assailant preferred—and summon him out for . . . what? It was far too cold to have sex out here. Even the thought of baring the requisite bits of flesh made me shiver.

If I couldn't get laid, I might as well stop thinking about it or I would eat myself up with frustration. I certainly wasn't going to wake him up if sex was out of the question. The last thing I wanted to do was to talk to him.

I passed the church, skirting the areas of the churchyard that were lit up by floodlights. The stone walls glowed a pale orange—warming, like firelight—and even the shadows cast were more peaceful than eerie. Nothing stirring on the Lesser Swinfold front. And my bed was calling me. All I had to do was negotiate that damn drainpipe without waking up the entire household. I rounded the concrete toilet, noticing once again the absence of any stink of old piss and beer—this was ludicrously incongruous for a Londoner—heard a faint noise behind me and turned halfway around, just in time to receive a violent blow to my head.

Even as I staggered under it, I knew how lucky I had been. If I hadn't turned, I would have taken it full to the back of my head and probably been knocked unconscious. As it was, my head was ringing, my vision fuzzy and my right shoulder, which had taken most of the force of the blow, was in such screaming pain that I didn't think I could use that arm.

I could barely even make out the shape of my attacker; their back was to the streetlight, and I was still dazed. Still, it looked as if there was only one person. At least I wasn't seeing double. I retreated around the side of the toilet as fast as I could. The blow to my shoulder must have paralysed a nerve in my arm; I could hardly move it.

Whack! My assailant lunged around the corner of the toilet, hitting at me with a big tree branch. I jumped back and took the blow glancingly on my other forearm. I was so busy dodging the attack that I couldn't even look around me for anything I could use as a weapon. I doubted there would be many other sticks lying around; I hadn't noticed anything on the green as I'd strolled around it. There was often a little man pottering around during the day, raking up leaves and any debris into a wheelbarrow—

It was shocking how thoughts danced through your brain when you were under attack, the adrenaline going crazy, fizzing all your senses up to the maximum. Well, comparatively speaking. My skull was still sore and fuzzy and my layers of sweaters, though some insulation against the blows, were hampering my movements, making me slower and more clumsy. I shook my head, trying to clear it a bit, and as the stick came towards me again I tried to block and grab it all at once. The figure holding it was just a black blur, a pale stripe of face under a dark hat, which didn't help much. So they were white. Great. That was very helpful. I hadn't seen a black face the entire time I'd been in Lesser Swinfold.

With only my left hand in use, I was struggling, but I managed to swing my body around to use its weight as extra heft on my arm. For a moment I thought I had the stick, or at least had wrenched it out of my opponent's grasp. I threw myself into the effort with everything I had, swivelling around. That was a big mistake. The twist strained at my injured arm so badly that I cried out in pain, and my left hand fell away from the stick.

I took another crashing blow across the shoulders. I doubled over, knowing that I was losing badly now. Forget fighting back; I had to run for it while there was still time. I feinted, lunged and then dashed in the opposite direction, towards Emma's house, scrambling painfully on to the churchyard wall. I couldn't remember where the gate was and didn't have time to look. I had nearly vaulted over, injured arm notwithstanding, when something grabbed at my foot. I kicked out wildly and felt the grasp loosen, my foot landing on a soft target. There was a muffled cry. Good. I hoped I had got the bastard in the face with my boot.

But then the stick caught me on my leg, and, already off-balance from the kick, I tumbled off the wall, bumping my bad shoulder as I went down heavily on to the tarmac of the road. The sweaters might have saved me from breaking anything, but I rolled on to my right arm and yelled out loud in pain. There was a bright light in my eyes, and I thought I was seeing stars. Was this concussion? I could hardly see anything except the light, blinding me, and I scrabbled around on the ground, hopelessly vulnerable, a roaring in my ears, knowing that, if my attacker was over the wall now and raising the stick to come down on my head, there would be nothing I could do to defend myself. The clamour in my ears was as loud as a train engine. What the hell was happening to me?

And then brakes squealed, the lights shining right into my face, and I heard a car door slam.

"Sam!" Hugo's voice yelled. "Are you OK?"

"Yes!" I yelled with all my strength. It was a lie, but that didn't matter. "Get them! Go after them!"

I could hear pounding footsteps on the road and panting breath. For a moment I just lay there, catching my own breath, letting my heart slow down. I couldn't remember my head having ever hurt this badly, apart from the time I hit it on a car handle and knocked myself out when I was kidnapped. Then full consciousness swept back, and I realised what I had done. I had sent Hugo after a murderer. If he was killed, I would have it on my conscience for ever. I got painfully to my hands and knees and grabbed at the bumper of his car to pull myself up. The bonnet, hot under my hands, was a shock to the senses. Leaning on the car, I tried to make out what was happening, but my vision was still cloudy, and the more I stared, the worse it got. I was nearly crying in frustration.

Lights were going on in the neighbouring houses. Or maybe they had been on already, roused by the noise of the fight.

"Help!" I yelled into the night. "Murder! Help! *Murder!*"

I felt very self-conscious. But it worked.

23

I HAD HAD PLENTY OF THEORIES ABOUT THE IDENTITY OF my attacker: Chrissie, Andy, Tamsin, Laura or Priscilla, protecting her son's honour, not to mention her own. But I was completely wrong. I hadn't guessed anywhere even close.

"*Sheila*," I said in disbelief the morning after. I remembered Hugo frogmarching her back along the road, the watchcap she had been wearing half off her head from the struggle, a bruise starting on her cheek from where I had kicked her, and I was as incredulous now as I had been then. It was wounded pride as well. I must have been really off my guard to let myself be nearly killed by a woman in her late fifties.

I didn't make this remark to the assembled group. Tom would immediately have pointed out how sexist and ageist it was.

"I don't understand why she didn't stab me," I said for the fifteenth time.

"Maybe she was going to whip out a knife when she had you unconscious," Lurch suggested.

"Nobody understands anything, from what I can make out," Hugo said impatiently. "That's what we're all waiting for—some information."

Sheila had been too hysterical the night before to be questioned. She had spent what remained of the night in a police cell and, according to Gail's contact at the station, was due to be questioned this morning. The contact had promised to ring Gail once she knew what was happening, and Sheila's solicitor was also a good friend of someone at Gail's firm and could be relied upon to give the bare bones of the case to him. The countryside was a small place.

"Ow," I said, shifting in my seat. I was wearing an elastic bandage, which was more like a moulded shoulder-piece, to keep me from using my arm while the nerve damage healed; unfortunately, it had to be worn next to the skin, so I had no visible signs of physical suffering to show off. "All I can think about right now is all the sodding cockroaches I have to make. I have to keep this thing on for at least two weeks."

"I already told you, Sammy. I'll do 'em after class. I got a couple of mates there who can help me. With the basics," Lurch added quickly. "I wouldn't let 'em do anything but the kits and the wheels. They ain't got the experience."

Hugo exchanged an amused glance with me at Lurch's air of superiority. It was practically the first normal contact we had had since last night. I couldn't decide whether it made me feel better or worse.

"Anyway, if you'd stayed in bed like you said you were going to, none of this would have happened!" Tom snapped.

"We don't know that!" I said defensively. "If she was going to go for me, she'd have found another occasion to do it."

"But maybe she wasn't going for you," Tom persisted. "Maybe it was just that you were skulking round the house."

"Oh, come on. No-one tries to kill someone just for sneaking round the house at three in the morning."

"Someone who's already killed two other people isn't exactly going to be rational by the third victim, are they?"

"Oh, for fuck's sake, will everyone just shut up?" Hugo said loudly. He didn't have to raise his voice much, simply project it. Someone who could act on the RSC's main stage and have his words reach right to the top of the house had no problem riding over a couple of people sitting next to him. "You've been sitting here theorising for hours, and it's completely futile! No-one knows anything! Could we please talk about something else?"

At that moment the doorbell rang. We looked at each other in wild speculation.

"I'll go," said Hugo, rising gracefully to his feet. "Anything to get away from you lot."

"Oh yes, come in," he could be heard saying wearily in the hall as he swung open the door. "Thank God I only have the most minor role in this drama. I expect you want to question everyone all over again."

"Not exactly, sir," came the unmistakable voice of officialdom.

A plain-clothes officer, accompanied by two uniforms, one a WPC, trooped into the living room and examined the occupants with a quick, trained gaze. I wondered why there were so many of them.

"Is Mrs. Emma Warwick at home, sir?" the officer said to Hugo.

"Yes, I believe so," he said, taken aback. "She's still in bed, isn't she?" he said to us.

I nodded. "Sheila gave her some sleeping pills last night. Tom looked in on her after Sheila was arrested, but she was dead to the world." I double-took. "Oh my God—you don't think—"

Tom, reading my train of thought, jumped up, looking terrified.

"I thought she was asleep! I thought I heard her breathing! I could have sworn I heard her breathing! Surely Sheila wouldn't kill her own *sister*?"

He clutched at Gail, who had stood up too.

"But maybe she was in a coma!" he said distractedly. "They take a while to work, don't they? Oh Jesus, *Emma*—"

He tried to dash for the stairs, only to be caught by the male PC.

"We'll handle this situation, if you don't mind, sir," he said politely.

"But you don't think—"

The plain-clothes officer nodded at the WPC.

"WPC Davies and I will just go upstairs and check out the state of play. If you ladies and gentlemen would be kind enough to wait down here. Which room is Mrs. Warwick's?"

"Top floor," I said.

"Thank you, miss."

"But—" Tom struggled, but to no avail. Finally, he calmed down enough for the PC to guide him back to the sofa.

"There's nothing you can do, sir. Any of you," he assured us. It was obviously meant to be reassuring.

"But what if she's . . . Shouldn't we call an ambulance?" said Gail, looking baffled.

"All in due course, Miss Christie."

"Ms.," Gail muttered automatically. "But look, why can't you at least tell us—"

The PC, for the first time, looked uncomfortable. Gail broke off, as we could hear footsteps coming down the stairs from Emma's room. Plenty of footsteps, and measured ones, no panic.

A small procession appeared on the main staircase. First the plain-clothes officer, his face set and sombre. Then, to our great relief came Emma, followed by the WPC. Emma looked dazed and her clothes were a mess, as if she had pulled them on at random. She looked over at us, her face contorted.

"Emma!" Once again Tom jumped to his feet, and once again the male PC planted himself by the newel post to stop Tom's rush towards the stairs.

"You're OK!" Tom said happily. "Thank God! Let me through, won't you?" he said impatiently to the PC.

"I'm sorry, sir, that won't be possible right now."

There was a long pause. He looked over to his boss, who said, "Following a statement made to us by her sister, Mrs. Warwick is under arrest for the murders of Janine Burrows and Ethan Summers. We are taking her into custody. And yes, she's been charged," he said in Gail's direction.

"But—but—" Tom stammered, for the twentieth time that morning.

"You bitch! You bitch! I'll kill you!"

I think we had all forgotten about Laura's presence in the room. It was much too easy to do that nowadays. She had been curled up in the window embrasure, rocking away, seeming as usual to pay no attention whatsover to the events unfolding before her. Now, finally, her protective carapace of indifference had burst. She threw herself towards Emma, eyes blazing, hands out like claws.

"You bitch! You killed Ethan!" she screamed.

It might have been easy for the PC to restrain Tom, but a half-crazed avenging girlfriend was a different matter entirely. Laura had shot past him before he could react. Desperately, he grabbed at her arm as the WPC put herself in front of Emma.

"Miss—Miss, please, this isn't the way—" he choked out as Laura's flailing fist caught him in the neck.

"Get off me! Get out of my way!" she screamed, wriggling like a mad thing. With awe, I watched her shake him off as if thirteen stone of policeman meant nothing to her. Emma, looking unutterably weary, watched her come, unmoving, seeming not to care if Laura tore her apart with her bare hands. Had they been alone, that would probably have happened. Laura was out of her mind with rage, and she looked as if she wouldn't stop till she saw blood.

With considerable bravery, the WPC caught one of Laura's upraised hands and tried to twist her arm behind her back. Laura caught her in the chest with the other fist and nearly sent her fly-

ing. The plain-clothes officer, either out of the need to see that
Emma didn't make a bolt for it, or simple cowardice, did not
enter the fray, and the two PCs between them struggled frantically with Laura, her red hair whipping between them like a flag
of defiance, blotches of colour luridly bright on each cheek. One
hand made it almost as far as Emma's face, clawing at it; the
plain-clothes officer moved Emma back just in time to avoid four
deep parallel scratches down her cheek. Emma herself wouldn't
even have budged to avoid them.

"Let me go! Let me go!" Laura kept howling. Even the pitch
of her voice was frightening: deranged, or maybe just primitive,
like a wild beast.

Opposite me, Gail Christie stood up. She picked up a vase of
chrysanthemums, and for a moment I thought she was going to
try to brain Laura with it. Then she dumped the flowers,
advanced on the mass of panting bodies and threw the water in
the vase straight into Laura's screaming face.

It was like a slap to a hysteric. Laura collapsed between the
PCs like a rag doll, dragging in her breath in huge gulps and letting it out in harsh gasping sobs. They held her for a while, looking at each other over her head, trying to decide whether or not
she was still dangerous; then, by consensus, they let her slip to
the ground in a heap.

"Ethan," she moaned, her voice ugly and distorted with grief.
"Ethan, Ethan, Ethan . . ."

It was like seeing a character from *The Trojan Women*, literally consumed by grief, come alive in front of us. Nobody, not
even the police officers, could move until Laura had finally
wound herself down, the hands covering her face dripping tears.
Hugo was staring at her, spellbound. And I knew why; he was
wondering if anyone could get away with that excess of emotion
on stage. Most people would have minded this trait of his, but I
never did. I had seen enough bad things to know that one should

be grateful for any trick you could use to distance yourself, to keep from being devoured by them.

· · · · · · ·

"I think that's the first time she's had a really good cry since she found him," Lurch said, when we had got Laura to bed with a cup of herbal tea (Tom) and two of Emma's sleeping pills (me) inside her. Without Emma or, as latterly, Sheila to assume the maternal role, we were having to manage as best we could. It felt like one of those children's books where the parents die in the first chapter and the plucky kids have to cope all on their own to avoid being taken into care. "About time she let it out, eh?"

Trust Lurch to put matters into perspective.

"Well, that's one way of looking at it," Hugo said dryly. "Alternatively, she might just have had a nervous breakdown before our eyes. But let's take the glass-half-full option, shall we?"

I clicked my tongue to reprove him. We had more important things to think about right now.

"So tell us everything!" I said to Gail, who had just got off the phone with the partner in her office who was a good friend of Sheila's solicitor. I imagined the news flashing like lightning through an enthralled Lesser Swinfold and all the surrounding villages. Bush telegraph, smoke signals, drums beating, pony express.

We settled around Gail like a group of expectant children waiting for a fairy tale, our faces all turned to hers. Tom was still in shock. I think he imagined that Gail would explain that it had all been a silly mistake and Surrogate Mummy would be home soon to cook dinner.

"Emma's confessed," were Gail's first words. Tom slumped in his chair. I patted his knee reassuringly without bothering to look at him. I didn't want him to throw a scene and distract us from the narrative.

"How come?" Hugo said intelligently. "Was there any evidence?"

Gail grimaced. "Sort of, I suppose. But that would be pretty nasty to get. They'd have to dig up her husband."

"Fuckin' hell, did she do him in as well?" Lurch was agog.

"No. That is," Gail corrected herself, "I have no idea. No-one's raised the subject. The point is that apparently he was the father of Janine's little boy."

My jaw dropped. I actually felt the muscles loosen.

"The picture!" I said, as excitedly as if we were playing a quiz and I had just won the million-pound question. "The photo! I always thought there was something familiar about it—that head-scratching thing Walter was doing! Pitt does that all the time!"

Gail nodded. Hugo looked bored.

"Could you translate for the rest of us not in the dizzy heights of Sam Land?" he drawled.

"It was a photograph of Emma's husband scratching his head. It's identical to the way Pitt does it—the same facial expression, everything. They tilt their heads to exactly the same angle. I'd never have spotted the resemblance just on that, though," I admitted.

"Sheila told the police she had always suspected Janine and Walter," Gail explained. "Emma hadn't the least idea. But then Tom invited Janine and Pitt to the New Year's Eve dinner, and Emma recognised Pitt's mannerisms. Apparently, he looks very like old baby photos of Walter. And it was common knowledge that Pitt's father was a mystery."

"And Janine had a thing for older men," I commented. "Though Walter was pushing it. He must have been nearly four times her age."

"So Emma killed her?" Hugo prompted.

Gail turned to Tom.

"You saw Emma when you came back to the house that night, didn't you?" she said. "And told her that you'd had a fight with Janine?"

Tom looked horribly abashed.

"I was really upset," he mumbled. "I did cry on her shoulder a bit. And then she made me some Ovaltine and sent me off to bed."

"Why didn't you tell anyone?" Hugo said. "It would at least have fixed the time when you got in. Better than nothing."

Tom hung his head.

"Because you heard Emma go out, didn't you?" I said, jumping to the obvious conclusion. "And you wanted to protect her."

"I just thought—" he said feebly. "The next day she told me she'd gone round to Janine's. She said she had some silly idea about telling her what a great bloke I was, or something. But she said that when she got there the lights were off, and she realised that it wouldn't work anyway, so she just turned round and came back home."

"Decidedly thin," Hugo commented.

Tom was wounded.

"I never thought for a moment that *Emma*—" he protested.

"I knew there was something you weren't telling me," I said crossly. "I can always tell, Tom. I was really worried for a while. You went all furtive, I thought it was something much worse than that."

"I couldn't tell anyone," he said helplessly. "I mean, *Emma*—I thought she was only trying to look after me—"

Gail made a sympathetic noise. Tom stared at her as pitifully as a six-year-old who had just been told that Father Christmas didn't exist, there was no Tooth Fairy, and Mummy and Daddy were getting a divorce.

"In a way, she was," Gail reassured him. "Apparently, she'd had some fantasy about you marrying Janine and bringing Pitt to live with her."

"Playing the doting grandmother to her husband's son," Hugo said. "Well, better than nothing, I suppose."

Gail nodded.

"Emma told Janine she knew that Walter was Pitt's father. Janine said she wasn't interested in Tom—sorry, Tom"—She reached out and touched him briefly—"and that she wanted Emma to stay away from Pitt because she found the whole thing very uncomfortable. Apparently, she—Janine—threatened to move away from the village now that Emma knew about Walter. She said she'd been thinking about it for some time anyway, and this was the last straw."

"And Emma hit her," I said. "And then grabbed the toolbox."

"Hubby playing around with a girl young enough to be your granddaughter," Lurch said disapprovingly. "Enough to send anyone round the bend."

"She probably hadn't taken that in completely till then," Hugo mused. "Maybe she was so concentrated on this happy fantasy of one big happy family that she hadn't really let herself be aware of her husband's betrayal."

He stared at me pointedly on the last word. A nasty little silence fell. Tom cleared his throat.

"What about Ethan?" Lurch said quickly.

"He was up late," Gail said, "and heard her go out and come back in. Apparently, he didn't actually believe that Emma had killed Janine. Like practically everyone else, he thought it was Tom, and Emma was protecting him. So he wasn't as careful around her as he should have been."

"I don't understand," I said. "Why did she have to kill him? Was he blackmailing her?"

"Can't you guess?" Gail said. "The police finally managed to get into his computer. He was writing a memoir about being involved in a real English-country murder case."

"Bet it would have sold well in America," Hugo said. "They love that kind of thing over there. Though we do need a titled detective and chippy working-class sidekick. Lurch, fancy going into partnership?"

Lurch gave him the finger.

"Let's wait till you get knighted, mate, shall we?" he said nastily.

"Those phone calls of Ethan's!" I said suddenly. "The trip to London! Was he seeing publishers?"

"Getting an agent," Gail said. "They found the e-mail correspondence. Ethan was writing a proposal to take to publishers. They interviewed his agent. He said he could have sold it for an awful lot of money. The subject matter's original, and memoirs are very big right now." She looked at Hugo. "Especially in America, apparently."

Hugo's expression was extremely complacent.

"It seems a big risk to kill him just for that," I said. "If he didn't have any actual proof she did it."

"Emma overheard him talking to Laura that evening about the book," Gail said. "Apparently, she was scared that Ethan would start snooping around to find as much material for the book as possible and decided to kill him before that could happen. The photographs of Walter, for instance. There were albums everywhere."

"At that rate, she might have gone on killing anyone she thought might suspect her," Hugo said morbidly. "One by one. Laura would probably have been next."

"I'm just surprised Emma didn't smash up Ethan's laptop," Gail said reflectively.

"She couldn't," I said, thinking it through. "That would call attention to it. She must just have been hoping that Ethan hadn't written much yet. But if she destroyed the computer, that would point directly to the memoir."

"Hang on, she had an alibi for Ethan!" Lurch said suddenly. "She was with Tom!"

"Tom said he kept falling asleep during the film," I explained, having already thought this out. "I never connected with it at the time, but how unlikely is it that Tom should fall asleep during a James Bond?"

"I was surprised myself," Tom piped up.

"She must have given you a sleeping pill or two in your drink and slipped out while you were snoring. Even if you were asleep, you'd be hearing the dialogue, and that would make you think you'd seen more of it than you had. I'm always doing that. And then, when she was alibi-ing you, she was covered too. Very clever. Especially as no-one would think of suspecting her anyway. She must have done the same for Laura. She told me she'd had a glass of wine with Tom and Emma, and she looked completely knocked out that morning."

"She could have bloody done it when I was in the nick," Tom grumbled. "That would've got me off the hook completely."

"You can scarcely expect a murderess to tailor her schedule to yours quite that conveniently," Hugo said.

"And then Sheila found out," Gail said, "or Emma told her. And Sheila was immediately nervous of you, Sam. You have a reputation for catching murderers."

"Only when they get so annoyed with her they try to put her out of her misery," Hugo said sarcastically. "She just stumbles around making a nuisance of herself till she gets on everyone's nerves. Beside her, Dr. Watson looks like Hercule Poirot."

Normally, though containing quite a few grains of truth, this would have been no more than banter, and I would have countered indignantly with a list of my few deductive feats. But there was a razor edge behind every word Hugo said to or about me today. I knew he was trying to provoke me, and I wasn't going to let that happen in front of everyone.

Lurch fidgeted awkwardly.

"And then Sam spotted this photo," he said. "That's the one that was missing downstairs, right?"

Gail nodded. "Sheila took it away and moved the others closer in. But when Sam mentioned it, Sheila panicked. She eavesdropped on you talking and thought Sam might go out last night after all."

"God," I said in self-disgust. "I thought it was so peaceful out there. I didn't notice a thing."

"It's 'cos it's the countryside, innit?" Lurch said in mitigation. "And it's so pretty. It don't seem real that people are getting killed here, does it?"

"Who was throwing the stones?" I asked.

"No idea," Gail said, shrugging. "But hopefully that'll stop now Emma's been arrested."

"Yes, but it couldn't have been someone who thought Emma had done it," I said. "I mean, if even we didn't suspect her . . ."

Everyone else was equally baffled. Months later Gail was to find out that it had been Jamie Rickson, the local boy who was keen on Janine. Convinced that Tom had killed her, bolstered in this belief by Ethan's murder so shortly after Tom had been released on bail and furious about being questioned by the police, he had let off steam by breaking some glass. He finally told some of his friends, who passed the story on till it became common knowledge; it became a sort of village joke: right house—wrong person.

"Sheila must have been desperate," Hugo said with a certain amount of pity. "Such a stupid thing to do, and where would it get her? For all she knew Sam might have shared her mythical suspicions with all of you already."

"She told them everything this morning," Gail said. "Barry—

that's her solicitor—said he couldn't get a word in edgewise, she was so relieved to get it off her chest."

"One can't blame her for wanting to protect her sister," Hugo observed.

"Tell that to my shoulder," I snapped, regretting once again that my bandage was concealed beneath my clothes. "It hurts to buggery."

"But you just love those painkillers, darling, don't you?" Hugo said so icily that the temperature in the room dropped five degrees.

Lurch stood up, muttering something about having to pack his rucksack. Tom offered to walk Gail out to her car. In a bare minute I was alone with Hugo. I couldn't even meet his eyes. The silence was thick with unspoken words. I felt their weight pressing against me and ducked my head.

"I must be getting back to London," Hugo said eventually. "I have a rehearsal tomorrow."

I knew him well enough to be aware that this was a lie, or at least an extension of the truth.

"But you're exhausted," I said, playing for time. "Maybe you should rest a bit."

"No, thank you," he said with chilling politeness. "I'll be fine. It's just a two-hour drive."

We had been up all night, what with making statements and taking me to hospital. I was running on adrenaline and even that was wearing away. Still, if Hugo said he was all right to drive—oh, I was being ridiculous. He just wanted to get away from me as fast as possible, and I could scarcely blame him.

"Why did you come?" I said, unable to resist the impulse. "I mean, I don't see why—"

It had come out all wrong. I meant to ask him if there had been something he had wanted to say to me, and I had ended up sounding as if his journey had always been doomed to futility.

"Why, to pay my debt, of course," he said in tones of great civility.

"Your debt?"

"You saved my life once. Now we're even. The slate is clean. Perfect timing, don't you think?"

I wasn't going to let him get away with putting things that neatly.

"How come you were driving past at three in the morning?"

Hugo looked at me levelly. Despite himself, I could see the pain in his eyes.

"I haven't been sleeping well," he said, "if you must know. So last night, past midnight, I decided it was ridiculous just to lie awake in bed thinking about you, and I drove down here. Don't ask me what I was expecting to happen, because I haven't the faintest idea. I made very good time and then when I reached the village I felt absurd. I knew one of the doors would probably be open, and I could sleep on the sofa, but I'm rather too old for that kind of student behaviour. So I just kept driving round. It wasn't bad, actually. At least I was doing something, keeping in motion. I went round the green every so often, seeing if there were any lights on in the house."

"I heard some cars," I remembered. "When I was hiding in the bush. That must have been you."

"How typical," Hugo said on a sigh. "If I'd only used my knowledge of your character for a few minutes, I would have known that there was nowhere you were more likely to be than hiding in a bush at three in the morning. Anyway, on one of my loops round I nearly ran over you, and you know the rest."

He stood up, smoothing down his trousers automatically. No matter how tired he was, Hugo would always pay attention to his clothes. He was letting his hair grow, and it was brushed back from his face, just long enough to be secured with a tie at the nape of his neck. When Hugo slicked his hair off his face he seemed unapproachably austere, the long, slightly arched nose and high cheekbones standing out in relief. He looked down his nose at me. Hugo was very good at that.

"Apart from that little accident of fate, it would seem to have been a wasted journey, wouldn't it?" he said.

I couldn't say anything. There wasn't anything to say. It felt as if there was a gulf between us as wide as the world.

"Is your young swain still hanging around?" he enquired.

This must be killing him. I knew that he just wanted to walk away without asking any questions, but he couldn't help forcing me to tell him how things stood. It would be a real blow to his pride.

"No," I said finally. "Been and gone."

"He can't have been much good, then," Hugo observed with biting accuracy. "How disappointing for you."

He pulled on his coat, turning up the collar.

"I don't know if I would have preferred it if you'd picked someone a little less callow," he said. "But on the whole, I think not. It seems to sum up the whole sorry state of affairs. Your appalling juvenility. Grabbing at whatever you want without any thought of the consequences. You can't live like that for ever, you know." He sighed. "Or perhaps you can. But I can't."

Lurch tumbled down the stairs, rucksack slung over his shoulder.

"Ready?" Hugo said to him.

"Yeah."

Now it was Lurch who wouldn't meet my eyes.

"Lurch?" I said in disbelief. "I thought you'd be coming back with me! I was going to have a sleep and then push off this afternoon."

"Yeah, well. I knew Hugo was going back so I asked him for a lift. Nothing to keep me here now, is there?"

"I'll call you tomorrow," I said, clutching at straws. "About the cockroaches."

"Yeah, whatever." He grabbed his anorak from a peg and was gone out the door. Hugo paused a moment to raise one hand to me.

"Any last words?" he inquired. "My God, Sam, I've never seen you so tongue-tied. How unusual. I expect I should take that as a sort of compliment. Well, I shall consider my goodbye to stand for both of us."

The front door shut behind him. I watched him walk across the lawn, the tails of his ankle-length black overcoat blowing behind him in the wind. Alan looked like a student in his coat, gawky and shy, but Hugo, haughty as ever, made his look like a cape thrown around his shoulders, swirling around his lean body. His hair was silver-blond in the winter sun.

I knew what Hugo had wanted me to say, and I knew that he would take me back if I did. He wanted to hear that I was prepared, if not to move in with him, then at least to put our relationship on a more serious footing. The thought of what that meant—where that eventually led—sent cold shivers down my spine. Alan had meant nothing to me beyond a brief fling, but he symbolised much more than that. If I did what Hugo wanted, I wouldn't be free any more. I felt claustrophobic just thinking about it. It wouldn't be fair to Hugo. Even though I had behaved appallingly to him, I couldn't guarantee that it would never happen again. Despite the fact that I was overwhelmed with guilt whenever I thought about it.

And that was a great victory Hugo had won. Practically nobody had ever managed to make me feel guilty before. Even the man I had killed. But what seemed to me like a huge defeat, or at least a concession, was just a drop in the barrel to Hugo. What he was asking of me was something I had spent my whole life rejecting. And he knew all this already. In our last fight about this, I had asked him to cut me some slack, and he had told me that he had been doing that for the last two years, and it was time for me to meet him halfway.

I understood everything he was saying. I just couldn't do it. And because I couldn't, I would probably lose him for ever. If I hadn't already.

He descended the stone steps, passed through the gate and was gone. I never cry. But now I put my head in my hands and burst into tears, not romantic-heroine tears but big aching ugly sobs, like Laura's, which felt as if they were being wrenched directly out of my guts. I wanted to cry until I had exhausted myself so much that I couldn't think of anything else.

I didn't succeed. I couldn't stop thinking about him. I was sitting in the very house that had been at the centre of all the upheaval of the last few weeks. Two people at that New Year's Eve dinner had been killed by the hostess, and her sister had been arrested for assault. But all I could think about, as I looked back to that evening, was that it had been the moment when my relationship had started to crumble. Two murders, God knew how many lives ripped apart, and my only concern was the ruin of my love-life.

I had always known that I was selfish. But simply knowing it didn't help. It didn't help at all.

Art-chick-cum-sleuth Sam Jones
("outrageously hip [and] voraciously sexy"—*NEW YORK TIMES BOOK REVIEW*)
**encounters more than enough deadly mysteries to keep life
exciting in four more novels by Lauren Henderson:**

BLACK RUBBER DRESS
0-609-80438-3
$12.95 paperback (NCR)

FREEZE MY MARGARITA
0-609-80684-X
$12.95 paperback (NCR)

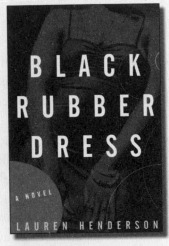

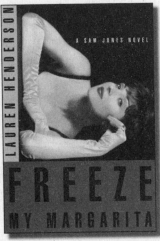

STRAWBERRY TATTOO
0-609-80685-8
$12.95 PAPERBACK (NCR)

CHAINED
0-609-80865-6
$12.95 paperback (NCR)

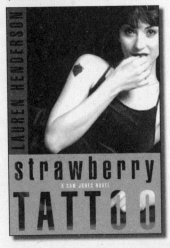